Fast & Wet

Kat Ransom

*to Victoria,
Part II ♡

Kat Ransom*

Fast & Wet
Copyright © 2019 Kat Ransom.

All rights reserved.

Disclaimer: This is a work of fiction. The characters, incidents, and dialogue are drawn from the author's imagination and are not to be construed as real. Any resemblance to actual persons, living or dead, is entirely coincidental. Any references to historical events, real people, or real places are used fictitiously. Names, characters, and places are products of the author's imagination.

For information on getting permission for reprints and excerpts, contact: authorkatransom@gmail.com

Prologue

"The most important things lie close to wherever your secret heart is buried, like landmarks to a treasure your enemies would love to steal away. And you may make revelations that cost you dearly only to have people look at you in a funny way, not understanding what you've said at all, or why you thought it was so important that you almost cried while you were saying it. That's the worst, I think. When the secret stays locked within not for want of a teller but for want of an understanding ear."
- Stephen King

One

Emily

Soft cotton sheets cling to my skin even though it's only May and the oppressing Florida summer heat hasn't arrived yet. My perspiration causes them to catch and pull against my back as I writhe under his hands that trace over my naked body.

Up my outer thigh and across the flat of my stomach, his rough hand cups my breast, and he lowers his mouth to take my nipple. He's so gentle, yet I'm heady with desire.

"Cole," I moan and run my fingers through his short chocolate hair and push my hips upward, desperate for more contact from his long, lean body covering half of mine.

"I'm right here, baby," he whispers around my nipple as his hand trails south, and his fingers discover my outer lips with a feather touch. Up and down, he traces me as my wetness seeps out and draws his fingers in.

The moment two fingers caress my swollen clit, I buck up and gasp. "Feel how wet you are for me, baby?" He whispers and sucks the hollow of my collarbone.

"Kiss me, Cole," I pull his head up, and his lips capture mine. His hot tongue pulses into my waiting mouth as his fingers work me into a frenzy that makes my hips and legs wiggle.

I've pushed the sheets and blanket down with my squirming. My only cover now is the scratchy denim of Cole's jeans, one of his legs over mine, and his naked chest draped over my torso.

The soft waves rocking the boat on Old Tampa Bay keep rhythm with my hips rising and falling to meet his hand. Fooling around on his dad's docked yacht is something Cole and I often do, but tonight is different.

He's become my everything. My savior, my best friend, my boyfriend, my lover. He's the keeper of my secrets and my freedom from disquiet.

Memories of all our private moments, our late night talks, our secrets, our kisses, wash over me as my heart rate picks up, and coherent thoughts are driven from my mind.

"I need you," I whimper on an exhale as I grip his strong forearm and encourage his fingers to dip inside me. He obliges with a groan, and two long fingers slip into my slick channel. My neck arches, and I drive my head into the pillow from pleasure.

"So fucking tight, my gorgeous girl," Cole whispers my favorite nickname into my ear as he nips the lobe and grinds his hardness into the side of my hip. His thumb moves back and forth over my clit as he works me deeper. "Come for me."

I reach down and cup his hard dick through his jeans, "I want to come with you."

A throaty, primal growl reverberates against me as he bites my shoulder then soothes the spot with the flat of his tongue. "Come for me first."

I whine and grip his cock tighter, my face screwing up in a pout. No more waiting, begging, no more pushing and pulling—I need him. "Cole, please."

A dark, sexy smile overtakes his face as he watches my urgency grow. He's amused by how badly I want him.

"I don't want to hurt you, let me take care of you first," he takes a nipple back into his mouth and sucks the taut peak. "Give me what I want, and then I'll give you this," he says as he rocks his hips harder into me.

My mind is racing, and I try to shut down rogue, distracting thoughts, and focus on his hands, how good he smells, the feel of his weight against me. I can't think about consequences right now.

I want this, I want him. I want all of him, and I want to keep him forever.

He sucks my bottom lip into his mouth and drags his teeth over me.

I unbutton his jeans, drag his zipper down, and slide my hand over the warm, thick bulge in his boxers that I want so badly. He hisses and his eyes snap shut as he rocks into my hand with the same tempo his fingers plunge into me.

Watching how good that makes him feel builds my confidence, turns me on even more. I raise my hips and focus on the heat building in my core.

"That's it, Em, so beautiful," he breathes and works me faster.

I feel myself get wetter and wetter, and I can't control it anymore. My body tightens, and I grip Cole's shoulder hard. I'm moaning and whimpering louder and louder as I start to cry his name.

His mouth covers mine, his tongue plunging into me to silence me as I come apart on his fingers and shudder as the tremors run through me.

He moves his body over mine, careful to support his weight, as I'm still panting deliriously. I push his jeans and boxers over his narrow hips. He kicks them down with his feet, and I feel his naked length fall against my stomach. Reaching between us, I grip it and feel the heat, how silky his skin feels.

Cole reaches for the nightstand and rips a condom open with his teeth. "Put it on me," he hands it to me as he stares down at my face from above me. His blue eyes are dark and hooded, his face covered in a glossy sheen of perspiration.

I love making him so hot, so out of control. It makes me feel like a goddess to do this to him.

I slide the condom over him and watch his brows furrow as he tries to keep control of himself. I don't want him to. I want him to lose control with me. I want to give him what he needs.

I want to *be* what he needs.

He holds himself up on his elbows next to my head and kisses me softly as I feel the head of his dick line up with my entrance. We're doing this. I'm finally doing this with Cole Ballentine.

The guy everyone wants, I get him. He's mine.

He pushes the head of his hardness into me, and I gasp and claw his shoulder. "Relax, baby, let me in."

I drop my knees wider as he holds himself still, softly kissing me, licking my neck. His eyes are watching mine for the green light. I lift my hips to take more of him, and he pushes in further. "Cole," I squint my eyes and grip him tighter, fingernails digging into his sun-bronzed skin.

"Look at me, Emily," his hands move into my hair, and he forces my

4

head straight to look into his eyes. "Feel how hard I am for you?"

I nod and run my hands across his gorgeous face. I watch his eyes dance and flicker along my face, the hunger inside them turning me on even more.

I want this to be good for him.

I want him to know how I feel about him.

"Make love to me, Cole."

"Are you sure, baby?"

I've never been so sure of anything in my eighteen years of life. In this moment, my feelings are concrete, my desire and need for him unwavering. "I'm yours, take me."

A surge of blinding, stinging heat overtakes my body as he makes a steady thrust into me. I cry out just as Cole smashes his mouth over mine, and my legs try to snap shut over his narrow hips. "Oww, fuck," I whimper into him from the sting, the burn of his size stretching me.

"I got you, I got you," he whispers softly, his thumb wiping away one tear that has started rolling down from a corner of my eye. "Let me move, baby, I'll make it better."

I release the grip my knees have around him and open myself up.

Cole starts to move, slowly pulling out of me. His eyes watch mine closely as he pushes back in. Within a few strokes, the pain subsides and turns into something else. The feel of him dragging against my walls, filling a place I never knew was empty, starts to tingle and loosen.

"Cole," I moan and grip his hard ass, pulling him into me. Oh god, this feels good when I relax. This is an intimacy between us, unlike anything we've shared before.

"You feel so good, Em. So tight on my cock."

I feel myself flush from the dirty words he's speaking to me. I raise my hips up to meet his, trying to match his cadence at each rock into me. I run my hands up and down his muscular back. He groans when I trace my fingernails over his shoulders.

I watch all of his cues and commit them to memory. He likes it when I say his name, when my nails come close to piercing his skin.

I feel silly, but I try to remember all the things porn stars do, the way their bodies move. I want him to be addicted to me. I want to rock his world, take us to the next level. I want him to love me and never leave me.

When I squeeze and clench my walls against him, he growls and drives into me deeper. I lift a leg around his waist, and he puts an arm under my knee to hold it there. "Oh fuck, Em, you were built to take me," he grunts into my breasts. "Feel me deep inside you, gorgeous girl?"

"Yes," I cry and arch my back. The way he talks to me turns me on even more. I feel powerful knowing I'm doing this to him, driving him to speak this way. "So good, Cole, you feel so good."

"You're so fucking beautiful, Emily. Jesus, look at you," he lifts up and takes in my heaving chest, my rock-hard nipples and breasts bouncing with each of his thrusts.

I take his head in my hands and bring him down to kiss me, overwhelmed with the sweet words he says to me. My handsome Cole, hard body sliding in and out of me, deep blue eyes watching my skin pebble. This belongs to me. I think I'm the one who is addicted.

My toes curl, and I run them up and down his calf, flexing with each push into me. I'm so overwhelmed with emotion and the pressure building up inside of me. "Cole," I take his cheek in my palm and look at him.

"Yeah, baby?"

"I love you."

Deep cerulean pools stare back at me, his eyes darting back and forth between mine. He doesn't say it back. His body has stilled, I see his Adam's apple bob from swallowing, but he doesn't say it back.

Naive girl.

I know then that he's already made his decision.

He's going to leave me.

"Don't stop," I move my hand to his hip and bury my face in his chest so he can't see me.

"Em," he mumbles softly into my neck, the regretful tone of his voice confirming what his eyes already gave away.

"Please, Cole," I wrap my arms around him and clench my teeth to keep the tears at bay. "Let me have you while I can, then."

He stays still inside me until my hips moving up and down spur him to continue. He brings a hand between us, and his thumb starts to run over my clit, up and down, then big circles.

I smash my eyes closed and push my head back into the pillow. I focus on the physical feelings and will the thoughts away. I concentrate on how he feels moving in and out of me, the way his rough thumb feels caressing me. I bury the ache in my heart.

My calf muscles tighten, and I feel a spasm in my core begin to quake. "Cole," I pant and thrash my head from side to side.

"Em," he whispers just above me.

I keep my eyes closed and fixate on the feeling of him deep inside me. If I angle my hips a certain way, he hits the spot inside of me that makes my body jerk and tense up.

"Please look at me, Em." I can feel his body stiffen. His muscles lock up, and the sweat on his body mixes with mine. I know he's close, and that pushes me past the point of no return.

I'm afraid to look into his eyes, but I want to watch him come inside me. A freight train hits me as my orgasm takes over. I force my eyes open as I clench down on him.

Behind his dark lashes, his pupils expand and search mine. Then his whole body stiffens, and a roar comes from deep within him, "Fuck!"

I shudder and tremble against him as tremors run through me, and he rocks against my pelvis a few more times until he's empty and heaving and panting.

I wrap my arms against his shoulders and pull him down on me, moving one hand into his damp hair to cradle his head against my chest. I don't dare move because when I do, this moment will be gone.

We will never be the same.

We're both silent as our breathing returns to normal. There are no words left to be spoken.

As I run my fingers through his hair, I listen to the soft waves hitting the boat, the frogs singing their evening mating songs along the water's edge. The sheets are soaked, soreness returns to my body.

But it's the ache in my chest that is inconsolable.

He's leaving.

Two

Emily

The sun is beaming down rare warmth in a cloudless sky above the University of Cambridge. If I were the typical college student in the States, I'd be outside taking advantage of the uncharacteristic summer weather.

Most likely, I'd be on summer break by now, drinking cheap tequila on a beach. I'd be creating regrets, making bad decisions that would make for fun party stories for years to come.

I'm a little envious but will never admit it.

Instead, I'm at a century-old cafe outside the university, eying a flat white that was just set before me. The barista really outdid herself this time with the leaf design of the microfoam floating on the surface.

"Kudos, Klara," I tell my favorite barista, who is also my roommate. "I can really see a leaf on this one."

"Leaf?" She throws her hands up in frustration and huffs a breath of air to get her blond bangs away from her eyes, "That's a cat!"

I smile and blow on the hot coffee before taking a sip as Klara collapses in a chair beside me at our table. There are perks to having a roommate who works at the cafe, mainly free coffee, even if the foam designs will never be museum-worthy. "Delicious, either way," I take a gulp. "At least this one doesn't look like a dick again?"

"I get good tips on the dick ones. Any leads yet?" Klara nods to my open laptop set in front of me.

8

Part of the university's program is pairing international students up for housing. Klara is from Sweden and has a gorgeous, thick accent. She tells me I have a thick American accent.

We taught each other all the fun four-letter words in our languages, though Klara has me beat, by far, since she speaks fluent English, like most young Europeans, and I only remember what I learned in high school Spanish.

"I'm meeting Professor Tillman soon," I say as I check my watch. "He said he has exciting news, so I'm hoping it's a job opportunity. Otherwise, no, I'm just answering emails."

"More on the paper?" Klara asks as she rests her tired head on her elbows on the table.

Klara is working part-time at the cafe plus trying to wrap up her Master's degree in Energy Technologies. She is exhausted more often than not. I was able to finish my degree on schedule, whereas she's running behind and into overtime now.

The Master's programs at Cambridge are no joke, even compared to what I was used to as a mechanical engineering undergrad at MIT. But it's a nine-month program, versus two years in the States, so after weighing all the pros and cons, I took the plunge.

If I didn't have Mom and Dad footing the bill, I'd have been in the same boat as Klara, having to take a job to support myself and struggling through the coursework. I'm grateful to them that I was able to focus on my studies, and with my shiny new degree in hand, it's time to get my head down now and find gainful employment.

Except, I'm distracted.

"Yes, more people emailing about my paper," I smile and glance at my inbox where emails from another researcher and a tire manufacturer await me today.

My individual research project to graduate with a Masters of Materials Science in Engineering was chosen by the academic staff. At first, I was skeptical of the concept: Chemical Advances in the Compounds of Tire Manufacturing.

But it turned out to be fascinating because, as we say in the MSE program, everything is made of something.

What the world considers simple hunks of rubber have a fascinating inner private life, to me, anyway. Hundreds of seemingly insignificant raw materials come together, bond at a molecular level, and create something unprecedented, secure, and durable.

Better than the individual components alone.

My research project went big, diving into hydrocarbon chains within antizonants, oxidative reaction mechanisms, and solubility of rubber compounds. It went so well that Professor Tillman and I published a paper in the Journal of Materials Science theorizing a possible new stable hydrocarbon bond that has the potential to drastically reduce tire degradation.

Longer lasting tires, fewer tires sent to landfills, safer tires on every car on the road—it could be massive.

Nerd. At least I own it these days.

"Just lots of questions on the research, no job offers," I tell Klara, who is rubbing her temples. She mutters something in Swedish under her breath when a toddler in the corner starts wailing at the top of his lungs.

I'm sure it wasn't kind, Klara has a dark sense of humor and little patience. I watch the little boy have a tantrum and find myself a little envious again. Wouldn't it be grand to scream and wail every time you were tired or slighted? Just get it all out and move on with your life?

I do better at computer models and chemical formulas than analyzing the inner workings of humans. At least science makes sense, it's black and white. You create or fix something and then move on. Case closed.

Not so much with humans.

"Skitstövel," Klara sneers at the boy and mutters.

I repeat the word trying to get the pronunciation right. "I don't know that one, what is it?"

"Poop boot," Klara thunders in the boy's direction. "Bastard," she sneers.

I choke on the coffee I was just sipping, almost launching microfoam out of my nose as I laugh and reach for a napkin. "Klara!" I scold her as the boy's mom gasps at Klara's menacing glance and outburst. "You're going to get fired," I giggle across the round table.

"Ja, ja, ja," she cajoles and waves her hand. "There is only one choice. You get a job and support us," she taps the screen of my laptop.

"I'm trying, I'm trying. But if you get canned, we'll have to pay for coffee."

"Unimaginable," Klara shudders her shoulders at the thought.

I do have to get a job, though. Quickly.

Now that I've graduated, my student visa is only valid for four months. I have to get a real job if I want to stay in the UK. And I do want to stay.

Maybe not here, perhaps not so close to London. That's a little too close for comfort.

Maybe something in Wales or Ireland. Scotland would also be delightful. Minimally, something several hours away from London.

Not that London isn't lovely. It is.

But I can't stay here.

I've done well the past ten months to avoid London at all costs, but I can't do it forever, hiding out in Cambridge sixty miles to the north. Bad enough I have to come up with constant creative excuses not to join Klara on weekend benders in the city.

In many ways, I've missed out on the quintessential college experience, being holed up in my room, buried in books, spending my weekend in the labs instead of being young and having fun. I wonder if I'll regret that one day, doing anything at all exciting like I used to.

Then again, school is safe for me. I'm good at it.

Usually, I blame my strict parents for my reclusiveness and cite Major General Walker's notorious lack of tolerance for shenanigans. But a twenty-five year old not being allowed out by mommy and daddy, who are three-thousand miles away, is lame, even for me.

I let out a long, audible sigh.

"What?" Klara asks, picking up on the change in my demeanor.

"Mmm, nothing," I shrug my shoulders. "Just remembered I need to call my parents back."

"Ugh," she rolls her eyes.

Apparently, the Swedish have a different parenting style, which doesn't involve hovering, authoritative discipline, or constant reminders that failure is not an option. Klara was given freedom as a child, allowed to explore and experience the world, make her own mistakes.

I was… not.

My parents love me, and I wouldn't be where I am today, a master's graduate from one of the finest educational institutions in the world, without them. A tingle of guilt stabs at me, but I sometimes wonder what it would feel like if mistakes were an option.

But, they aren't, and I learned that lesson the hard way when I didn't listen and made the biggest mistake of my life. One that continues to haunt me, in secret, every day, wakes me up from dreams and infects my mind even though it's been almost six years.

The mistake who lives in London.

In his fancy fucking apartment with his fancy fucking girlfriend-of-the-week.

Stop it, you crazy person.

"Ladies," I look up and see Professor Tillman pulling up a chair to our table.

I was so zoned out in my self-inflicted neurosis that I didn't even notice him come in. He's in his customary tweed jacket with elbow patches and carrying a leather portfolio. With his bushy gray hair, he could pass as an original Cambridge founder, but he is brilliant, and I have tremendous respect for him.

"Professor Tillman," I stand up to meet him, but he motions for me to stay sitting and takes a seat.

He's extra perky today, his eyes bright and his shoulders dancing back and forth. He looks like he's ready to dance a tango.

My stomach grows tense hoping he has good news for me today. Maybe someone has picked up our research and wants us to continue our work. Then I could stay here forever.

"Emily, Emily, Emily," he teases. "One of these days, you will start calling me Roger."

"Sorry, Doc," I smile back at him. "Old habits die hard."

I was taught from a young age that you call someone by the name they earned, not the name they were given. Hence why Dad is still Major General, and Doc is the least formal name I can bring myself to call Professor Tillman in respect for his earned PhD.

"Ms. Bergner," he turns toward Klara. "Only two courses left to go, the end is in sight now."

"Ja, Emily has been helping me in Advanced Energy Transformation. It's in the bin now," Klara smiles.

"Bag, it's in the bag now," I lovingly correct her. "Bin would be bad, bag is good."

"Ha," Professor Tillman chuckles. "You're lucky to have my star pupil as a tutor, Ms. Bergner. I have every confidence that it's in the bag now."

"Ah, bin, bag, as long as I graduate," Klara shrugs and pulls her blond ponytail tighter. "Back to the coal mines," she says, winking at me as she stands to go back to work.

I nod at her, she got that colloquialism right.

I need to research what her poop-boot phrase from earlier means, in more detail. Is it poop on a boot, like one stepped in it? Is it a boot full of poop—that would be horrifying. A boot made entirely out of poop? That would be gross and structurally unsound.

"Emily, I have wonderful news," Professor Tillman leans in toward me and catches me off guard, going off in one of the many tangents my mind dreams up at any given moment.

He unzips his portfolio and starts pulling out papers. He's beaming, and my excitement grows. "Is it about the paper?" I bounce in my seat.

"Better! Well, it started with the paper, of course, so many emails and phone calls, Emily."

"I know, I have one from the research and development department at Echeleon Tire today asking about the hydroperoxide radicals."

"You aren't giving our secrets away, are you?" He snickers.

"No, of course not" I shake my head. "I was hoping they'd offer me a job, but they just have more questions. Still, how exciting."

"Pffft, Echeleon," he rolls his eyes and waves his hand as if they're rubbish. "We can do better than that, Emily."

Better than Echelon? They're one of the top ten tire manufacturers in the world. "What is it?" I ask him, unable to control my excitement a moment longer. The suspense is killing me.

"You have an interview!"

"An interview? For a job? With who?" My pulse picks up, and I feel my palms start getting clammy.

It's really happening. After years of working diligently toward this, studying into the late hours of the night instead of binge drinking, after getting into my chosen program at Cambridge and relocating to Europe, it's finally happening.

"Only one of the most advanced engineering roles available at one of the most prestigious young companies in London," he rambles with frenzy in his voice. He's almost hysterical as he shuffles papers and beams at me. "I'm so proud of you, Emily!"

"Oh my god, what is it? You're going to give me a heart attack!"

Maybe it's SpaceX, they're a prestigious young company. Or GeoTech, they were advertising for a polymer engineer in their London lab. Or, he said it started with the research paper. Maybe it's one of the British auto manufacturers.

Professor Tillman finally passes me the papers in his hand as my heart is ready to beat out of my chest. But he hasn't let them go.

As I have one hand on them, he continues, "Now, it's just an interview, I can't promise you the job. But I know a higher-up, and well, he owes me a favor. They read the paper, this job is unexpectedly open, and, of course, I told them you'd be perfect."

Manners be damned, I snag the papers out of his hand and try to control myself from dreaming of the next step in my career, the new and exciting opportunity I begin now.

No.

No, no, no. What the hell is this? Some kind of sick joke? Am I being punished for something I've done in a past life, despite not believing in reincarnation? Maybe this is a sign I should start.

"Can you believe it?" Professor Tillman smacks the table and taps the papers.

"No," I mutter, staring at the lob listing.

No, I cannot believe it.

There is a sinking feeling in my gut, it radiates down from my chest. I have diligently avoided this for ten freaking months, and now the logo stares me down like I'm an animal trapped in a cage.

This is just… well, it's goddamn ridiculous, is what it is.

"Imperium! You have an interview with Imperium, Emily!" I lift my face and see Professor Tillman's eyes as round as saucers.

Shit shit shit.

How am I going to get out of this? I'm not doing this shit. I'm not ready.

"Umm, I don't know about this," I start fidgeting with the papers and creating plausible excuses as to why I will absolutely never, ever attend this interview.

"Don't be nervous. I know it's an enormous opportunity, but you would be perfect for this role. They'd be foolish not to snap you up!"

"Right," I clear my throat and stall, fight the panic from within. "It's just that, I'm not really interested in Formula 1."

I only watch every free practice session, qualification session, and race, in secret. I only have fake usernames on the F1 subreddit and a few other social platforms created to indulge my neurotic behavior, which, at this point, can only be described as cyber-stalking.

But I'm not interested.

"Nonsense, half of the engineering students are here to land a job in Formula 1. And you, my dear Emily, are on the fast track in! Do you know how lucky you are to be considered just out of college?"

Professor Tillman is right, of course. An overwhelming number of students are here chasing dreams of F1. London is surrounded by six of the most successful racing teams, and Cambridge has several degrees catering to the specialized industry. This part of the UK is even called Motorsports Valley.

But I did not sign up for that. I came to Cambridge *despite* the proximity to everything F1.

I'm here running *away* from my F1 dreams.

F1 nightmares, more like it.

"Thank you for the recommendation, truly. I'm sorry, this just isn't right for me, though." I push the papers across the table back toward him and do my best to remain professional, polite, sane.

"Not right for you? What are you on about? It is a Tire and Performance Engineer position, and it's available immediately, in the middle of the season. It's custom made for you, did you read the description?" Professor Tillman's bushy brows are furrowed, and his face is getting red. I've never seen him angry before.

I glanced over the description. If it were at another company in another industry and, preferably, on another continent, it *would* be perfect.

"I'm not qualified," I stammer in a desperate attempt to get out of this. I want to slink back to my flat and reassess my life choices over a stiff drink.

"Don't insult me," Professor Tillman barks in an uncharacteristic, bitter tone. "I am your advisor and professor, and my name is listed alongside yours on that research paper. If you feel unqualified, then that is a reflection upon me."

"No," I shake my head, and my jaw drops in horror.

Shit. The last thing I mean to do is insult him. Not even because doing so would be monumentally stupid for my career, but because I value Doc's opinion and hold him in such high esteem. He has been one of the best things about coming to Cambridge. He has taught me so much.

"What is this about, Emily? I have never known you to run away from a challenge."

Ha, if you only knew.

I can see the disappointment in the gray of his eyes, and I look down into my mug of flat white that's still steaming.

The foam has almost all dissolved into the coffee. It shouldn't have denatured so quickly, not at this temperature.

I glance at Klara, working the cappuccino machine behind the counter, pushing a button over and over and cursing at it. I know why she cannot make good foam art. She's overheating the milk, melting the lipids, and destroying the hydrophilic ends of the protein chains.

"Emily?"

"Sorry, Professor," I snap back to attention and wring my hands together under the table, desperate for an acceptable excuse to offer him.

I'm allergic to racing fuel.

My religion does not tolerate motorsports.

I have cranophobia, fear of helmets.

Is there a fear of heartbreak and rejection? If not, there should be, and I should be allowed to cite it.

I deserve to cite it.

"Listen, I was young once and nervous about leaving academia, too." Professor Tillman's shoulders soften, and he attempts to reassure me, but he doesn't understand. "This is a position that will challenge you, and maybe that frightens you. But you need to be challenged to be fulfilled. I believe in you, and you're going to ace the interview. You have a couple of days to prepare and, if I know you, you will use them wisely to strategize."

"A couple of days?"

Oh, hell, no.

"Yes, as a favor to me, you are fast-tracked to interview this Friday at 9:00. I wrote it down for you, see?" He flips the paper and shows me the details. "Edmund Lloyd, Engineering Director, that's who you'll meet. Surely you've heard of him?"

"Uh-huh," I nod and force my lips to rise in a quivering smile. I've heard of him because I see him on TV, too. I read about him, also.

"Wonderful, just wonderful!" Doc' claps his hands together. "What an opportunity. Promise me good tickets when you get this position, Emily. I knew you were destined for greatness, I just knew it."

His smile has returned, and he radiates pride back at me now.

Oh, bloody hell. What am I going to do?

Three

Seven Years Ago - Florida

"Baby you need a break so let's just run away. Well I'm tired of coding Perl, tired of VBA, Maggie throw your law books away. Turn on, tune in, drop out, give up with me." Cracker - Turn On, Tune In, Drop Out With Me

Cole

"Please get back in the boat before a fucking alligator eats you."

"There are no alligators here, Cole. I'm much more likely to be eaten by a snake," she tries to flatten her lips, but I can see a corner of her mouth quirk up, just a tiny bit.

She knows exactly what she's doing to me, she always does.

I'm right here. Come in the water and chase me, Cole.

I'm trying not to dump this ridiculous orange kayak while reaching for Emily. She's stubbornly keeping herself just out of arm's reach, wading in the clear, shallow waters of St. Petersburg's Weedon Island.

Her long brown hair is even darker than usual, waterlogged, and slicked back against her head. It floats out around her shoulders when she submerges herself. When she pops back up from under the water, it drips off her eyelashes, and the sun catches the drops, glistening all over her sun-kissed skin.

I want to lick every drop of it off her as soon as she gets back in the kayak. The monstrosity looks like an oversized hunting vest, complete with yellow oars so that displaced tourists and drunk kids can be spotted by helicopters when they don't return home from their kayak adventures.

Or when they get eaten by alligators.

"I have a snake in the boat for you," I mumble to myself.

Dangling precariously over the side of the kayak, I manage to reach her fingers and start to pull her back to safety where there are no alligators, piranha, or swamp creatures, and the only snake posing a danger to her is in my board shorts.

The kayak starts teetering from side to side.

"Em," I warn her. She's brought her feet up to the underside of the boat, clutches my hand, and bites her lip mischievously. "Don't you do it."

When I surface for air, the kayak is flipped over, the yellow oars float aimlessly nearby, and our once-dry clothes are sinking. Our little cooler is floating nearby but has sprung open and liberated empty soda cans.

But Emily is laughing, her smile lighting up the shadows of the mangrove trails, and the darkest corners of my world.

Like the last several weekends, Emily has dreamt up a new adventure to embark us upon, and while I've lived in Tampa most of my life, I've never kayaked the mangroves before. Or any of the other undertakings, experiments, games, or projects she's so keen on.

She thinks she's dragging me to all these adventures, and, if I'm honest, I let her think that because I want the brownie points. But besides getting to spend time with her all day, she's also making me live a little beyond the only other obsession I've ever known—the track.

It's only been a month or so since she finally relented and started speaking more than one-word answers to me, stopped running away all the while begging me to chase her.

Once she did, we were late for every class. I was entranced with her every word and couldn't end a simple conversation with her when the bell rang. And as soon as she saw me, her face would light up. The girl spoke in *novels* like she'd been waiting her whole life for someone to listen to her.

Like that someone was me.

Eleven minute drives home from school became four-hour, two-hundred-mile road trips around Florida. And now that we've shifted from friend-zone to *more*, and I'll be goddamned if some starving, sneaky anaconda or blood thirty crocodile is going to steal her from me.

I'd chase this girl across the earth and through the ends of time.

"Oh no, it seems as though I've capsized our vessel," she giggles and lets out a snort. An actual snort.

There is something about making her laugh, making her smile. The quiet girl at school who ignores everyone, who stares out the window all day like she's dreaming of being anyplace else.

She makes me feel like I take her there.

The girl who pays no attention to the teacher but still aces every test. There's something so powerful about me being able to make her eyes go from dull and disinterested to full, dancing, and dazzling.

I get to do this for her.

I'm not just worth something when I'm with her, I feel like a fucking god. She's so incredibly smart and kind, and unique. She talks about things that matter. I don't know what the hell she sees in me, because Emily Walker is a good girl, not the usual kind who see bragging rights when they look at me. No, Emily sees something else. She looks at me like I hung the moon—and I need more of it.

Testing the depth, my feet hit the soft earth below me, and my toes sink into the silt, giving me enough traction to drag Emily through the water and up against me. Her palms flatten against my chest, and she looks up at me through her wet lashes, a tremor running through both of us and arcing between our bodies like electricity.

"Looks that way, gorgeous girl. Kayaking is not your forte." I rest my hands on her midriff, my thumbs caressing her hip bones. She's treading water trying to stay afloat, her feet not reaching the ground. Grabbing her behind her knees, I wrap her legs around my waist to anchor her.

She inhales sharply, then whispers, "Good."

"Why is that good?" I sink down to my neck in the water and hold onto her, doing my best to keep my dick where it belongs and not make her uncomfortable. She's not like other girls.

Her fingers expand over my chest. I can feel her energy seep through my pores and send a bolt of heat through my spinal cord.

"This is the only time I get to fail. It feels good."

"It feels good to fail?"

"Maybe that's not exactly it," her hands grip my shoulders for support as a small boat goes by and sends a wave rolling into us. "It feels good that I can try whatever I want, and there are no consequences. You aren't disappointed that I dumped our kayak. Are you?"

"No," I chuckle and kiss her forehead.

Hell, she could sink the US Naval fleet, and I wouldn't be disappointed in her. I'd be helping her launch the torpedos.

I know plenty about consequences, though.

"Is that why we do this stuff every weekend? So you can screw up," I ask her, letting my hands trace up and down her back.

"Partially," she looks over my shoulder and nods before giving me her big, brown eyes again. "I mean, I do like learning new things too, but I don't know. I just... we can be bad at things together, and no one cares."

"If this is you being bad, Emily Walker, I need to up my game," I wink at her and watch a rose blush creep up her chest and neck.

"You know what I mean," she lowers her head to my shoulder.

I can't keep my lips from grazing the tiny smattering of freckles that dance across her shoulder.

I do know what she means, though, because my world revolves around consequences. Different from her consequences, but what do semantics matter?

Failing most certainly does not feel good in the Ballentine household, though.

"Is that what I am to you, too? Your experiment with being bad?" I don't know what I'll do if she says yes. While I'm okay with being used by most chicks for fulfilling their daddy issues, that isn't what I thought Emily and I had.

"No, I didn't mean it like that," she fires back at me, her eyes going round and searching mine like she's waiting for me to crack, to bleed, before her. "You're not an experiment. You're also not as bad as you think you are."

"No?" I tug her waist against me, partially because I want to teach her how she can *really* be bad, partially because I want to feel more of her. And partially because I need more clarity before I lose more of myself in her if we're not on the same page. And I'm not above forcing honesty out of her.

"You just want me to think you're bad," she smiles and rubs herself against me.

Fuck, this girl is going to destroy me.

"No one thinks I'm *good*, Em."

And I do mean no one.

Everyone at school knows I'm just biding my time until graduation, fulfilling the mandatory obligation before I move on, doing the bare minimum. I stay just this side of being arrested most nights because while Stanley Ballentine doesn't give two shits about what I do or *who* I do, an arrest record *would* interfere with his plans for me, and there *would* be consequences then.

"I do, and I like that I'm the only one who gets to see it," she smiles and nips my bottom lip.

The hint of her jealousy turns me on more than is probably emotionally healthy, but that's never been my strong suit. Plus, what am I supposed to do when this beautiful girl is biting my lip and grinding herself on my dick that's barely containing itself behind some thin polyester?

I wish I could kiss her sweetly like she deserves, because even when Emily is bad—she's good—but, instead, I kiss her like she's my next meal and I haven't eaten in a hundred years.

With her legs locked behind my back, I absorb the taste of her-- sunshine and a trace of the Dr. Pepper that now floats down the river. Throw in a hint of a good girl wanting to be very bad with me, and it's like heroin in my veins.

"Yo Ballentine," someone yells behind me just as a splash hits me in the face, and Emily's lips pull apart from mine. "Your kayak is floating away."

My chest puffs up like a rooster preparing to defend his flock against a hawk. I move Emily behind me as I turn, grabbing the football Chuck Dixon has launched at us. Three kayaks make their way closer to us, and the cackling of drunk girls echoes through the mangroves.

"Hi, Cole," one of them waves at me and tries to stand in her kayak with Kyle whats-his-face.

"Sit down, Brittany," Kyle yells at her when the kayak starts to wobble.

I toss the football back at Chuck and issue them my customary greeting, "What's up assholes?"

"Party at Bryce's tonight, you coming?" He asks while their kayak parade creeps slowly down the river in front of us.

"Maybe," I answer him, keeping one hand on Em's legs that are still wrapped around me from behind.

I have no intentions of drinking shitty beer at Bryce's tonight when I have this goddess wrapped around me, wrapped up in me, wrapping me up in her.

"Come on, man, we haven't partied in weeks."

Uh-huh, see the aforementioned goddess.

"You should come, Cole," one of the other chicks bats her lashes at me. She pushes her chest out, then peers around my shoulders and purses her lips at Emily, "Hello, Emily."

"Hey," Emily answers from behind me, disgust echoing from her voice.

"Want me to get your kayak, man?" Chuck asks as they float past it.

"Nope."

"Leave the lovebirds alone, dude," Kyle laughs as they finally pass us.

"Bye, Cole!" The three girls wave and giggle.

As soon as they're out of sight, I spin back to Emily and vow to murder those pricks when I see the crestfallen look on her face. I was very fucking clear with them.

"They still leaving you and Makenna alone?"

"Yep," she tries to unwrap her legs from me, but hell no. Not over these jealous assholes, anyway.

"I like those legs right where they are."

"You should go to the party," she sighs.

"Do *you* want to go to the party?" Because that's the only way I'm going.

"No," she shakes her head. "The Major General wouldn't let me, anyway. He thinks I'm at Makenna's house right now, but that won't work all night."

I groan. This asshole treats Emily like she's made of porcelain, like she's not a straight-A student, a girl who thinks deliberately overturning a kayak is naughty.

I mean, I can't blame him for not wanting his pristine daughter hanging out with the likes of me. But Emily is smart and capable and doesn't deserve to be kept in an ivory tower. She doesn't deserve having to sneak around just to go kayaking or lie every weekend to spread her wings a little.

"How long do I have you for?"

"We've got time," she smiles and throws her arms around my neck. "Do you have to go to the track today, too?"

She's getting goosebumps up and down her arms, so I walk us into the sun. Slinking back down in the water, I run my hands over her to warm her up. It's ninety degrees out, but the girl is perpetually cold. "Yeah, I need to get some laps in."

"Can I come with again?"

"Absolutely," I can't fight the grin that overtakes my face at her wanting to come to the kart track with me again.

"Stanley won't be pissed?"

"Fuck him." Stanley will most certainly be pissed. I'll catch more shit about it from the old man, but it's well worth it to have Em with me all day, beaming down at me in the bleachers, looking at me like she wants to climb me when I'm in my race suit.

"We should go, then," she kisses me, and I fight the urge to keep my vise grip around her waist when her legs fall off my hips.

Wading downstream to the kayak, I drag Emily behind me. She's laughing and floundering about trying to stay above water. She goes quiet when I right the kayak and throw one waterlogged shoe back inside that was floating nearby.

"Cole..."

I turn around, and Emily has one of the yellow oars raised in her hand, her eyes are enormous, and she's watching the shoreline a few feet away.

My eyes dart to where she's looking, "Is that..."

"I think it's an Eastern Diamondback, maybe."

I reach slowly for her and pull her away, the snake moving over mangrove roots and watching us. Its tail is rattling, and its forked tongue is visible from how close we are.

"Get in the boat, Em," I whisper, because I don't know if you're supposed to be quiet around snakes or make noise, like bears, but quiet seems appropriate.

Emily moves to the side of the kayak, and I put myself between her and the snake, its beady little eyes never leaving us. Emily tries to lift herself in the kayak, but it just wobbles and thrashes from her efforts.

"Stop, stop, stop," I put a hand on her. Every time the kayak rocks, the snake gets agitated and bobs its head around, tracking the movement, inching closer to us.

"You get in and pull me up," she breathes, the nerves and fear in her voice audible. She's still wielding the oar like she's going to bash the snake to death.

"I'm not leaving you in the fucking water."

Ever so slowly, I move the kayak, so it's between the snake and me. That only seems to piss it off even more. Maybe these damn things are like bulls, and the bright color is enraging it, fuck if I know. But, at least now, I have a barrier between Emily and the serpent I knew was lying in wait for her since she dove from the goddamn kayak earlier.

"Okay, I'm going to get in and pull you up," because, as usual, Emily's advice was the smart choice.

Moving as slowly as I can, I lift my torso onto the kayak. As soon as I start swinging my legs over, the water displacement from the kayak sinking a few inches rushes at the snake. It falls into the water and heads right toward us, its head and tail above water, his body propelling him forward.

Moving faster than I ever have, I throw my legs over the kayak and grab at Emily to haul her up. But she's screaming and smacking the water with the giant yellow oar like Jaws is after our boat.

Despite her wild attacks, I'm able to wrap my arms around her shoulders and haul her over me, lying flat in the kayak, so we don't flip the damn thing again.

"Are you in?" I yell in a panic, trying to make sure her legs are on board and aren't going to get chewed off by this devil creature.

"I'm in, I'm in," she pants. "Can it still get us?"

Hell if I know, I'm not Steve fucking Irwin. But that snake is going to be a pair of boots long before it reaches Emily.

"Stay still," I take the oar from her and sit up. Finally, my eyes find the bastard on the other side of the river, making its way back up onto more mangrove roots.

"He's gone," I tell her.

She sits up and starts rubbing her thighs, which are red and scuffed up from me dragging her over the side of the kayak in a panic. "Damn it, Em, you could have been hurt attacking it with the oar. What the hell?" I inspect her legs. She's going to have huge bruises.

"It was coming at us!"

I shake my head and run my palms over the red marks on her legs. "Are you okay?"

"I'm fine. I didn't hurt it, did I?"

This girl... death of me, I swear to christ.

I take her face in my hands and give her the kiss she deserves, the sweet one, the one that tells her how amazing she is, how special she is, how good she is.

"I'm supposed to rescue *you*, you know."

Those gorgeous brown eyes meet mine, the ones that haunt my dreams and make things in my chest tighten and constrict unnaturally. "You did," she breathes around my mouth. "You do, every day."

Four

"When the stars were right, They could plunge from world to world through the sky; but when the stars were wrong, They could not live." - H.P. Lovecraft - The Call of Cthulhu

Emily

"Oh, no," Makenna's eyes go wide, and her hand flies to her mouth as soon as the video chat connects. Her face takes over my laptop screen.

"Oh, yes," I reply and move the half-drunk glass bottle she's staring at further toward the camera lens.

My good friend, Sailor Jerry, only comes to visit during times of extreme emotional duress. The honorable seaman always brings along his ninety-two proof friends and eventually whisks me off into a spiced rum dreamland where Cole Ballentine ceases to exist.

I haven't seen Jerry for a long time.

Not since Makenna and I last met up in the States and, in an Everclear induced stupor, we decided to see if Cole's old cell phone number still worked.

Sailor Jerry would never have allowed me to dial that vintage number I purposely never deleted.

Everclear, however, that nasty bitch will turn on you.

The number worked. Why the hell did he never change it after all these years? I met with the haunting sound of his voice for the first time in so long, hearing my name leave his lips again.

Emily?

Em?

Is that you?

I hung up without uttering a word, and that was the last time Jerry took me to bed and made me forget.

I'm not a big drinker, too much of a control freak. But desperate times call for desperate measures.

And I am a desperate woman.

"It finally happened? You saw him?" Makenna's hands are still on her cheeks, partially hidden under plumes of her long, curly black hair.

"Worse," I mumble.

"Shit. Okay, let me see what I have," Makenna grabs her laptop and takes me along with her through her apartment in San Antonio, Texas. Her refrigerator light comes on. "I don't have Sailor Jerry, but I have merlot. It'll have to do." She returns to her bedroom with a bottle of wine, no glass.

This is not a night for civilized drinking.

Makenna is my best friend and one of the only people who knows the real me, flaws, failures, and all. Another military brat, we both found ourselves in Tampa when our fathers were serving at MacDill Air Force base.

The Cole Ballentine Years for me, in retrospect.

Makenna was was just another shy, nerdy girl used to being the new kid in school, used to being picked on and uprooted from her home every year or two.

We tend to stick together, those of us who feel like we never really belong anywhere.

Makenna was the weirdo who withdrew into art and is now a brilliant photographer. Back then, the Florida humidity wreaked havoc on her gorgeous curls and set her up for a host of cruel jokes and nicknames like "Bush Beast." It got worse when she burnt large swaths of it off while trying to straighten it into submission.

I was quiet and introverted, the perpetually new kid everywhere I went. People thought I was shy, but that wasn't it. I just had nothing to say to them.

School bored the hell out of me, the other kids annoyed the shit out of me, and they deemed me "creepy" even though I was the blandest girl in school with my dull, straight, brown hair and generic brown eyes.

I wanted Makenna's bouncy curls, and she wanted my stick-straight locks. The grass is always greener, but all the grass is dead and dried up in high school when you're not in the popular crowd.

Knowing what I do now, I probably should have listened to my gut back then with Cole. He was so far out of my league it took him months to convince me he wasn't setting me up with an elaborate hoax when he kept trying to talk to me, sitting next to me in class, showing up at my locker.

Tall, cool, popular, wealthy father, hot car, obscenely handsome—everyone thought he had it all. He walked those halls, and you'd swear he was Moses parting the Red Sea.

He owned every room he walked into. Every angsty teenage girl desperate for a fixer-upper bad boy lined up to drop her panties with one sexy smirk.

Yet, he wanted me. I may have made him chase me down and prove it because the concept was outlandish at the time.

And he did prove it, relentlessly.

Funny thing, it turns out everyone is an insecure disaster in high school. No one was immune. What you see on the surface is never what lurks below.

Cole's life was a thousand times the mess mine was, he just hid it better, dealt with it better, coped better. Both of us camouflaged who we really were, but when we were together, we fit. We clung to one another.

He put an end to the reign of terror Makenna and I endured, straight away. Teenage me thought he was my soulmate, that we'd be together forever.

Now?

Well, now he's just the reason I'll have a hangover in the morning.

He's also the reason I'll be perpetually single if I don't stop subconsciously comparing every other man to him or driving them away because it's better to do the leaving than to be left.

I fill Makenna in on the pending interview with Imperium this week, and she doesn't speak until half her bottle of merlot is gone. "Obviously, you have to go," she twiddles her fingers.

She's still thinking of ways around it, whereas I've resigned myself to it at this point. There is no way out of it without disrespecting Professor Tillman and jeopardizing my professional credentials with him and, therefore, the university.

"I do, but it's just an interview, right? I won't get the job. The odds of me seeing him at corporate headquarters must be slim to none." I'm not sure if I am trying to convince Makenna or myself.

"We need contingency plans. What if they offer you the job?"

"I thought of that, so I will blow the interview, totally cock it up," I nod, spurred on with my ploy by spiced rum.

"I don't see you being able to blow an interview, but okay," Makenna shakes her head. "The real question is what you'll do if you run into him."

"Do you think kicking him in the balls is too extreme?"

"Not at all. That would be ideal, actually. You'll get your revenge *and* get blackballed by the company. They'll probably issue a restraining order," Makenna nods.

This is making way too much sense as my head gets foggy, and the room begins to spin.

"It's been six years, Makenna, what is wrong with me?" I wrap my hands around my friend Jerry and take another swig. I have actually researched this extensively, looking for a reason why I cannot get over Cole Ballentine.

I am a highly functioning, smart, capable woman, for God's sake. My eyes and hair may still be dull brown, but I've filled out pretty nicely, I think. I've been out with other men. I've had unfulfilling sex with some of them.

None of them ever do it for me, though. Not physically, not emotionally, not anything—it's like all the electricity has been cut, and I've been working off a back-up generator for six years.

Certainly, none of them haunt my dreams or make me replay memories over and over like a motion picture in my mind.

I could date a million men, sleep my way across the UK, and none of them would make me feel the way Cole did. None of them would ever know me the way he did, none could light my soul on fire the way he did with one glance.

None of them would ever hurt you as much, either.

"Please," Makenna sputters, sending merlot down her chin. "I'm still hung up on Doug Masters, and he was a world-class douche."

"Total douche," I agree with a bob of my head. "Remember when we put methylene blue in his soda and made him piss blue for a week? What a little bitch," I giggle like an idiot.

Doug's biggest ambition in life was making bongs out of large vegetables, and my beautiful, creative friend was far too good for his dumb ass.

"Umm, *you* put methylene blue in his drink. You always rose to the occasion in times of crisis. Me? I sat around crying for weeks on end like a loser."

"Mmm-hmm, that's right. Don't mess with my crew," I waive my Sailor Jerry at the screen. I'm such a gangster. "If you're a loser, though, what the hell am I, Makenna?"

"Please. At least I only have to see Doug when I Facebook creep on him. You have to see Cole on TV, in magazines, watch him flaunt around with hot wom... sorry," she cuts herself off when she sees my face go ashen.

"It's okay," I blink. Part of me is relieved to hear someone else fess up to Facebook creeping since I am guilty of that, as well.

Because you are a crazy person.

"I mean, really, most people don't have to deal with that shit, Emily. It's not right."

She has a point. I've considered it before but thought I was pacifying myself.

When most boyfriends leave you, they fall off the face of the earth. They crawl back under whatever rock they emerged from. They don't go on to become successful F1 drivers achieving their dream all over NBC, Sky Sports, and ESPN every week.

First-loves change us all, I suppose.

They leave a mark on your heart and soul that fundamentally alters your chemistry. An indelible blotch etched deep inside that can't be scrubbed away no matter how much Sailor Jerry you scour it with.

Maybe you only get one true love. Perhaps you give so much of your heart away that there is simply nothing left for anyone else.

Would Makenna be haunted by Doug to this day if she had to see him on the cover of magazines every time she went to the grocery store?

If I'd ever felt the same about anyone else, I might get over it. Maybe I need to try harder.

Logically speaking, Cole is just another bundle of DNA walking around the planet. A stupidly handsome bundle of DNA, but flesh and bone just like everyone else. There is no science supporting the concept of soulmates or eternal love.

I've looked.

Magic and fairytales do not exist. Certainly not in jolly old England, like I once hoped.

I wish my heart understood logic and reason, but it continues to beat to its own drum without regard for cold, calculating science. It's filled with the all-consuming consequences of giving itself over, entirely, to someone who was supposed to protect and cherish it.

"I'm being an idiot," I mumble.

"You're the smartest person I know, shut the hell up," Makenna fires back, which makes me giggle more.

I need to stop drinking, I'm not a giggling kind of girl.

"I still want your curly hair," I smile and touch the screen like I'm petting her. Shit, I'm drunk.

"There's enough of it to go around, I'll ship you a pound or two," Makenna's chin drops as she burps. "You know what? Fuck him, Emily."

"Fuck him? Like you think I should fuck him again? That sounds nice," I close my eyes and imagine fucking Cole again.

Those few months we had together after my first time, spending every day together culminating in being naked in his arms, they're never too far out of my mind. He took the last little piece of me and, from that day forward and ever since, Cole Ballentine has owned every cell in my body.

Stolen them.

That was right before he accepted the offer to the Imperium Junior Driver Program and moved to Europe, leaving me all alone in swamp-ass-Florida.

Why I can't turn the feelings off, I will never understand. My brain and my heart have long since given up being friends. I know love isn't a choice, but you'd think self-preservation would kick in after enough time, and it would heal.

Sometimes I think it has, but then I'll see a photo of him, or a video, or a race. I'll swear I see him in a crowd, a flash of those electric blue eyes. Then I'm right back in high school with my best friend, my first and only love, with the man who still owns me.

He just doesn't want me.

I mean, that's what I have to believe because he left me with no other option that will satisfy my brain. After he became my everything, Cole Ballentine ghosted me. He made me promises, he made plans for us even after he left. He held my heart in his hands and swore me his forever. And then he just... stopped.

He stopped returning calls, texts, emails. There was no reason, no explanation given. There was no big fight or breakup. There was only a cold, abrupt, silent end to my world and I was left alone to fill in the gaps of why.

WHY WHY WHY

Three little letters can cause so much destruction. And when asked of humans, of love, I get no answers.

Maybe I seek answers to WHY in science now instead. I get answers then, indisputable facts of WHY something is the way it is.

"No, don't fuck him-fuck him. I mean like fuck that rotten sewer rat," Makenna clarifies. She's slurring her words too. It makes me feel better that I'm not the only drunk idiot right now.

"Maybe I will fuck him-fuck him. And then I'll leave *his* ass this time," I shake Sailor Jerry at my screen.

"Yessssssssss," she hisses and raises her bottle in solidarity.

I'm not thinking clearly, at all, but boy would it be nice to enact this plan and get properly fucked again for a change. How glorious it would be to come home after sex and not have to arrange a second date with Mr. Hitachi and his Magic Wand because the first man can't get the damn job done.

"If I can't get over him, I may as well get under him, eh, eh?" I snort.

"Now, now, Emily, what would the Major General say?" Makenna puts her hands on her hips and tucks her chin down, performing her best impression of my overbearing father in his customary, rigid stance.

I cross my arms over my chest and lower my voice to mock him, "Live up to your potential, Emily. You lack self-discipline, Emily. I won't let you throw your life away on that loser, Emily. Failure is not an option, Emily." I felt like one of his cadets for most of my childhood.

"Mom would support my fuck-him, plan," I drop my arms and sigh. Not that I would ever discuss this with her, but Mom loved Cole. She still loves Cole.

When Dad tried grounding me and removing all of my privileges after finding out Cole had deflowered his pristine daughter, it was Mom who listened, sympathized, and never tattled when I simply snuck around instead.

It never dawned on him that when parents make their children lie, their children simply become excellent liars.

I honestly don't know how Ava Walker has remained the dutiful wife of Major General Thomas Walker all these years. They're polar opposites.

And contrary to another American colloquialism, the only opposites that attract in real life are magnets. Line up a magnet's North Pole to another's South Pole, and they'll cling to one another. North to North, though, they repel and push each other away.

"Do you think my parents are like magnets?" I squint at Makenna.

"I've had too much wine if this is some science shit, Emily. Speak English."

I'm really drunk and having deep thoughts about magnets.

Pathetic.

I shake my head and dismiss the silly thoughts about imaginary forces drawing Cole and I together or pushing us apart, even though he's now only an hour away from me.

Nope, there were no force fields in play.

Just Cole leaving then forgetting all about me within the first month as his new life in Europe got more exciting. Nerdy, naive Emily Walker back at home was left behind.

I don't dare admit this to even Makenna, but I don't even hate Cole for it. I'm mad at myself for being so stupid. This, Formula 1, was Cole's dream.

His dad moved to Tampa just so Cole would have access to the best karting tracks and coaches in the States. He was always on this trajectory. It was me who interfered, and I simply could not compete.

It's easier to pretend to hate him, though.

I wish I could.

Five

"I'm standing in your corridor, I wonder what I'm waiting for. The leaves are drifting out to sea. I'm waiting for you desperately." - Cracker - I Want Everything

Cole

It's 8:45 am. I have more adrenaline coursing through my veins than before the start of a race waiting for the lights to go out.

I pace back and forth in front of the large windows in Edmund's office, stopping every few seconds to watch the parking lot for signs of her arrival.

"She didn't confirm the interview?" I ask my Engineering Director for the third time.

That isn't like her. Something's wrong.

"Same answer as the last two times," Edmund rolls his eyes and goes back to his computer screen to study the latest computer model the aerodynamic team sent up.

Edmund Lloyd's been our chief engineer since I came to Imperium as a teenager. He's an old-school kind of guy who cut his teeth in the Formula 1 of years past. He's worked with legends of the sport and is a traditionalist who preferred the old ways of doing things. He'd rather have raw horsepower than hybrid engines. "There's no replacement for displacement," is his favorite mantra. We've all heard it ad nauseam over the years.

Every year that F1 introduces different technical rules that he has to adapt to, he loses more hair. This year, it's a new tire manufacturer,

33

Concordia, that has his hairline receding even further, and the shiny bald spot on the top of his head has grown exponentially. The whole team has been struggling to get the most performance out of Concordia rubber.

I don't pretend to understand it all. I drive the car and can tell them what feels right, how the car reacts and responds to me. But why? I leave that to smarter people.

People like Edmund Lloyd and Emily Walker.

"I still don't understand this," Edmund raises one eyebrow at me suspiciously. "Just a friend from high school, but you're going to wear a path through the floor with your pacing. Since when do you pace?"

I stand up straight and crack my neck.

Get a grip, asshole.

I don't understand what the hell I'm doing either. I should have thought this through better. I should have gotten my ducks in a row first.

Ever since Emily moved to the UK ten months ago, I've been on edge, out of sorts. She's throwing a wrench into my system, disrupting all the ways I've occupied my mind over the last six years.

Why did she move here?

I may have casually mentioned Emily to Edmund after one of the latest meetings discussing why the new tires suck and they talked about bringing an expert aboard. The tires are degrading, wearing down, quicker and more explosively than they should. We just can't get them to work right. I may have left him a copy of the research paper Emily wrote at Cambridge. I didn't understand half of it, but our factory engineers were salivating over it.

I wasn't expecting Edmund to know the Professor Emily worked with on the paper and to line up an interview with her today. This was all abysmal planning on my part. What did I think would happen? What was I even hoping for?

I was bad for her then. I'll be worse for her now.

But, like a selfish prick, like someone possessed by a cosmic pull, I can't stay away from her.

Not when she's an hour away from me in her little two-bedroom apartment on the fourth floor just off the university campus. Not when she goes out with some asshole for dinner or drinks or coffee and lets him kiss her goodnight. Giggles at some bullshit line that he feeds her, smiles at him like she used to smile at me.

Oceans separated us before. Damn good reasons separated us.

But now?

My neck is stiff, and I crack it again.

It's 9:01, and she isn't here. She isn't coming. Emily Walker is not a person who shows up late.

Hell with this. I need this shit like a hole in the head.

It is what it is, it's not meant to be. I am who I am, God knows I can't change it. And Emily shouldn't be with me now any more than she should have been years ago. No matter how much I want her.

"I need to be in the simulator. Sorry about the no show," I tell Edmund.

He shrugs, never looking up from his computer, and I leave his office to make my way downstairs to the Sim. I push the elevator button repeatedly before I give up and take the stairs to my left.

"Sim time, dickhead," Dante, my teammate, pops out of an office and slugs me in the shoulder.

"Heading down now. Hurry up so I can kick your ass, as usual."

Dante faux laughs and points at me like the concept is hilarious to him as we head into the stairwell. Dante and I came up through the Junior Driver Program together, and we get along better than most teammates, considering our job is to beat the other one every race.

On the track, we fight like hell, but off, we've become damn good friends. I had no one when I left Florida. Despite Dante being from Italy and having a huge Italian family who dotes on him like he's the chosen one, we have a lot in common. We both grew up here, thrown into the ring as boys, and left to our own devices and coaches to become men.

"Ciao, Evelyn," Dante croons and winks at one of the office staff who's walking up the stairs as we walk down.

"Morning, boys," she blushes and sweeps her eyes over us both.

"New haircut?" He runs a finger through Evelyn's shoulder-length blond hair, "Bellissima."

I smack him in the shoulder as Evelyn bats her lashes at him. "Let's go."

He turns back down the stairs but not before sizing up Evelyn's ass as she continues up the stairs. "I need to get laid," he mumbles and adjusts himself.

"What's it been, forty-eight hours?" Dante goes through women like most people change their socks.

Not that I'm judging or suggesting that I am any better.

I'm not.

"Sixteen hours, but who's counting? What's happening with the hot little red-headed number?"

"Nothing. Same shit, different day." I assume he means Nova, who the gossip magazines claim is my on-again-off-again tennis-star girlfriend who just left London. We're only "on" when our geographic locations match up, and then it's far from a relationship.

"It's true what they say, yes, redheads are freaks in bed?"

"More like batshit crazy, in this case." Dante laughs and makes an assortment of lewd gestures like the crass asshole he is.

Nova's Russian and likes it about as cold and ruthless as I do. Serves us both well until she inevitably goes off the deep end.

We hit the main floor and open up the stairwell door at the far end of the building lobby. Sunlight beams in from the wall of windows, and I squint at the brightness. Tall potted plants and trees stand between trophy cases that line the massive open-air lobby.

Imperium is relatively new in Formula 1. It hasn't been around since the 1950s, like some of the original teams, but we've done well regardless. They're all about young drivers, innovative tech, cutting edge design. We tend to attract the younger generation of fans. Our merchandise is all bright green and matte black. It brings in the high energy, extreme sports crowds.

"Now that's an ass," Dante stops. He looks down a hallway to our right and holds up his fingers in a square as if he's taking a photo.

I look up, and my breath escapes me. I feel organs shutting down.

Emily is standing at the end of the hallway facing away from us and staring out a glass exit door. Her long brown hair is almost to her waist, which is wrapped in a grey asymmetrical skirt. She's shifting from foot to foot on heels that accentuate her naked, toned calves. She runs her hands down her sides and over her pretty clothes.

She's nervous.

"Ask the gods, and you shall receive," Dante makes the sign of the cross over his heart and looks to the ceiling before he takes a step toward Emily in the hallway.

I put a hand on his shoulder and fist his shirt, "No." I drag us a step back behind a giant palm tree as Dante twists his face up like I've gone mad.

"I saw her first. What do you say in America, shotgun?"

"Shut the fuck up," I push him back into the wall and keep watching Emily between the palm leaves.

"That's her," I growl while holding Dante against the wall, my eyes never leaving Emily, who continues to fidget and look at her watch.

"Her? Ohhhh," it finally dawns on Dante. "That was today."

I nod.

What the hell is she doing? I check my watch, it's almost 9:15, and she's on the ground floor hiding in a hallway. Of course, I'm hiding in a goddamn palm tree like a pussy, so this is a fine predicament.

Fuck that.

I step out from behind the palm tree, put my hands into my pockets, and stroll to the entry of the hallway she's in. Dante follows and stands silent next to me as we watch Emily from twenty feet away.

As if she can feel my eyes boring into her, like she also feels this electric wire connecting us, she stops fidgeting and slowly turns her head.

That's right, baby, you feel me here?

Her big brown eyes meet mine, and she holds my gaze as her body turns toward me. Fuck, I haven't been this close to Emily Walker, up close and personal, in years. She was always beautiful but now...

Now, her curves are on fire. Her silky cream blouse drapes over full round tits, and she walks toward me with a sway to her hips of a woman who is very much all grown up.

I'd swear my blood has stopped pumping because my limbs are suddenly numb, yet I can hear the *whoosh-whoosh* of my heartbeat in my ears.

She brushes her long hair over her shoulder and picks up a black leather portfolio bag from the ground, her eyes never leaving mine. One corner of my mouth turns up in a smirk as she gets closer.

"Emily," I greet her in my best bedroom voice. Her name rolls off my lips, muscle memory returning as I say it aloud, not just in my head for the billionth time.

She has a thin gold chain around her neck that hangs off her collarbone. I force myself to keep my hands in my pockets when I catch a trace of her familiar smell. It's something clean and fresh like sunshine hitting laundered sheets hanging in a garden or some girly shit.

"Cole, how nice to see you," she smiles and crooks her head a bit like she's surprised to see me here.

Bullshit.

"Been a long time," I let my eyes run down her neck and past the first couple of buttons undone on her blouse. It's been at least a thousand years, but who's counting?

37

"Ahem," Dante elbows me in the side. The prick is still here. I don't want to waste the few words I get with her on Dante.

"Emily, this is Dante Renzo, my teammate. Dante, this is Emily Walker, an... old friend from high school." I tip my head toward Dante for the introduction, but don't take my eyes off Emily. I couldn't even if I wanted to.

Dante takes Emily's hand and kisses the back of her fingers, "Ciao, Emily, Pleasure to meet you." Emily smiles at him sweetly. I'm going to rip his head off for that, later.

"Nice to meet you, Dante," she takes her hand back. "So, you both work here, then?"

You know goddamn well I work here.

"Yep, what brings you to London?" I ask since apparently she still wants to play these games.

"Small world, I have an interview for an engineering position," she answers in a tone that is way too chipper to be genuine.

"Is that so," I say as a statement, not a question.

"Unless, of course... would that bother you, Cole?" She cocks her head to one side and blinks her long lashes at me.

Dante lets out a muffled snicker beside me.

I crinkle my brows at her.

Then her lip quivers the tiniest bit, her tell.

"Bother me," I laugh, "that's hilarious. We were just teenagers having fun. No harm, no foul, right?"

No harm, my ass. The countless hours I've spent keeping track of her, watching her across an ocean, pining after her—and she still wants to play cat and mouse games with me.

Did you think she was going to leap into your arms, asshole?

"Perfect, glad to hear it," she clutches the leather strap of her bag and puts it over her shoulder. She checks her dainty gold watch, "I'd better go. Dante, nice to meet you."

She reaches to shake his hand, and being the opportunistic tool that he is, Dante kisses the back of it again. The fact that *his* lips get to touch her skin infuriates me.

"I hope to see you again soon," he whispers.

"I'd like that very much," she smiles back at him. "Cole, nice seeing you," she nods to me, keeping her hands very much to herself when dismissing *me*.

I take a partial step out of the hallway entry so she can squeeze past me, "Good luck, gorgeous girl."

Her smile drops faster than light the moment she hears her pet name leave my lips.

That's right, baby. You want to play games?

She sizes up the gap between Dante and me that's blocking her exit path to the lobby, and even though I feel like I will literally die if another day passes without touching her, I stand farther back and let her through. I may play our familiar games—the ones she loves so much—but I won't go that far in manipulation.

Dante and I both turn to watch her walk away into the open lobby, where she stops at reception and gets directions. My feet stay planted, my gaze locked on her until the elevator doors close. They steal her from me, and then she's gone, on her way upstairs to meet Edmund.

Only then do I suck in a breath and feel air return to my lungs.

And then I shove my best friend into the nearest wall. "Your smarmy lips never touch that again, asshole."

He smiles, showing me all of his white teeth, and lets out a bellow of a laugh. "Man, you have to step up your game if you want to get that back!"

"What are you talking about?" My hands are on my hips, and my breathing is still all jacked up. I don't need to hear whatever Dante's brilliant advice is.

"You were a dick! You have to woo women, talk sweetly to them, speak to them in the language of love," he whispers and kisses his fingertips.

"Shut the fuck up," I shake my head at him.

"Like this," he approaches a planted tree in the lobby and starts delicately petting a long green leaf, cooing at it, "Bellissima, mio amore, senza di te la mia vita non ha senso." He starts making kissy noises at the leaf.

"The hell is wrong with you?" I watch him romancing the potted plant as two mechanics walk by and take in the scene.

"I will teach you, you'll see. 'Gorgeous girl,'" he mocks my American accent. "Try tesoro, cuore mio, polpetta."

"Meatball? You want me to call her a meatball?" I've picked up some Italian from Dante over the years, though polpetta probably came from restaurant menus if I had to guess.

"If you want her to feast on your meatballs ever again, yes," he nods.

Jesus Christ, this guy.

"She likes gorgeous girl," I mumble and shuffle my feet. Part of me is keenly aware that I am now discussing wooing Emily with Casanova here who wants me to call my girl a meatball.

Also, I haven't decided yet if I am wooing Emily. I don't woo.

Not anymore.

I wouldn't even know how to woo anymore.

"Hmm," he thinks as we leave behind his latest girlfriend, the potted plant, and continue through the lobby, "smart girl like that probably wants you to appreciate her mind, not her body. Maybe luminoso?"

"She knows she's smart, doesn't always know she's beautiful," I sigh and think of all the times she trusted me with her insecurities and fears. All the times I kissed them away and showed her just how goddamn gorgeous she is.

"Interesting," Dante nods.

"Pro-tip, you douche, smart girls want to be called pretty, and pretty girls want to be called smart."

My girl, she's both.

"This is brilliant, I'll try that out tonight," Dante slaps me on the back.

"You do that."

Dante keeps walking past the elevators and doesn't notice that I've stopped and am waiting for the damn thing. Finally, he looks back, wondering why I'm not following him to the simulators. "Tell the guys I'm sick or something," I shrug.

I have bigger concerns right now.

Ninety minutes later, I burst through the door of Edmund's office. Emily has finally left the building, though I can still feel her energy buzzing around me.

"What took so long?" I've missed my session in the simulator and will have to make it up later.

Screw it.

"That was amongst the strangest interviews I've ever done," Edmund scratches his gray beard from behind his desk.

"What does that mean?" I plop down in a chair in front of his desk and lean forward, waiting impatiently.

"Well, she's either a total ball-buster or she doesn't want this job," Edmund crooks up his head and looks out the window.

I was afraid this was going to happen, that she'd turn the position down to avoid me. She probably has hundreds of companies recruiting her. Though she is also now perfecting the art of ball-busting, which is new.

"Did you offer her the position?"

Edmund inhales deeply, "Well, we'd be stupid not to. Mechanical engineering bachelor's from MIT, Chancellor's Excellence in Engineering Award at Cambridge, her Master's thesis in tire composition could bring the specialty experience we need. God knows we can't figure out why the bloody Concordia tires are such rubbish," he throws his pen onto the desk. "Roger Tillman says she's brilliant."

"Yeah, yeah, I know—did you offer her the position?" I roll my hands for him to get on with it. Everyone knows Emily is brilliant. I know every accomplishment and degree and award she's won for the last six years.

I know them by heart.

"I did, even though she was twenty minutes late, and it was like pulling teeth to get her to talk about her achievements."

She wasn't late. She was downstairs hiding at 9:00 am.

"And then she demanded nearly double the salary," Edmund rubs the bridge of his nose.

I grin proudly at that attempt. Good one, Em.

But I'll pay her salary demands out of pocket if Emily thinks that's going to get her out of working here. Now that she's this close, now that I have spoken to her again, there's not a decision left in my mind. I have no choice.

"I think I got her, though," Edmund grins like the Cheshire cat.

"How?"

"Took her for a tour of the factory and the lab. It's what sold me on F1 when I was recruited out of university. Her eyes lit up," Edmund makes dazzle hands with his fingers.

Our labs and factory would make anyone's eyes light up. It looks like a spaceship with all the computers, instruments, and manufacturing equipment. The wind tunnel in the aero lab, all the beakers and chemicals in the fuel lab, the molding and injection lab where we make most of our parts and 3D print components. I should have thought of that.

"Then what?"

He laughs, which sends him into a coughing fit but then recovers, "Then we went through the composites lab. She seemed to like the carbon fiber process the most, though she told me we can get the resin curing time down if we raise the atmospheric pressure in the autoclave, and she wanted to know the exact chemical structure for our materials. She's got balls."

That's my girl.

Edmund twirls around in his chair and steeples his hands, "I like her. She'd fit in. Imperium needs bright, young minds and big balls. I'm an old man. I can't keep up with all this technical shit anymore, and I won't be around forever."

"So, is she hired, or what?" I ask and wish he'd get to the point already.

"Ball's in her court," Edmund shrugs. "I made the offer, she has until Monday to accept, or we'll keep looking."

Monday.

That leaves just the weekend for me to convince Emily Walker to take this job, to stay in London, to stay with me.

I did my part, don't run now, Em.

Six

Emily

There are very few problems in life that I have not been able to solve through science and data. But with a spreadsheet before me outlining the pros and cons of accepting the job at Imperium, I'm stuck at the concept that things aren't always so cut and dry.

The pro-Imperium column is extensive:

The most incredible labs I have ever seen.

Opportunities for advancement in materials science that could revolutionize the auto industry and lead to road safety and green Eco-solutions.

Travel the world.

Absurd salary package they inexplicably agreed to.

PhD reimbursement.

Work Visa, would not have to return to the US and do not want to deal with Dad.

One of the most innovative companies in the UK, future opportunities endless.

Klara could quit the cafe.

And then there's the cons column:

Cole Ballentine.

I spent all day running a dozen different types of charts and models issuing scores and giving weight to specific priorities, but if there's one thing I hate in science, it's bias.

No matter how hard I try, I am looking for data that proves what I want it to, not the truth.

And after Friday, after seeing him in person for the first time in almost six years, the only truth I know is that I am not over Cole Ballentine.

I don't know how to assign him a score for the impact he has had on my life. It would surely be biased.

Part of me hoped when we'd see each other again, I would snap out of it. Nothing would happen, I'd feel nothing, and I'd realize I was only a naive teenager back then. I would hop and skip away, and the rest of my life would be rainbows and unicorns.

But I didn't imagine the chemistry we've always had. I wasn't overblowing the way he makes my organs somersault or my brain misfire. Time has changed nothing. If anything, it's magnified the intensity of all the emotions swirling around inside my chest.

Now, I've been reminded that they're all still there. All the feelings, the anger, the hurt, feeling like a piece of me is missing, and I will never be whole or structurally sound without it—all still there.

It was all I could do to plaster the fake smile and confidence over myself while he stood tall before me, cool as a cucumber, and dared to tell me we were just kids having fun.

It wasn't fun when I was heartbroken, couldn't eat, couldn't sleep, and was ready to give up going to college to follow him to Europe. It was not fun when my life went to hell in a handbasket, not fun at all.

I felt like a fool when he said that. I wore a new skirt and heels and walked into that building with my shoulders back, ready to face my demons. Ready to take my life back and get over this shit.

That lasted all of fifteen minutes.

Seeing him online, in photos, or on TV did not do him justice. How unfair that men never fail to get more attractive as they get older. The tall, lean eighteen-year-old I last saw has turned into a broad-shouldered, muscular *man* with a chiseled jaw and the confidence of a reigning king.

His neck and traps doubled in size since he was karting in Florida. The results of his F1 training to withstand extreme g-forces now rise out of his green and black Imperium tee-shirt. His forearms were thick, corded, and developed. It was hard not to stare at either when I saw the muscles flexing in the hallway.

I used to be able to tell when Cole was stressed or upset by watching his neck muscles tense. But cornered in the hallway with him, I was too afraid to gawk the way I wanted to. I've always been a 'neck girl' and a part of me, a part I am very disappointed in, wanted to lick and

44

bite that neck again.

I hate that what I really wanted was for him to throw me over his shoulder and drag me back to his lair. Even after everything.

Weak, weak, weak, Emily.

His brilliant blue eyes are the same, though.

Looking into those cobalt pools sucked me right back in, reminders of the ocean water, the days we spent at Florida beaches wrapped around one another in the rolling waves. They brought back all the feelings I'd sworn to myself I would never allow myself again.

Every inch of him seems to hold a memory I've stored in the recess of my mind. They're flooding back to me now that they've been rekindled for even the briefest of moments. The more I try not to think about them, the more vivid the recollections become as if my body is operating at some primitive level focused only on its survival.

I'm pissed at myself for letting him affect me like this. I'm disappointed in *me*. I was doing pretty well, on the surface, until he went and called me 'gorgeous girl.' Then the dam broke, and the riptide was set free.

Naive girl.

Still, I've paced my flat half the day, run the data, and there's no excuse I can feed myself for not taking this job. Further, I'm not going to run away anymore or stay hidden in my own little world. He doesn't get to win.

Sick of this shit.

So very, very sick of it.

I am better than this. He doesn't get to ruin the next six years of my life, too. *He* is the one who left *me*. *He* can hide from me if anything.

I pick up my cell and dial Mom to tell her the news. If I tell her, then I can't back out of the job at the last minute. It will become real, and there won't be any going back. I need to take control.

"Hi, honey," I can feel Mom smiling through the phone at me the second she answers.

"Hi, Mom."

I stall for the next ten minutes or so, chatting about the London weather and trivial nonsense. She tells me about their latest move to Delaware to the Dover Air Force Base

I've lost track of the number of moves at this point. Even if I wanted to return to the States, it's not like I have a home there. My old bedroom was packed up and discarded half a dozen transfers ago.

I often wonder why Mom puts up with the military life. Once upon a time, she was going to be a chemist. It was her who made me fall in love with the sciences as a little girl. But instead, Mom opted for the life of a military wife, supported the Major General, and raised me.

Finally, I force myself to concentrate on the task at hand and bite the bullet if, for no other reason, then to move past the growing pit in my stomach.

"So, I got a job offer."

"You did? And here we've been wasting time talking about your boring old parents. Tell me all about it? What company has snatched you up?"

"Imperium," I blurt out without hesitation.

Take that, bandage. Ripped you right off. I mean business.

"Imp... you mean...?" Mom pauses.

"Yes, Imperium. The F1 team."

"Oh," there's a long, uncomfortable pause where my mother smartly chooses her next words, "that's wonderful, honey. What position were you offered?"

"Tire and Performance Engineer," I proudly state. If I fake my confidence long enough, perhaps I will even start believing it myself.

I tell mom about the position and the laboratory, and all the things that I remind myself are exciting about this job, but I know she's politely ignoring the elephant in the room.

Eventually, there is a silent pause that I refuse to fill, and Mom is forced to spit it out, "And... will you be okay with Cole being there?"

"Yep," I lie. "I saw him before the interview, in fact."

"You did? How did it go? What did he say?" There's panic or pity in her voice, hard to tell which because both are warranted.

I'm certainly not going to tell her I was both incredibly turned on and then later dry heaved in the parking lot. Because I can't even explain how my body pulled that hat trick.

How do you explain when someone sucks away all the air in the room, turns your brain into mush, both excites and terrifies you? Why is a part of my body willing to cast aside the years of torment and still gravitate toward him like fire sucking in the oxygen it needs to burn?

"It was fine, Mom. It was a long time ago, and it's time to move on. He's certainly over it, he said we were just kids having fun."

"I see," I can hear her swallow. I'm sure she does not want to have to pick up my broken pieces again if this goes south.

"I met his teammate," I switch gears.

"Oh, Dante Renzo? He's a looker."

Part of me hates that Mom keeps up with Cole's career enough that she knows his teammate's name and knows that Dante is a classic tall, dark, handsome type with a swoon-worthy Italian accent.

"He was nice," I say, even though I could have sworn I saw Cole tense up when Dante kissed my hand. I was trying not to look at him too hard, though, so I can't be sure.

"You haven't heard from the Ballentine's, have you, honey?"

"Hell no. Why?"

Technically, I've *never* spoken to Kristy, Cole's mother. I only saw her in person a few times and in photos. She was hauntingly beautiful and gave Cole his stunning turquoise eyes. Stan, on the other hand, only spoke to me when I'd run into him at Cole's house. I wasn't worth his misplaced rage, he saved that all up for Cole.

"Oh, no reason. I saw Kristy not long before we moved and wondered, is all."

"Really? What was she doing?"

This is weird, Cole's mother was never around for long when we were teenagers. She was forever flitting in and out of his life, leaving a trail of destruction behind.

His dad had plenty of other women coming and going, but his mom was mostly absent. As far as I know, the last time she was spotted, was around the time Cole left for Europe.

"Just shopping at the grocery."

I wonder what's going on with that mess, but that brings me to another point we need to address. "What is Dad going to say about this?" Mom may love Cole, but Dad... does not.

"Oh, you leave the Major General to me, honey," she reassures me.

"He's going to lose his shit," I reply.

My father made it abundantly clear what a disappointment I was to him when he finally found out about Cole. He wanted to believe it was Cole who talked me into having sex when it was quite the opposite, and we were both consenting adults.

Little did he know how consenting I actually was. It was me who had to convince Cole to finally take my V-Card. One does not share those sorts of details with their military father, though.

Still, he stormed into the Ballentine household to talk 'man-to-man' with Stanley about controlling his bad-influence son. I wish it was just the one time, but they went at it time and again. Because that's what the Major General does. He treats everyone like a cadet who needs to obey and get in line.

Yes sir, Major General, sir.

When Cole moved to Europe, I didn't just lose him. It was the final straw that severed any warm feelings I had for my father, too. At the lowest moments of my life, Dad regularly threw it in my face that he warned me this would happen.

He was right, I was wrong. He'd ask me if Cole called that day. I'd admit no, and Dad would literally say, 'Good. I told you so.'

I never felt like daddy's little girl, but rubbing salt in my gaping wounds was more cruelty than I've ever formally forgiven him for.

And then there were the fights about Cole between him and Mom, which just added more stress to the worst time in my life. Out in the garage, yelling at all hours of the night about it. Cole was like a nuclear explosion that leveled the whole damn neighborhood.

"Your father just wants you to be happy, honey," Mom says for the billionth time in my life.

"Well, then he should support this decision and not give me shit because this is an amazing opportunity, and I'm taking the job."

Look at me, growing a backbone today. I hang up with Mom feeling like a proper adult.

I'm reading the bottle of the magic hair product Klara has lent me while I finish preening in the bathroom. Whatever is in this stuff, my hair is on point. It has full, beachy waves and swirls around my shoulders like whitecaps inside a tide pool. It smells like bottled sin.

No more straight, dull, brown.

Don't analyze the ingredients on the bottle. This is a new you.

Much to Klara's shock and delight, we're going out tonight.

It is Saturday night, and she thinks we're celebrating the job offer that I informed her I would be accepting. Not only will I have a job, but this is a celebration for Klara, too. She's inevitably going to get fired from the cafe with her propensity for swearing at small children. I'll be making enough at Imperium to cover our rent when that happens so my Swedish friend can finish up her masters stress-free.

Then we can *both* get on with our lives.

In my new self-imposed and improved mind space, though, we're mostly celebrating my determination to turn over a new leaf. I'm not going to be held hostage emotionally anymore with romantic fantasies of unrequited love and memories from half a decade ago.

I have to face this head-on, take control back.

I've told Makenna, my mother (who has undoubtedly told the Major General by now, as well,) and I've emailed Professor Tillman that I will be accepting the job. All I need to do is call Imperium on Monday and formally accept the offer.

There's no going back now. There's only going forward, and that's what tonight is about.

I'm wearing the new heels I bought for my interview and a green, form-fitting off the shoulder v-neck dress with sleeves and little bunches around my waist. It hits mid-thigh, and it's scandalous. Not just scandalous for Emily Walker—it's naughty. Klara calls it a "fuck me dress," and I bought it months ago, the last time I thought I was going to get over Cole Ballentine.

I never wore it then, it's way outside of my comfort zone, but I'm rocking it tonight.

Just kids having fun, eh? It's high time this kid had fun, then.

"This one," Klara hands me a tube of lipstick from her impressive collection. It's called 'Vengeance,' and it is blood red.

"Perfect," I smooth it over my lips and smack them together, fluff my hair one more time, and then take the first step out of my flat door toward the new me.

Seven

"Sitting alone tonight, waiting for the sunshine. Sometimes I kneel and pray, hoping someday that you'll be mine. But she's so many miles away, I've got so many things to say. And all of the games we'd play don't matter anyway." - Everlast - This Kind of Lonely

Cole

A couple dozen people dance and grind on each other in my living room to a bastardized remix of Joy Division's *Love Will Tear Us Apart*.

It's not an unusual Saturday night, per se, I just find myself in no mood for it. I don't even invite these people over most nights, they just show up. I recognize some guys from the team, but I've never seen the majority of these people before.

I don't know them, they don't know me.

I'm avoiding them all, brooding outside on my terrace overlooking the River Thames. The Battersea Bridge lights cast a haunting glow onto the water below, and the sprawling mass of city twinkles in the distance.

It took me a long time to get used to living in London. It's a city that's both very hard to love and very hard to hate. It's filled with extremes, and there's no escaping it. It pulsates at all hours of the day and night, and I've gotten so used to the clouds that I start to resent the sun when it makes a rare appearance.

I spent the day wracking my brain about Emily and still have no answers. The only thing I know is that I don't want her to leave London even though I'm more miserable with her here. When she was at home, in the States, there was distance and an artificial separation I could rationalize.

She never left my mind, but she wasn't breathing the same air as I am. She wasn't close enough for me to drive an hour and watch her turn her bedroom light off at night before going to sleep. I didn't look for her face on every street corner or in every car I passed on the road.

And every once in awhile, if I tried hard enough, I could distract myself from her memory. I never allowed myself to believe I could have her back.

But now, and for the past ten months, she's everywhere around me. No amount of distraction gives me even a moment of peace. My head is filled with what-if's. Her coming to London was her siren summonsing possibilities I'd long since written off as plausible. Now, she's here but she's graduated, and she could leave again, so I'm forced to deal with that reality.

She was in school for the better part of the last six years, and I had reasons for not contacting her, then. Now, if I'm frank with myself, I question if those reasons are still good enough. And that's what's eating me alive.

We aren't kids anymore. She should be able to make her own decisions, make up her own mind. Granted, that means I would have to give her all the information so she can do exactly that.

That may kill me, but I can't live inside this stagnant holding pattern forever. Emily either needs to be in my life, or I need to find a way to get past her. I can't lie to myself and make excuses anymore. She can't leave London without me knowing for sure, one way or the other.

I push myself off the metal deck railing overlooking the river and flop onto the stiff outdoor sofa. There's a small propane fire burning in the middle of the deck table, and I turn the switch off before one of the drunk mystery people inside burns my apartment down, next.

The giant sliding glass door opens, and a wave of music rushes out when Dante and two women draped over him pass through and invade my outdoor area.

"There you are," Dante bellows and splashes his cocktail onto the deck. He's shitfaced, I can tell already.

He takes a seat on the matching sofa across from me, and one of the girls following him slides in next to him, one bare leg thrown over his thigh. She's licking his neck, and he's paying absolutely no attention to her. The second chick darts to the deck railing to take selfies against the river backdrop.

"Did she take the job?" Dante asks me.

I shake my head, "Not yet."

At least not as of a couple of hours ago when I texted Edmund, and he reiterated that he would let me know as soon as he hears from her, either way.

"Damn. Bella," he calls to the selfie chick and waves her over. "My friend here has a broken heart, can you believe it?"

On cue, Selfie Sally struts over and I give Dante a death glare as she plants herself in my lap and puts her arm around my neck. "That's terrible, who would do such a thing?" She coos and runs her hand over my face.

"A brown-eyed American girl," Dante answers her on my behalf.

"Oh, are you American, too?" Sally asks, her hands running up and down my chest. She sounds like she's from Manchester, and by the looks of these two, Dante has picked up another couple of models, or wanna-be models, from somewhere.

"Yep." I'm entirely too sober for this shit tonight.

"Buy me dinner, and I'll make you forget all about her," Sally squeaks.

The very suggestion that this girl could make me forget Emily offends me, even though I have attempted her theory several times over in the past. It doesn't work. "For what? You'd only pretend to eat it anyway."

Sally pouts at me.

"Dude, don't be rude," Dante scolds me and slurs his speech.

I look around Sally's rack to Dante, "You don't find this tiresome at all?"

"You're mad! Find what tiresome?"

I look at Sally and take her chin between my fingers to prove my point, "Sweetheart, what's my name?"

"Mmmmm," she thinks, or she tries to, "Captain America!"

"Uh-huh, and what's his name?" I point to Dante, whose girl is still wrapped around him and oblivious to the conversation.

"Whatever you want it to be?" Sally asks.

"Damn fine answer!" Dante bellows.

I lean back into the couch and run my fingers over my eyebrows.

"What's your problem, man?" Dante grows serious and taps the vampire latched onto his neck to scoot off so he can lean forward on his couch.

"No problem," I lie. There are a million problems.

"Bullshit. You see her once, and you're a total soft cock now."

I grab Sally's hips and drag her off my lap, depositing her on the couch next to me. She pouts for a millisecond before scampering to the railing for more selfies with her friend.

Dante is right, not about the soft cock, but about my bullshit. A week ago, Sally, or whoever, would have been bent over the deck railing she's so fond of.

Then I had to go and poke the sleeping bear.

"Lock the place up when you're done, will you?" I stand up to head inside.

"Where you going?"

"To talk to her."

Cambridge is about an hour away, so I have a fair amount of time to consider what I want to say to Emily. How I want to say it.

She has every right to be pissed at me, but maybe she will understand why I left. Maybe she will understand why I stayed away, though I don't want to hurt her more. I definitely will if I tell her everything, and some truths are not mine to tell.

Either way, I am an adult, and she is an adult, and both of us should be free to make our own educated decisions.

Given how sassy she was at work the other day, I'm pretty sure she will tell me to piss off, but I chased Emily down once and made her listen to me. I can do it again.

Pulling up to her block that's lined with old brick buildings housing off-campus students, I can see from the street that her flat lights are still on. I assume she's home because, well, Emily is always home on Saturday night. She's still a good girl, unlike the path I've gone down.

It's all the more reason I should stay away from her if I were a better man.

Finding a parking spot on the street, I back my car into the space and remember the first time I found myself here. I didn't mean to turn up, it was like I was compelled here. She had just started at the university, and I was quickly reminded that Emily was better off without me. But there was something inside me that just had to see it for myself, to know for sure.

So, every now and again, when the pull became too strong, I'd come see for myself. Check on her. And, sure enough, Emily was alive and well. She had friends and a roommate and would sit inside a cafe nearby reading on her Kindle for hours. She studied, she tutored other students, she was doing what she came here to do.

She wouldn't be doing that if I were in her life. So, I stayed away.

Once in a while, some guy would pick her up at her front door or walk her home. It was then that I had to fight myself to stay in the car. Because they were all the kind of guys that Emily should probably be with. Post-grad guys who wore suits and could talk about physics or engineering with her. Guys who would be gentle and treat her right.

Guys who didn't come with a shitload of baggage.

Not guys like me who learned from an early age, and still have it instilled in me every time my father shows up, that it's okay to beat women and children, then throw them out when you're sick of them. I kept myself firmly inside of my car all those times I saw her with another guy because I refuse to be that guy. I refuse to saddle her with someone like my father.

As much as it guts me, if she's happy without me, then I won't stand in her way.

I will stab a knife through my own heart before I ever become my father and lay a finger on a woman, but it's part of my DNA, isn't it? My very birth was a result of what he did to my mother.

I hate that I've followed in his footsteps with a revolving door of women. Mine are consensual and leave satisfied, but it's long since been satisfying for me.

And I am not proud. I hate sharing any traits with my father at all.

The last woman who not only knew the real me but liked me for it was Emily Walker. Everyone since wants Cole Ballentine the wealthy athlete or, like Selfie Sally tonight, they don't even need to know my name. A penthouse on the river or a three-hundred-thousand dollar sports car is enough for them.

She's the only one who saw real worth in this fucked up shell of a body. Maybe she still does.

As I'm about to get out of the car, the lights in Emily's flat go out, so I hang tight. A moment later, the front door to the building opens, and her tall, blond roommate comes out, and she holds the door as Emily follows behind her.

What the fuck is she wearing?

Both of the girls are dressed in tiny little dresses and sky-high heels, which is not unusual for her roommate, but... I have never seen Emily like this. My heart is racing not just because she looks absolutely incredible, but also because I am shocked by this new look.

This is not an outfit that says, 'let's have dinner and a pleasant conversation about current news in materials science.'

My plans of finally having an honest conversation with her are put on the back burner. It's dark out, it's nearly 11:00 pm, and they're both walking down the sidewalk alone.

They make it to the end of their block and turn left. I don't want to be a creeper, but I follow far behind the girls in my car and watch where they're going. I'll just make sure they get there safely.

Then you'll probably make sure they get home safely four hours later.

Several blocks later, they both enter some dance club called 'The Jungle.' I can hear the bass thumping from the street, and there's a bouncer outside sitting on a stool who quickly checks their IDs and lets them inside. The windows are blacked out, but neon red and green strobe lights flash to the sidewalk when the heavy door opens.

This is not at all what I was expecting when I left London tonight.

After half an hour of stewing, I can't take it anymore. I root around in the backseat and find a hoodie and a baseball hat and throw them both on. I look like the Unabomber, but I don't want anyone to recognize me. I don't want to cause a scene. I don't want to sign autographs or take selfies. I just want to talk to Em, *really* talk to her. We could always talk, about anything.

When the sidewalk is clear, I walk up to the bouncer with my head down.

"ID," he waves his hand, bored stiff on his chrome stool.

Damn it.

I pull out my wallet and hand him my ID. He looks up at me standing before him. His eyebrows come together as he recognizes my name, and now the face, hidden beneath my hoodie and hat.

I snap my ID back out of his hands and replace it with a stack of fifty-pound notes. "Not a word."

The bouncer nods in understanding, no media, no paparazzi, "Have a nice night, Mr. Ballentine."

I open the door and do my best to keep my head down while I try and make it through the wall-to-wall crowds of drunk university kids. Why is she here? Emily loves music but hates clubs.

There's a DJ on stage and a crowd of people dancing before him, a horseshoe-shaped bar on the other side of the room. It's dark, save the flashing strobe lights, and I make my way to the nearest wall.

I don't see Emily anywhere, she's shorter than a lot of the people crammed together with their arms up on the dance floor. There's no sign of her at the bar.

My eyes scanning below the brim of my hat, a light flashes across a tall blond head in the crowd, her roommate. I follow the wall closer and keep in the darkness, moving around the occasional couple mauling each other.

Eventually, the crowd parts in the right way, and I see Emily's long hair spinning around. Her eyes are closed as she dances to the beat, a drink in a red plastic cup in her left hand. I watch her, transfixed, as she rolls her hips and raises her hands above her head.

Her shoulders are bare, the hollows of her collarbone and her long neck illuminating every time lights pass over her on the dance floor. She's intoxicating, otherworldly. I can't take my eyes off the way she's moving her hips, every curve on display in that tiny dress.

What would she do if I joined her out there? Wrapped my arms around her, like I used to, pulled her tight against me—does she want me even a tenth of how badly I want her? Would her muscle memory kick in, too?

I make my way toward her onto the dance floor, the odd elbow hitting me and person bumping into me as I make my way through the crowd. Emily's roommate passes right in front of me, pulling a man behind her. She whispers in Emily's ear and passes the man to Emily.

Emily smiles up at this guy, a tall blond who looks her up and down.

I know that look in his eye.

Emily raises a hand and wraps it around his neck. He drops a hand to her waist and pulls her body close to his.

My blood runs cold as I watch the two of them start dancing together. His knee parts Emily's legs, and he lowers his head to her neck, whispering something in her ear. She raises her head and laughs, her fingers tickling the hair at the base of his neck.

His hand lowers to her ass. He pulls her in even tighter, the two of them writhing and grinding on each other.

Watching this unfold ten feet away from me as if in slow-motion is the most excruciating torture I have ever experienced. Every cell in my body wants to rip this guy's filthy, groping hands off of her. I want to throw her over my shoulder and get her out of here.

Emily isn't here to talk tonight. Not to me. Not to anyone.

Who in the hell is this woman?

It hits me like a runaway freight train through my chest.

This is not my Emily.

This is not the good girl I knew who looked at me like I hung the moon, the girl everyone thought was quiet but had more to say than anyone I've ever met. The Emily I know—the one I loved—was more comfortable in my old tee-shirts than fancy dresses. She wore minty lip gloss and had the lightest dusting of freckles across her face that you'd only notice after she'd been in the sun all day.

Emily liked small groups of close friends, not big groups of associates. She liked curling up with books, not strangers.

Emily hated parties and clubs. She sure as shit wasn't into grinding on stranger's thighs in seedy nightclubs or drinking cheap liquor out of Solo cups. The Emily I know would have kneed this guy in the balls for grabbing her ass like this.

But yet, she's smiling and laughing and touching him as much as he's touching her.

My Emily is gone.

You stupid motherfucker, you're too late.

I turn to leave as she spins, and there's the briefest flash of recognition in her eyes. But then my back is turned, and I'm lost in the crowd on my way out the door.

How could I be so stupid? It's been years. Of course she isn't the same person.

I'm not.

This is the first night in six years where no matter where I am in the world, regardless of what continent I am on or who is next to me, I am truly alone.

There is no one now.

Eight

Hockenheimring — Hockenheim Germany

Emily

I've been thrown into the deep end of the pool a little bit, but I know how to tread water—figuratively and literally—indefinitely. Honestly, I'm pretty excited to be here in Germany at my first race with Imperium. I wasn't expecting to be this pleasantly surprised.

Maybe things are finally looking up. It's about time.

After I accepted the formal job offer and completed all the HR paperwork and Imperium helped me file for the right work visas, I only had a few days at the factory until all the personnel left for the German Grand Prix.

I spent them meeting the team of engineers. There are over twenty of them who work in the factory on different car components and areas of performance, plus more on-track engineers like myself who will travel to each race.

Then there are a million designers, logistics staff, aerodynamicists, hospitality, IT, media—thank god we all have name badges that control our access into factory areas so I can look at everyone's name until I memorize them.

The Composites team, though, I am in love with it.

I spent so long actively hiding from Formula 1 that I never realized this industry is at the cutting edge of materials science. Many of the teams even produce aviation and aerospace components. As thrilled as I am to be in Germany for the first time in my life, I can't wait to get back to London and the factory.

Plus, I haven't seen Cole at all, besides some very brief sightings around the track today. I've been able to keep my emotions in check. I'm doing it.

I am in my element learning so many new things. I don't have a moment of free time because I'm studying build sheets and industry regulations trying to get caught up.

This was the right decision.

I owe Professor Tillman an email update and will make sure to thank him. I feel like I'm moving forward in my life, not looking back. I'm surviving with, and despite, Cole.

I can do this.

I know I will see him more this weekend. I do have to work with both drivers directly on tire performance, but I feel like I'm handling it better than I expected. According to the crew, the drivers are swamped with media and sponsor engagements most of the weekend anyway.

Maybe this is just what I needed, to be thrown into the pool and forced to swim.

On Friday morning, I'm sunning myself on a cushy cream-colored outdoor sofa and studying 3D models in the Imperium on-track motorhome. Every team has a traveling, portable building that takes the crew all night to set up, and Imperium's is nothing short of an engineering marvel.

Three stories in height, all the walls are dark, one-way glass. It has everything from a full restaurant-sized kitchen to my favorite area—a rooftop hospitality area that can host parties and can even convert into a swimming pool. There's a full bar up here with a fancy-ass coffee machine.

I see no reason to ever leave this safe haven.

"Ah, there you are," I look up from my new laptop to see Edmund coming up the stairs.

"Hi there," I smile.

I like Edmund. He's an old school nerd. He looks like he's past retirement age with his grey beard and wrinkles, but he reminds me of university professors. Like he has a lifetime of experience and knowledge that I'm eager to extract.

He's also been abundantly kind answering my sixty-five million questions, so far.

"Let's head down to the garages," he waves me over.

I flip my laptop closed, and we leave the motorhome to trek to the trackside team garage. According to the schedule, the cars will be running free practice sessions today, so this will be my first time seeing all the parts in motion live and in-person.

As we walk to the garages, Edmund introduces me to a few people we run across, and he points out all the other teams, nine, plus us. There is a shocking amount of media everywhere. I've seen it on television, of course, but in person, it's a wild hive of buzzing activity, cameramen dragging cables and microphones with them.

Thankfully, very few people want to talk to engineers, so they never spare Edmund or I a glance. They're more concerned with the occasional celebrity they come across, or a driver, of course. These are the people who make all the videos and clips of Cole I've watched over the years.

Stop it. You're doing good.

The garage bays themselves are nothing short of impressive, either. Walking into the back entrance, there is a private area with a restroom and two smaller rooms that I suppose the team can meet in, or the drivers can change inside.

Then, moving toward the track is a private viewing area with stools and televisions of track action and one entire wall is composed of rechargeable headsets. Edmund picks a fully charged unit off the rack and hands it to me as we walk past.

Beyond are two concrete bays where the cars sit and a frenzy of mechanics and pit crew bustle around. Racks of tires catch my eye. They're all wrapped in individual covers and numbered. I've been learning how strict the tire regulations are.

Each team only gets a certain number of each tire compound, there are rules about when each can be used, rules about how much they can be inflated, at what temperatures they can be run. There are rules upon rules upon rules. I haven't been able to glean much information on the actual structure of the tires online yet, but there simply hasn't been enough time.

"I want you to spend today on the pit wall with us," Edmund says, and he leads us past the garage bay to an extended covered workstation that runs parallel to the pit lane. A dozen computer monitors sit elevated on a wall with five stools facing them for different race engineers and strategists. The track itself is right in front of us and the garages behind.

It's so easy to get caught up in the grandeur of it all, being right on track smack dab in the middle of this elaborate festival of speed.

Edmund points to a seat, and I take a stool next to him after more introductions. I'm taking in all the data running across computer screens in front of me. It shows everything from local weather to screens showing the performance and status of each individual component on the car. There are even intercom systems in front of each stool that allow us to speak with drivers or the factory back in London.

I'm fiddling with the tech so much I jump when a car fires up behind me in the garage. Dante is inside his car already, the pit crew makes sure the coast is clear, and then he pulls out.

Cole is just about to step into his car in his black and green race suit and helmet. His helmet this race is silver and black, an elaborate geometric pattern all over it. He likes to change them up frequently with new designs and colors.

My eyes run up and down Cole's tall frame. There's a bulge visible in his tight-fitting race suit, and as he prepares to get into the car, he turns around briefly, and it's obvious he's adjusting himself before getting into the cockpit.

I can't tear my eyes away, I'm not even aware of my surroundings.

You hear about these moments when people say that time stops, and the world fades away, and it always sounded like embellishment—or psychosis—but it's real. There are simply times when the body's needs override the brain's orders.

Cole turns back, and I know I've just been caught staring at him. I can only see his eyes through his helmet, but he looks right at me with those impossibly blue orbs. I see the corners crinkle. Then he winks and climbs in the car.

Damn it.

This is the first time I've been close to him this week, and I've already been caught checking him out. I'm reasonably sure my jaw was open. I'm surprised I'm not drooling.

No other man does this to my body, no one else makes my mind shut down like this. It's like a switch he has complete control over. One flick of his finger and it's lights out, no more racing thoughts, no more analysis or thinking. My lizard brain takes over, and its sole purpose is physical need.

Survival.

Edmund taps the headset sitting on my pit wall station, "Start listening to the drivers and their feedback and comparing it to your data sets."

I put the clunky headphones on and move the mouthpiece away

from my chin. I won't be adding to conversation today, I'm just here to learn right now.

With both cars on track, the data on my computer screens comes to life—wind flow measurements over parts of the vehicle, brake temperatures, downforce measurements, fuel levels, tire life models. The monitors spit out hundreds of data points in real-time as the two cars go around the flat track in the Rhine Valley.

It is seriously impressive.

"Okay, Cole, Strat Mode 11, please," I hear Edmund issue the command over the headset to run a practice program. There's a cheat sheet taped to the counter telling us all what the Strategy Modes mean this weekend. It's kept confidential so that other teams don't know each other's plans.

It looks like this mode is our standard race pace setting, and I'm starting to see patterns in all of the data before me. I can almost see the tire temperatures, PSI, and degradation changing before me as the cars increase their speed and payload under cornering. Dante's car and Cole's car differ entirely as they're both running different tire compounds.

Both Dante and Cole respond over the radio several times, providing feedback on how the cars feel, reporting oversteer or understeer, asking for changes of settings. I have a lot of jargon to learn.

A tingle runs down my spine every time Cole talks over the radio, I can hear his breathing right in my ear, and it's like he's whispering to me again. I swear I can feel his breath on my skin.

I only look up from the monitors when Cole passes us on the track each lap, a flash of green and black, and then he's gone. This is worlds different from all the days I spent watching him at karting tracks, a bunch of guys and a few girls zipping around in go-karts.

That was fun. This is engineered insanity.

I can't help but feel a little proud of Cole. Regardless of everything else, he's worked hard to get here, and he's made it.

I'm also still wondering why he winked at me.

I could have sworn I saw him Saturday night at the club Klara and I went to, but I'd dismissed it and assumed my eyes were just playing tricks on me again. God knows they've done that plenty over the years.

Before I know it, both free practice sessions are over for the day. I've asked Edmund a litany of questions, and I have downloaded the day's data set to my laptop so I can continue analyzing it tonight.

I need to keep myself busy because as much as I was focusing and paying attention, I entertained a whole mess of inappropriate thoughts about Cole. Ideas about his deep voice and that tight little race suit.

Those ideas, and so many other strategic plans about how I'm going to deal with him, need to be on the back burner.

"Oh good, Emily, I want you to meet someone," Edmund grabs my elbow as we re-enter the garage area, and I try to ignore Cole and his personnel crew standing in the back.

A very well dressed man in a tailored suit smiles at us and makes his way to Edmund and I. "Edmund, hello," he calls in a lovely French accent and shakes Edmund's hand.

"Olivier, this is Emily Walker, our new Tire and Performance Engineer. Emily, this is Olivier Gaspard, Motorsports Director for Concordia Tires. You two will have a lot to talk about, I'm sure."

"Ah, Emily, I have heard so much about you," Olivier takes my hand and holds it in his large, soft hand. His dark hair is perfectly mussed, and his crisp white button-down pops off the blue suit that looks like it costs more than my first and second cars, combined.

Olivier must be in his mid to late thirties and is very easy on the eyes.

"Nice to meet you, Olivier," I smile and pull my hand back because there's an extended shake happening and I don't want to seem weird already on my first day on track.

"I have so many questions on the paper you published in the Journal of Materials Science."

"You read it?" I ask and blush a little being put on the spot like this. I mean, I guess it makes sense, but I am still so humbled that the paper picked up so much traction from international companies.

"Oui, of course. Very impressive!"

Great, now I'm blushing more as Olivier, the handsome, rich dude in an expensive suit, starts speaking French at me. "I can't take all the credit, I was a co-author with my Professor."

"Nonsense," Edmund interrupts. "Emily's going to be brilliant for the team. The next generation."

"Oh, you aren't finally giving in to the idea of retirement, are you?"

"Ehh," Edmund mumbles, "one of these days, I'll take my pension and learn to play golf."

"Emily, s'il vous plaît, are you free to have a coffee with me? I'm sure you have as many questions as I do," Olivier smiles at me with perfectly straight, white teeth, his oversized gold Rolex reflecting the sun's rays.

"Is that okay?" I ask Edmund. I do have a running tally of questions in my head, and, as I understand it, Olivier is the official representative of Concordia that's at each race and available to all the F1 teams.

"Yes, yes, go," Edmund says. "I want you to learn everything there is to know. You know the challenges with this season's tires, so I expect you'll be spending a lot of time with Olivier."

"Okay."

Olivier and Edmund shake hands again, and then Olivier points the way through the garage so we can exit the rear door. We make our way back to the private team areas where all the motorhomes and hospitality suites are. I let him lead because I'm not sure where he wants to meet.

On the way through the garage, I catch Cole watching us. I *feel* Cole watching us. He's surrounded by his physio and personal assistant. I recognize both from television but have not met either yet.

He doesn't glare or wink. His eyes just follow me as I walk through the garage.

I really don't want things to be weird. Weirder.

You were looking at him, too. Stop reading into things.

Outside, the afternoon sun is shining. There's the same bustle of activity—crews walking up and down the service road between all the portable buildings.

I smile a little bit to myself. I'm in Germany and just spent the morning on the pit wall of an F1 track, and now I'm meeting with the Director of an international manufacturing company.

Besides that one little winking incident, there's been no embarrassing moments. No mental breakdowns. I did not die. I think it's okay to pat myself on the back a little.

Olivier leads us into a Concordia motorhome along the row of team buildings and holds the door open for me. It's every bit as posh as the Imperium motorhome, but not as young and hip. This is more timeless with cream leather sofas and gold accent pieces.

"Have a seat, I'll fetch us coffee. Americano for you, I assume?" Olivier directs me to a sofa in the main room.

"Depends, do you have a fancy coffee machine in here, too?"

"Of course, complete with a barista. We are a French company, after all, Emily," Olivier smiles.

"In that case, a flat white, please."

Olivier nods, and I take in my surroundings while he's gone.

I know that Formula 1 is perhaps the most wealthy sport in all of the world. Each of these motorhomes cost nearly ten million dollars to construct, each car can cost fifteen or twenty-million to build, but seeing it in person is quite different from reading about it or seeing it on TV.

I learned a lot about racing and motorsports through Cole when he was karting in high school, and that alone was ridiculously expensive, but nothing like this.

This is like Russian oligarch money. If history is any lesson, no good comes from this much concentrated wealth.

"Mon cher," Olivier hands me my coffee on a dainty saucer, and I let out a laugh when I look at the microfoam floating on top. It's a cute little race car. I'd love to take a photo for Klara, but I don't want to embarrass myself by acting like such a rookie.

Because cool things like this happen to me every day.

Olivier takes a seat next to me on the sofa. As I take a sip of my coffee, I can't help notice that he's staring at me.

"So, I've spent a lot of time talking to Edmund about the tire performance issues, and I'd like to jump in and learn as much as I can right away," I blurt out to avoid this staring-thing that's happening.

"Ha, plenty of time for that. Tell me about yourself, Emily."

Olivier is turned towards me. He's sitting on one leg, has one hand over the back of the couch, and while I know the French tend to be a bit more... relaxed than Americans, this is not a work pose I'm familiar with. This feels like he's at a lounge choosing women for the evening.

"Umm, well, I graduated from the University of Cambridge earlier this year, and, as you know, my thesis was in tire..."

"No. Tell me about yourself, Emily. What do you do for fun? What brings you joy?" Olivier interrupts me.

Brings me joy? What kind of Oprah Magazine bullshit is that?

"Oh. Well, I love to read. I spent a lot of time at the beach when I lived in Florida and in California. Umm, I've recently really gotten into cooking. I want to look into cheesemaking, in fact."

Olivier lets out a burst of laughter and interrupts my rambling stream of gibberish, "Cooking and cheesemaking?"

"Yeah, it's kind of..." I pause. I don't want to tell Olivier, this suave wealthy guy, that something about creating a finished product out of raw ingredients and the science that goes into baking, particularly, appeals to me. Or that I like it when the thing I just made gets eaten and makes someone happy. "It's just relaxing."

It's something simple, fun, and the worst consequence of failing at it means a full trash bin and no one but me knows.

"Well, then you must come to France. Best food and cheese in the world."

I nod and tuck a strand of hair behind my ear nervously, "Next year, for sure. I just missed the France Grand Prix."

Olivier goes back to his staring. I feel awkward, and I'm pretty sure he was making fun of me when I brought up the damn cheese.

As I do in these situations, I divert right back to my comfort zone, "I haven't been able to find the materials data for Concordia's F1 tire line. Is that something you can get for me?"

"The materials data?" He quirks his head.

"Yes, the build sheets, the chemical processes, information on all of the polymers and…"

"I'm afraid that is all proprietary, Emily," he shakes his head and sits up on the couch from his relaxed position.

"Proprietary."

"Yes, it means the information is…"

"I know what proprietary means," I interject a little too quickly.

Shit, that was defensive, and I practically barked at him. I'm a little edgy about being one of the only women in the paddock at all, and I have a short fuse for people assuming I'm an idiot because I happen to have tits. "Sorry, what information can you share then?"

Olivier stands. I guess coffee time is over. "I'll be happy to send you all the information available, mon cher."

I take my cue to leave and stand up. Shit got awkward quick.

Cheesemaking and proprietary information, ugh.

"My card," Oliver passes me his business card. "Don't hesitate to contact me with any questions or concerns. I'm sure we're going to be seeing a lot of each other, Emily. Welcome to the paddock."

He smiles warmly at me again, and now I'm not sure if he's upset with me or not. I hate feeling awkward like this. Sometimes I wish I could flip my own switch and stop thinking so much.

"I don't have a business card yet, but I can give you my email?" I say as we head to the door.

"Your email?"

"For the tire information."

"Oui, right. I'll get it from Edmund."

"Okay, thanks. Nice to meet you, Olivier."

He nods and holds the door open for me, and I make my escape.

Cheesemaking.
Good lord, Emily.

Nine

"So hard to find my way, now that I'm all on my own. I saw you just the other day, my, how you have grown." - Van Morrison - Brown Eyed Girl

Cole

"Why do you give them your number?" Dante asks me as my phone lights up again and again on the coffee table between us. "Rookie mistake."

I sit forward on the couch on the rooftop deck of the motorhome and grab the phone. I haven't looked at it all day. But now qualification is over, the sun is about to set, and things have quieted down the for day. And I need to deal with this.

I come up here to the rooftop to relax. It's one of the only quiet places available around the track, but the constant lighting up and buzzing is getting old, and this is a problem that isn't going to go away on its own.

I glance through the thirty-six messages and roll my eyes.

"Stage-five clinger," Dante says as he throws his feet up onto the table across from me.

"Seriously," I groan and dial the number.

Of course, she answers on the first ring and embarks upon her tirade.

Ninety percent of the time, Nova is a sane and reasonable woman. I have always been exceedingly clear that this is not a relationship and, ninety percent of the time, she is in agreement. It's the other ten percent of the time that's the problem.

Like now.

"Nova," I try to interrupt her rant that slips between English and Russian. "Nova, listen to me. I don't want to do this anymore."

I pull the phone away from my ear at her high pitched scream. Dante's eyes go wide, and his shoulders rock in laughter at my predicament. I don't think he's ever spent more than one night with the same woman, so this is hilarious to him.

"Stop yelling."

She does not stop yelling. I'm going to have to talk over her.

"Nova, I need you to hear me. We can't do this anymore. We don't want the same things. I've told you this."

Dante makes the motions of playing a fake violin.

Nova is now crying.

"No, we don't. I'm sorry, Nova. That's not going to happen." I try to combat every point she makes, and I'm trying not to be a dick, but my patience with this is running out. Lately, every few months, it's the same thing. "We are never getting married."

"Married?" Dante blurts out in horror, and I kick his foot.

"Shut the fuck up," I mouth at him.

"You don't love me. You don't even know me, Nova." Nova's well acquainted with my dick, but that's about it. "Okay, well, I am not in love with you, and I never will be," I clarify when she doesn't accept my first argument.

A stream of Russian profanity courses through the line. I don't want to be cruel, but this has to stop. This is why I don't touch anything that even resembles a relationship anymore.

"Nova, it's over. For good. Stop calling, don't show up. It's over. Do you understand?"

When an ear-piercing "fuck you" reverberates through my phone and the line goes dead, I assume she finally understands. I toss my phone back onto the coffee table and pray it's quiet for the rest of the evening.

"Jesus," I groan.

"She's going to cut your balls off, man," Dante laughs. "This about the brown-eyed girl?" This has been Dante's nickname for Emily since she started at Imperium as if she's the Van Morrison song.

I haven't heard that in years.

"No, this is about Nova being a bunny boiler."

That's at least half-true, anyway. This isn't the first time she's brought up getting married. We've never so much as gone on a date, it's ridiculous for a multitude of reasons. But especially because I've long since given up on the concept.

I haven't had an emotional connection with anyone since I left home, since I left Emily. I tried, for a while, then I gave up. Sex was sex. I'm not going to deny I've had a lot of fun, but that extra layer was never there again.

At some point, it didn't even make the loneliness go away anymore, either.

Dante checks his watch, "I'm out of here, you coming?"

The sun is down, and the stars are just starting to come out. I just want to sit here alone in the quiet for a little bit before I leave for the hotel. "Go ahead, I'll catch you later."

Dante leaves, and I lie down on the couch, put my arms behind my head, and watch the stars above me start to twinkle and come out for the night. I used to do this a lot and think about it being the same sky that Emily was under somewhere else in the world. She could see the same thing I was if she were doing the same.

I reach behind me to stuff a throw pillow under my head, and something hard falls out. It hits the deck next to the couch with a thud. Glancing over the couch, I pick it up—Emily's Kindle. I know it's hers because she has a black leather cover on it that makes it look like an antique book.

Back on the sofa, I arrange my pillow and lie back down. Let's see what Emily's reading. It'll probably be tales of organic chemistry or a how-to book on splitting atoms for fun and leisure.

I flip open the cover, and the on-screen book advertisement is a sweaty naked dude's torso, "*Abs of Thunder*—Marcus Wolf is a wealthy playboy, and he takes what he pleases in this 5-star steamy series of office bad boys."

I laugh to myself, fucking Amazon.

I swipe the Kindle open, and it's on the end credits for whatever book Emily's just finished, so I click the home button.

Her library looks like a Google image search for abs.

Swipe, swipe, swipe—pages, and pages of books with dude abs. Motorcycle dude abs, guy in a suit abs, guy with his arm around a chick in a bra abs. I spend two hours a day in a gym, and I have never seen so many abs.

Emily Walker is into smutty books now? Fascinating.

I go back to the home screen and look at some of the titles to see what she's into these days.

Taking What's His
My Filthy Billionaire Boss
Surrender to My Control
Rock Hard Racing

Hmmm, Rock Hard Racing, you say?

Tapping on that icon, I settle into the couch while the sounds of the paddock die down for the night, and the sky continues to darken.

Ugh, it's about NASCAR, lame.

Nevertheless, I want to know what Emily's been reading all those times I saw her in the coffee shop. I start reading Charlotte and Steel's torrid love affair.

Who is named Steel in real life? This is ridiculous.

Three chapters in and things are getting serious. Charlotte is in trouble, her ruthless boss is on her case, and she needs this job to pay for her mama's kidney transplant. Is Steel going to pussy out and let that happen? He's been trying to get into Charlotte's pants, but she needs this job, damnit.

"Just pay for the operation, you douche," I mutter to myself.

Another couple of chapters breeze by, and Charlotte is now spread eagle on Steel's tongue, and everyone's loins are burning, bosoms are heaving.

I picture Emily reading this stuff every night as she tucks herself into bed, getting hot and touching herself. She always liked me talking filthy to her, I guess I shouldn't be surprised, but I can't stand the thought of other guys talking to her like that.

Did the guy she was dancing with at the club take her home and say this shit to her, too?

"Is that my, oh my god, what are you doing?" I hadn't even heard Emily come up the stairs onto the deck.

"Give me that," she tries to swipe the Kindle from me, but my arms are much longer. I hold it out of her reach as I lie on the couch with her hovering above me.

"I'm just getting to the good part," I smile. Even under the moonlit sky, I can see Emily's face turn bright red and a flush start to overtake her neck.

"This isn't funny," she holds her hand out, expecting me to hand her the Kindle back. There's a slight tremble to her fingers.

"No. Nothing is funny about Charlotte's mama needing a kidney transplant. This is serious," I bite my inner lip and try to keep a straight face.

"Cole," she covers her face with one hand.

I put one hand up to keep her from snatching the Kindle and bring it back down before me with the other. "Ahem, now then," I start reading aloud. *"Charlotte panted, her thighs quivering from the assault of Steel's tongue on her wetness.*

'Yes, Steel, yes,' Charlotte cried.

Hearing her cries of ecstasy, Steel dragged himself over her naked body and lined his thick cock up with her entrance.

'You want my stick shift, baby?' He taunted her."

"Oh my god," Emily flops down onto the couch across from me and covers her face with both hands.

"You know, this is not the most technically correct in its depiction of NASCAR," I look over at her.

"That's not the point," she takes her hands away from her face and pouts.

God, I love seeing her blush. So many little things I've missed about her.

"No, I imagine it's not," I can't help but smirk at her.

I keep reading aloud and sneak glances at her out of the corner of my eye.

"'Give it to me,' Charlotte whispered. 'Give it to me hard, Steel.'

'Beg for it, beg for me to fill up that pussy,' Steel growled.

'Please,' Charlotte whimpered.

Steel thrust forward, his massive girth penetrating her and filling her up like no other man could. He moved in and out, his pelvis slamming into her like a piston, and Charlotte's wetness began to seep down her thigh."

"See, right there. Pistons don't really slam. They're very smooth and more like they rock… in and out of each cylinder. You're a mechanical engineer, you know how pistons work." I look at Emily and dramatize my words, speak them slowly.

"Oh my god, I hate you," she's redder than ever, but I can see her biting her lip, trying not to smile. It's the first time in a long time I've made her smile, even if she's hiding it.

Before I have time to think through what I'm asking or the ramifications of her answer, I blurt it out. "Do you… hate me?"

She leans back to the couch and wraps her arms around herself. Her face turns away, and she looks off into the distance.

Please say no.

Eventually, she brings her head back and looks down at her lap, then shakes her head, "I should."

"But, you don't?"

She shakes her head again like she can't make herself say it aloud.

I drop her Kindle to my chest and turn my body to face her better. Even the head shake is a win, and a tiny bit of the heaviness inside me lifts.

"I hate what you did, though," she adds after a moment.

"I hate what I did, too."

"Good for you," she fires back at me.

Okay, then. I knew it was coming. Emily can be angry. She *should* be angry.

I need to switch gears before she walks out. "Not what I expected you to be reading," I tap the Kindle on my chest, "not that there's anything wrong with it."

"Yeah, well, I'm not the same person you used to know," she says defensively, still mad. "Are you?"

"No," I admit.

What a fucking mouthful.

I picture her dancing at that club and all the things I've done over the last several years, things I would never want her to know or learn about. Things I am not proud of.

"I don't want this to be weird, Cole," she says after a long quiet moment. I can see her formulating her resolve before my very eyes. "We have to work together."

I sit up, drop my legs off the couch, and nod as I turn to face her. "We used to be friends once."

"You want to be *friends*?" She emphasizes the word friends like it's the most disgusting thing she's ever heard.

"I'm asking what you want."

"I don't think I can be your friend."

I take a deep breath and try to reign in my thoughts, try not to show my disappointment. Still, even if there is only one percent of hope, I don't know how to give up. Not with most things, and definitely not with her.

It may be naive, but I want to believe there's still something there within her, something lying under the pain and anger. Sitting this close to her, hearing her voice, looking into those deep brown eyes again—I have to try.

"How about just being friendly, then?"

"Friendly?" She asks skeptically.

"We do have to work together, like you said," I shrug. "We're going to have to communicate and spend time together."

She thinks about it for a moment, takes a deep breath and nods, "Okay."

I smile and lean back. Sometimes one percent is enough. Nothing is over until it's over.

This is a start.

"I have questions," she pulls her knees up underneath her on the couch and looks at me.

My heart drops.

It's too early for the questions I'm afraid she'll ask. I'm not prepared, and if we get too deep into the past right now, she'll run.

Emily doesn't run from commitment. She runs when failure might be an option, and when it carries consequences that she can't accept. I think I might just be her worst-case scenario now.

"Some of the things you say in the car, on the radio, I don't understand what you mean," she explains.

Oh, thank christ. Just car questions.

"Like what?"

"You said the rear felt loose."

I spend a minute telling her about understeer and how we can change the wing setups, how it affects cornering in the car, but she cuts me off after a minute or two.

"I know the definition of it, Cole. I need to know how it feels."

"How it feels?"

"Good engineers listen to needs and wants and then create a solution. I know what all the parts on the car do, or can do. I don't know how it feels to drive the car, and I need you to explain it to me. So when you say it feels loose…"

I rub my chin and think about how to describe the feeling to someone who's never driven a Formula 1 car. Only a handful of people on earth will ever experience it, and it's not as easy as one might think to put it into words.

"It's not sticky. It's like there's no foundation when it's loose. It's like the car pushes itself around, doesn't do what I ask. Like it slips out of my hands, and there's nothing I can do about it."

Like you.

"And then you don't trust the car heading into a corner," she says.

I can almost see her mind working. As gorgeous as Emily has always been, she's absolutely brilliant, and it turns me on as much as her body does.

She's probably the reason I have no tolerance for ditzy chicks. The bar has been set so fucking high.

"Right, it makes me lose confidence like I'm going to spin and lose everything. It makes me hesitant to go as deep in the corners or push as hard when I don't know if the car will be there for me."

Like you.

There's a long pause where we both just stare at one another. I wish I knew what Emily was thinking. I wish I knew if I stood up and walked to her and took her face in my hands and pressed my lips to hers—that she'd be there with me.

I'm not convinced she wouldn't knee me in the dick. More likely, she'll quit and then be out of my life again.

Too soon.

"Your tires wear for shit when the car is loose," she finally snaps her eyes away from mine and says.

"Good thing you're on the case, then," I laugh.

She smiles, cautiously. So cautious.

"Did you get anything helpful from Gaspard?" I ask, treading very lightly over the rocky terrain of Emily's palpable anger and trepidation.

"Gaspard?"

"Yeah, Olivier from Concordia," I do my best French accent of his fancy name and try not to roll my eyes. Guy's as smooth as glass.

"Oh. No, not really. I think I upset him or something," Emily crinkles her eyes up and twists her lips.

"Why? What happened?" My hackles are immediately up like I have any business at all feeling protective. But I am. This industry is brutal, sometimes.

"Nothing, really. I asked for some info he said was proprietary, then I went off on a tangent about wanting to learn cheesemaking," Emily shrugs and purses her lips like she's embarrassed.

"You want to learn how to make cheese?" I smile.

God, she's adorable.

Every week, Emily was learning something new when we were together. It was never dull or boring with her in my life. One week she'd want to learn to surf, so I'd take her to the beach, and we'd do a lesson together. The next week it would be pottery, and she giggled all night at my *Ghost* reenactment attempts.

Candle making, rock climbing, whatever it was, we did it. All that mattered was that she was happy, and I was with her. She drew the line at my suggestion of skydiving, but I'm kind of glad she refused because I was secretly terrified, too. Going a couple hundred miles per hour is excellent, on the ground. Not free-falling through the air.

"It's stupid," she drops her head.

"It's not stupid," I shut that shit down. No one in their right mind would ever call Emily stupid. "Cheese is goddamn delicious."

I will take you to learn cheesemaking. Please let me take you like we used to.

Her face lifts, and her slight smile is back. I still feel like a million dollars when I make her smile.

"The metalworking class was still my favorite," I tell her, and she starts fiddling with her long, brown hair as she makes the connection, remembers all the times that are flashing through my mind, too.

I don't think I've ever been so turned on in my life as watching Em weld shit in that class, her safety mask on, fusing steel together like a total badass. We absolutely sucked at it, which was half the fun for her.

To my right, I hear footsteps coming up the stairs, and we both glance over.

"Hey," Liam struts up and interrupts us. It's just as well, I can't rush her.

"Emily, this is Liam, my physio. Liam, this is my friend Emily," I wink at Emily when I call her my friend.

Baby steps.

"Nice to meet you," Emily stands and shakes Liam's hand. He's a particularly tall bastard and hovers over her.

"You too, welcome to the team. Let me know if you need anything," he smiles at her.

"Mmm-hmmm," I stand to join them and give Liam the death glare. Liam is only too happy to offer his massage services to pretty women, though he does a lot for the rest of the team, also.

"Time to go," Liam checks his watch and announces.

Liam is the Fun Police, officially. He sets sleep schedules, what I eat, all the workouts, and generally tries to keep distractions down and performance up.

"Apparently, it's my bedtime," I tell Emily, and all three of us start to walk toward the stairs.

As Liam heads down first, I whisper over my shoulder at Emily, "Don't leave me hanging. Does Charlotte's mama get the new kidney?"

She bites her lip and shakes her head, long brown hair swirling around her, "You'll have to read the book."

Ten

Emily

The schedule on race day is jam-packed. Long before the race even begins, at sunup, the mechanics and engineers are all at it in the garage, ensuring every T is crossed, and I dotted. Then, not ten minutes after the race, the breakdown process begins, and most of us fly home.

Dante and Cole have a million pre-race obligations and routines, so I don't even see them until it's a few minutes before the national anthem starts. That might be a good thing since I keep replaying last night in my head.

I called Makenna as soon as I got to my hotel and told her about talking to Cole on the rooftop and my absolute mortification of him reading my romance novel aloud.

I wanted to die of embarrassment nearly as much as I wanted to climb on top of him on that outdoor couch.

Lying there all stretched out like a jungle cat bathing in the moonlight, equally wild and untamed thoughts overtook me. Fiction is the closest I've ever been able to get to recreating sex with Cole Ballentine.

I've only been with a few other guys, but even when I was very clear with them on what I wanted, it wasn't the same. It was beyond dirty talk—that just came out like a joke with other men—I would end up laughing and couldn't get into it.

It didn't turn off my mental switch. I didn't trust them enough.

Then he had to go and be sweet about the stupid cheese, too. Cole

78

never once made fun of my rambling thoughts or bizarre ideas. He never minded when I went off on tangents. He embraced them, made me feel comfortable. And so, years ago, I opened up to him and showed him the most honest version of myself.

And then he left, of course.

For six years, I've imagined what it would be like to talk to him again, be in the same space as him once more. I've envisioned everything from clawing his eyes out to jumping his bones.

But when I got the chance? Ninety percent of those thoughts left me, and I was sucked into his vortex.

It's like he wields a pocket dimension where space and time become irrelevant, and he's a black hole sucking me into him. He's been this way his whole life. You couldn't miss Cole in a crowded high school hallway anymore than you could miss a supernova in the night sky.

Makenna still thinks Cole and I need to have sex to get him out of my system. Even if some part of me wants to believe that, it's a ridiculous idea.

Six years and thousands of miles haven't gotten him out of my system. Then again, what I've been doing isn't working, and you know what Einstein said about insanity—it's doing the same thing over and over and expecting different results.

Stop it.

The German national anthem finishes, and the circuit is packed with seventy-thousand fans. It's a gorgeous, sunny day, and I'm excited to experience my first race in person.

I'm more excited to see tire data from an actual, full race. Every team gets their choice of three tire compounds today, soft, medium, and hard. It seems simple enough.

I won't be on the pit wall during the race, my regular station is in the rear of the garage with a few other engineers and our computers, but we're all in contact via our headsets. Making my way past the mechanics and cars, I head toward my zone when Dante and Cole enter through the back of the garage.

They both look very focused, but everyone else is clapping them on the back or telling them 'good luck' as they walk by, so I wait to take my seat.

"Good luck," I tell Dante.

"No luck needed, bellissima," he smirks at me. God, he is an endearingly cocky bastard.

Cole is behind him and pauses to smile at me, clearly waiting his turn for me to acknowledge him, too. "Good luck, have fun," I tell him. As soon as he gets what he wants, he resumes his pace, and the crew get both guys into their cars.

I may, or may not, watch him walk away.

Dante and Cole get secured in their cars. I throw my headset on, then tuck into my spot at my computer. I can hear both drivers going through their rituals. Edmund gives them instructions, updates on weather, and wind speeds.

In just a few minutes, both cars pull out of the garage, and I'm hit with pangs of nervousness and find myself chewing on my thumbnail. I see several other people tapping their feet and fidgeting, it's not just me.

The whole pack of cars does their formation lap around the track and then line up on the grid waiting for the lights to go out. For a moment, it is silent in the garage, and the tension is palpable.

Then the start lights on the grid drop, and all twenty cars rumble, roar, and push past one another, zinging past our garage on the straight.

My eyes dart between the data on my computer screen and the monitor above it that shows live action of the cars on track. I need to look at this data and watch it, but I'm also compelled to watch the TV screen. I want to see how Cole is doing, but I'm also suddenly more nervous than ever before.

Be logical, Emily.

Serious accidents are infrequent. Safety is unparalleled in this sport.

I know this. I've researched that heavily already, years ago, and many times since. It just feels so much more real now, in person.

Several laps go by, and both of our boys are doing reasonably well for themselves in fourth and fifth place. The cars have spread out around the winding track. I can relax a little bit, not be so afraid that some other driver will cause an accident. There's always one asshole acting like a torpedo on track, ruining shit for everyone else.

Dante's on the medium compound tire, and it's rated by Concordia for twenty-five laps, but his tire data is showing more wear than they should at this stage. Edmund catches it too, as I hear him over my headset tell Dante to cool the tires and change some settings.

That's no good, it means he'll have to slow down. Accelerate less, slow down more gradually, go softer into the corners. I can see why the tire performance is critical here, and I start running some numbers to see if we can artificially manipulate the tire temperatures.

I also start watching Cole's data, he's diving into corners and quick on the uptake—he trusts the car, right now.

I smile.

Then I decide I need to really need to dig into the differences between all these tire compounds. It's two nearly identical cars, yet only one is chewing up rubber.

I use the lull in track action to walk around the garage and take a look at our rack of tires in their black heating jackets. Temperature looks right, every tire has a unique identifying number on it and is labeled for the specific driver. Even though I can't tell anything just by looking at the slick black rubber, I run my hands over several of them.

Olivier hasn't gotten me that materials data yet. I want to know what's inside these babies.

"Dante, box this lap. Box, box, box," his engineer calls over the radio instructing Dante to come in for a pit stop.

"It's too soon, we'll lose track position," Dante answers.

I run back to my computer and look. Dante's right, he isn't scheduled to come in for a pit stop yet, but his tire life is showing as virtually gone.

"Copy that, but you're losing time, box this lap," his engineer tells him again.

"I can do a few more laps," Dante argues.

I see an engineer on the pit wall throw his hands up in frustration. Clearly, Dante is always cocky and doesn't like to follow orders.

Sure enough, Dante zooms right by the pit lane entrance and zips past us in the garage. Just after he passes us, there's an awful screech, and a plume of black smoke waifs past our line of sight.

I look up to the monitor, and one of the cars on another team has just had a massive blowout. Chunks of rubber fly in all directions as the tire disintegrates like it's taken a grenade to the sidewall.

The yellow car skids, then moves to the side of the track to get out of the way, its metal rim sparking against the asphalt before he makes it to a run-off area.

"Yellow flag, Sector One," Edmund tells both drivers, so they know to slow down and use caution in that area.

Good lord, the carnage the tire has made looks terrible on the television monitors. The tire coming apart and flopping around has torn up the floor of the car, and the driver is pissed as he gets out. Pissed, but he's okay.

This shit is scary in real life, damn.

In two laps, the track marshals have removed the battered yellow car, and our engineers tell the boys the track is clear.

Dante again passes the pit lane entry and continues defying his engineers. I wonder if all the drivers have this much ego. Cole certainly did even when he was just eighteen.

All the computer data on Dante's car looks good. It's just tire life that's the problem. I wonder if the engineers in the other team are thinking the same thing as their dead car gets wheeled back to their garage. I'm wondering what settings we can tinker with on our end that may help.

I'm chewing my cuticle when the data on my screen blows up, bright red lights and error messages flashing.

I see it on my computer before I look up and confirm it on the television monitor. Dante's car goes off at a corner. He sails into a gravel trap as his rear left tire comes apart in strands and flings huge pieces of rubber everywhere. The car kicks up a plume of dust, and the gravel thankfully does its job. It slows Dante down significantly before the car knocks sideways into a barrier wall and rocks to a halt.

"Cagata pneumatici! Vaffanculo a chi t'è morto," a very long string of what I'm assuming are Italian profanities come through my headset as Dante's car comes to a stop.

I need to learn more languages.

"What is he saying?" I ask the engineer sitting next to me.

He lifts one of his earphones off his head and says, "Umm, more or less, these bullshit tires can go fuck corpses. More or less," he shrugs.

"Are you all right, Dante?" Edmund asks him.

"Yes, yes, I'm fine. These piece of shit tires should not come apart like this," he yells back.

Edmund tries to calm him down over the radio, but Dante is right. All tires, especially high-performance tires like these, are designed to fail in safe ways. They should not implode like this. Is this what's been happening all season?

Typically when I watch races at home, I'm only paying attention to Cole. And I'm also usually hiding in my bedroom, so the rest of the world doesn't know exactly how *not* over Cole I am.

I want to see that damaged tire.

I check the monitor and see Cole's doing fine out there, his data looks good. I watch as the marshals work on getting Dante's car onto a wrecker and wait with my hands on my hips as the tow truck starts it's slow progression back to the garage area.

Dante makes it back before the tow truck and storms through the garage, hurling more Italian inside his helmet. He shoves a door open so hard it bounces off the wall behind, then escapes through the rear of the garage. I need to talk to him about what happened, but not now. Angry Dante looks a little scary.

Eventually, the car makes it back on the wrecker, and I'm clamoring to get near it as it gets lowered to the ground from the truck. A crew of our mechanics is waiting to assist, and once the car is on the ground, I start inspecting the tires.

They're beat to shit, they're hot, but I need to really look at them.

Our crew gets the car on a dolly, and mechanics get to work on removing the tires and cooling the brakes, so they don't catch on fire. As I'm waiting for a tire to be removed, a team of Concordia reps in white shirts appear with a rolling metal rack.

"I'm sorry, I don't remember your name," I tell the mechanic removing the damaged tire. "I want that tire." I point to the shredded tire that blew apart on Dante.

"I'm Mark, but what do you mean you want this tire?" The mechanic asks.

"I mean, I want it. Give it to me, please," I make a motion with my hand to give it the hell over.

Mark looks at me like I'm nuts.

I find myself pissed off. Dante could have been hurt.

I don't know if it's the tire's fault or what happened, but I intend to find out. I do know that I should not be looking at a tire that looks like shredded chicken, for god's sake.

"Uhh, I can't give you the tire," Mark argues.

"What? Why not?"

One of the Concordia reps wheels the rolling rack and takes the tire from Mark. The other reps start taking tires from the other mechanics as they are removed from the car.

"All used tires return to Concordia immediately for inspection," some little nitwit Concordia chick who's crept up next to me says.

"Inspection? Well, I want to inspect them first," I snap back.

Don't start with me, bitch. You have no idea what I'm dealing with this week.

"Sorry, that's not how this works," she sashays her head.

"Mark, is this true?" I turn to him.

Mark looks like he is afraid he's going to get dragged into a catfight at any moment and is none too pleased about it.

"Yeah, sorry. Those are the rules," he confirms.

Salty tire bitch gloats at me as the fourth tire is loaded onto their rack to be wheeled away. All these stupid rules, who comes up with this garbage?

"Fine," I squint at Tire Bitch, and I pull my cell phone out of my pocket.

The other Concordia people have started wheeling the tires away, but I jog after them and start taking photos as I chase them. I'm just aiming my phone in the general direction of the damaged tire and holding the shutter down.

"You can't do that," Tire Bitch argues.

"Mark," I yell back to the mechanics. "Is there a rule about me taking photos?" I run backward.

"Not that I know of," he bellows.

"Ha!" I sneer at Tire Bitch, who rolls her eyes at me and instructs the other three Concordia reps to pick up their pace.

I chase after them like a crazy person until I have taken what feels like a hundred photos. Hopefully one or two will be useful.

Then I make my way back to Dante's wrecked car, which is being wheeled into the garage bay now. First, I check the ground where it was lowered off the truck, and damn, no rubber chunks are lying around.

I wonder if I can get some off the track later, but no, those efficient German marshals have long since swept up all the debris.

Damn it.

I want the materials data from Olivier.

I check the television monitors and my computer again. Cole has come in for a pit stop while I was chasing manufacturer reps around like a nut, but everything looks good for him.

I look over at Dante's car, the carbon fiber pods are smashed and splintered, the front wing is dangling off, the floor of the vehicle is bent up at an unnatural angle. According to the data, he hit the wall at 93 miles per hour, and the impact was nearly 14g. A couple more and the g-force sensor in the car would have tripped, and Dante would be taken to a medical center for a mandatory check.

If Dante had been in a normal road car, he'd be dead several times over.

This could have been Cole.

By the time the race has ended, I've chewed my cuticle enough that it's bleeding. I barely knew what place Cole finished in because I was overwhelmed with him just coming back in one piece.

No matter what has happened between Cole and me, I don't think I could handle it if he got killed out here. I know the dangers, obviously. I've always known but seeing it creates a pit in my stomach.

I want to slap him and shake him and ask him a thousand questions about how he could have done what did to me, but I don't want him dead.

I wonder if this is how Mom feels being married to a military husband, though Dad has long since even gone up in a plane, much less been deployed.

I'm probably blowing things out of proportion. Dante is fine. I have no idea where Cole is, but he's also fine.

Breathe.

The only thing I can do is do what I do best. Put my head down and figure out what is going on with these tires. Even if they're not faulty, there has to be some reason the team can't get them to work right.

And if they're not working right, for any reason, they aren't safe.

Eleven

Emily

"Enhance. Enhance," I joke to Zane, one of the factory engineers who's helping me in the lab today as we analyze my tire photos. We have them pulled up onto an oversized monitor hung on the wall.

"It's not CSI, Emily," he says. Zane is American, too, so we've been making jokes us Yanks would know.

"Maybe we need to turn the lights out and look with flashlights, that's when you find all the good clues."

Most of my pictures are trash, blurred beyond recognition because I was jogging when I took them. But there are two that might be useful if only Zane would enhance like television shows indicate we should be able to do.

I've spent the better part of my time between races digging up as much information as I can because Olivier still has not sent me the promised materials data. I emailed him a reminder and got an out of office notification.

I even found a French student at Cambridge to help me request the patent information Concordia has on record in France, but that's going to take twelve weeks or more, and now I have to tutor someone else for the favor. But, without a tire from this season in hand, preferably a destroyed tire, I'm on my own to ferret out clues.

But I'm not going to be underestimated. I've had enough of that to last me a lifetime. I am smart and damn good at what I do. To hell with anyone who wants to put me in a corner and thinks otherwise.

"Wait, go back one photo," I tell Zane and move closer to the giant

86

wall monitor.

He clicks back one photo and blows up the image. "What?" He asks, fixing his glasses to look closely.

"Can you zoom in any more right here," I point to a corner of the image.

Zane tries, but the resolution blows out if we zoom in any more. "What are we looking at?"

It's hard to tell because this is a shitty cell phone photo, and most of it is blurred, but there might be something. "Right here," I tap the monitor, "what do you see?"

"Cracks in the rubber?"

I nod. I really want someone else to see what I see, though, because it could be nothing, and I don't want to bring bias in. And I am definitely biased now after Dante's accident scared the bejeezus out of me.

"I don't get it," Zane finally shrugs. In fairness, he did not spend nine months of his life learning everything there is to know about tires. He spent his graduate year learning about computational fluid dynamics, which also sounds fascinating if I'm honest.

"Do those cracks look random in pattern to you, or do they run perpendicular to the grain?" Both of us have our noses pressed into the monitor and are cocking our heads from side to side, trying to figure it out.

"Perpendicular. Maybe?"

"Ugh, you're no help, Zane," I put my hands on my hips and step back.

"What does the crack orientation have to do with anything?"

"The way the cracks form tells a story. Perpendicular cracks can be from ozone…"

"What are you guys doing?" Zane and I both jump and spin around to find Cole with one eyebrow cocked, looking at the magnified tire photo on the wall, and my smattering of papers spread out around me like a tornado has been through.

"Looking at cracks," Zane shrugs.

"As one does," Cole smiles at me with that panty-melting grin he does so well.

I've seen Cole a handful of times at the factory since we've been back. He's being pretty professional, I have to admit. He's conveniently available when I've had questions, but he isn't underfoot or making me uncomfortable in any way.

A couple of times I've caught myself wishing he were around more, actually, but I've been pushing that down and trying to focus on work. Because I'm good at *that*.

"What's up?" I ask him. His hands are in his jeans pockets, which just makes his pants tight in that area, and I try not to glance down. He's gotten scruffy since we've been home for the last several days, and it makes him look even more impossibly rugged.

"Dante said you wanted me to tell you when I'd be in the simulator?"

"Oh yeah, I forgot. When are you doing that?"

"Now."

Has his Adam's apple always been so pronounced?

Good lord.

"Um, okay, let me just grab my laptop," I start scrambling around looking for my computer and find it buried under a stack of research papers I printed off at the University about other auto sports projects.

Cole stands still as a statue just watching me, an ever-present smirk on his face. Every time I've bumped into him, he's smirking or smiling at me. I don't know how I'm supposed to be hateful when he's always polite. I was expecting him to be confrontational when I arrived if anything.

Nope, he's playing the perfect gentleman, instead.

I was hoping to be confrontational, myself, if I'm honest. I have years of rage I would like to get out. But we're both being professional, and it's oddly unsatisfying. I feel robbed of wanting to punch Cole in the face or kick him in the balls like I'd always envisioned.

Walking out of the lab together, we need to go up a flight of stairs since the lab is in the basement. Reaching the stairwell, Cole extends a hand so I can go first. Again, the gentleman. Maybe he's matured, grown up.

No sooner do I think that when I feel the hairs on the back of my neck prickling. We're halfway up the stairs when I stop and glare at him over my shoulder. He's right behind me.

"What?" He asks.

"I feel like you're looking at my ass."

"You would not be wrong," the corners of his eyes wrinkle, and he continues his grinning.

"Stop it," I scold him. "You go first." I step aside on the stairs so he can move past me.

"Now you're going to look at my ass," he says as he steps past and leaves a trace of his cologne to swirl past me.

It's not the same cologne he used to wear. It's better.

"I am not."

I absolutely am.

"Mmm, I think you are," he teases.

I ignore him because anything else I say is only going to encourage him. He holds the stairwell door open for me, again, as we exit into the lobby.

When we walk past the hallway where I first ran into him, he asks, "Why were you hiding the morning of your interview?"

"I was not hiding, I was here early and just wandering around," I feel goosebumps climb over my skin.

Liar, liar, panties on fire.

"You were twenty minutes late for your interview. You were hiding."

"My watch was broken."

"Okay," he chuckles at my ridiculous excuse.

I sigh and will myself into being an adult. I can be more mature and grown up too, I suppose if I must. "I was trying to bomb the interview."

"Because of me," he states, not so much asking, but confirming.

I nod. There's no point in denying it. Cole's not stupid, and he knows me better than anyone.

Or, he did, once upon a time.

"Are you uncomfortable around me?" He asks. His head hangs down as we walk as if he's embarrassed.

It's a question I should have to think about, but I don't. Cole's always made me feel comfortable, like a cozy pair of slippers that you slink into. My answer leaves my mouth immediately, "No."

As we continue to walk through the lobby and toward the Simulation room, I pay attention to my thoughts, how my body feels. I'm not uncomfortable at all. I'm relaxed, there's a calmness inside of me. Now that I recognize the feeling, I can't remember the last time I didn't feel awkward or have thoughts racing through my mind.

Probably six years ago.

I was here with Dante earlier in the week, but the Simulator room still makes me do a double-take. There's a partial, mock F1 car raised up on a platform in the middle of the darkened room on four hydraulic legs. In front of it is an enormous one-hundred-eighty degree vision screen so the driver can experience what he'll see on the track.

It looks like a theme park ride, but six times as expensive.

Running along the side of the room is a control station, and I plug my laptop into the data portal as Cole climbs the stairs into the cockpit and settles in. He's running the Hungary track simulation today since that's our next race.

I get the program pulled up, and the screen comes to life, the mock car rises up into the air. The program starts running as if the car was on the grid at the front of the race.

Data starts pouring in as the car rolls and pitches like a real car would. I watch Cole's fingers snap the paddle shifters behind the steering wheel, watch where his eyes go on the screen, and how the car responds.

"Why did you do that?" I ask when he fiddles with a setting on his steering wheel, and the data points change.

"I like this suspension setup better."

I huff and stare at him, he knows I need more than that.

"This track is all cornering and precise braking. I need the car with me. Adding more negative camber makes it… tighter," he speaks his words in chunks as he goes around the track on screen and the car rocks and shakes.

I just noticed he bites his lip when he goes around corners. You'd never see that under a helmet.

"Do you do that because you're nervous in the corners?" I ask. That would make sense with the tire problems.

"Do what?"

"Bite your lip."

He smiles and slowly runs his tongue over his bottom lip before answering me, "Just concentrating. You're making it difficult."

"How am I making it difficult?" I'm just standing here!

"Looking at my ass, looking at my lips, it's distracting."

I glare at him then look down at the controls before me. I fiddle with the brake controls, turn them way down.

Cole swings into the next corner on the screen. I hear him hit the brake pedal a few times, and then his virtual car sails off into the grass. The hydraulics of the platform jump around and rock the mock car violently back and forth.

I crack up laughing and think I even snort.

It feels so good to laugh with him again, like an eraser rubbing on those tarnished parts of my heart.

"Real nice. That's real nice, Em."

I continue snickering as I reset the computer, and Cole starts fake-driving again, but I'm hung up on him calling me Em. No one else ever has, except one short-lived boyfriend and I asked him to stop it.

We run through several programs and dozens of laps. Cole's doing well explaining how the car feels, and I have all kinds of notes. This next track is known to be very hard on tires, so it's essential I understand as much as possible, and Dante was not as helpful in the Sim.

Dante is all one-word answers and has a hard time expressing how something feels versus facts. At one point, he tried mansplaining downforce, and we had to have a little chat.

At this point, I think I have everything I need from Cole in the simulator, but I'm enjoying watching him and talking to him, even if it is about the car. He thinks he's clever, but he's been sneaking plenty of innuendos into his descriptions.

The car feels tight, the brakes are so hot.

When he tells me how stiff and hard the suspension is getting, I tell him he sounds like Steel from my ridiculous book.

"Steel's an asshole," he replies.

"Oh, really?" I laugh.

"Yeah. He could have just paid for the kidney in chapter one, told Charlotte he was in love with her, and she wouldn't have been forced to choose between him and her job."

"Well, that wouldn't be very dramatic then, would it?"

"I guess there had to be some plot to further all the sex scenes."

"Wait," I say as I move from behind the desk and stand right next to the elevated car, "how do you know Charlotte had to leave her job?"

"I read the book," he says flatly, still going around and around the track on screen.

"You read. The book…"

"Mmm-hmm," he says, biting his lip into a chicane.

"Why would you do that?"

"The suspense was killing me."

"Cole…"

The car stops on screen, and he looks down at me from his elevated seat, "I read it because you read it. Just wanted to know more about the new you."

I feel something shift in me, something dangerous. A small crack forming in my foundation.

I turn my head away from those lethal blue eyes looking down on me and stare at the Imperium logo on the wall, instead.

Cole pulls himself out of the seated car and stands up, then begins his descent down the stainless steel stairs attached to the platform. "Up you go," he says when he reaches the bottom.

"What?"

"Up you go. You want to know how it feels, so, get in," he points upward to the cockpit.

"I can't, is, is that allowed?"

"Who gives a shit? Live a little, Em."

I look at Cole, then look at the simulator, look at Cole, look at the Sim.

Oh, fuck it.

I climb up the steps apprehensively, but Cole's right behind me and helps me get into the cockpit. He shows me all the controls I'll need, tells me how to work the paddles and all the controls.

His hands run over mine as he puts them on the steering wheel, I can feel his breath on my neck as he bends over me to explain everything.

"There's nothing you can break," he reassures me. "Just have fun."

Cole goes back down the ladder and restarts the computer program. The screen changes to starting position on the Hungarian grid. The lights go out, and I stretch my leg as far as it will go to mash the gas peddle down.

The car jerks forward, and I let out a squeal as the platform moves and shakes.

"Shift," Cole laughs, my steering wheel showing me I've maxed the RPMs.

Oh hell, I was still in first gear. I shift into second, and as the first corner comes up, I hit the brakes, and the whole car rocks forward like it's just hit a brick wall. The car sputters and dies.

"Shit!"

Cole is laughing hysterically now but restarts the program, and I try again.

I can make it through two or three corners and in gears one, two, or three before I manage to destroy the virtual car. I lose track of how many walls I run into. At one point, I somehow manage to overturn the car.

"Fuck, I'm gonna piss myself," Cole cackles.

"I want to make it one full lap around," I call down to him.

This is a hoot, even if I am starting to get motion sick from bouncing around in this circus ride.

"Is the real car this hard to drive?" I ask as I'm halfway through one full lap without death or destruction, even if I'm only going twenty-five miles per hour, and *all* of my engine warning lights are on.

"The real car is much harder, baby."

Rounding the final corner, I find myself biting my lip, too.

"Ha! I did it! I am the world champion!" I throw my arms into the air as I cross the finish line. One lap in just seventeen minutes.

Total rockstar.

Cole climbs back up the ladder and helps extract me from the car. Even getting in and out of these things is difficult.

"Well, did it help you understand the car better?" He asks me at the bottom as I fix my hair that's become disheveled with all the commotion.

I quirk my head to the side, "You know, I wasn't thinking about it."

He beams at me, the corners of his smile damn near reaching his eyes.

Our eyes flicker back and forth between each other in the darkened room.

Cole takes a big breath in, blinks, and then breaks our gaze. He turns behind the desk, "I'll print out your data set for a souvenir."

"More like a badge of shame," I take the papers as they come out of the printer. It's so bad it makes me laugh again. Good thing I went into engineering as I have no career potential as a Formula 1 driver.

We gather up my laptop and my printouts, and as soon as we leave the room, I realize it's now dark outside. Hours have passed inside the simulator room.

"Walk you to your car?" Cole asks.

"Okay, just need to grab my stuff." There's more security around this building than Fort Knox, yet I tell myself the prudent thing to do is to let Cole walk me to my car.

"You excited for Budapest?" he asks as we step outside into the warm, muggy night air.

"I am. If there's time, I want to buy some paprika, and there's a restaurant I've always wanted to go to." There probably won't be any time, if the last race was any indication, but I want authentic paprika for my arsenal, and this restaurant has been on my bucket list for a while now.

"What restaurant?"

"I can't pronounce the name, but it was on Anthony Bourdain's show."

Cole nods, and we talk briefly about how much we both felt the loss of Anthony Bourdain. I don't know why his death affected me so much, I think I admired the way he lived his life and enjoyed the small things, lived in the moment.

"I think he's why I started cooking," I tell Cole.

"You cook now?"

"When I can." We've reached my car, and I unlock it and open the door.

"You're amazing. Good night, Em."

"Goodnight. Thanks for that," I point back to the building.

"Any time."

I get in my car, and he shuts the door. I give him a little wave as I pull away and notice in the mirror he's still standing there watching me drive away.

I'm halfway home before I realize he called me 'baby' today.

Danger, Emily, danger.

Still, I find myself tapping the steering wheel to music and singing to terrible pop songs as I make my way back to Cambridge. Today was a good day, and that's all I want to think about.

When I get home, I post my horrendous simulator data print-outs to the refrigerator with food-delivery magnets and laugh the entire time I explain to Klara what the hell they are.

"You're happy," she grabs my hand and smiles.

Twelve

Hungaroring — Budapest, Hungary

Cole

"You did what?" Edmund's eyes go wide, and he sets his coffee cup down with a heavy clink.

"They were not very nice about it, either," Emily says as she pulls her long chocolate hair behind her head, twists it up, then sticks a pen through it to hold it in place.

Fuck, that's hot.

She looks like a sexy school teacher when she does that. Her long neck is exposed now, and I can almost see her pulse ticking beneath her skin.

"What do you mean they weren't nice about it?" The caveman inside me perks up when Emily says the other teams weren't exactly friendly with her.

All weekend, she's been hell-bent on talking to the other teams to see if they're having tire problems, too. They are, but Em has quickly discovered that everything is a secret in Formula 1. Teams don't share data, strategies, or intel. Not when there are billions of dollars at play. It's every team, man, or woman, for themselves.

"They didn't do anything," she clarifies and gives me a knowing look that tells me to calm down. "They just acted like I was a dumb girl, and a strategist from a certain Italian team suggested I'd be better at fetching them all coffees than worrying about tires."

The fork in my hand falls to the table in outrage. Those pricks.

"Ahh, to be young again," Edmund chuckles and looks around the hospitality area of our motorhome where I'm grabbing a pre-race snack, and Emily is taking advantage of any free time to talk shop.

It took Edmund about three minutes after Emily started to put the pieces together about us. He doesn't mind that I schemed him and Emily into this job since he's thrilled with her anyway, but he's promised to keep my secret. Emily might think she only got the job because of me. It would hurt her pride and fuel bullshit ideas like this crap that women belong fetching coffee.

She's dealt with it her whole life as a woman in STEM fields.

"Ignore them," Edmund continues. "Their strategists can't find their way out of a paper bag."

Emily whips out a thick, spiral-bound notebook, pages and pages filled with her delicate, girly handwriting in blue gel ink. She's very particular about her pens, and when one goes missing, she gets stabby.

"Do you know what these tires cost? It's absurd," she flips to a page in her notebook. "Twenty thousand dollars for a single race."

I nod, sounds about right.

"Did Olivier get you the information?" Edmund says like he has a frog in his throat, then he starts coughing hoarsely. "Excuse me, coffee down the wrong pipe."

"Yeah, he sent me commercial brochures. PDFs that anyone can download from the Concordia website," Emily purses her lips and scowls. She even asked Edmund to get the info from Olivier, and this is what he sent in response.

"I don't know there's much more I can do, myself," Edmund says to Emily. His eyes are watering from coughing, and he dabs at them with a napkin. "I can talk to the bosses, but they'll probably tell me to deal with Olivier."

"He won't give me a straight answer."

Emily's met with Olivier a few times now, he's been hanging around the garage being Mr. Smooth French Guy all over her. If I didn't know Emily so well, I might be jealous.

But he treats her like arm-candy, dismisses anything she says with a laugh. He treats her like one of the attention-seeking celebrities or models who walk up and down the paddock.

Dumbass.

I'm standing back and letting Olivier dig his own grave. He's doing a better job of it than I ever could, all on his own.

Edmund checks his watch and clears his throat, "Twenty minutes left. I'll meet you both in the garage. I need to go find something for this cough."

"See you there," I tell Edmund and try to suck down another liter of water before the race. It's especially hot today, and Liam has been on a tear making sure the whole team is adequately hydrated.

"Do you know what they do with the tires after the race?" Emily asks me, her face incredulous.

The sassy, determined tone of her voice turns me on more than she'll ever know. She's the most beautiful when she's like this—confident, strong, assured. I could listen to her talk about tires, math, chemistry, or cheese—all day long.

It still has the same effect on me it did years ago. It drives out all the other bullshit from my mind. When I'd hear Stan's voice in my head telling me what a piece of shit I was, what a moron I was to not hit every apex on the kart track, or how I was blowing the opportunities he'd given me, it was Emily who chased the thoughts away and replaced them with the excitement she felt over learning something new.

Dear old dad is supposed to grace me with his presence at the next race, too. I need to figure out how to manage that because I don't want Stan anywhere near Emily. He probably already knows she's here, given how many voicemails he's left me.

Not that I've listened to a single one.

"They're supposed to analyze them," I answer Emily about the used tires.

"They burn them, Cole. They shred them, then burn them and use them as fuel at cement factories."

"Is that normal?" It sounds bizarre, but what do I know.

"It's not abnormal, but it's rather convenient, isn't it?"

"Can I do anything to help?"

Emily takes a deep breath and smiles at me across the table. "Just don't get yourself killed out there."

"No pressure," I smile back.

She let it slip the other day that Dante's crash scared her, but then she quickly reigned herself in. I don't like that she's upset, but a selfish part of me does feel good knowing she's thinking about me enough to be worried.

That she doesn't want me dead.

Everything has been going better than I thought it would with Emily. Sometimes, it's like we've slipped right back into who we used to be with each other. Other times, I catch her pulling back. We haven't talked about the past, though, and I know, eventually, we're going to have to if I want her back.

And I want her back.

I need her back.

She's been back in my life for a month, and it's like giving a starving man one bite of steak. I want the whole goddamn t-bone, the entire cow. All of the cows, the herd, the ranch.

"Stan's going to be in Belgium," I blurt out in response to the persistent rogue thoughts in my mind about moving fate along. There's not much I enjoy doing slowly.

"Oh," her face falls.

"Just wanted to warn you. I'll do my best to keep him away from you."

I wish the prick would just stay home in his Florida McMansion with whatever woman he's terrorizing this week, but Belgium is his favorite race. He comes back every year to relive his glory days and act like he isn't a washed-up has-been.

He drove that track once as an F1 reserve driver when the primary pilot was injured. He never lets anyone forget it.

"Does he know I'm here?" Emily asks and fidgets with a long strand of hair that's fallen out of her bun.

"I haven't told him, but probably." I'm sure he's seen her on TV, heard gossip through the rumor mill, and that's what all my voicemails are about.

"Does the Major General know you're here?" I ask about her own asshole father.

"I haven't told him, but assuredly," she clones my dysfunctional statement with a frown. "I told Mom," she adds.

"How'd that go?"

She shrugs, "It's not like we're together."

Knife to the heart.

Stab stab stab.

Her dad and mine should really run off together. They can make one another miserable and leave the rest of the world alone. Too bad they also hate each other.

You should be able to banish people to remote islands, like in the old days.

I want to continue this conversation, I want to tell her we aren't together *yet*, but I need to head to the garage and get in the car in a few minutes.

Save it for tonight.

"My mom said they saw your mother," Emily mumbles and looks at me with her big, brown eyes. There's a mixture of apprehension, pity, and curiosity swirling around behind her long, dark lashes.

"Recently?"

"I guess."

"What did she say?" I take my Imperium hat off and run my hand through my hair. The last thing I need is her showing up again, here, there, or anywhere.

Emily's been given enough reasons to hate me without the piece de resistance.

Emily hunches her shoulders up, "They didn't talk to her."

I bet.

Mommy Dearest is probably out of money again if I had to guess. I sure as hell haven't sent her any since I blocked her and cut her off years ago. Apparently, getting abused by Stan is worth whatever cash he tosses at her from time to time.

It's not that I blame her for leaving Stan. That was the correct thing to do. But allowing me to be born, since she hates me so much, the product of what I am—then hating me for it my whole life—isn't okay.

Leaving a child alone with Stan when she'd finally found a backbone was not the correct thing to do.

Her part in the last six years without Emily was most definitely not the correct fucking thing to do.

She thought old Stan was going to be a Formula 1 driver, but she hitched her wagon to an abusive prick who didn't have the talent or dedication to make it. He ended up being successful in sub-prime mortgages where he could prey on people in other seedy ways, but she was gone by then.

Fuck the both of them.

"Sorry, I shouldn't have mentioned it before the race," Emily sees my frustration and, in the blink of an eye, she puts her hand on mine on top of the table.

Like an autonomic body reflex, muscle memory, my fingers wrap around her's, and she gives me a little smile.

This is how it all started, isn't it?

At first, I just thought she was this smart, gorgeous girl—she intrigued me, challenged me. She was the first girl who said no to me, wouldn't go out with me, told me to 'piss off,' if I remember correctly.

Then we disappeared within each other, saved the other every night, every weekend.

Before she can pull back from me again or overanalyze it, I pull her hand to my mouth and softly kiss her fingers. I stand up from the table and throw my hat back on, "Ready?"

Don't think, Em, just feel.

"Yep," she stands and joins me, and we walk to the garage together. She's quiet like I knew she would be. She's thinking about the tiny kiss on her hand, and I can practically see the questions and comments swirling above her head, like a comic book character. But I won't push her.

Inside the garage, I pull up my race suit as the crew hustles to get every last-minute detail finalized. Emily grabs a headset off the wall, and Dante grabs me to head out onto the track for the national anthem.

My mind is anywhere else as I stand on the track under the sun listening to a big guy in a tuxedo sing while a woman next to him plays a violin. I can still feel Emily's skin against my lips, and I have to stifle the twitching in my dick when I think about running my lips all over the rest of her body.

Don't be the asshole with a hard-on lined up in front of cameras while the national anthem plays.

The musical torture ends, and all the drivers head back to their garages. Dante is still in a pissy mood about the last race, not that I blame him. All the championship race points we've earned have been compromised this season, he's just much more of a hot-head than I am about it.

Liam hands me my helmet in the garage. In bold reds and deep blues, the colors of Hungary, I like its design this race. The reds remind me of the paprika I know Emily wants to pick up before we leave.

I give the helmet a once over, even though I know what I'm looking for is there. It's always there, hidden somewhere. I flip it around in my hands and find the initials hidden inside the swirl of a flour de lis, *EW*. Then I can put it on my head and strap it down.

As I tighten the chin strap, I see Emily out of the corner of my eye in the back. She's biting her fingernails again and watching me from behind her computer station.

Flipping my visor up, I walk to her. She drops her hand from her mouth and peers up at me from her stool. If I didn't have this helmet on, I don't know that I'd be able to stop myself from taking her head in my hands and kissing the hell out of her.

She sucks her bottom lip into her mouth, and I raise my eyebrow at her. I'm going to have a fucking hard-on in the car now, no getting around it. She knows what I want, though.

"Good luck, have fun, go fast," she smiles, her cheeks glowing a soft shade of rose.

"Go fast, today?" I smile at her addition to the pre-race commentary she started, not that she can see me grinning like an idiot under my helmet.

"As professional advice from your engineer, yes. Go fast," she nods.

Go fast. I'm going to go so fucking slow, baby. So torturously slow when I finally get my mouth on you.

"Duly noted," I wink and turn around.

With my back turned, I have to adjust myself in my race suit before I step into the car, and I hear her snicker behind me.

Just you wait, Emily Walker.

I'm sweating my balls off after the race. My fire suit is stuck to my skin, and my hair is soaked. Hungary never used to be this hot. Fuck all those people who deny climate change.

"Drink," Liam hands me another water bottle that he's thrown a nasty electrolyte tablet into.

"I am, christ," I mumble around the water bottle.

"You lost four kilos, drink more," he stands, watching me like a nun waiting to smack me with a ruler. "And one beer tonight, that's it," he folds his arms across his chest.

He's like an Australian schoolmarm, this guy.

I roll my eyes at him, but I'll do what he says, unlike Dante, who lives to terrorize his physio. I don't particularly enjoy working out for hours every day with Liam barking at me, but now that I know how much my girl likes abs, I may be listening to Liam a little more than usual.

Plus, he's been taking good care of her like I asked, keeping her hydrated and giving her melatonin and other shit to help with the jet lag.

We start walking back to the motorhome, and I unzip my race suit down to my waist, these fireproof things are unbearably hot.

Mila, my PA, jogs to catch up to us and hands me my cell phone and starts rattling off all the updates she has for me. No press to do, which is good, we can get out of here earlier.

Mila's in her mid-thirties, and I thought she was going to quit the time a tabloid published a rumor that we were sleeping together, but she had Imperium threaten to sue the publisher, instead. She's a tough German lady like that.

"Reservations all set? I ask her.

"They normally don't take reservations, but they cleared the top floor for you."

Excellent. Mila gets shit done. I don't know how she pulls some of this stuff off, but she never lets me down.

"Change her plane ticket home tomorrow?"

"Why do you ask?" She snips at me in her thick accent, "You know better."

"Just checking, calm yourself," I tease her and put an arm around her shoulder. She shrieks and throws my sweaty hook off.

Inside the motorhome, it's buzzing with the crew already starting to break gear down and pack up. Most of them will head straight to Belgium to set up for the next race.

It takes me a few minutes to find Emily, fiddling with the coffee machine, as usual. Girl's got a caffeine addiction if I've ever seen one.

"Hey," I step up beside her as she's attempting to froth milk.

She turns her head, and her eyes widen and travel from my head down to my waist. The milk steamer is still hissing and blowing, though her mug has wandered off it, so I flip the switch off.

"Sorry, I'm gross," I look down at myself, my white fire suit stuck to me, sweat dripping from my head.

I see her throat constrict as she swallows hard. "What's up?" She asks, her voice cracking.

Emily Walker, are you turned on right now?

"Emily, Emily," I hear someone call in a French accent. The very tone of this guy's voice is smarmy.

I look up, and that cockblocker Olivier is rushing across the lobby of the motorhome.

"Ugh," Emily groans, "he gives me the creeps."

"There you are, mon cher," Olivier butts right in and invades her personal space despite the visible cringe on her face and the clear step she takes away from him.

I see the way he looks at her, she's gorgeous. I can't blame him there. But a real man would back off, listen when her body language says 'nope,' not try to intimidate her. But before I can step in, Emily's inner badass comes out.

"Olivier, I need that information from you," she starts in on him immediately.

"Yes, of course. I'm trying to get it for you. You know how scientists can be," he chuckles.

I watch Emily's head jerk back, and her eyes scowl.

Fuck, this guy can't get out of his own way to save his life. His charming rich guy in a five-thousand-dollar suit act may work with most chicks, but Emily is not most women.

"Would you like to have a drink with me this evening, Emily? We can discuss it then."

Oh, hell, no.

"She has plans," I bark, and I know I sound like some kind of alpha asshole, but enough is enough.

Emily's head tilts toward me then snaps back to Olivier. "I have plans," she agrees.

Good girl, baby.

"Oh, I see. Another time, then. Perhaps in Brussels," he suggests.

"Sure," she mutters, utterly unimpressed with his bullshit.

God, I love this woman.

We both watch Olivier slink away and get lost amongst all the people piling into the motorhome.

"What are these plans? My flight leaves in a few hours," she takes a sip of the coffee still in her hand.

"Not anymore, your flight leaves tomorrow morning now."

Her eyebrows raise, and she looks at me for clarification, skepticism whipping around her, but I can see the curiosity burning equally as bright.

"You need paprika and dinner at Belvarosi Disznotoros, first." I'm sure I butcher the pronunciation, but she gets it.

"From *Parts Unknown*," her eyes widen.

I nod and grin at her, see the excitement on her face.

"Cole…" she puts her coffee down and drops her head, and I know she's overthought things again.

More likely, she's doing the smart thing and staying the hell away from me, but I can't do it anymore.

I need her.

"We can bring Dante or Liam, Mila, anyone you want, if you're not comfortable," I tell her. I really don't want any of them around, but if that's what it takes, then so be it.

She looks around the room, and her wheels turn for a second while the pit in my stomach expands and wraps itself up into a knot.

"No, that's okay. We can go."

That quick, my gut unravels, and I stand a few inches taller. "I need to shower and change and then we can go. Is your luggage here, or do you need to go back to the hotel first?" I ask and scan her black Imperium polo and tight little green shorts.

"I need to change?" She looks down at herself.

"I can bring security if you'd rather not."

"Oh," she shakes her head, "I forgot that you're a famous person," she says, and I notice a faint trace of redness creep up her neck. "My suitcase is here, I can change."

I don't remember the last time anyone said anything like that to me.

It's been years since I was just a guy talking to a gorgeous woman and not Cole Ballentine, the Formula 1 driver. It would feel like going home if home was a concept I ever knew.

I let her know that Mila will take her luggage back to her hotel room, which has been extended for one more night, and I'll meet her in twenty minutes.

I am taking my girl out on a date for the first time in six years.

"You want to take a scooter?" I ask again when she points at one of the little Vespas in the parking lot instead of the Ferrari I've been using this weekend.

"It's so European."

She's officially the first woman I've ever met who is not impressed with a Ferrari and wants to take a beat to hell Vespa scooter on a date instead.

The marshals drive these things around the track, and the one she's pointing at is scuffed, dinged, and looks like it's been run over by a garbage truck. They leave the keys in them because no one would even bother to steal one.

And it's pink.

"Oooookay," I shake my head. "I need to grab you a helmet then."

"Why, are you going to let me get hurt?" She hops on the back of the tiny scooter and sasses me. I can't help but wonder if there's more to that question than meets the eye, too.

"No," I will absolutely not let her get hurt.

And I'm not going to interrupt the fun, flirty thing she has going on right now and read more into her question. So I throw my leg over the tiny pink scooter and feel the suspension sag with both of us on it. It probably can't exceed thirty miles an hour, anyway, piece of shit.

As soon I sit down and feel her against me, her legs covered in tight, white capri pants, the scooter is the last thing on my mind. I do go slow and avoid every pothole on my way into Budapest, though.

Her long hair is whipping around us, and when she tries to tie it up, she leans against me for support, and it's fucking heaven.

True to her word, Mila has had the restaurant block off its small upstairs loft eating area. I was expecting the place to be fancy but should have known better. It's cafeteria-style and cost about ten bucks US. It's perfect.

After the staff takes a few selfies with me and has me sign something for their wall, Emily orders a schnitzel the size of a surfboard, and I carry it all upstairs on trays for us.

Emily puts away nearly the whole damn plate, and I finish off what she left because Liam isn't here to scold me, and this shit is good. She has a couple of beers, and I stick to my one, not so much for Liam, but because now I'm driving her around on the ridiculous pink thing parked on the sidewalk out front.

It's dark by the time we thank our hosts and step out. With my hat down, we stroll through downtown Budapest relatively unbothered, save one or two people who recognize me and want photos. Emily doesn't seem to mind.

We make our way to the Danube, and stroll along the shore, watch the city lights twinkle on the Pest side of the river, take in the parliament building on the Buda side. Past the Shoes on the Danube memorial, the crowd thins out, and it's just us ambling in the dark, talking, and laughing.

She tells me about Klara and updates me on Makenna. I tell her stories about all the trouble Dante and I have gotten into over the years. We find paprika at a street vendor, and I stuff it into my pocket for her. At some point, our hands brush together while we're walking. Her pinky finger links with mine, and I'm not letting it go for anything in the world.

She stops to take a panoramic river photo, and I let her walk a few paces ahead. I take out my own phone and snap some pictures of her. She's so beautiful, the twinkling city lights dancing in her eyes and her hair blowing around in the breeze.

All these years, I never stopped loving her, not for a second. It was always her.

"What are you doing?" She turns and finds me taking photos of her while I lean up against a lantern post.

"Nothing," I grin.

"Let me see," she reaches for the phone, and I hold it up high out of her hands as she wiggles. Trying to grab it, she puts her hand on my chest for balance and leans against me.

I feel like the world stops turning, it's just her and me along the river, a soft glow of light illuminating her face. My hand with the phone drops to my side, and she looks up at me to see why I've suddenly quit teasing her.

Our eyes meet for the briefest of seconds. Without conscious thought, my phone falls to the sidewalk, and my fingers are in Emily's hair, pulling her to me. I bend and press my lips to hers, so soft and full.

Her hands wrap around my neck, and she stands on her tiptoes to reach me, leaning into me as I prop myself against the lantern post behind me. Our mouths smash together in symphony. The taste of her floods my memories and washes over me as my tongue runs along her bottom lip. She opens for me, her tongue dancing with mine as the inferno builds.

My hand on her neck, I trace her jaw with my thumb and angle her head to kiss her deeper. Her fingers run through my hair, and she lets out a soft whimper that makes me want to devour her, combine my cells with hers, and fuse our two bodies into one.

It's like my heart remembers how to beat again.

As her tongue chases mine, I feel her desperation, her need matching my own. Her body rocks into me, and I can feel her hard nipples against my chest, and I spread my palm across her perfect ass and pull her into me harder.

She moans into my mouth at the feel of how goddamn hard I am for her. Curvy hips swivel and rotate into mine with sweet torture.

I wrap my fist around her long hair twice and tug her head back so I can finally get my lips on her long, smooth neck that's been in my head all day long. Kissing and licking from her collarbone to her earlobe, taking it between my teeth and nipping gently, I want to devour this woman.

"Cole," she pants before her lips are on me again, her hands a panicked frenzy clawing at the base of my neck, through my hair, then they're up the back of my shirt, and I hiss as she digs her nails into my skin.

She wants me as much as I want her. This is her body language saying 'yes, yes, yes.'

"Fuck, Em, my gorgeous girl," I moan and slip my knee between her legs. She doesn't hesitate to push her core into my thigh as she pants and continues to clench at any flesh she can reach. She's fucking on fire, and it's been so much pent up longing, so many years of need building between us.

We're both volcanos that have been simmering and heating up below the surface before the whole mountain top blows up and sends molten lava into the clouds.

My tongue swirls with hers when I worry I'm being too rough with my fists tangled in her hair. But then she sucks in my bottom lip, drags her teeth over it hard, and the taste of copper hits me.

Jesus Christ, this girl. I'm gonna blow in my pants for the first time in my adult life, at this rate.

"Oh my god, I bit you," she takes half a step back, puts a hand to my lip, and sees a tiny flash of red on her fingers.

"Mmm-hmm," I moan and push her hair behind her ears.

Unfortunately, her little act of vampirism brings her back into the moment, reminds her that this is happening, and she takes another half step away. There's a flash of fear and panic in her eyes.

"Em, don't," I reach for her hand.

She pulls her hand away from me, which feels like a freight train plowing through my rib cage.

"We can't do this," she wraps her hands around herself, and her eyes get glassy, her hair whipping around as the night breeze picks up off the Danube.

"What do you want, Emily? Tell me."

I need answers, direction, hope. I can't have her and not have her. If she tells me there's no chance, no way, I need to know. I don't know how I'll deal with it, it would snuff out any goodness, any light left inside of me.

"I don't know," a tear falls down her cheek, and she looks out over the river.

"Stop trying to think, tell me how you feel." I take a step toward her, and she doesn't retreat. I wipe her tear away with my thumb.

I fucking hate when she cries. It makes me feel totally powerless, yet there's nothing I wouldn't do to make it stop.

"Is there any room, at all, in your heart for me, Em?"

"Room?" She turns back to me, and her shoulders heave, tears begin pouring from the corners of her eyes, "It's been empty and hollow all these years without you."

"Baby," I pull her into me and squeeze her tight, wrap my hand around her head and hold it to my chest. She locks her arms around my waist and clutches me as she cries, tears soaking through my shirt. "I'm sorry, I'm so fucking sorry, baby."

I don't think I can ever tell her how sorry I am, and I hope she never knows the depths or all the reasons why I'm so sorry. That would only cause more tears.

"I don't know what to do. I don't know what I want. I want to be mad at you. I'm *supposed* to be mad at you," Emily mumbles against my chest.

"It's okay," I kiss her hair.

I'm plenty mad at myself for both of us.

"I need time to think about everything."

It's been six long, awful years. I don't know how much more time needs to pass, but if that's what she needs, that's what I'm going to give her. This is all my fucking fault, anyway.

But for right now, I celebrate the win that she isn't running away from me. Her arms stay around me, no running despite the consequences she fears.

I pull her away from me and push her wet hair back from her face, "We'll take it slow, okay? As much time as you need. You set the pace."

She nods then buries her head back into my chest.

Eventually, two Budapest police officers show up in their little blue sailor caps, and Emily has to convince them that I am not molesting her, which is funny on our walk back to the scooter but wasn't funny at the time.

I was fairly certain there'd be photos of me being arrested *and* riding a pink Vespa in the papers tomorrow.

Still worth it.

Thirteen

Circuit de Spa-Francorchamps — Brussels, Belgium

Emily

Everything is a mess.

My head is still swimming in confusion over Cole and making out with him like teenagers in Budapest. I don't know what came over me, I was like an animal.

Something about him calls to my body with primal, animalistic attraction. He makes me feel raw and primordial like no man ever has. I like nerdy, bookish Emily well enough, but around Cole, I turn into a fiend, desperate for him to corrupt me.

I bit him, for god's sake!

"I've been avoiding him," I update Makenna, who has been texting me non-stop for updates since I fessed up to falling off the wagon in less than two months. Six years of steely resolve, gone.

"Bitch move," she counters as if I don't know this.

"It's awful. He just stares at me, all hard and dominating, with his stupid sexy smirk like he knows it's inevitable, and he's just biding his time."

"Yeah, that sounds horrible." I can feel Makenna's eyes roll across the cell phone waves.

It's a shitty, rainy weekend in Brussels, and I'm hiding from everyone under a huge pine tree. Mist and the occasional raindrop filters down onto me through the pine needles.

Everything about this weekend sucks.

"Stan is here making everyone miserable, he's making everything worse," I whine.

I hate it when I whine. I pride myself on not being a whiner, but that's precisely what I am right now.

I need more coffee.

"What is that glob of snot doing there?"

"Irritating everyone, mostly. Running around pretending to be a big man in the paddock even though no one even knows who he is."

Cole's dad is, essentially, a failure. He wasn't even a one-hit-wonder. He drove one professional race, which he lost, and then got canned. So he lives vicariously through Cole and has inflicted trauma, pressure, and abuse on him for years.

Nothing was ever good enough, no mistake ever went unnoticed or unpunished.

I hate him with every fiber of my being.

"Did he say anything to you? Do I need wine for this?"

"Isn't it about 7:00 am there?"

"So?"

I wipe the mist off my forehead and pull the hood of my Imperium rain jacket up more. "Cole and Liam are trying to supervise him, but yeah, as soon as Cole got in the car, Stan started in on me. He told me I was 'all grown up' like a total creep."

"Eww," Makenna makes retching noises.

Stan has been a man-whore as long as I've known Cole. We tried to spend as little time as possible inside his house when we were together because, nine times out of ten, some half-naked new woman would be wandering around. Sometimes more than one.

I hate that he grew up like that and I hate that, over the years, I've wondered how much Cole inherited those traits from his dad. Cole's been with a lot of women, there have always been photos and stories online.

I'm jealous, I know it. I have no right to judge Cole. But I don't even know if he is still with the Russian tennis player he's been linked to and here I'm kissing him on the streets of Budapest.

"Yeah, and then he said he hopes I'm actually helping his son this time and not distracting him from his goals," I finish telling Makenna about my encounter with Stan.

"Oh, fuck him."

"Right? He's the one distracting everyone. Cole has been storming around all weekend slamming doors. Liam is pissed because Cole is pissed. Edmund is pissed because the whole team is on edge."

I don't even tell her that I've missed two calls from the Major General.

And, I feel like I'm making it all worse by continuing to run and hide from Cole like a baby. I just wish I had the answers. I need time to sit down and concentrate, to think this through, but I haven't had a chance.

I can't just ignore the fact that Cole left me, broke my heart—obliterated it.

Are we even the same people anymore? How could we be? When he left the States, he was eighteen. Now, he's almost twenty-six, he makes millions of dollars per year, has his pick of women and has traveled across the globe a hundred times over.

Have I changed?

"Which one is Liam, again?"

"Australian physio," I remind her.

"Is he hot?"

I huff, I have too much on my mind to think about Liam. "They're all hot, okay?"

"Are they hiring any photographers?" She giggles.

"I wish. It would be nice to have another girl here. Maybe you can visit me soon," I tell her, but then I need to go. Qualification is starting soon, and, like it or not, I need to face the music.

I shake the water off myself and emerge from my hiding spot under the tree. I probably look like a homeless person.

Up ahead, I see Liam walking down the service road on the way to the garage and, he has enough sense to have an umbrella, so I sneak in underneath it with him.

"Hey. You look cold. Are you cold?" Liam feels my cheek.

"I'm fine, you don't have to babysit me," I nudge him with my shoulder.

"Boss says I do," he smiles back at me.

"I'd rather you worry about him."

"I hate when his dad is here," Liam says knowingly. It has been a tense two nights, and we'd all like Stan to return to the troll bridge he lives under.

"Where's he at, anyway?"

I hope he isn't in the garage during qualification. Qualification is stressful enough as it is, the drivers are at max speeds with no fuel in the cars, and now it's raining. It creates a lightweight rocket ship with no grip, and then Belgium thought it should open up the skies to make matters worse.

"I left him in the beer garden with a bottle of whiskey and two grid girls. Hopefully, that entertains him long enough to stay the hell away."

Cole has to be so embarrassed. For a short while, Stan was acting as Cole's manager and, I'm sure, taking a chunk of his earnings. I only got the online gossip blog story version, but from what I read, Cole's job was at risk if Stan continued to manage him.

Cole fired him and hasn't had a manager since. I can only imagine the third world war that must have caused. I wish I could have been there for him. Maybe I should have contacted him, I don't know. But he's the one who left me, refused to take my calls, or respond to my letters.

When we make it inside the garage, I shake off my soaked raincoat and take my seat. It's damp, cold, and grey. I rub my hands over my arms to get rid of the goosebumps.

The drivers are running wet tire compounds today because of the rain, so I'm eager to see how they perform for the first time. Edmund's had me working with the aerodynamic team the last several days, then he was out sick for a while, so I haven't had as much time to harass Olivier about the information I still don't have.

I feel Cole enter the garage before I even see him, my heart rate picks up, and my senses go on high alert. He and Dante stroll in, both tall and full of swagger, though I can tell Cole's still on edge. He's been cracking his neck all weekend and does it again now.

Dante's either in a good mood or trying to cheer Cole up. I see him make a hand gesture like he's squeezing melons and Cole chuckles with his eyes down and shakes his head. Liam notices Cole's neck cracking tick, too, and Liam—always watchful—swoops in and starts feeling Cole's neck muscles.

Cole slaps his hands away, and the two of them start laughing and joking, and it makes me happy to see Cole smile again. They chat for a second, then both turn to look at me.

I don't even pretend that I'm not staring anymore, there's no point. I couldn't stop myself if I wanted to, Cole Ballentine is beautiful.

I quirk an eyebrow up at them both, they're clearly talking about me. Then Cole struts over to me. He walks like an alpha predator moving through the jungle, and I forget to breathe.

His eyes are intense and locked onto mine as he crosses the garage.

He reaches the stool I'm sitting on, shrugs his *dry* Imperium jacket off, and slips it over my shoulders.

I peer around Cole's frame and scowl at Liam for tattling. He shrugs and throws his hands up.

"Better?" He asks, running his hands over my arms to get me warm. He has no idea how warm I'm getting from him touching me.

He's being obscenely sweet to me, he's been nothing but respectful since we got home from Budapest, following my lead in all of our conversations. I asked him for time, and he's given it to me, and I've been acting like a bitch.

Figure your shit out, Emily.

"I'm sorry," I look around and whisper to him quietly, so no one else hears us.

"You have nothing to be sorry about, gorgeous girl," his palm comes to my cheek, and he runs his thumb along my bottom lip as if there are not thirty people flitting around the garage. He's looking at me like I'm the only one here, and he doesn't give a shit about anything else.

If we were alone, I'd suck that thumb into my mouth and swirl my tongue around it.

"I'm figuring things out," I tell him.

"I know," he beams with confidence.

Then he's off, getting strapped into the car, and I wrap his jacket around me and breathe in his smell enveloping me.

The first qualification session nearly gives me a heart attack. All the cars are struggling for grip on the wet track, sliding around corners, and one of the other teams loses a car into a wall, which red flags the session.

It's still raining during the second session, and I don't understand how there are so many rules in F1, yet they let these guys race in a monsoon. Several cars have spun out or gone into the grass.

I'm gripping Cole's jacket around me and rocking in my stool, on edge, watching the wet tire data come in. The way they work is so different, their tread designed to push water and dry the track.

"I can't see shit," Dante complains over the radio.

The cars are kicking up so much water spray that it's making it impossible for the drivers to see well.

This is madness.

On my computer screen, I see Dante's brakes lock up, and I look up at the television monitor. His front tires are locked, but the car is still skidding into the La Source hairpin. In the blink of an eye, the backend of the vehicle spins. It's pointing in the wrong direction on the track, then round and round he goes.

I add to the collective gasp of the crowd, audible even in the garage, and leap from my stool. Two other cars are barreling at Dante, skidding, and trying to steer around him.

An engineer next to me grabs my elbow, all eyes are on the television monitors. Dante's spin finally comes to a stop after two rotations, and the other cars narrowly avoid hitting him.

It all happens in seconds, but it felt like an eternity. Dante is yelling over the radio, more Italian swearing, and I don't blame him. This is insanity. They need to delay qualification before someone gets hurt!

The television monitor eventually shows Cole's car rounding a turn, thank god he's okay. I storm out of the garage to the pit wall and pull one earphone off Edmund's head.

"They have to delay this," I plead. "Everyone is going off, they're going to get killed!"

He turns toward me, and there's a warmth in his eyes I've never noticed before. He wraps one arm around my shoulder, "They've driven in much worse, it'll be okay."

Worse? This is ridiculous. This is some macho bullshit, right here, that's what this is.

Edmund pats me on my shoulder, and I make my way back into the garage. I need to calm down, I need to breathe.

Both our cars stop in the garage for a brief moment as we wait for the third and final qualification session to start. I want so badly to go to Cole's car and, I don't even know what. Shake him, kiss him, drag him out of the car?

You cannot do that. He needs to concentrate.

And his stupid dad has been here all weekend upsetting him. I've been acting like an asshole.

This is terrible.

Both cars leave the garage again, and I'm on the verge of a panic attack. All I can do is stand here wrapped in Cole's jacket and pace. I can't even look at the computer monitors, my eyes are glued to the television as I watch all the cars struggle and slide.

Cole starts his timed lap, and the cameras follow him through the corner Dante spun in. He nears the steep hill into the most iconic turns in motorsports history, Eau Rouge and Raidillon.

It's such a steep incline that drivers can't see the other side of the hill, they just have to point the car in the right direction and hope the road will appear in front of them where it should be. If the conditions were dry, Cole would take those turns flat out at over three hundred kilometers per hour and 5gs.

He can't possibly do that in the rain.

A brief glance at my computer monitor tells me he is.

A chain of cars blasts up the hill into the corners. I can barely breathe. Cole is one second behind a car which hits the peak of Raidillon when it loses its grip and begins to spin in the middle of the track. Cole can't even see him as he reaches the summit, headed straight for the disabled car.

"NO!" I scream.

I register that there are voices in my headset, but I don't know who they are or what they're saying. One-second goes by as if it's an hour. Cole sees the disabled car as he crests the hilltop, locks the brakes up, and pitches the car sideways.

The car turns violently and skids rear end first, the screeching of tires piercing the air and plumes of blue smoke filling the television monitor. His car sails backward into the runoff area and smashes into the yellow and red tire barriers. The whole back end of the vehicle scrunches up, bits of debris fly everywhere. One of the tires is pointing straight up into the air.

"Cole!" Yelling at the monitor, I turn to race out of the garage to run up the hill toward him.

"Hey, hey," Liam wraps his arms around me from behind and tries to hold me still.

I thrash against him, and he lifts me off the ground, "Let me go," I wail.

"It's okay, he'll be okay, it's okay," he chants and puts me back down, but he won't let go of me.

I don't know when they started, but tears are streaming down my face.

"You all right?" I hear Edmund's voice through my headset.

I hear Cole take a few gravelly deep breaths on his radio like the wind has been knocked out of him, and then finally, after both a few seconds and a lifetime, I hear his voice, "I'm okay."

I break down and lose my shit in the middle of the garage, as Liam holds me up. I don't care who sees me or what they think, I only want to see Cole get out of the car.

Liam hustles me to the back of the garage, my eyes glued to the television monitors as we walk. Cole finally flings his head restraints off, then pulls himself out of the car, and I sob against Liam.

He's okay. He's okay. He's okay.

Marshals are already on the scene, and a medical car zooms up the hill.

"They're just there as a precaution," Liam soothes me. "See, he's walking around, he's okay."

I nod into his side and suck in snot as he leads me out the back of the garage. "I need to see him," I gurgle.

"I know, come on. Mila will tell him to meet you in his room. He just needs to get checked out, all right?"

Liam leads me into Cole's private room in the motorhome, and I dry my eyes and take deep breaths. "I'm sorry," I tell him. I'm sure I'm acting like a dramatic cow, but it was so violent, so fast.

Cole's room is on the second story of the motorhome. It's small but efficient with a bed, desk, mirror, and a small closet. One wall is floor-to-ceiling privacy glass that I know no one can see in.

Liam sits with me on Cole's little bed as I collect myself and calm down. He's saying that everything is okay, that it's okay to be scared, and I know he's being kind. But I just need to see Cole.

It feels like hours pass, though I know it's only been minutes when the door flies open.

I don't think. I launch myself into Cole, throw my arms around his neck, and my tears and sobs become hysterical again. He wraps one arm around my waist and lifts me up so he can take a few steps into the room. Liam moves around us, I hear Cole thank him, and he closes the door.

"It's ok, baby, it's ok," Cole holds me and runs his hand down my back. He's soaking wet, and I'm squeezing him so hard I could break his ribs.

His ribs.

I pull back out of his arms and frantically run my hands and eyes all over him, his arms, his torso, his shoulders, his face. I tear at his race suit to get it open. I need to know he's not hurt.

"Em," he takes my head in both his hands and lowers his face to peer into my eyes, "I'm ok. I'm ok."

"Cole," I whimper, my eyes filled with burning tears.

He presses his lips to mine, soft but lingering. I cling to his neck. He kisses me, sweetly again, "It's okay."

"I could have lost you," I choke out.

"Impossible," he pecks me again and wipes my tears away. He

pushes my wet hair back behind my ears, his eyes inspecting mine.

"Are you really okay?" I go back to running my hands over his chest and arms.

He turns with me and sits on the edge of his bed, pulling me to stand between his legs, "I'm ok now," he smiles and kisses me sweetly again with his hands on my hips.

So many little kisses, they slow my heartbeat yet speed it up in a different way.

Tracing my hands over his face, my thumbs brush though the stubble along his jaw. His deep indigo eyes follow mine. I can't look away. It's like stepping back in time when everything was stable and good, and I felt safe and loved. When I felt complete.

I could have lost him. I have Cole in my hands, after all of these years, everything I've ever wanted, and I could have lost him again.

I lean forward and drag my lips over his, kiss the corners of his mouth softly, kiss the hard ridge of his jaw.

I need him like the air I breathe. I don't need to think about it, thinking has done me no good over the past six years. I just need this man.

Working my fingers through his drenched hair, I press into him, and our lips collide. I ease my tongue into his mouth, desperate for more of him, and as soon as I do, Cole's arms drag me in, and he takes over. As hard as I'm pushing, he's pulling, our lips and tongues a frenzy of need.

All I can feel is electricity surging through me, a fundamental life-need to have his skin against mine and be utterly owned by this man. His hands sweep through my hair, and he jerks my neck back, his hot tongue caressing me. He bites the sensitive skin between my neck and collarbone, and sparks ignite inside me.

His breath is ragged, and I'm desperate to inhale all the oxygen I need. I reach a hand between us and cup his cock, hard and thick pressing inside his race suit.

"Cole," I moan as I squeeze him tighter. His grip in my hair intensifies, his lips racing over every inch of my throat.

"You want this, Em?" He growls into my neck.

"Yes," I pant.

His hands drop from my hair, and he pulls my shirt over my head. He drags me back between his legs and rips my bra down to expose both my breasts.

I clutch his head as he sucks one nipple into his mouth, swirls around it with his tongue, then drags his teeth across it gently. Every cell in my body begins to hum.

He moves to the other nipple as I throw my head back and claw at the base of his neck. Sliding my hands across his broad shoulders, I start ripping open his race suit and push it off his shoulders.

I grumble at the fire suit underneath and claw at it to get it over his head.

He stands and pulls the white undershirt over his head. I'm tremor stricken by the look in his eye, the way he's sizing me up. I take a step backward like an antelope retreating from a lion staring it down. His shoulders are heaving, and his skin is glistening with rain. A bead of water runs from his wet hair down the side of his neck.

His eyes are traveling the full length of my body, and when they meet mine again, I take one more step back. I bite my lip and whimper for him.

Come get me, Cole.

A mischievous grin spreads across his face, his jaw ticks, and then he's on me.

He slams me up against the far, glass wall, and my body responds before my mind can catch up to it. I hitch a leg up onto his hip and dig my hands into his hair as he sets to attacking my neck. Teeth snap the sensitive skin, and then his tongue soothes the sting.

I cannot control my moans and gasps until he covers my mouth with his. He has a hand behind my knee, and I'm digging into the back of his thigh with my ankle like I can climb him and get closer.

He's pushing me so hard into the wall, grinding his pelvis into me, and I can feel his hard length pushing on my belly. He runs a hand behind my head and grabs a fistful of my hair, using it to hold my mouth still so he can kiss me like he needs to.

He's so hard and forceful and animalistic. I'm whining and groaning and whimpering into him, every cell in my body begging for him. I think he's pinning me to the wall so hard that my feet are off the ground.

"Oh god," my head hits the glass wall when I jerk in pleasure at the warm heat of his mouth, and his tongue circling my nipple. Not losing a beat, his hand shoots up behind my head, and he cushions it from banging into the wall again.

That small gesture of protection, his measure of control needed to notice something so insignificant amidst this inferno, it's too much. "Cole, I want you."

He rocks his hardness into me and looks me in the eye, "Yeah? Tell me what you want, gorgeous girl."

I'm speechless, unable to move my eyes away from his, as his warm palm skates down my throat onto my chest, and his thumb flicks over a hard nipple. "You want me to kiss you here?"

"Yes," I arch my back toward him as his mouth sucks my nipple in.

His hands trace over my stomach, and he unbuttons my pants. The zipper comes down, he slips his fingers into my panties, and he cups my pussy. I jerk upward. "You want my fingers here?"

"Yes," I whine and writhe.

"Get this shit off." He tugs my pants and panties down in one swift tug. I kick off my shoes and step out of everything. He snaps my bra off, his eyes running up and down my naked body.

"Cole, please," I whisper. I can't stand him not touching me. His eyes are telling me he's going to do filthy things to me, and I want them badly.

"You need to get fucked, gorgeous girl?" His black and green race suit is still dangling from his hips, his chest naked, sculpted. A perfect dark trail of hair leads my eyes from abs to the distinctive bulge in his pants.

I nod at him, bite my lip, and slide my hand from a breast down the length of my body until I slip my fingers inside my slick folds.

He pulls my hand away and sucks my fingers into his mouth, "This belongs to me." He cleans my fingers off, then spins me around and pushes me face-forward into the glass wall.

His cock presses against me from behind. His arms wrap around me, and one hand returns to my pussy as his fingers slip inside. "Oh, god," I moan as his fingers swirl across my clit.

"You want me to fuck you up against this window, baby? In front of all those people out there?" He takes my chin in his other hand and makes me look where there are dozens of people below us, ten feet away.

Oh, Jesus Christ, he's going to make me come in two-seconds just from his fingers and talking to me like this. I look down on the people below us and can't believe I am doing this, but I have never wanted anything more.

It feels filthy, and I can't get enough.

His foot spreads my legs, then two hard fingers plunge inside me. My body heaves against his, and he pushes me forward into the glass, his fingers sliding back and forth inside me. Guttural moans and gasps escape my lungs.

His thumb starts rubbing my clit, and I brace myself on the window as my thighs start shaking. "Come on my fingers, Em. Ride my fucking hand."

"Oh god, Cole, they're going to see us," I gasp and look at all the people just outside under their umbrellas.

"As wet as this pussy is, I'd say you like it," he licks up the side of my neck and bites my earlobe.

"Fuck me," I beg.

"Yeah, you want to be a bad girl?" He bites my shoulder while his thumb keeps working my clit.

"Yes." So bad, I want to be so very, very bad.

"Bad girl like you were at that club in that fucking green dress?" He adds a third finger, and I clench and gasp, his hand is slamming into me so hard, his middle finger hitting that perfect spot inside. His left arm wraps around my neck and shoulder, and he holds me tight against him.

"That... that was you," I whisper and remember the night I thought I saw him. But I'm so close to coming I can't think straight.

"It was always me, Em," his thumb pushes down harder, and I lose control as an earthquake overtakes me, tremors rip through me, and I dig into his forearm that's still working my clit.

Cole's left-hand rises to cover my mouth as I scream and pant his name, and then my legs turn to jelly, and I go weak.

He catches me and spins me around to deposit me on the bed. Scooting up onto the bed, I try to pull him over me, but he pulls my legs back down off the side of the mattress. He pushes my legs open and kneels on the floor between them.

My breath is ragged as Cole starts kissing his way up my inner thighs.

"Were you thinking about me when you fucked him?" He nips me.

"I, I didn't."

His tongue caresses my folds, and I just came thirty-seconds ago, but I need more of him. I pull his head into me, but he grabs my wrists and holds them against the bed.

"No?"

I shake my head, my hair twisting up and covering my face.

"Why not?"

I raise my hips up, desperate for his mouth, he flattens his tongue and makes one slow swipe through me.

"He wasn't you."

He growls and buries his head between my thighs, kisses me all over.

"More," I plead.

"I waited six years to taste this perfect, wet pussy again, Em. I'll take my fucking time," He takes one slow pass through me again. "I'm gonna lick and taste until you're begging to come on my face."

"Oh god," I pant and fall back to the bed as he starts lapping at me, running his tongue up and down from my entrance to my clit. "When, when did you get so filthy?"

This is like Advanced Dirty Talk, compared to the 101-level course we took together so long ago.

He covers my whole core with his mouth for a second, his tongue flicking back and forth across my clit. Then he pauses and looks up at me over my heaving chest, "When you taught me, the way you blushed and got so wet for me the first time I took you."

Oh, hell.

He wraps my legs around his shoulders and holds my thighs as I raise my pelvis and push against him. The stubble along his jaw adds to the delicious friction between us, and when he thrusts three fingers inside of me, it's a magical blend of pleasure and pain coursing through me.

He sucks my clit into his mouth I buck into him. He grips my thigh so hard I'm going to have bruises tomorrow, but god I want them. He pushes me back onto the bed with his mouth.

"Don't stop," I pant, my calves locking up and clenching around him.

He moans into me and fucks me harder with his hand, sending my whole body rocking back and forth on the tiny bed. In two more flicks of that magic tongue, I'm quaking and squeezing his head between my thighs, my hips pivoting off the bed.

"Oh fuck, Cole. Yes, oh god," I thrash my head back and forth, and he has to release my thigh to cover my mouth again so that every person in this paddock does not hear me screaming his name.

As the shudders and aftershocks run through me, Cole stands and pulls his fingers out of me. He traces them over my sweaty body, runs two fingers across my lips, then pushes them into my mouth.

He leans over me and kisses me with his fingers still in my mouth, the taste of my arousal swirling between us. He kisses me languid and slow and returns his hand to my pussy, cupping it in his palm as we come down.

"Bare now," he smiles against my mouth.

"Mm, you like?"

"Fucking love it, gorgeous girl."

Every time he calls me that I feel a rush of warmth inside me. It's like slipping into a warm embrace, a cocoon of security and love.

"I need to shower and meet with the team. Take a nap," Cole kisses me gently, sweetly, then stands up.

"You're leaving?" I sit up and look at the bulge still very much present in his race suit.

He watches me while he reaches into his pants and adjusts himself. I'm wholly insatiable, and seeing him so hard, touching himself in front of me, I want him inside of me.

"I'll be back. Sleep, baby."

He pecks me on the forehead then slips out the door.

I fall back against his pillow and sigh, then tuck myself into his blanket, bringing it tight up under my chin. All of his bedding smells like him, and I'm so exhausted from the cold, the rain, the accident, and the best orgasms I've had in six years that I fall asleep within moments.

Fourteen

Cole

Not even Stanley Fuckface Ballentine can knock me off my cloud today.

I've given my girl multiple orgasms. The first two in my room in the motorhome yesterday. She rode my face in her hotel room last night and passed out before her head even hit the pillow. And this morning, there was an incident involving my fingers inside her pants in the company car that would only be described by HR as exceedingly inappropriate.

"You're pathetic, man," Dante shoves me in the shoulder as we walk to the garage to start the race today. The team worked all night to rebuild my car, and we're good to go.

"Maybe if you weren't such an asshole, you'd be smiling, too," I keep grinning as we head into the garage.

"Yeah, that's never happening."

Liam hands me my helmet in the back of the garage, and I give Dante some more shit before I check my helmet. It takes me a minute, but then I find it hidden inside the Imperium logo, which fades into an American flag, *EW*.

I'm not putting it on yet today, though.

"Engineer Emily Walker," I call through the garage. Emily's head spins from her stool in front of her computer station, and she turns bright red. "Ms. Walker, I have a question about my tires," I bellow and try to keep a straight face.

Liam snorts and leaves me alone to my antics.

"What are you doing?" Emily shushes me, and I pull her into me and kiss her like today's our last day on earth.

"Okay, that's out of the way now." I pull my helmet on and start strapping it down, all the while staring at her expectantly.

"You're ridiculous," she smirks.

I roll my hand that she should get on with it.

"Good luck, have fun, go fast…come back to me."

"Wild horses couldn't keep me away, baby," I wink at her.

She pulls my head down and kisses my helmet where my mouth is hidden behind it. Hell, I like that a lot.

I walk to my car to get in and see that fucking Stan is harassing Liam. He's got a beer in his hand, which he can't even have in here, and Liam's trying to get him out the door. I've had enough of this guy's shit. He doesn't get to infect and ruin things again, anymore.

No more.

It's a new goddamn day.

"Get the fuck out, or I'll put you out, old man." I bark at him through my helmet.

Liam puts his hands between us even though I'm perfectly in control.

"I'll deal with it," he tells me.

"Don't you talk to me like that, boy" Stan slurs his words and staggers.

"Call security," I look at Liam and zip up my race suit.

"Security? You can't call security on me! They know who I am."

I snicker and begin putting on my race gloves. Fuck this guy, he's not worth busting my knuckles up for. He's not worth much of anything. Security can bounce his ass out.

"Come on, Stan, let me take you up to hospitality. We've got a keg of local beer tapped. It's good shit." Liam puts a hand around Stan's shoulders and tries to herd him out.

"Yeah, okay," Stan mumbles and looks at me like I'm the biggest piece of shit on earth. He's told me that enough times, I know the look.

"Liam?" I call to him as he escorts my drunken sperm donor away. He turns his head, and I point to my eyes then point to Emily.

He nods. He knows I don't want Stan anywhere near my girl ever again. His drunk ass had better be on a plane by the time this race is over. I can deal with a lot of things, but I won't tolerate him near Emily.

I make a mental note to give Liam a bonus for dealing with this trash. Maybe bring his family in for the next race or something.

Emily has seen Stan be led away, but I don't think she could have heard us, so I just wink again and give her a thumbs up, then climb into the car.

Fuck you, Stan. Not today.

The track is dry today, the sun is out, and the car is, for once, doing exactly what it should. I'm sure that's, in no small part, thanks to our sexy new engineer. I freaking love this track, one of the all-time classics. Flat-out corners, long straights, elevation changes—it's perfection.

"All right, fuel and tires look good, Cole. You can push now. Repeat, push now," Edmund comes through the earpiece in my helmet, and I close the gap to the car in front, who happens to be Dante.

For the better part of several laps, Dante and I squabble back and forth, wheel to wheel. I'd pass him, then he'd pass me, but I'm finally in front of him and pulling a lead now.

"Tell him to stick that in his cannoli," I laugh over the radio.

"Uh, copy cannoli message," Edmund replies, trying to be serious.

With two more laps to go and no one close behind, this is a second-place podium for me if I can bring it home, and the car is rock solid. It's never over before it's over, but I can back off and relax just a little.

"GG," I say over the radio and hope Emily registers the code since I'm not that big of a pussy to call her gorgeous girl over the radio so it can be broadcast in thirty-six countries. "The car is tight as hell, so smooth through the corners."

There's a long pause, and then I hear the crackling in my ear and her voice, quiet and nervous about her first time talking on the radio, "Yes, I see that from your data. Tight and smooth."

I hear the garage laughing before Emily releases the button to speak to me. I love that they all love her, too. And they should, she's the last one to leave the factory every night. She's thrown herself into this circus, embraced it, and has been working with damn near every team at Imperium. Because she's a total badass, even if she doesn't always know it.

A meteor could not wipe the smile off my face as I cross the finish line in second. I do a little bob and swerve with the car to acknowledge the crew standing along the race wall, cheering and hooting as Dante and I bring both cars home.

We pull the cars into parc ferme, wave to the fans, and get mobbed by our teams behind metal crowd fencing. All the pit crew and engineers hug me and pat my helmet, but I'm looking for her. She's a few people deep, but I grab her hand and pull her forward to the fencing. She takes my helmet, plants a kiss on my visor, and squeals.

I get about ten-seconds with my crew, and then the FIA is pulling me away to get weighed and hustle to the podium ceremony. It's a massive win for Imperium to have two drivers on the podium, and the whole team is damn near rioting on the ground beneath our platform. There's going to be one hell of a party in Brussels tonight, I'm sure.

I'll be having my own party, after the private chocolate making class course Mila arranged for Em and I, of course. I don't even care how much shit Dante is going to give me about it.

I'm wooing.

It seems like an hour passes before all the media and hoopla is over and Dante and I finally head back to the garage. He's already making plans for drinking and fucking his way through all of Brussels tonight.

Emily's not in the garage when we walk in, but the crew is looking at both of us like something is wrong. We look around in question, then we hear it, Stan yelling and carrying on from the back room.

"Goddamn it," I toss my helmet down and storm into the back room, Dante in tow.

Stan is piss-drunk, yelling and swearing at Liam, and a couple mechanics who are trying to corral him out of the building before he makes more of a scene.

"I told you to get the fuck out," I point at him.

"You don't tell me shit, you little pissant," he lunges at me but stumbles.

Liam is trying to reason with him, but you can't reason with a career alcoholic.

"Second-place, that the best you got?"

"Someone call security," I yell back to the crew behind us who is watching in horror.

I'd like nothing more than to knock Stan's teeth out and curb-stomp him, but I'm more of a professional than he ever was, and he's done jeopardizing my career. I'm not going to be on the news for brawling with my father in the team garage.

"You worthless little shit," he gets in my face despite Liam trying to pull him back. "Too busy chasing pussy instead of winning."

"Watch yourself," I shove him back.

"Always were more concerned about that dirty whore…"

That's the last thing I hear before I drive my fist into his face, and Stan flies back, hitting the concrete. I don't feel it on my knuckles, I don't hear the commotion of the guys circling around, I don't feel Dante's hand across my chest holding me back.

I don't feel any of it for several beats until sound returns to my ears, and Stan rolls over gurgling, blood gushing out of his nose on the floor. Security rushes in behind us, and, unanimously, the whole crew tells them that Stan attacked me.

They've got Stan handcuffed on the ground, and he's spitting blood out, sweating and screaming—all the insults I've heard a million times before—but I don't give a shit.

Finally, you're in cuffs, dickhead.

"Banned." I clench my teeth and tell security, "He's never to step foot on any track ever again." They nod and drag him to his feet and haul him out the back door.

Goodbye, prick.

Someone slaps my back hard, and I turn.

Shit, our team boss, Silas, is next to me, and I have no idea how long he's been there.

"Good race today, boys," he crosses his arms over his chest and grimaces at the blood on the floor. Then he takes a deep breath, shrugs, looks to Dante and me, and says, "Drinks on me tonight."

Dante and I look at each other as Silas walks away then Dante busts up laughing. There's absolutely nothing funny, other than our team boss shrugging off the blood on our floor, but something about the stress of it and the way Dante is struggling to breathe from laughing so hard, now I'm cackling like a hyena, too.

"I need to clean that up," I laugh. I'm not asking a cleaning crew to deal with Stan's mess.

"Ey, where's a mop?" Dante yells as our crew disperses.

No one offers us a mop, but Dante and I find some towels, shop rags, and gasoline cleans up blood pretty well, we learn. In a few minutes, we've got it wiped up, and both of us have tears in our eyes from laughing so hard.

We're washing our hands in the sink in the back when the exit door flies open again, and Emily sticks her head inside.

"I need help," she looks at us and waves us over.

We both think Stan's done something else and rush to fling the door open, but when we do, Emily is trying to lug a twenty-five pound used tire inside. She's covered in brake dust and is black from the dirty rubber.

"What are you doing?"

"Hurry up, I need this tire," she drags it another few feet, and I go grab it from her and haul it in through the door.

"Where did you get this?" Dante asks as the tire flops onto the floor where Stan's blood just was.

"I stole it." Emily's out of breath and panting.

My eyes go wide, but she continues, "It was on a rack waiting to go into the Concordia truck."

"Em, these are all numbered, they can't go missing," I run my hands through my hair.

"Shit," Dante mutters. He knows as well as I do that this is fucked up. Silas isn't going to laugh about *this*.

"I'm going to give it back, just help me," she says as she jogs into the garage bay where the mechanics are working to break down and pack up the cars and gear.

Dante has the good sense to haul the tire into the bathroom to hide it while I chase Emily into the garage. She's rifling through tool cabinets like a madwoman. "What are you looking for?"

"I don't know, a plasma cutter or a saw or something." Drawers are flying open left and right.

"Plasma cutter? What the fuck?"

She stops, puts her hands on her hips, "There are no rules about what conditions the tires must be given back in, Cole. I checked."

"Jesus Christ."

I think for a minute then find one of our wheel-gun guys who always has one of those oversized pocket hunting knives on him. He's some kind of survivalist or whatever those prepper types refer to themselves as. He's outside sealing up a metal freight container.

"Hey, uhh, Jeff, can I borrow your knife for a second?"

"Sure," Jeff pulls it out of the holster on his belt, because of course, it needs its own holster and hands it to me. "I'm telling you, everyone needs a good knife, Cole."

"Uh-huh, thanks," I run back into the garage and drag Emily into the back room.

The door to the bathroom is locked, and Emily bangs on the door.

"Who-eeees-eeeet?" Dante calls from inside.

"Open the fucking door," I growl and look around to make sure no one sees this.

He cracks the door, grinning like a psychopath, and Emily and I rush inside and lock it behind us.

I open up the knife, "Okay, what are we doing?"

"I need a chunk of that tire, through the middle, like this big," she holds up her hands for size.

"Right..."

Dante rotates the tire and kneels on it to hold it steady as we formulate our plan of attack.

"Don't cut my dick off," he jokes as I force Jeff's ridiculous knife into the tire and start hacking at it. It is every bit as difficult as I expect it to be, and we've bent the shit out of Jeff's beloved knife.

"Hurry up," Emily whispers.

"Hurry up," I look up at her, "you want to do this?"

"Give it to me," Dante takes the knife and starts sawing.

We've got about half of it done when the doorknob wiggles and someone knocks. All of us go silent for a second before Emily calls out, "We're in here!"

"Uhh, we?" A voice behind the door asks.

Shit. All three of us look at each other. Emily's hand goes to her mouth, we don't know if this is a regular crew person or Concordia.

"Oh, Cole, give it to me," Emily blurts out in a panic and starts banging the wall and moaning.

"What the fuck?" I whisper, but she just shakes her head and shrugs.

Dante snorts, "Yeah, take this cock, Cole. Choke on it..."

I slug him in the shoulder, and he falls off the tire onto the floor laughing his ass off and moaning.

"Fuck the both of you," I take the knife back and keep sawing.

"Uh, I'll just come back later," the voice from outside the door says.

"Okay yeah, much later," Emily moans and keeps banging until she's sure the mystery person leaves, then she abruptly cuts off and snatches the chunk of rubber as soon as we've got it free.

"We have to get this back on the rack," Dante stands and opens the door, peeking out.

The coast is clear, and all three of us sneak out of the bathroom. We open the back door to the garage, wait until it's clear, and then we start racing down the service road toward the Concordia truck.

"Tire bitch," Emily grabs us and points.

We duck behind the eighteen-wheeler and see a short Concordia rep in her white, pressed shirt, carrying a clipboard, and headed toward the truck where the rack of tires is at the back waiting to be loaded.

"Her name is Tire Bitch?" Dante whispers.

Emily nods as we all watch the Concordia girl. She's headed right for the truck, and it's painfully obvious one of the tires is missing.

"You two owe me," Dante mumbles, then stands upright, slicks his hair back, and strolls out from behind the truck. Emily and I watch, our hearts racing, as Dante swaggers up to Tire Bitch, takes her hand, and starts kissing it and cooing at her with his usual Italian bullshit.

She giggles at whatever nonsense he's feeding her, then he takes her face in his hands and smashes his mouth against hers.

She drops her clipboard. Her arms wrap around Dante, and he spins her around, so her back is to us.

"Stay here," I tell Emily, then I race the mutilated tire to the rack and hoist it up without making a sound.

Dante's watching me out of the corner of his eye with Tire Bitch's tongue down his throat, her eyes closed, her hands grabbing at him. I move to the far side of the semi-truck then round the hood to Emily, who's watching the shit-show.

Once we're clear, Dante pulls Tire Bitch off his face, says something to her, then turns and walks away. Her face is covered in black tire soot from his hands, and she looks lovestruck.

"Poor little Tire Bitch," Emily whispers.

Fifteen

Emily

"Emily, this is... highly unusual," Professor Tillman says as he looks into the brown paper bag I've brought into his office today.

I'm absolutely exhausted from jet lag and travel. I'm supposed to be off work for the next few days, but this can't wait. I'm not making any progress on figuring out why everyone seems to be struggling with this season's tires.

It just doesn't make sense. Sometimes, some compounds seem okay. Other times they shit the bed. Olivier has been of no help. While he's plenty underfoot, he's entirely useless, which is even worse.

If someone is useless, the least they can do is make themselves scarce.

"I know, but I need your help. Imperium doesn't have the kind of lab needed for this, and I can't do it at work anyway, for obvious reasons," I plead.

"Certainly not," he agrees.

"Will you help me?"

He's still for a long time, staring at the eight-inch chunk of tire Cole, Dante, and I stole. His eyebrows waggle from side to side every few seconds, he takes a few breaths, and I know this could go either way.

"It's important to me," I break the silence. Doc looks up from the bag and rubs his chin. "People could be hurt. Someone I... someone I care very much about could be hurt."

He drops the tire back into the brown paper bag and leans back in his chair.

Damn it, he's going to tell me no.

I can't blame him, I probably sound like a crazy person, as usual. This is stolen proprietary property, and I'm asking him to use the university laboratories to melt it down, tear it apart, run chemical tests on it, and find every secret hidden inside.

Secrets I'm starting to think Olivier and Concordia don't want me to know.

"It's okay, I understand," I hang my head and start to stand. I'll find another way.

"I didn't say no," he interrupts.

I sit back down.

"If this university can deal with the hellfire we caught in the 1970s when we created the first test-tube baby, we can certainly fiddle with some tires. Off the books, of course."

"Of course," I smile.

He reaches back in the bag and starts examining the hunk of hacked up rubber. "These are totally different from mass-produced tires, I'm sort of curious, myself."

"We'll have to separate all the components into their raw materials."

"Change the predictive model software," he adds.

"Anionic living polymerization."

"We'll have to bring in a chemist for that," he starts tapping his fingers on his desk. "I know someone."

"They're meant to fall apart, deliberately, to make the races more interesting. But the way they're breaking down, something is failing. I just don't know what."

"Well, let's see what's inside and start there. It could be nothing, you know."

"I know." Logically, I know this. But part of getting to an answer is eliminating other possible options, and I'm looking in every nook and cranny yet coming up empty-handed.

"It'll take time. I'll call when I learn anything. And I expect tickets to the Silverstone race," he laughs.

"Complete with paddock passes," I agree.

On my walk back home, I can barely keep my eyes, open but I want to tell Cole the good news.

If I'm honest with myself, I don't like being home anymore. In Cambridge, he isn't across the hotel hallway from me. He isn't prowling around the paddock or motorhome where I can ogle him, smell him, sneak into a corner office and taste him.

It's gotten to be fun, exotic, whimsical, almost—seeing all these cities with Cole. I don't know what this means for us, and I don't know how I feel about it, but I'm doing my best to live in the moment. Be casual. Be smart.

> **Emily: The eagle has landed. I miss you.**
> **Cole: Good job, baby. Get that sweet ass over here.**
> **Emily: I'm exhausted. Zzzz. What are you doing today?**
> **Cole: I ate all the chocolate we made and Liam's making me run an extra 15 miles.**
> **Emily: That's what you get.**
> **Cole: I've got something to give you.**
> **Emily: More chocolate?**
> **Cole: Even sweeter on my tongue.**

I'm blushing when I get home and throw on pajamas, Cole still sending me more and more graphic messages. At some point, I succumb to my heavy eyelids and fall asleep on him.

"Emily?"

I wake, in a daze, to knocking on my bedroom door. It takes me a few minutes for my head to stop spinning and figure out where I am. Nope, not a hotel today, I'm home. It's dark out.

"Emily," Klara sing-songs at me from outside the door.

I crawl out of bed and stretch as I open the door, yawning. God, I needed that nap.

"There is a race car driver at the door," Klara announces, wagging her eyebrows.

She knows of Cole, she knows I'm doing *things* with Cole. But I've never told her, or anyone besides Makenna, the whole story.

"Oh my god," I peer down on myself in my blue flannel pajamas that featuring dancing pancakes. I run to the mirror, and it's every bit as bad as I imagine, my hair is sticking up, and I have raccoon eyes.

I look like a deranged mental patient.

"You have to stall him," I beg Klara and race to the bathroom to do whatever I can to fix this mess.

Brushing my teeth at the speed of light, I hear Klara walk back to the front door and let Cole in. I listen to them introduce one another and chit-chat for a second, and then there's a knock on the bathroom door.

"Em," his deep voice fills the tiny space of our hallway.

"What are you doing here?" I crack the door and try to peek my head out, but he sticks his foot in the gap immediately and pushes it open.

His gaze runs up and down my hideous ensemble then returns to the abomination that is my bed head.

He looks like he just stepped out of a high-end fashion ad in his dark jeans and untucked white button-down rolled up to the elbows so the whole world can see those delicious forearms.

He has that appearance like he just rolled out of bed, too, but a smoldering, casual look that is entirely intentional. His hair is supposed to be a little disheveled. The more he runs his fingers through it, the better it looks.

Why does he always smell so good?

And I look like a runaway asylum inmate.

"God, you're beautiful," he whispers.

"Have you been drinking?"

From the way he's inspecting me like he's going to devour me, I know he has not. But he's very much drunk on something else, lust.

"Pancakes," he smirks, running his long fingers across the buttons of my pajama top and unbuttoning the top one.

I take his hand and lead him into my bedroom, shutting the door behind us. I'm not that awful of a roommate to subject Klara to the dirty things I know are going to come out of Cole's mouth when he has that gleam in his eye.

Cole walks around my room slowly, running his hand along my dresser and knick-knacks, taking everything in. He grazes my jewelry box then sees the little metal stick-man. He picks it up, and it seems so small in his hands now.

"You kept this," he glances at me and spins the steel figure in his palm.

I nod and take a seat on the corner of my bed.

Cole made the little figure out of scrap steel during our metalworking class. Its head is a big machine nut, and it's attached to a large bolt, and it has spindly little legs. At the time, I teased him that it was an accurate depiction of him—how big his head and ego were.

I couldn't bear to have photos of us out all these years while I was trying to forget him, but it felt wrong to have nothing, too.

Cole puts the figure back on my dresser. "What else did you keep?"

He takes a few steps back to me and starts slowly unbuttoning my pajama top again.

"Nothing," I lie.

I wonder if he has any mementos of me left in his fancy penthouse. Probably not. I'm sure his other girlfriends would have shut that down. I know I would have. Plus, he's never been sentimental like I am.

"You left me hanging," he bends and kisses my neck, pushing my top off my shoulder.

"I feel asleep," a warm flush overtakes me as Cole pushes me back to the bed and slides his hand into my top to cup one of my breasts.

The texts we'd been sending earlier had gotten downright lewd. The last one I remember from him was a very graphic description of how hard and aching he was for me. There's something intensely satisfying about having the power to do that to him. Knowing that he drove here in response.

Knowing that he's been here before, outside, watching Klara and I walk to that club. Instead of feeling creeped out, I like it. I like that he was watching.

He kneels over me on the bed, and the heat of his breath covers me as he runs his tongue around my nipple ever so slowly.

"Turn the light off." No one needs to see this, my pancake pajama nightmare.

"Fuck no."

"I'm a mess, I look like an idiot," I push his shoulders back.

He takes my chin between his thumb and fingers and makes me look at him. "You're stunning. You've only gotten more beautiful over the years."

I blush and swivel my eyes since he's holding my face still. I'm suddenly self-conscious looking like this while he looks like, well... him.

"What?" He asks.

"You could have any woman you want," I mumble, embarrassed to even say the words. I hate sounding like an insecure girl, but sometimes it's hard not to be one. He hasn't made that any easier over the years.

"Good. Because the one I want is you," Cole pushes me back down onto the bed and scoots me up, so my head is on the pillows, and he's hovering above me. His eyes are electric blue and won't leave my face.

I force myself to look at him again. "We're out of control, Cole. What are we doing?"

"You're setting the pace, remember? You tell me," he lowers his head and gently kisses my neck, grazes my collarbone, then starts kissing lower and lower down my chest.

His touches are feather light today, so different from how aggressive he usually is. I want to discuss what's happening between us, but instead, I find my thoughts escaping me and my fingers in his hair.

He swirls his tongue around my belly button and kisses along the waistband of my pants, his fingers sliding them down one excruciating inch at a time and hips lips following.

"Fucking pancakes," he says and then kisses my core through the flannel. "Sexiest thing I've ever seen."

"I find that hard to believe," I laugh.

And also mean it. I've seen the girls he's dated, the six-foot leggy pro tennis player with fiery red hair, for one. I highly doubt she wears button-up flannel pajamas.

She probably has a collection of leather and kinky vinyl shit, thousands of dollars of lacy La Perla. I'm making good money now, maybe I need to up my game. Tomorrow Klara and I can go lingerie shopping. She got fired and has nothing else to do besides study, anyway.

"Where'd you go?"

Cole's staring up at me, and I realize I've zoned out.

"Sorry, guess I'm still tired," I lie again.

I don't like that I keep lying to him about the fears in my head, but I'm afraid to bring them up. I'm so scared that it will be the end of this.

"Go back to sleep then, baby," he inches up and kisses my stomach and starts to move off me, but I push him back down.

"After," I smile. I don't care how sleep deprived I am, or what random thoughts run through my mind, I'm never turning down Cole's mouth between my thighs.

I may be a lot of things, but stupid isn't one of them.

"You sure?"

"Uh-huh," I raise my hips and playfully shove his head back down where it belongs. This man's tongue is addictive.

More feeling, less thinking.

"Vixen," he lowers back down and kisses along my pelvis, sliding my pants down further.

"Stay the night with me?" I want to sleep next to him, stay wrapped up in him. He's always gone in the morning on race weekends, all of his obligations getting him up at the crack of dawn.

He doesn't answer, but his mouth and tongue are doing all the talking, instead, as I arch into him. Everything is soft and slow tonight, sweet torture as he brings me to the edge then pauses, over and over.

Once his fingers join the assault, though, there's no stopping it, and I remember coming at least twice while biting my pillow and trying not to be the roommate from hell.

I remember being held close in his arms, against his chest, breathing in his scent, being encased in his warmth.

Being so content and sated.

And then, when a beam of warm sunlight came through my blinds and woke me, I felt all around my cold bed, and I knew he was gone again.

Sixteen

Emily

Some things are not quite right with Cole and me, besides the obvious. Waking up alone this morning, Cole absconding into the night again, is not sitting well.

I've been focused on trying not to overthink things, not make them unnecessarily complicated, and to be cool and casual. It's also not the easiest thing to talk about, and frankly, I thought I was being silly, imagining things.

But something is not adding up, and I'm afraid I might know what it is. If I'm right, I can't continue sticking my head in the sand.

"This is really weird and too much information, but I need your advice," I tell Makenna as I pace my bedroom. It's the middle of the night in Texas, and it was rude of me to call, but she'll forgive me.

God knows I've done it for her.

"No such thing as TMI. Spit it out so I can go back to sleep," she mumbles in her groggy voice.

"Well, for starters, he won't fuck me," I blurt out. There's no other way to say it.

"What."

"Just what I said."

"But you said... you told me about all the times..."

"Yeah, he gets me off, like, over and over, but it never goes any further." I try to clarify, running my hands over my face in embarrassment.

"Is he... hard?"

138

"Very, all the time. That's definitely not the issue." All equipment is functional, highly performing, top of the line, by all appearances.

"Well, he said you could go slow. Does he know you want it?"

I stop pacing and look up at the ceiling, "This is so embarrassing, but yes. I have specifically said, fuck me, I want you inside of me, so on and so forth."

"Maybe this *is* too much information," Makenna giggles.

"It's not funny."

"Okay, okay, so then what happens?"

"He keeps, you know, doing what he's doing until I have enough orgasms to pass out. He orgasms me unconscious every night. Like, with his hands and mouth."

"Umm, wow, okay. On the one hand, that's kind of amazing, but yeah, on the other hand, weird. From what I know about Cole, he's never been one to pass up sex."

"Exactly, he's insatiable. And then when I wake up in the morning, he's gone. Every time. Last night I asked him to stay the night, he ignored me, and you know, did it again, and when I woke up, he was gone."

Makenna lets out a groan, and at least I know I'm not the only one who finds this bizarre. I'm not imagining it.

"I hate to say it, but it kind of sounds like you're the mistress," she finally adds.

I slink back down to my bed, the weight of Makenna confirming my fears hitting me. "Oh god," I murmur.

"I mean, I don't know. But if Dr. Phil is to be believed, if he isn't getting it from you, he's getting it from someone else, right?"

"You know he's not a real doctor, right?" I'm grasping at straws, I don't want to have these thoughts. But I can't ignore them anymore, or ignore the apparent lack of Cole's interest in bringing his dick to the nightly orgasm parties.

Or that he leaves right after every time.

Or that I am a girl with plain brown hair and plain brown eyes who wears flannel pajamas.

Naive girl.

"I'm not going to be some skanky mistress, if that's what this is," my fists ball up as I clench the cell phone in my hand.

Hanging up with Makenna, my blood pressure continues to rise as I pace. All these years, all the women I've seen him in pictures with and on television come back to haunt me.

I let myself get sucked back into his undertow, and I've been avoiding the hard talks with him. I didn't want to rock the boat. I was happy for the first time in years, and I thought that I could move past it, chalk it up to being young and foolish maybe, but not as his side piece.

Or worse, someone he feels guilty about hurting, so these are sympathy orgasms every night, and he returns home to the hot Russian tennis bitch afterward.

I throw on clothes and pull my hair into a high ponytail. I make myself a little presentable because if *she's* going to be there when I show up, I'd prefer not to look like a total loser.

An idiot in pancake pajamas.

"Klara?" I call when she walks past the bathroom.

"Ja?"

"Random question. What's it mean when a guy will fool around but won't actually have sex with you?"

She squints her eyes at me in the bathroom mirror as I coat my lashes in mascara, "Like he's just toying with you?"

I nod. Is that what Cole is doing?

"I guess he's just not that into you?"

My gut sinks.

I couldn't compete with his world six years ago, I guess that hasn't changed. But *I* have, and I'm not putting up with it anymore.

The entire way to London, I am stewing and growing more irritated, angrier. I don't know if he's home or who might be there when I get there. I've never been to his condo, but I want answers today.

Right now.

My plans to storm to his door and beat on it are thwarted by a doorman who won't let me into the elevator until he calls Cole. I feel slightly cheated out of the plan I had cooked up in my head on the drive here, but I'm quickly allowed to proceed up.

Of course, you have a doorman, this is your world now.

My heart is racing as the elevator moves to the top floor. If there's another woman here, it's going to be awful. I try to get ahold of myself.

The elevator dings and the doors open. I'm expecting to have to walk down a hallway, but the elevator doors open to a private lobby for Cole's condo. I barely have time to notice the sleek wood floors and clean, modern design because Cole is standing there waiting for me.

He's barefoot, shirtless, and in a pair of thin gray jogging pants with his hands stretched straight up onto the door molding above him. For a flash in time, I am stupefied from the sight before me. I will myself not to stare at the prominent V along his hips.

"Good morning, gorgeous girl," he flexes before me, all stretched out and looking like a Greek statue with a sexy smirk on his face.

"Don't you 'gorgeous girl' me," I bite, step off the elevator, and move past him.

His smile fades, and he spins around behind me to close the door.

I stomp into the condo as he follows, asking me what's wrong, what's going on.

I don't know what I expect to see or what I'm looking for, but the size and space of this condo are overwhelming. Spanning the entire floor, three walls are floor to ceiling glass, and the far wall, overlooking the river, is open and letting the breeze pass through. There's a huge deck outside.

Highly polished wood floors gleam under soft white recessed lighting. Cream sofas and chairs are accented with pops of navy blue and gray accent pillows and dark rugs, giving a very masculine feel to the vast open-concept space.

Like everything else, it's so much more tangible and impressive in real life versus what I saw online when Cole gave an interview at home years ago.

"What's going on, are you okay?"

In the middle of his living room, seeing no one else lingering about —though I have not seen the bedrooms—I spin around and can feel how red my face is, how angry I am. Everything I have been trying to ignore bubbles to the surface.

"Why won't you fuck me?" I yell and don't even care how ridiculous I sound.

"What?" Cole's head jerks back and his brows furrow.

"You heard me," I cross my arms and stand my ground.

"What the hell is this about?" He takes a step toward me, but I hold my hand up, and he stops.

"You do everything else short of actually fucking me, then you leave. Every time, Cole. Am I just not what you want, or am I the other woman?" I force myself to spit out my hostile words even though I feel my eyes getting watery, and my voice falter.

He brings his hands to his head and runs his fingers through his hair. He looks confused and mad, which is just great because that's exactly how I feel, and I'm sick of it.

"You think I don't want you?" He says like he cannot believe the words coming out of my mouth. Like I'm a crazy person for suggesting such a thing.

"Is that why Cole? I'm not some model or athlete."

I throw my arms out to my side. My voice carries throughout the cavernous, open space. Surely if there was anyone else here, they'd hear me yelling. The Tennis Bitch would probably have stomped out by now and beat me with her racket.

"Don't you dare pull that shit," he yells back and points at me.

His chest is heaving, and his muscles are tense, and I'm taken aback by his anger. I was the one who was going to be angry and yell today.

"What the hell is going on, Emily? Since when are you the insecure, jealous type?"

"Since you made me that way!" My anger flares up like gasoline on a fire. I'm fighting the tears hard, but they're just a drop away from spilling over the dam, a flood is about to ensue.

He drops his hands to his hips, where his jogging pants are riding low. His shoulders sag under the realization that we're talking about this now. Like he hears the hurt in my voice that *he* caused.

"You left me, Cole! And then you spent the next six years parading around with beautiful, exotic women…"

"I was single, Em," he interrupts me. "You were with other people, too."

I don't know how he knows what I was doing, but he isn't wrong. Our proclivity certainly wasn't equal, if we're talking semantics, though.

"Is that why you won't have sex with me? Do you have a girlfriend?" I peer over his shoulder toward a hallway beyond the kitchen that must lead to bedrooms.

"Jesus," he huffs and starts pacing. "You think I have a girlfriend, that there are other women—what—hiding in my bedroom right now?"

I shrug and twist up my face because it sounds ridiculous when he says it like that, and I know it.

But I also don't trust that there isn't another woman.

Or six.

"Go look then," he waves his arms around. "Go on!"

"Fine," I cock my head in defiance and start down the hallway. Several doors line each side of the hall, the first being a restroom and a spare bedroom.

"How about in there? Any chicks in there?" He asks for every room

I stomp into.

There's a gym. There's a room with wall to wall helmets and trophies inside and a desk. The master bedroom is bigger than my whole apartment, twice over, in Cambridge. Its walls are all windows opening onto the deck area and dark gray curtains. Mostly I'm noticing the bed, though, and the obvious one side of it that has covers thrown back and pillows used, the other side still pristine and made up.

"Better look in the closet, I may be hiding them in there," he snarks.

"Don't you gaslight me!" I spin and yell back at him.

"I am not fucking gaslighting you."

"No, you aren't fucking me at all, are you?" This has devolved into a spiteful yelling match, but it's overdue, and we're going to do it.

"You want to know why?"

"Yes," I state authoritatively and cross my hands over my chest again, waiting for his answer.

"Well, let's see, the first time in the motorhome, after my crash," he starts listing, "I was so full of adrenaline I was afraid I was going to hurt you. And I wasn't going to fuck you for the first time in six years in the goddamn motorhome."

His voice is getting more irritated as he continues his list, "Then in your hotel room you literally fell asleep on top of me. Then what? Oh, the car. Yeah, asshole that I am didn't think that was the appropriate time, either. And then the jet on the way home with Liam and a dozen other people on the plane. The airplane bathroom didn't seem like the most romantic of choices. But fuck me, right, what a prick I am?"

"What about last night?" I ask quietly, staring at the floor. I'm starting to feel like a giant asshole, now, when he puts it like this.

I didn't use to be like this.

He sighs and paces across the plush, cream carpet in his bedroom before turning back toward me. "It's been six years, Em. Do you know how many times I pictured it in my head? Us getting back together? I just wanted…"

"What?" I whisper.

His eyes watch me, the blue reflecting the sun's rays coming in through the glass as the sun moves high into the sky. "I just wanted it to be perfect," he shrugs.

Both of us stand there silently for several beats as the first wave of brutal honestly hits us.

"There are no other women now?" I ask sheepishly. I need to know

143

for sure. I want to hear the words.

He steps toward me and takes my face in his hands, forcing me to look at him, "No. There's only you. It kills me that you think I'm like that, that I would cheat on you."

The waterworks have slowed, but the well isn't dry, and I feel moisture seep from my eyes again. "You have to understand, Cole. You left me, you hurt me."

He nods and hangs his head. His shoulders are slumped, and I know he's ashamed. "This is just about other women?" He asks quietly, staring at the ground.

I don't like his use of the word 'just,' like it's a minor detail.

"I've had to see you with all these other girls, all these years. I don't want to be insecure or jealous, but… it's hard. I'm not like them."

Both of his warm palms cover my cheeks, and he looks me in the eye with a lingering intensity, "You listen to me, and you listen good. I have been with a lot of women, Emily. *A lot.*"

I force my eyes away, I don't want to hear this.

He brings my face back to his, "You are the only one I want. The only one I have ever felt this way about. You're *not* like them. None of them meant anything. You mean everything. Okay?"

He's waiting for me to answer, but tears are streaming down my face. I need to blow my nose, and this has not gone how I was expecting it to. I came here to yell and catch him cheating, and now I'm a blubbering mess.

There's just so many years of emotions battling inside of me.

"You're the most beautiful woman in the world, Em. You're my gorgeous girl. Okay?"

I nod and wipe my face in my sleeve, "In pancake pajamas," I mumble.

He smiles and drags me into his chest, kisses my head. "I love your pajamas, and they *were* the sexiest thing I've ever seen."

I wrap my arms around his narrow waist and feel his warm skin against my face. I should probably apologize for being so obnoxious and searching his home like a psycho.

"I know I did this. I'll do a better job of making you feel secure, okay?"

"You don't have to do that," I speak into his chest.

"I want to."

"Why do you leave every night?" I ask while my face is still buried, and he can't see it. Part of me wants to quit while I'm ahead, but the other part wants to conquer the mountain and send the insecure, sniveling, whining girl inside to her grave.

He takes a deep breath, then sits on the edge of the bed and pulls me onto his lap. I swallow hard, sniffle, and Cole helps to wipe away my tears while I will myself to pull up my big girl panties.

"I've never spent the night with anyone else. It was always just sex. I don't know where we are, Em, and…" He pauses and thinks a second, "I'm fucking terrified."

"Of me?" I can't help but let out a laugh.

"Yes, of you," he wipes another tear away and pushes a strand of hair that's stuck to my face away, "you scare the shit out of me."

All these years, I felt like he had all the power. He was the one who left, and I was the one rejected. To hear Cole say these words now, it feels like we are on the same page again, being honest and raw with one another again.

"I'm scared, too," I admit to him. "I don't know what's going to happen or if this will work. What if I'm always afraid you're going to leave again?"

I can't go through that again.

"I won't. I know I left, and I take all the responsibility for it. I was young and stupid, but that doesn't make it okay. But, I was always with you, Em. I never changed my phone number so you could always call if you needed me. My email is the same. I tried so hard to let you know I was always here. I was wrong to leave, but it was always you."

He kisses me sweetly, then stands and takes my hand. "I want to show you something."

Cole leads us out of his bedroom, across the hall, to the room with his trophies and helmets. Sleek glass custom cabinets hold what appears to be a hundred or so helmets, dozens of trophies from around the world, and empty bottles of champagne from podium ceremonies.

He pulls the first one off the top cabinet on the left and hands it to me. "My first F3 race, Donington Park. I was just a teenager."

I move it around in my hands, inspecting the Union Jack design. I can see why it's special to him, but I don't get his point. "I don't understand."

He rotates the helmet and taps where his name is emblazoned along the middle. I study it closer. Where his finger is, I see *EW* in chrome, blended into the design. You'd never see it if you weren't looking.

"My initials?" I glance up at Cole.

He puts the helmet back, moves a few paces down the cabinet case, and pulls another helmet off. "My first F1 race, Melbourne. I was twenty-one then."

I take it from him and look all over. Finally, I see it, *EW*, in a slightly darker blue than the other colors.

"Barcelona, I was twenty-four," he hands me the next one, and I find the same. Four or five more helmets, he shows me my initials on every single one, over all these years, across all these continents.

Here I thought he wasn't as sentimental as I am.

"Cole," I whisper, another godforsaken tear running down my cheek and making my eyes sting. This is not the same variety of tears, though.

"It was always you, baby. Always."

Wrapping my arms around his broad shoulders, I press my lips to his and feel his strong arms pull me in. We're clinging to one another, pulling and gripping, like our lives depend on it. There's a hint of morning coffee on his tongue as it parts my mouth, and I open to let him explore.

When his face drops to the curve of my neck, licking and sucking, my tears are replaced with an overwhelming need to be closer and closer to him. Lifting one leg up, he slides a hand down and hoists me around his waist. My legs instinctively wrap around him.

He pushes me up against the door, our kisses so desperate we bang into a display case on the way. The way he's kissing me, possessing me, I know he feels it. I know he's right here with me.

I know I never stopped loving him.

"Bed, Cole," I moan around his mouth, and I feel his lips turn upward. "No more perfect. Now."

"Yes, ma'am," he walks me across the hall back into the master bedroom and sets me to my feet next to the bed.

I kick off my shoes while he pulls my shirt over my head. My hands run over his smooth pecs, and I can feel his heart hammering, his chest heaving with breath as he unbuttons my jeans and shoves them down. Unsnapping my bra behind me, he catches the straps and yanks it off my arms until I'm nearly bare before him.

"Take off those panties and show me how wet I make you."

I hold his stare and slide them slowly down my legs, then hand them to him. He smirks, inspects them, then drops them onto a dresser behind him.

Cole has always been in charge in the bedroom, since our very first time, and the way he's breathing now, the way his eyes command mine, I know I'm in his control.

Completely exposed, he holds my chin with one hand, his gaze scanning me from my toes, up my legs and torso, over my breasts, and then he makes a full circle around me, soaking my body in. "So perfect," he whispers into my lips when he's made a full rotation.

Shoving his sweatpants down, I kiss his chest, and my hands graze his hard ass before tracing around to the front of his hips. I let my fingers slide down his hard shaft before I grip the base with my hand, and Cole lets out a hiss into my neck and drags his teeth across my skin.

A bead of precum forms on the tip, and I use my thumb to spread it across the broad purple head then stroke him, squeezing him as hard as I remember how he likes to be touched. He bends to kiss each of my nipples then pulls away. He walks to the nightstand beside the bed and pulls out a condom.

"Put it on me," he hands me the packet, and I go to work, remembering this intimate part of our past.

He could tell me to do cartwheels right now, and I wouldn't question it.

I slide the latex over his heavy dick, feeling the heat and the velvet skin as my hands glide over him. His fingers dip inside my pussy, and he whispers filthy comments in my ear about how drenched I am for him before he pushes me back onto the bed, and his body chases mine.

Supporting himself on his elbows, he attacks my mouth, and the head of his cock rubs up and down my clit, sliding effortlessly back and forth through my slick folds. I need him inside of me so badly I can barely breathe, my fingers gripping and clawing his back, desperate to feel him.

Cole's left-hand grips my ponytail, and he jerks my head back before grinding down on me hard, his control slipping and his breathing picking up.

"You feel that, baby?"

"Yes," I whimper in response.

"That's how much I want you."

The fingers of his right hand dig into my ass, and he pulls me into him harder. He pumps over me a few times, our motions growing more frantic.

"So long I've waited to bury myself inside this sweet pussy." His hand slips between my legs, and his fingers start working me, his teeth marking my neck and breasts as we writhe against each other.

I can feel his need growing by the second, his body tensing, every muscle in his toned and cut body flexing.

"Cole, goddamn it," I take his wrist in my hand, "I need you. Now." I feel like I will implode without feeling all of him inside me.

In a swift movement with his hands on my hips, he rolls over onto his back and places me on top to straddle him. Holding the base of his cock up for me, he folds his other arm behind his head, and those blue eyes shimmer at me. He smiles, knowing exactly how desperate I am for him. "Take what you need, baby."

With Cole guiding the tip, I slowly ease myself down onto him. An inch at a time, I have to start and stop, rock side to side, before I can finally sink all the way down.

We both groan, and the sweet burn of Cole filling me comes back for the first time in years. It's so much better than I remember as I start moving up and down on him.

Somehow he's even bigger and fits me even better. Fills up all the space inside of me like we were custom made for each other.

His fingers press into my hips, and I watch his face, his mouth open and head pushed back into the pillow. I can see his jaw tense, and his teeth clench, and I know he's fighting the urge to throw me to my back and fuck me as hard as he wants to.

I love doing this to him, making him struggle against his control.

He rocks his hips up and thrusts into me every time I press down. "Fuck, that's it, gorgeous girl, ride my cock."

I build a rhythm, holding myself up with my hands on his chest, then lean back, arch my spine, and support myself against his thighs. I moan and breathe his name.

He sits up and takes a nipple in his mouth, pulling it in with his lips then dragging his teeth along the peak.

"You need to come for me, baby, I can't hold..." he takes my ass and pulls me onto him harder and harder.

Biting my bottom lip and relishing feeling so powerful, I run a finger over my clit then bring it to his lips. He sucks in my finger, the fire in his eyes as he watches me burning intense. He's close to losing it.

And I need him to.

I lean down over him and drag my tongue from the hollow of his throat up his neck and hover just above his lips, "Did you miss fucking me?"

His only answer comes in the form of a growl and hands tightening even more around my hips.

"Show me," I bite his lip.

Before the words have left my lips, I'm on my back. Cole slams into me and knocks the air out of my lungs. My fingernails dig into his shoulder, and I gasp.

I feel the head of his cock drag against my walls as he slowly pulls out then thrusts back into me so hard the bed rocks. When I open my eyes, he's watching me, storm clouds brewing in those blue skies, threatening to unleash a storm.

"Did you miss this big dick filling you up?"

"Oh god, yes," I moan as he continues to drive into me then languidly pull out, over and over again.

Nothing, no one, has ever felt as good. Nothing has ever been anything but a pale imitation of the chemistry we have.

"More, Cole," I beg.

He bites my earlobe and whispers, as if he doesn't want to break the spell, the fantasy, "It's been six years, Em, I don't want to hurt you."

Cole was always aggressive in bed, and I wonder how much more so he could be now. He's mentioned this twice, but I know he'd never hurt me.

Not physically.

Even more, I want everything from him. I want one hundred percent of Cole, nothing less than his body, heart, and soul.

I am not eighteen anymore, I am not a good girl, and I want it all from him.

I run my fingers through his hair, scrape my nails down his scalp, along his neck, and across his toned back.

"I'm yours, Cole. Give me everything you have. I've waited forever for it."

His eyes flicker, and a low primitive rumble comes from his chest, and then I am hit with the force of a tidal wave slamming into me. Throwing my hands up, I brace myself from being pounded into the headboard when he lifts my legs over his shoulders.

"Fuck, Em, fuck," he pants.

He's so deep inside of me, hitting places inside of my I was unaware even existed. I clutch for oxygen in between thrusts and crying out his name, a hellfire burning inside of me.

"Don't stop," I plead when I feel the crescendo creeping higher and higher.

I feel myself grow wetter, my walls clenching around Cole's heat inside of me. My nails dig into his flesh, and I bite his shoulder, crying out as the salty taste of his skin stings my tongue.

Cole lets my legs drop to his hips, and I wrap and lock them around his waist. His hands fist my hair, and he sucks the skin of my breast hard enough to leave a mark.

He drops a hand between us, and his thumb starts to circle my clit with expert precision.

"Oh god," I cry. I am so close to exploding, the pressure inside me well beyond boiling point and ready to shatter into a thousand pieces.

"That's it, baby," he growls in my ear. "Give me that cream, come all over my cock."

"Cole," I scream and arch my back off the bed, my head thrashing from side to side as his gravelly voice in my ear sends me over the edge.

His pace picks up, his hips firing into mine. The sounds of our skin slapping together join with Cole's grunts. "Keep coming, baby, give me more."

"Oh Jesus," I clench down and dig into his shoulder with one hand, the headboard with the other.

My legs writhe, my body filled with spasms and aftershocks and unending ecstasy. An unintelligible cry escapes my throat as I stretch my neck and my hips twist and thrash underneath him.

"Give me more, baby, a little more."

My throat goes dry and cracks from the intensity of my cries. Beneath my legs, I can feel Cole's thighs thrusting, his calves and feet digging into the bed for purchase as the bed rocks and shakes like we're going to crash through the glass wall and drown in the river below.

It would be a good death.

I don't know if I am going to be split in two or come again, but my body jerks forward, and it hits me again, a wave of pleasure all at once rising from somewhere deep within that only Cole knows how to unlock. I loop my limbs around his slick body and scream, holding on for dear life, my whole body shaking.

"Fuck Em, I'm..." Cole's mouth hangs open, and his face twists up into a beautiful, exquisite work of art.

"Give it to me," I grip his ass and pull him hard, thrusting my hips upward to meet his.

He lets out a deep roar, thrusting as he explodes, and I feel his warmth fill the condom as my hands run down his back, slick with sweat.

He kisses me deeply as he slowly pulls out and I suck in a breath at the sting of being so stretched, a dull burn filling the void.

He pushes himself down and drops his head between my thighs, and his hot tongue covers my entrance, his heat and moisture soothing the delicious ache.

"Cole," I squirm and let his hair wind through my fingers.

"Shh, let me," he says against me, the warmth of his breath across my bare skin relaxing me. I can't possibly come again, but this is somehow more intimate and affectionate, to be comforted and cherished like this.

The way he goes from aggressive and dominant to gentle and sweet, I get the best of both worlds, and I feel like I'm cloaked in adoration, shrouded in safety.

When I release a long, audible sigh and my legs fall limp to the bed, he kisses my outer lips softly and creeps back up my body, peppering soft kisses all along the way until he reaches my mouth.

"That was perfect," I reassure the worry he expressed earlier, and he rewards me with a smile that reaches his ears.

"You're perfect, gorgeous girl," he kisses me again. "Did I hurt you?"

"Mmm, only the good way."

He rolls over onto his back and stretches his long legs out. He pulls me into his chest. I throw one leg over his and snuggle into him while his arm holds me tight.

"I'm not leaving, and you can't make me," I mutter against his skin and take in how good he smells. He's insane if he thinks I am not spending the night tonight, and I'll lie on top of him forever so that he has to stay put if I need to.

He chuckles, his ribs visible as his breathing slows "Good, move in. Never leave."

His comment catches my attention for a second, but then he lets out a yawn, and I decide to let it go as a simple post-sex uttering.

I trace my fingers along each groove of his six-pack marveling in how gorgeous his body is, like a sculpted statue that belongs in a museum. Except I don't want to share it with anyone else.

"My abs ab-by enough for you?" His eyes are closed behind his long, dark lashes, but he has a sarcastic smirk on his face. The abundance of abs on the covers of my romance novels has become a silly inside joke between us.

"Ab-a-licious," I kiss his nipple.

Seventeen

Cole

My eyes aren't even open yet, but I can smell her, the familiar clean linen and floral scent, in my bed. My face buried in a pillow, I smile, roll my shoulders, and stretch my limbs out.

I don't feel her pressed up against me anymore and reach my hands out in both directions—ice-cold bed.

Flipping over and scanning around, she isn't here. The light in the ensuite bathroom is out, and I don't hear the water running.

"Em?"

Crickets.

Seriously? She took off? After searching my house yesterday like the DEA looking for a stash, bitching *me* out for not staying the night, she's the one who's done the leaving this morning.

Serves me right, but I thought we were done playing these games. The ones where she runs and I chase her.

Throwing on a pair of boxers briefs, I take my frustration out on the dresser drawer by slamming the shit out of it when I see her panties from yesterday still lying on the top. I throw open the bedroom door and go in search of my phone to call her.

We're never going to get anywhere if we can't move beyond the past.

I apologized—not for everything, she doesn't even know the half to it—I told her I'd do better. I meant it, whatever it takes, yet she wants to get even and leave m...

Shit.

Rounding the hallway corner, I see her in the kitchen. Her back is to me, and she's in front of the stove mixing a bowl of god knows what. There are pots and pans everywhere. It smells like heaven.

She's in one of my tee shirts—and nothing else. Her hair's up in a ponytail, and it's bobbing violently, long brown hair swishing across her shoulders from side to side as she bends her knees and sways her hips back and forth to whatever is playing through the earbuds she has in.

She starts singing along with her music and spikes a pinch of salt into her bowl, Emeril Lagasse style. "When you haven't been where I've been, understand where I'm coming from. While you're up on the hill in your big home, I'm out here risking my dome, just for a bucket or a faster ducket. Just to stay alive yo' I got to say fuck it. Here is something you can't understand, how I could just kill a man. Here is something you can't understand, how I could just kill a man."

This is the funny thing about Emily. On the surface, she seems like the well-behaved, scholarly daughter of a military family. Just below, though, is someone with so much more depth, someone rocking out and singing Rage Against the Machine and begging me to do filthy things to her all night long.

It's an unbelievably hot combination.

She is really getting into it, rolling her head from side to side, wiggling her shoulders up and down, that perfect ass of hers becoming more visible as her shirt hikes up every time she bounces around. I can hear the bass and beat through her earbuds and take a seat at the breakfast counter, perfectly content to watch this show all damn day.

Finally, she spins around while singing and jumps at the sight of me. I love that instead of being embarrassed, she beams back at me, pulls her earbuds out, and slinks between my legs on the kitchen stool.

"Good morning, handsome," she wraps her hands around my neck and lays those sweet lips on me.

"It's better now," I grab a handful of her ass and pull her between my knees.

"Did I wake you?"

"No, you were gone when I woke up," I raise an eyebrow at her.

"That's terrible," her long eyelashes flutter at me, her big brown eyes dancing with mischief. "What's that like?"

"I didn't like it." Her sass earns her a slap on the ass, and she squeaks, prancing back to the stove.

"What is all this?" I ask as I grab a cup of coffee she has brewing and sit back down at the counter. I didn't know I owned this many pans and utensils.

"Breakfast. There are veggie egg muffins in the oven. Thought those would be good for you to grab before you work out in the morning. Flourless banana pancakes because Liam put the kibosh on regular pancakes, and then a southwest turkey and egg skillet thing."

"Where did you get all of this?" I don't have this much food in the house, I don't think. Also, she actually consulted Liam on what I eat?

"Concierge offered to get it for me when I asked where the nearest grocery is."

"They do that?"

"Apparently, and apparently you pay for it," she waves a wooden spoon at me.

"Huh," never knew that. "Well, thank you, baby. This is… nice."

"I like to do it, and I'm in love with this kitchen," she smiles and waves her arms around at all the stainless appliances I've never used. "There's no food in this apartment, though. What do you eat?"

"Liam brings meals in little containers once a week."

Her face wrinkles up. "You can't live on that. When's the last time someone made you a home-cooked meal?"

I rub my neck and think about it. The sperm donor never cooked, and my memories of Mom, mostly her screaming that she hated me, and she never wanted me, were not exactly a scene out of Leave it to Beaver. "Never?"

"What do you mean, never?"

I shrug. Emily looks like someone has kicked her dog.

"No one's ever made you breakfast?"

"No. I usually just make a protein shake."

"Dinner?"

"I nuke one of the containers from Liam."

Something about this concept seems deeply offensive to her.

Who the hell would I cook for, myself? I'm not home seventy-five percent of the time, and all this work for one person's meal sounds like a miserable endeavor. No thanks.

She slides the last banana pancake out of the pan, which, I have to say, looks like a pretty legit normal pancake. "Thanksgiving. Surely you had a turkey and stuffing and cranberr…"

"Nope," I interrupt her and sip my coffee.

She turns the stove off and rounds the counter, putting her hands on my thighs. She's actually upset about this.

"It's not a big deal, makes me appreciate you cooking all the more," I try to kiss her but, she pulls back.

"Cole," her eyes are searching mine. "Christmas dinner?"

"Em," her eyes are growing glassy, and now she's looking at me like *I* am the dog who's been kicked. "It's fine, let's eat." She lets me pull her in closer by the backs of her thighs, and I nuzzle her neck. "Or I could just eat you," I try to lighten the mood, but also, fuck food, I could sustain life on Emily in my bed.

"It's not fine," she pulls back. "I should have made you come to my house for the holidays."

"So the Major General could rip me to shit? Yeah, that would have gone over well."

Fuck. There's a tear ready to spill out of Em's eye at any moment. I didn't mean to ruin this sweet thing she's done this morning, and I wasn't vying for sympathy. It's really not a big deal.

"He would have let you."

"He would have poisoned me."

I think she forgets how much her father hated me then, and his opinion of me has not improved any over the years. It's gotten infinitely worse.

But she doesn't know that.

"What have you done on all the holidays since you left?"

Stalked your social media then drunkenly fucked nameless women until I passed out, mostly.

"Nothing," I answer, instead.

Her hands circle my shoulders, and I feel her tears hit my skin. "Don't cry. Come on, I want to eat whatever you made. It smells delicious."

"I should have made you come to my house. I should have called you. I should have been there for you."

You couldn't have been, baby.

She lifts her head and looks at me through her wet eyes, "Thanksgiving is in a few months. Can we spend it together?"

"You're not going home?"

"No, I want to be with you."

"Your dad's gonna be pissed."

"I don't want to talk about him," she snaps, and her fists ball up.

I don't want to talk about him either.

Ever.

Thanksgiving has never been anything but another day to remind me that I have no family, no one to really give a shit. Not even a phone call from old Stan. I understand why Mom doesn't call, I'm just a walking, talking reminder of what Stan did to her.

Same with Christmas, another day where everyone else is with their loved ones, and those with no one sit around feeling like lepers. Last several years I turned my phone off so a part of me couldn't even wonder if it would ring. I knew it wouldn't, but I'd find my subconscious waiting for it anyway.

"Baby, if you want to spend Thanksgiving here, I'll find you the biggest turkey in London. I'll get one of those deep fryers, and we can burn the deck down. Whatever makes you stop crying."

That brings a smile back to her face, and my heart's rhythm restores itself.

"I could cook the shit out of Thanksgiving dinner in this kitchen," she chuckles and wipes her tears away.

I stand up and snatch her little body up against mine. "Fucking the shit out of you in this kitchen sounds much more fun," I breathe into her neck and kiss the soft skin all down her nape and collarbone. This cooking in my tee-shirt thing she has going on is doing something for me.

She pushes her ass back into me, sighs as my hands travel up the inside of her shirt along her smooth skin. I take one of her perfect tits in my hand and glide the other down to her naked, bare pussy.

"Can we get a Christmas tree?"

"Hop on the counter and spread your legs and I'll kidnap Santa Claus for you."

"Breakfast," she giggles, pulls away, and flits to the oven, leaving me standing here with a raging hard-on.

Emily starts plating up a breakfast feast, but seeing her so emotional about being alone for the holidays sits in my stomach like a lead weight. They mean something to her. Being with me means no more family holidays, and I don't think she understands that.

She couldn't.

She wants to give them up now, this year, because it's novel and she feels sorry for me, but I don't think she realizes there would be no more Thanksgiving dinners with her family. No presents on Christmas morning with her mom and dad.

No turkey, no Christmas stockings, no Santa Claus, and no goddamn eight reindeer.

I've never had it, so I'm not giving anything up. You can't lose what you never had.

But Emily, she's always had that normalcy, those happy memories, and traditions, and it'd be one more thing she'd sacrifice to be with me.

"Do you like your job, Em?" I ask as I shovel mouthfuls of her cheesy egg goodness into my mouth and try to act casual.

Or is that another thing I've taken from you, your chosen career?

When she answers, I don't think she's faking. Her eyes light up. "I love it," she grins around a forkful of pancake. She starts discussing the engineering marvels of the cars, the advancements F1 brings to other industries, and all of the things that get her motor turning. "Plus, I get to be with you."

That makes me feel better, like less of a selfish prick. Less of an abomination.

"This was really good, thank you for doing all of this." I've stuffed myself, and eating Liam's meal prepped mystery containers is going to be more difficult going forward.

"You're welcome. I like doing it. It's fun." She starts gathering up plates and dishes and piling them in the sink.

"Leave those, baby, I'll do them later."

"Deal," she saunters over to me and runs her palms up and down my chest. She's so beautiful, so soft, so smart and sexy. She's everything I fell in love with years ago, but even better now.

"What do you want to do today?" She links her hands together behind my neck.

"Make you happy."

She thinks I'm kidding when she kisses the tip of my nose and says, "You do make me happy." But, then her eyebrows furrow as she notices my face doesn't match her playful grin.

"All I've done lately is make you cry." Two days in a row now, that I'm aware of, and who knows how many more when I wasn't there to watch it.

"You're being dramatic, that's not all you do," her palms cup my cheeks, and her thumbs run across my jaw, bristling through the stubble that's a few days old.

"*I'm* being dramatic?" I cock an eyebrow up and suggest that, possibly, maybe, ransacking my apartment looking for other women may have been a touch more dramatic than my statement.

"You do make me happy," her eyes watch mine, the black of her pupils moving back and forth between mine. "You make me laugh," she plants a light kiss on my lips. "You make me feel special and safe and wanted," her mouth moves to my neck, and she traces her tongue around the edge of my ear.

"I want you more than anything in this world." I run my hands from the side of her tits down her torso and to her hips. I fucking love these perfect hipbones and how my hands fit around them.

"You know all of my secrets. You're my best friend," she continues the trail of her mouth over my skin, and I feel a pang of guilt that there are still plenty of secrets, but it would only hurt her to learn them.

And it's getting hard to concentrate with her mouth on me.

"You fuck me to sleep every night and give me the best orgasms I've ever had," her teeth latch onto my shoulder, and she pinches one of my nipples.

"Jesus,' I hitch and slide my hands under her shirt.

"You and your magic dick make me let go. I feel like I'm someone else, or actually, like I'm finally myself."

"This magic dick?" I take her hand and put her palm over my cock, which is rock hard and throbbing for her.

"Mmm-hmm," she moans and cups me, her fingers dancing gently over my balls. "It's different with you."

"How?" I push down the thoughts of her being with other guys and concentrate on how good her hand feels on me and the handful of her ass in my palm.

"I feel like I can completely let go, give myself to you. Like my walls come down, and I can just *be* because I trust you. I can relax and be naughty with you."

"You want to be naughty..." I rub my thumb over her nipple, already a stiff pink peak for me.

"Filthy," she whispers into my ear and squeezes the base of my cock, hard.

"You're killing me, baby." The things I want to do to this woman, she has no idea.

"Oh yeah?" She pushes off my chest and grabs my phone where it's been charging on the kitchen counter, then comes back. She swipes up on the screen, pushes a button, and hands it back to me.

She's turned the camera on, and it's set to record video, the red dot flashing at me. "What are you doing..." I eye her suspiciously.

I like the new, naughtier Emily. I like her a lot.

"I want you to be able to watch," she pulls me off the stool and drags my boxers down my legs. She bites her bottom lip and adjusts the phone in my hand so that it's pointing down at her as she sinks to her knees.

"Jesus Christ, Em."

"Watch," she whispers.

Her palm wraps around the base of my cock. She runs her tongue along the ridge of my shaft from the root to tip, her eyes sweeping up and watching me.

I suck in a deep breath and lean against the breakfast counter. Holy shit, my gorgeous girl has only gotten one thousand times hotter and bolder.

Her tongue circles the tip, and she puckers her lips over the very top, teasing me.

She's going to be my undoing.

I reach down and pull the shirt over her head so she's naked and I can watch all of her tight little body below me. Her nipples are pink and pointed, and her tongue goes back to stroking my length up and down. My gaze travels back and forth between Emily and the camera as I imagine watching this over and over again.

"Suck, baby," I grip myself and move the head of my dick to her lips.

Never taking her eyes off me, she opens her mouth, and I watch her lips go round and sink down my flesh as her hand wraps around the base.

"Fuck," I throw my head back and moan, but I bring my face right back because I can't help but watch her. Her cheeks hollow, and she whimpers around me as she tries taking me deeper and deeper.

Her hand pumps my base up and down. Her wrist circles in time with the strokes of tight lips on my shaft. She brings a second hand up to gently cup my balls and tries taking me all the way.

"Yeah, just like that, gorgeous girl," I hiss as I feel myself hit the back of her throat. With my free hand, I wrap her ponytail around my fist twice and guide her head over my length. Through the camera phone, I see her eyes flicker with passion as my chest heaves and the pressure builds inside of me.

"Slide your fingers into that wet pussy and touch yourself."

She moans around my cock, the vibrations sending electricity up my spine, and she widens her knees on the floor. She pulls her mouth off my dick with a pop and runs her hands down her chest, squeezes her tits, and drops one hand to that beautiful pussy.

"Fuck my mouth, Cole."

If I thought I was addicted to Emily Walker years ago, screwing around hiding from her parents, dry humping each other, and making out in cars, this is next level.

This is like being addicted to oxygen, there's simply no life without it.

Guttural moans escape me as I drag her lips back over me and start thrusting into her mouth. Her fingers dip into her folds, and she starts circling them over her clit.

She's so goddamn wet I can hear the sounds her of fluids against her fingers as she rubs more frantically, her knees moving up and down on the floor, wiggling and writhing, chasing her own pleasure while giving me mine. I'm gripping the cell phone for dear life in one hand, her ponytail in the other.

Her cries and whimpers against my flesh intensify, her tight lips running up and down me as she sucks me harder and harder. I hold her head tight where I need it and thrust into her wet mouth. Her knees and thighs start to shake, her eyes snapping shut.

"You're so fucking sexy. Open your eyes, baby," I gaze down on her and see her eyes open again, watching me, looking into the camera. "Come on your fingers, then I'm gonna blow in that dirty mouth."

She lets a loud cry go from deep inside her as her fingers pick up, and she moves up and down on her knees like she's riding me. My fist tightens in her hair, and her whole body starts to tense up and jerk with spasms.

"That's it, baby, come for me."

Her lips never leave my cock as her orgasm hits her, and unimaginable sounds cry out around my dick. Her back arches and her fingers slow, then she grips the base of my cock again and stares right up at me through her damp lashes. I can't control it anymore.

"Fuck," I growl as I feel white-hot heat start to sear up from my inside.

Emily doubles down on squeezing me and moaning, sucking me with everything she has, and then the first wave of hot lava erupts from me.

Like a fucking champ, Emily takes me deeper and swallows every pump until I'm empty, drained, and panting, and I release my grip on her hair.

"Holy shit," I suck in a deep breathe and see her reflection on the camera phone. She licks me up and down, cleaning every inch of me with her tongue. She's smiling up at me, at the phone, like she knows she's the sexiest woman that's ever walked the earth.

I feel like I've been hit by a truck, in the best possible way.

She kisses my balls then plants a soft one on the head of my dick, and I help her up. She takes the phone from my hand and turns the camera off, smiling at the stupefied look on my face and tossing it on the counter.

"When did this happen?" I pull her into me and marvel at the perfect creature I get to hold in my arms. I don't deserve this, but there's no way I can live without it ever again.

"I've never done that before," she looks at the phone, then back at me. "I'm only like this with you."

"Thank Christ," I laugh, "I'll end up in prison, otherwise." I kiss her forehead and hold her tight to me.

"Delete it if you want, baby," I tell her. I don't want her to worry about this video existing, and she has every reason not to trust me.

"Nope," she kisses my throat, "I want you to keep it and watch it when I'm not here. That's your early Christmas present," she smiles.

Well, ho ho ho. Maybe there's something to celebrating the holidays, after all.

Eighteen

Emily

"Of all the things, I've missed this the most." My fingers brush through Cole's hair, his head resting in my lap. His long legs hang off the end of his sofa, and we've been lounging around all day, cocooned in blankets and each other.

We haven't turned the television on, listened to the stereo, or ventured out of his apartment, other than the trip to the grocery store I requested, in three days.

It's just been Cole and me, talking, laughing, cuddling, and christening every piece of furniture and room in this apartment.

The only entertainment we've dabbled in is reading each other smutty books that I send to his Kindle now, continuing our inside joke.

It's like I always imagined life with him might be, if those six years weren't stolen from me.

But they were, and I can't deny they've had an impact.

As much as I want to live in the moment, be the bigger person, and not dredge up the past, I don't want these lingering fears forever. I don't want them cropping up when I least expect it, invading my mind like a virus. I don't want to be insecure forever, waiting for the other shoe to drop. We're dancing around the topic—me more so than Cole—because sometimes it's easier not to shine a light in dark corners.

I don't want to lose him again.

But, if he leaves me again, it'll be even worse this time, and that's a darkness I can't walk into willingly. Fool me once, shame on you. Fool me twice...

Lazy blue eyes peer up at me. He looks so boyish and innocent with his head resting on my thighs. Every once in a while, his lips turn up in a contented grin. I don't need to ask him why, I understand how he feels. It's the warmth and comfort and contentedness of just being together, being whole again, being complete.

A part of me has been missing for years, and it's come home.

I trace my thumb over the scar above his right eyebrow, a tiny imperfection on his gorgeous face.

"Tell me about this," I slowly swipe my thumb across it again as his eyes close.

"Stan, you know that."

"I know, but you never told me *how* it happened." I've known about Stan being physically and emotionally abusive, of course, but Cole never wanted to get into specifics. I understood why, no one would want to relive those memories.

He lets out a sigh, "It's not a fun story, Em."

"I want to know everything about you, scars and all."

He shifts on the couch, and I feel his neck tense up underneath me as he stays quiet.

I keep running my hand through his hair, and, after a moment, his shoulders relax again, and he opens his eyes back up, looking at the ceiling.

"I don't remember how old I was, little. My mom was still around, so I couldn't have been more than six or seven. He was pissed at something I'd done at the kart track and was fighting with my mom. They were downstairs; I remember being in my room, and she started screaming for me."

"To leave?"

He huffs, his eyes swipe to mine for a split second, then go back to the ceiling. "No, not to leave. She'd call me to help her every time Stan would hit her."

My hands still in his hair, and I watch his jaw tense. "Help her? You said you were only six or seven."

Cole's shoulders shrug. "Ran down to help her. Stan had her on the ground, and she had blood on her face. Tried to pull him off her, screamed at him to stop. He turned on me, instead."

Bile starts creeping up in the back of my throat, and I feel a tremor run through my body. I shouldn't have made him talk about this. Maybe some things are better off living in the dark, where they belong. Where they can't infect the sunshine and light.

163

"The scar is either from the ring he wore or the coffee table he threw me into. Who knows."

His eyes close again, and I cup his cheek with my hand, trying to control the shaking and quakes of my fingers. I knew things were bad, but picturing the details in my head, Cole, as a little boy trying to help his mother, anger radiates through me, and pain seeps through my pores.

No one deserves that.

I know it makes me judgmental, and I have no right, but I don't know if I feel more hatred for his father, or for his mother. His dad threw the punches but his mother calling him into it, to redirect the blows? He was a child. He had no one.

"I remember it bled so much I couldn't go to school the next day, and then he was pissed about that."

"You didn't need stitches?"

"Can't get stitches, Em. Then someone might find out," he says bitterly. "He locked me in the hall closet, and the next day, when I did go to school, I had to tell them it was from a karting accident."

Leaning down, I kiss the scar gently and swallow hard to keep my emotions at bay. Memories of kissing small scars on his body, years ago, come back to me. At first, he told me they were karting injuries, too.

"By the time I met you, my mom had left, and I was old enough to fight back, so most of the hitting had stopped. Or, I could at least hit back."

I nod, remembering him saying as much—that his dad *used* to hit him. That didn't stop the emotional abuse, though. I witnessed plenty of that myself. "I'm not judging you, Cole, I just want to understand. Why do you still talk to Stan? He's a monster."

His hands scrub his face up and down. "I don't know. It's fucked up. Guilt, I suppose. Everyone tells you you're supposed to honor your parents, family is supposed to be some unbreakable bond. I wouldn't be where I am now if he didn't stay and put me through all the training and practice, pay for karting. I know it's wrong, but..."

I shake my head. Everything Cole has achieved is despite his father. He's earned it through hard work and discipline and has overcome every obstacle Stan threw in his path. And his mother who abandoned him to it.

He clawed his way out of hell.

"I don't want pity, Em," he misinterprets my expression.

"I don't pity you," I cup his cheek. "I'm proud of you."

His brows furrow and I feel his muscles tense, like it's painful for him to hear this, like he doesn't believe me.

Stan had been poisoning Cole against me the entire time we were in high school, and knowing he still has some influence on Cole makes me wonder how much he had to do with Cole leaving me.

I don't need one more thing to hate Stan for, and I understand why Cole has issues. It can't be easy to cut your parents out of your life, even if they're monsters. But it would make sense if Stan was the cause of Cole leaving me.

"Did Stan push you to break up with me when you left?" A pit forms in my stomach as soon as the words leave.

"Yeah, sure. You know how he was."

I nod, remembering. We avoided Stan at all costs, back then, because every time he'd see me, Cole would get screamed at about me being a distraction. Stan said I was a gold-digger, and I was just using him like Cole's mother did. Even though Cole was just a teenager when we met, Stan had already projected all of his fears, shortcomings, and vicarious aspirations onto Cole.

But, if Cole believed him then, and Stan is still in his life—to some extent—it can happen again.

"You believed him, though," I whisper, the gnawing in my stomach growing by the second.

"No," Cole reaches a hand up and makes me look at him. I hadn't even realized I turned away, afraid of what his eyes would tell me that his words would not. "Stan's a self-serving prick. I never believed anything he said about you and I will never let him near you again."

"Then, why?" Two simple words. Six years boiled down into a couple syllables. They're finally out into the open and swirl around us in space like smoke trails.

There are times when silence is comfortable, even needed. And there are times when silence is the loudest noise in all of the world. A sound so loud it shatters your eardrums, and the percussion deafens you.

As Cole sits up on the couch and runs his hands through his hair, thinking of his response, his silence is deafening.

"You see the good in people, Emily. It's one of traits that makes you so beautiful, inside and out. When we first met, I was a mess, do you remember?"

I nod my head. But Cole wasn't a mess, his situation was. Once he wore me down enough to let him in, I saw him the gem hidden inside of him. How strong and decent and protective he was, despite everything he had stacked against him.

No one ever listened to me the way he did, understood me, made me feel so cherished and valued. So safe.

No one ever believed in me the way he did, was so excited for all of my silly ideas or encouraged me to be myself and make all the mistakes I dreamed of being free enough to make. He had no expectations of me to be perfect. His affection was never conditional.

"The moment I met you, I felt this thing in my chest," he grips his shirt like it's physically painful for him, like the cotton is on fire. "I had this deep-seated urge, this *need*, to pull you into my arms, tuck you into my chest, and protect you from every danger in the world. You don't always see the bad in people. You don't see it in me." His face turns to me, and the blue of his eyes has gone glacial, "I had all the bad inside of me, Emily."

"What are you talking about?" I reach out for him, but he pulls his arm away from me like he's toxic, like his skin will burn me. His retreat cuts me open, a simple action as sharp as a paper cut that stops you in your tracks and lights your nerves on fire.

"I couldn't protect my mother, but I could do right by you. Keep you away from me."

Watching emotions ripple through Cole, every muscle in his body tense and taut, my head is swimming, drowning in emotions. Confusion as to what he really means—this alleged evil inside of him. Hurt for him that he is living with wounds and traumas inflicted on a little boy, and anger.

So much anger.

"You can't possibly think you are your father," I rasp between my teeth. The idea is absolutely preposterous. Cole is many things, but stupid is not one of them.

"Aren't I?" He stands and starts pacing the living room. "My great-grandfather, my grandfather, Stan—they were all the same. We've all got the same DNA. Why would I be different?"

Rage courses through my veins over everything that has been lost over the past six years. Not just our relationship but my self esteem, my sense of sanity, my confidence—it all took a hit when Cole ghosted me. It launches me to my feet. Getting right into his face, even Cole draws back when he sees my face shaking. "You tell me right now. You left me because you think you are your father? You were trying to protect me? From *yourself?*"

"You have to understan…"

"Answer me!" I scream at him, letting it flow through me like floodwaters destroying everything in their wake. "Is that why you left me?"

The dam is open. All those nights spent crying, alone, wondering what was wrong with me that Cole didn't want me anymore—they are rapids rushing through my veins, and they're ready to take down everything in their path.

No words are needed. Polar blue orbs stare back at me and give me my answer.

Without forethought, my body harvests all the pain, anger and sadness it's harbored all these years and it launches it upon Cole. For a split second, I want him to hurt just as much as he hurt me.

"You fucking asshole! You hurt me worse than anything you could have done physically! You did all of this so you wouldn't be like Stan but what you did was worse! You're a monster all the same, just a different kind!"

As soon as it's off my lips and I see the light in his eyes dull, the pain I caused, I'm disgusted by my horrible, hateful words. I've just realized his deepest fear, poked the hot spear straight through his heart.

"You… you think I'm worse than Stan?" He whispers with a haunting crack in his voice and he steps back from me as if his very presence might infect me.

"No," I take a step toward him and stretch my hand toward him but he takes another step away. "I didn't mean that. I'm hurt and angry, but I didn't mean it." Despite his retreat I need to be near him, reassure him.

He moves against the kitchen counter and when I try to put my hands on his waist he takes them in his own and slaps my palms again his chest. "Just hit me Em, it would hurt less. At least I'd deserve it, from you."

"No," I pull my hands down and wrap them around his hips. "I'm sorry. You are not Stan. I don't want to hurt you." I think I'm going to be sick. What is wrong with me?

He turns his back to me and continues pacing around the living room. I can see the muscles rolling under his shirt, tension cascading over him in waves.

I wouldn't want to touch me if I were him, but I can't stop the gravitational pull, and I wrap my arms around him from behind. "I'm so sorry. There's no excuse. I was so angry because all this time… You're not him, Cole. I'm so sorry. I'll leave."

"Goddamn it, I don't want you to run away again," he turns with me still attached to him and wraps his arms around me even though I don't deserve it. "Even if you wanted to leave, I wouldn't let you. I can't do it a second time, Emily, even if I should."

"You're not him," I plead. "You'd never hurt me."

"Haven't I already, gorgeous girl?" There's so much pain behind his eyes that it breaks me in two.

I know the answer to this question, I would bet my life on it, but I ask it anyway, so he can hear it aloud, "Have you ever hit a woman?"

"Jesus, no," his arms drop from me, and I take both his hands in mine. I won't let him retreat. "I would literally rather end my life than hurt you."

How can he believe these things about himself? All Cole has done, since the day I first met him, was protect me from everyone—starting with the bitches at school who tormented Makenna and me—and he's still doing it. Even now. Even with me.

"You aren't him," I take his face in my hands and force him to look at me.

"That's just one thing, Em. There are a million other reasons why I had to leave you and why, if I were a better person, I wouldn't have dragged you back."

"I didn't mean what I said. It's just… all these years I thought it was me, I wasn't good enough for you. I couldn't compete with your lifestyle. I wasn't a model. I was just the boring high school girl you forgot about. I wondered what I did, why I wasn't enough. I wished I was prettier or skinnier or just, *more*."

I've never seen Cole cry before, but his eyes are crinkling up and glassy as he listens to every fear and insecurity I've developed. Every reason I've given myself over the past six years for why Cole broke my heart and left me comes spewing out.

Before my knees go out and I collapse, he scoops me up and sets me on the couch. He falls to his knees before me, "If you never hear anything else I say, Emily, listen to me now."

His hands push my hair back. He moves his face within an inch of mine, and there's such an intensity to his stare that I couldn't look away if my life depended on it.

"It was never you. *I* am the problem. I let you hate me. I needed you to hate me. You deserve far better than me, but goddamnit, Emily, I

168

have loved you since the day we met, and I never stopped, and I can't fucking stay away from you no matter how hard I try."

"Don't say that about yourself. I lov..."

"No," he cuts me off and shakes his head, "don't you say it again. You don't know what you're getting into, and I can't take it."

"I know what I am getting into, Cole. I know you. I see you. You can't stop me from loving you."

God knows I have tried stopping myself from loving him for long enough. It doesn't work.

We're opposite ends of two magnets snapping together. No matter how much you force them apart, they spiral and spin and end right back up in the same place.

"Do you have any idea what you'd be giving up?"

Giving up? Does he have any idea what I've given up the past six years? Happiness? Fulfillment? The other half of my soul? What could possibly compete?

Reading the abject confusion on my face, he continues spewing all the reasons Stanley Fucking Ballentine has obviously filled his head with, poisoned him with, since the day he was born. "Your family, for one. There's never going to be Christmas morning at the Walker household for us."

"What? That's ridiculous," I start. I mean, he may be right, but I will deal with it. Eventually, the Major General will get over it. Or he won't, and that'll be his problem.

"Kids, Em. I'm never having kids. This ends with me. How do I deprive you of that and live with myself?"

"Cole, stop it." I don't understand where this is coming from, except that he has also had years to dwell, years to dream up as many imaginary scenarios as I have. He has had a lifetime of toxicity seeping into his pores, actually.

"I don't know if I even want kids," I shake my head.

I told him this years ago, he knows this. It's not that I don't like children or don't enjoy them, I just don't seem to have that gene that makes me want kids of my own. I've known it since I was a little girl. Cole and I talked about this one of the many nights we snuck out. We agreed that some people just shouldn't be parents. Like Stanley Ballentine.

"You wanted to go to college, didn't you? And you were ready to walk away from it to come with me."

"That was my choice, all of these are my choices. Not yours." At least this part of his argument is valid. I begged him to let me come with him.

In hindsight, I can see why my parents went through the roof over that, but it was my decision. I could have done my undergrad degree here in London, the same place I got my Masters degree.

Because the world cannot keep Cole and me apart. I don't believe in fate or magic, but even I cannot deny the forces that draw us together anymore. Whatever it is, it's bigger than either of us. It's bigger than any childhood traumas or prior heartaches.

He is the other half of me, and I know he feels it, too.

"You're not wrong, it was your choice. But I had to make choices, too. I didn't know if I was going to make it to F1. Ninety-nine percent of people don't. Stan didn't. I was never going to college. It was driving or nothing. If I failed, I'd be exactly like him, and you'd be fucked over, just like my mother. You'd end up resenting me. One way or another, I was going to hurt you."

Cole's head falls to my lap, and his tension, his energy, rolls off him in waves. All of this time, we could have been together. Because none of this has ever meant anything to me. I could have lived without all of it.

What I could not live without was him.

"I wish you would have trusted me," I bend down and kiss his hair, grieving for the loss of so much time wasted.

His head lifts, and a lock of hair falls over his eyebrow, over the scar I'll never see in the same way again. "I'm so sorry. I'll never forgive myself for what you went through. I tried to make it work, and then, fuck, you were in such bad shape and..." his head drops back down. "You were better off without me. I'd only keep hurting you. Ruin your life. Take away your family, your friends, school, your decision to be a mother, trap you."

I hate hearing these things come out of his mouth, he sounds like my father, for god's sake. "Do you think I'm stupid, Cole?"

I know how he will answer this question, but just like the last, he needs to hear it. His head jerks up, "What? No, of course not."

"Then you listen to me. Those are *my* choices, and *I* will make them for myself from here on out. Do you understand me? Jesus, Cole. I could have gone to University College or Imperial College in London. I got accepted to both, you knew that." In a last-ditch effort, I applied to several schools here in the UK. This didn't have to happen.

"I didn't know that," he shakes his head.

"I told you that, in the letters that I wrote to you. You'd already left, and you'd stopped returning most of my calls, but I still wrote to you, and I told you that, the day I got the acceptance letters."

"I, I never got any letters from you, Em."

"What are you talking about, I wrote you every single day?"

In my teenage head, I tried convincing myself that maybe he was just too busy to return calls. Then I thought maybe getting mail from home would remind him of me, like an old-time love letter in the post that would rekindle his feelings for me. I wrote to him every single day for months.

Cole wraps his hands around my waist and buries his head in my lap. "I never got letters from you."

It was so long ago. I definitely mailed them, but maybe I messed the postage up or got the address wrong. Though, you'd think they would have come back marked return-to-sender, or something. I guess it doesn't matter, nothing will bring those years back and what matters is now.

"Promise me you won't do this again, Cole. I need to hear you say it. My choices are my own, and you need to trust me to make them. I'm not better off without you. I am better *with* you. Promise me you'll respect my decisions, no matter what your inner voice tells you. I can't go through this again."

His head lifts, and his gaze penetrates me, melts away all the fears inside because no matter what Cole has ever said, his eyes always speak his truth. "I promise you. I'm sorry for so much but as sick as it makes me, I'm never going to be sorry that you're in my life again. I'll never let anything take you from me again."

Before I can argue with his fallacies of unworthiness again, his lips meet mine. All of the emotions whirling between us are conveyed with the passion he's kissing me with. What starts sweet turns needy and desperate, demanding my devotion and my forgiveness and my promises back to him.

I give in because there is no alternative for Cole and I. Because I don't want to live in a world without my other half. Going through life missing my soul, walking around like a ghost, going through the motions like a shell of a person—it's not really living.

No amount of time or distance ever broke the invisible chain binding us together, and there's no force in the world this strong, that I've ever found.

There's a reason I never got over Cole Ballentine. We were never over to begin with. Something inside of me knew it, even if my brain did not, and would not let me sever our chain.

Now I know, beyond all doubt, there are things in life that cannot be solved through science and reason. Some things have to be solved with your heart, your gut, your soul—and mine simply don't function in a world without him.

"I love you, Em. I never said it back that night because I knew…"

"I know," I kiss him back and swallow his words, swallow the pain inside him. I start telling him I love him too, I always have, but he cuts me off again.

"Please don't, let me earn it. No one has ever loved me before, and I want to be able to believe you. I just, I can't right now. Please just let me earn it."

I don't know how to convey to him that my love for him is absolute or how to describe to him how freely my heart gives it to him, even when it was without my will.

Real love is an unstoppable force that exists despite all odds, all obstacles. Even when you beg it to stop, beg it to dissipate into the night, love persists in its own dimension, pulling and dragging you back into its gravitational pull until order is restored to the natural world.

Love shouldn't have to be earned from someone like your parents, and I don't know that Cole will ever get it from his. Even if he did, it wouldn't be honest or true.

I know I can never replace that for him, but I can show him how much he means to me. I can shine a light into his dark corners and be his candle in the twilight.

"You know what a composite is?" I ask, and he raises one eyebrow at me.

"Sure, like in our lab. Making something out of a bunch of nothing."

I smile at him. He's right, but leave it to Cole to boil down the bread-and-butter of my engineering degrees into something so tangible and honest.

"Talk science to me, baby, you know how much it turns me on," he whispers into my ear as his lips runs down my neck.

He's not even being funny right now, he gets off on this, which proves the point I'm about to make, even more.

"A composite is two distinct and complex materials that combine to produce something so structural, so functional, that it can't be found in any other individual component."

He rests his forehead against mine, and I run my hands across his shoulders, down his pecs where I feel his heart beating, "Better together, Cole."

Nineteen

Autodromo Nazionale Monza - Monza, Italy

Cole

I should have let Mila book the hotel room.

But oh no, I was going to be sweet and romantic and put effort into wooing Emily correctly, do it myself.

We have a black-tie gala tomorrow night in Milan, I have a stylist and dresses coming for Em—I did ask Mika for help with those, I'm not that much of an idiot—it was going to be perfect and cinched with a beautiful hotel suite.

"It looks like a nursing home exploded," I look around in horror, throwing our suitcases on the bed, which is complete with a mint green and white gingham duvet. Or maybe it's a repurposed picnic tablecloth.

"It's not so bad. It's... certainly historic," Emily teases, taking in the framed drawings that line the walls. Each one is a person long since dead, most of them wearing white powdered wigs, likely from the last time this room was remodeled.

Some Mozart looking dude watching me go down on my girlfriend was not my idea of sexy-time when I booked the most expensive suite at the five-star hotel in Monza.

Ruffled curtains, so many frilly curtains, line the windows that let in enough light to really magnify the horror that is the wallpaper—pink and teal flowers with bluebirds. Red checkered couches sit next to antique end tables covered in doilies. There are enough vases for a funeral home starter-pack.

This is the least sexy hotel room I have ever seen, and I have seen a lot of hotel rooms.

I pull my phone out of my pocket and do what I should have done to begin with.

As soon as Mila answers, I get right to the point. "Can you please get us a suite at the Four Seasons or something?"

Emily spins around from examining a plastic apple on a bureau alongside some small, touristy bottles of olive oil and other random crap. "No, you don't have to do that, it's fine."

I hold up a hand because Mila's yelling at me, half in German, about how I should have listened to her, but fuck no, this is not fine.

I wanted to do something nice for Emily. Not put her up in Shady Acres.

"Surely, there is a suite left somewhere in this city."

Mila is checking, but she swears there is not.

Emily walks out of the bathroom and is biting her bottom lip, her cheeks red and puffed out from trying not to laugh.

"What?" I step past her, and then I see what she's laughing at.

"I don't care what it costs. The bathroom is 1970's yellow, it's like Big Bird's nest up in here. I am not a snob," I argue with Mila, who is now insistent every room in the city is long since booked up for the race.

My eyes crinkle up at the family tree of dead people on the wall when Emily takes the phone from my hand.

"Mila, the room is fine. Yes. Yes, I know. I'll tell him. You're right. Okay, thank you." Emily disconnects the call and sets my phone down on a table next to a tea set.

"You're kind of a snob," she stands on her tiptoes and kisses the tip of my nose.

Of course, to a woman who would rather ride on a dilapidated Vespa than inside a Ferrari, I might appear snobbish. I don't think that's necessarily the case, but toh-may-toe toe-mah-toe.

"Newsflash Em, nice things are nice. This hotel sucks."

"You're a grump," she pushes our suitcases to the edge of the bed and flops down, immediately groaning and clutching her lower back. "It's unnatural, it's like bedrock," she cries and inspects under the sheets like the mattress may actually be made of stone.

"Oh, screw this, come on," I grab both of our suitcases and gesture to the door.

Somewhere in this city is a hotel room that was not decorated by a Golden Girl and has a mattress that does not inflict pain when a small, 5-foot-something girl lies on it. I will find said hotel, and they *will* give me a room.

"There are no other rooms, Cole. Let's just make the best of it." She reaches off the bed for my hand and pulls me back to her. "We can camp out on the floor."

I peer down at the parquet floor, mostly covered in rugs that were obviously woven by the original twelve disciples, "Absolutely not."

"Are you going to crab the whole weekend?"

"I'm not crabbing," I crab at her.

"You crabbed at everyone on the plane the whole way here, you crabbed at the driver at the airport, now you're crabbing at me. Is it because of Edmund?"

I take a seat on the mattress, and Emily is not exaggerating—it's unnatural.

I'd like to lie and tell her I'm in a mood because of Edmund, yes. But that's only part of it, and the fact is, the secrets I'd like to bury forever aren't staying hidden anymore.

They're collateral damage from having Emily back in my life, and I knew I'd have to face the demons if I wanted her. I'm willing to face mine for her.

It's too bad I'm not the only demon in our lives. Funny thing about demons and devils and monsters under the bed—they seem to run in crowds and latch onto their victim like poltergeists imprinting upon a house some unsuspecting schmuck moves into.

Emily is that house, and it's because of me that the spirits won't lie peacefully.

After we had the last big blowout, there's one more thing *I* need to tell her. There's one more thing she needs to hear from *me*, and then I'll have to live with everything else, help her live with them if it comes to it.

I had, minimally, hoped to spring it on her in a lovely Italian villa, a penthouse suite, maybe liquor her up with champagne first.

Instead, I have this, this thousand dollar room that makes Olive Garden seem swanky.

Time for an exorcism.

"Edmund is half of it," I start.

Edmund is out sick, missing his first race that anyone can remember. I won't have my engineer on the pit wall, in my ear, for the first time in my professional career.

I'll get James, a junior engineer who is, by all accounts, a decent person, I'm sure. But it's not the same, and I don't know James. I don't trust James. Every time we get into the cars, we're putting our faith in the hands of the crew, people like Emily who can see data we cannot see from behind the wheel. We have to trust those people not to kill ourselves, or someone else, pushing the boundaries of speed, and frankly, common sense.

"And the other half?" She asks innocently enough, not knowing this is something I've never told another person about, ever.

I run my hands through my hair. "I at least wanted to get us a decent room and take you to dinner and…"

"Butter me up?"

I nod, I admit it.

Not that any amount of money dropped on a hotel or restaurant will change facts, but yeah, butter her up is exactly right. At least point out that I'm not a total derelict, I can support her, take care of her, point out my redeeming value.

If she gave a shit about fancy hotels or restaurants or cars, this might be easier. Then again, I wouldn't love her like I do if that were the case.

"I don't know how to say this. Some other people know, but *I've* never told anyone. I understand if it changes how you think or how you feel about me. I should have told you before, but now we're trying to make things work, and they're serious and…"

She interrupts my rambling and takes my hand in hers, "What is it? You can tell me anything, you know that."

Oh, if only I knew that.

Those are just lovely words you hear in movies and read in books. In the real world, you do not get to say *anything* and be accepted for it. In the real world, there are consequences.

"Did you… do something?" She asks when I've been silent too long.

"No, sorry. I just… this is one thing I did *not* do, for a change."

"If you didn't do it, then I can't be mad."

I hope she remembers those words in the future.

"There's no good way to say this. You know how my mom always said she hated me and resented me, didn't want me?"

"Yes, and it's her loss that she walked out of your life," Emily tries to console me and look in my eyes, but I'm fixated on a bluebird on the wallpaper because staring at that ugly fucking thing is still better than what I might see if I look in Em's eyes when I tell her this.

177

"It's because Stan raped her. I'm the byproduct. That's why she hates me, could never look at me. That's why she left. It's taken me a long time to come to terms with it, Em, but the shame... I was afraid people could look at me and see the evil embedded in my genes, they could tell I was broken and came from violence. I was afraid if I ever had a son, he'd be a rapist, too. Just, so much fucking shame. It consumed me."

On the plane, I had imagined I would feel the weight lifted off my shoulders when I finally released the words, but it's the opposite. Because that's just more silly shit that you hear about in movies.

Instead, I feel like the words are crushing down on me like a million pounds of shame trying to smash me through the earth's crust. I'm not an idiot, I know I didn't do the crime, and technically *I* shouldn't feel ashamed.

But shame is not reasonable, logical, or kind. It is nagging and relentless, and it destroys you from the inside out. It is ever-present. It makes you listen to it, it makes you believe.

I need her to know I didn't leave her because I wanted to. It sure as hell wasn't anything she did. It was because I was filled with shame, and I allowed that to be exploited. It was my mistake and one I'll live with forever, but never let happen again.

The room is so silent I can hear one of the dozen gilded antique clocks ticking as its pendulum swings.

"I'm not going to tell you I'm sorry, because I'm not sorry you're here or that you exist, and you're not looking for pity," she says softly, her thumb rubbing small circles over my palm.

I dare a glance at her out of the corner of my eye, and she's not crying or running away screaming.

"I wish you would have told me, of course," she continues, "but only so I could have told you sooner that it would never change how I feel about you. This doesn't define you, Cole."

"I mean, it pretty much does, though. It's the foundation of my very existence."

"That's just not true. Stan is a god-awful piece of shit, and I would never minimize your feelings, but I also won't sit here and let you believe this somehow makes you defective or damaged."

"I tried to get Kristy to press charges, looked up the statute of limitations. I offered to pay for an attorney or go with her to the police. She just laughed at me."

Emily moves off the bed and kneels before me, making me look at her. "I wish you could see yourself through my eyes, see what I see."

"I could say the same, gorgeous girl."

She curves her lips up and nods, "You're right. I'll do a better job of believing you if you'll try to believe me. Do you want to know what I see when I look at you?"

"I don't know, do I?" I grin at her, try to lighten the mood a little because I've had years to process this. I've had years of mental coaching, and years to make peace with the facts, as much possible. My only remaining fear was that Emily would look at me differently.

But she isn't looking at me differently, because that's the kind of girl Emily is. She'll criticize and beat the hell out of herself, but never anyone else.

"You're the strongest person I've ever met. You have no idea the resiliency and strength you have inside. You're kind and generous, you're funny and sweet. I know that you'd protect me with your life. You're the first person I'd pick in any emergency situation, take with on a deserted island. You love unconditionally. You've worked your ass off to get to where you are."

"You're getting carried away," I haul her up off the ancient rug— god only knows what its seen in its time—and she straddles my lap.

"I know the bad stuff is easier to believe, but you are a good man, Cole."

God, when she looks me in the eyes like this, she makes me want to believe it. She makes me want to be that.

"You know, when we were teenagers, I used to feel guilty." Her hands run through my hair. I can't fathom what she ever had to feel guilty about.

"I would whine and complain about my parents, my problems, and all the while I knew you were dealing with bigger issues, *real* problems."

"Your problems were just as real."

"And that's exactly what you would do. Be selfless." Emily leans in and kisses me, her soft lips finally shoving those weights off my chest.

"Do you really not feel any different about me?"

"If I were allowed to tell you that I love you, I would tell you it only makes me love you more."

"You're not allowed yet, though. I still have several years of wooing to make up for, and this rancid hotel set me back at least two months."

Sliding my hands up her legs, barely clad in thin little black leggings, I cup her ass and pull her over my thighs.

"Can I show you instead?" She waggles her eyebrows at me and then pulls her shirt off over her head.

Like I'm going to say no to that.

Sometimes words aren't needed, sometimes you can speak louder with your mouth closed. Now is one of those times, so I answer Em by dropping my mouth to the valley of her breasts and sweeping kisses along the soft curves.

She tastes like honey and resurrection and all the things that make life worth living.

"Know what else I see when I look at you?"

The way she's biting my earlobe and sucking on my neck, she could say I have three eyes and four arms, and I'd still take it as gospel.

"The man who's going to fuck you into next week?" I say around a perfect, rosy nipple I've just liberated from its lacy prison.

"I see the sexiest man on the planet, the one every other guy in my life has failed to live up to. The one who ruins all my panties because I am constantly soaked for him."

My fingers dig into her deeper when her breath tickles my ear, and then she scrapes her teeth against my jaw.

"Do you know how badly I want you? All the time? How much I need to feel you inside of me? How much I love it when you take control, throw me down, and fuck me hard?"

Her throaty voice, the way she's grinding against me, sends every ounce of blood in my body straight to my dick. Unsnapping her bra, I fling it aside and start to pull her leggings down her hips when she stands up and puts a hand on my chest.

"Get naked, Ballentine," she orders as she starts peeling her leggings down.

Fuck, I can see how wet she is when she loops her thumbs into her panties and slides them off. Her bare lips are glistening with it.

"Bring that beautiful pussy over here," I tap my chin, lift the hem of my shirt over my shoulders, and toss it aside.

Emily gives me a look that's oddly challenging, but equally seductive and devious. She turns and sits on my lap with her back to me. My hands instinctively cup her tits, run up and down the gentle curves of her hips, as she grinds her ass against my cock.

"God, you're beautiful," I kiss up and down her spine.

Wars were fought over women with just a fraction of what Emily has.

She moves her hair off one shoulder and tilts her head back to me,

"You make me feel beautiful."

Cupping her chin and bringing it to me, I drive my tongue into her mouth and slide my other hand down her body and between her thighs, her wetness coating my fingers. "You're dripping, baby."

"All for you," she turns around and pushes me down onto the mattress, then climbs over me, her hard nipples dragging against my abs and chest as she moves seductively back and forth down my body.

Every synapse in my brain is pleading with me to flip Emily over and drive into her. But watching her filled with confidence, licking up and down my torso, peppering hot kisses on my cock through my jeans, is intoxicating.

Unbuttoning and unzipping me, Emily tugs my jeans, and I raise my hips so she can pull them off. My cock springs free, and I stroke myself a few times, up and down, while Emily stands before me watching, eyes blazing, and her chest expanding with deep breaths.

"Let me feel how tight you are," I eye her and motion for her to sink that gorgeous wetness down onto me.

She shakes her head, "Come and take it."

Ah, cat and mouse time again. But this is different.

I know what she's doing to me and why she's doing it right now. By the way that she's staring back at me, daring me, she's caught on that I've caught on.

I raise an eyebrow.

"You want this, Cole, you're going to have to take it. You're going to have to believe me when I tell you I want you."

It's not that I don't believe her. I just needed to be sure, leave no margin for error.

Emily's my outlier, my exception. She's not another one night stand with a mutual agenda, practically drawn into a contract that made it crystal clear. After I learned how I came into this world, what evil lies in my genes, I needed the extra green-light from her.

I did want things to be perfect, I wasn't lying when I told her that—but the thought of hurting her, in any way, is unbearable. Better safe than sorry, it was easy to let her set the pace, take what she needed.

"I'm gonna come by myself if you don't hurry up," she taunts, fingers circling over her clit.

"Don't you dare," I growl.

"You have baggage, I have baggage. You are not the big bad wolf. I'm telling you I want you, and I don't ever want to be treated like a fragile little princess ever again. Make me hurt for you, Cole."

If Emily wants to throw down the gauntlet, we'll throw down the motherfucking gauntlet.

Rising from the bed, I prowl to her and take her chin in my hand. I stare down at her chocolate eyes, feel the heat swirling between our naked bodies.

"I won't settle for pieces of you, Cole."

"You want all of me?" I move her hand to my dick, hard enough to drive nails through walls, and she wraps her hand around the base.

Her eyes narrow, she squeezes me harder, "Every. Inch."

There is no denying the lustful haze in her eyes, the pulse I can see move across her chest and through her veins.

"Then bend over and hold on, baby," I spin her around and push her down over an antique dressing table with gold mirror in the corner. She waits patiently, slowly dipping her fingers in and out of herself, panting, while I find a condom in my wallet and slip it over myself.

She grips the sides of the table as I run my hands down her back, along her perfect, smooth ass that's arched up for me, "I need you, hurry."

"Spread your legs."

Like a good girl, she does exactly that. She breathes out soft moans and whimpers when I run my hand through her wetness, spread it all over her pussy and up to her ass.

She lifts her head and watches me in the mirror with swollen lips and lust filling her eyes. Her tongue moves along her bottom lip before she pulls it into her mouth. I hold her hips, line up my cock, and drive into her in one swift thrust.

She lets out a cry and grips the dresser tighter as it slams into the wall over and over.

"You like to be fucked hard, don't you?"

"Yes," she pants, "more."

Gripping her hips and pulling her into me, her body quakes and her movements become jerky, but she doesn't relent. She gives as good as she takes, rising up on her toes to try and meet each thrust.

I don't know what's a better view, watching my cock slide into her tight, hot pussy and come out glistening with her wetness, or the look in her eyes as she watches me in the mirror and pants, whimpers, utters muddled sounds.

"Oh god, don't stop," she puts a hand up against the mirror her head is slamming into.

"God's not here, gorgeous girl."

Bending over her frame, I kiss along her spine and taste her salty skin. Moving a hand between us to her ass, I run my thumb between her cheeks and circle it around her tight, puckered hole. Pushing just past the surface, I rotate my thumb inside her and watch her closely in the mirror.

Her face twists in pleasure and her tight walls clench down on my cock. "Oh my god, that feels so good," she presses her ass further back into my hand. I rotate my hips and grind my cock deep inside her, hitting that spot I know makes her scream.

As hard as I can push into her, she pushes back. She's squeezing and strangling me, swallowing me up and begging for more. My thighs burn as we slam into one another over and over and groans arise from deep inside my diaphragm.

"Keep going, Cole."

Leaning over her, I take her earlobe between my teeth, run my tongue around the soft skin, "Did you give this ass to anyone else?"

"No," she whimpers, "oh, Jesus, don't stop, I'm so close."

I know she is, I can feel every tremor and spasm as she clenches down on my dick.

"Come for me, then I'm going to fuck this tight, virgin ass," I stand back up and give it to Emily as hard as she's begging me to give it to her. The table may have survived the last ice age, but its days are numbered as it slams into the plaster, and the spindly, decorative legs start loosening and slanting.

"You want that?" I push my thumb in further and watch her muscles contract, sweat roll off her back.

"Yes, yes, please," she begs.

"Then, fucking, come, for me," I thrust my pelvis into her with everything I have. Emily brings the house down with an ear-piercing scream, her palms slapping the wall, then fists gripping the table, desperate for an anchor as she flies through her orgasm.

Her walls milking me, I let her ride out every spasm and quiver as she screams my name, then slowly pull out.

"Keep that ass up," I tell her, give her a stinging smack on one gorgeous ass-cheek, and grab a bottle off the bureau. Had I been more prepared, I would have brought lube, but this will work nicely too.

"Get back over here and make good on your threats," she wiggles her ass and taunts me.

"Such an impatient dirty girl," I slap her other ass cheek, and she moans in satisfaction.

The liquid hits her skin as I drizzle it down her crack and spread it around. "Olive oil?" She watches me in the mirror.

"Extra virgin," I grin down at her.

I line myself up and wrap an arm around her waist, work her clit, and kiss her neck until I feel her relax enough to push the head of my dick inside that tight ring.

She gasps and holds onto the table, her body melding with it.

"Relax, baby."

She unclenches, and I push slowly, so slowly. Her body gives in underneath me, her muscles softening in surrender.

"Holy shit, more," she pushes back, but I press a hand to her lower back to keep her still. Olive oil or not, I'm not a small guy, and I'm not going to let her impale herself. Emily likes pain, but the good kind. I'll give her all of that, the kind that makes her scream for me, but no real hurt.

Gently, I move back and forth against her, a little more each time, and her moans pick up.

"Jesus fuck, Em, you feel so good." There's so much pressure in my balls I don't know how much longer I can keep this up with her clamping down on me and making those soft, desperate whimpers.

Her hips are writhing and jerking as I fill her up and keep circling her clit with my fingers. "More," she begs.

Sinking all the way in, throwing my held to the ceiling and groaning, I slide in and out, deeper and deeper until my balls are up against her skin. Her head is pushed up against the mirror, exquisite pleasure written on her face.

"Just like that, yes, oh, Cole, I'm gonna come."

Her tight channel tries to strangle my cock. A gush of cream hits my fingers between her folds when another orgasm builds in her.

"Come with me, gorgeous girl."

Sweat trickles between us and mixes with the oil until we're sliding skin on skin. Every muscle in her body goes taut and shakes like there's an electric rod between us. She cries out for me, amidst every four-letter word and deity name her brain can muster.

Driving the table damn near through the wall, heat and boiling tension rocket down my spine, through my balls, and I'm coming in hot ropes inside her.

"Fuck," I roar, and I expect the mirror to shatter from the cries Emily lets loose with me.

She goes limp, the table taking her full body weight and half of mine as I lay my torso over her back. And then the fucking thing does give out, two of its legs caving in and sending the table, and us to the floor.

"I hope that was a reproduction," Emily laughs, "or you just bought yourself a very expensive, busted antique table."

Twenty

Five Years & Many Days Ago - London

Cole

"You have to stop calling her. Leave her alone."

My blood boils, my fists clench. I want to send this phone through the drywall. "You don't get it, I will never leave her alone. Give it up."

"You listen to me. If you love her, you will stay away from her. She is miserable! She's lost all kinds of weight, she can't even eat without throwing up. She has bags under her eyes and cries herself to sleep every night!"

"That's all the more reason I should be with her," I argue.

I can't stand the thought of Em suffering like this, it's unbearable. Nothing is worth this.

"You're only going to ruin her life, either now when she is young and can rebound and live a full and happy life, without you. Or, down the road. You'll turn into your father, cheat on her, divorce her, take away everything that matters to her."

"I would never do that," I shout.

"You don't have a choice, it's who you are!"

"No, I would never hurt Emily."

"Even if not intentionally, Cole, there's no denying it. Deviant behavior is genetic. It's literally in your DNA. You can't escape it. You'll only ruin her. She deserves better than that, and you know it."

"That's not true."

Fuck, it can't be true. I am *not* Stan. I would never, ever hit Em, cheat on her, fucking rape her. My stomach coils just thinking it.

"I'm sorry, but it's true. These are facts. After Kristy told us, I looked it all up. I will show you research papers if you don't believe me. You can't change what you are. You'll end up just like your piece of shit father and your whore of a mother. I won't let you take Emily down your trail of destruction."

"I love her," I blurt out because, in the movies, this changes everything. It makes insurmountable obstacles fade away into the ether.

"If you love her, you will stay away from her. You're toxic. If you loved her, you wouldn't take her away from her family, her friends, let her miss out on college."

"Then I'll quit racing and come home. I'll go with her wherever she wants to go to school."

"And then what, Cole? Really? You'll never be welcome here. So you're going to take away her family, her friends? You're going to deprive her of having children one day because you certainly can't pass on your defective family genetics."

"She doesn't even want children!"

"Yes, she does, you idiot. She only told you she doesn't because that's what you needed to hear. She's always wanted to be a mother."

"That's not… no," I stutter.

This can't be true, we talked about it. She even brought it up.

"Use your head, you know how kind and nurturing she is. You know she's plenty smart enough to tell you whatever she needs to."

Of course, she is kind and nurturing, but—would she lie? Fuck, we're only eighteen. It didn't seem like that big of a conversation to have at the time.

"This doesn't make sense," I pace back and forth in my bedroom, thankful Dante is not home to overhear this.

"I only want what is best for her."

"So do I," that's all I've ever wanted. But she… she was happy with me. I saw it. I felt it.

"She's my daughter, I have no reason to lie to you. If you were what was best for Emily, I wouldn't be making these calls to you. But you are not, will never, be good for Emily. You will *ruin* her life. I am begging you to do the right thing and leave her alone. Let her grieve and move on. Let her go to college. Let her meet a man who will take care of her, treat her well, raise a family with her."

"I can't," I slide down my wall and collapse in a heap.

"And that's how I know you're just like your father. Selfish, a ruiner, an absolute monster who claims to love someone only to destroy everything they care about."

Bile creeps up my throat, and I start dry heaving. "I'm going to be sick."

"If you stay away, I will protect her. I'll even update you on how she's doing, from time to time. I'll do everything in my power to ensure she gets the life she deserves. But you have to promise me, Cole. Stay away. Do not be your father. Don't let Emily end up like your mother. It *will* happen. You *will* do it her. Because you're *exactly* the same. Everyone knows it."

The phone slides out of my limp hand, vomit fills my mouth, and my heart stops beating.

Twenty One

"No matter how hard you try, you can't stop us now." - Rage Against the Machine - Renegades of Funk

Emily

I wish Edmund was here. Edmund would believe me. He *did* believe me. He knew there was something wrong with these tires, too.

"...a gross breach of protocol," Olivier bangs his fist on the table and glares at me.

His nice-guy act came to a rapid halt as soon as we stepped foot on the circuit grounds in Italy. No more trying to ask me out, no more 'oui oui, mon cher' bologna.

They've found the mutilated tire we hacked up, and now he's pissed.

"Do you have proof that it was Imperium who took the tire?" Silas asks Olivier. He's calm and collected, seemingly unfazed by Olivier's completely accurate accusation.

Unlike me, doing my best to be quiet and not implicate myself.

My foot starts tapping under the table. Cole moves his leg over next to mine and puts a hand on my knee under the table, still looking straight ahead at Olivier.

"Who else would it be besides her?" Olivier points at me. "The new girl, making weird demands for proprietary information, acting like she knows everything."

189

Out of the corner of my eye, I see the vein in Cole's neck pulse. While part of me would enjoy watching him climb over the table and choke Olivier to death, that would end badly for all involved. But he stays still, controlled, his thumb caressing my knee under the table his only movement.

"I have to say, I'm not sure why we're having this conversation if Concordia has no proof of who stole *part* of a tire," Silas folds his hands together on the table and gives Olivier a shit-eating grin.

Olivier bangs his hand on the table again and stands up so abruptly his chair flies back, "I *will* find out!"

Cole lifts his free hand and gives him a little toodle-oo wave, and Olivier storms out of the room, slamming the door behind him.

Now it's just the three of us. Given Silas has set back in his chair and his eyes bead between Cole and I, I know we're not out of the woods yet.

"Well?" he asks, crossing his arms over his chest. 'Tell me you at least got answers from the bloody chunk of tire you stole."

"Technically, the tire itself wasn't really stolen," Cole starts.

"Don't push me, Ballentine. Emily, what have you found?"

"We're still running tests, it takes time," I fess up. "The only thing I can tell you so far is that the hydrophilic silica levels seem very out of whack, but we need to identify all the other compounds and then simulate how they react with one another."

I don't tell Silas that I've been holed up having mind-blowing sex with Cole for days now or that I should probably be in Cambridge with Professor Tillman, speeding things up. I've been staying in touch, though, and well, even at the best labs in the world, things take time.

"Hydro-what, what the hell does that mean?" Silas purses his lips.

He may have stood up for his team in front of Olivier, but, apparently, one does not get to be Team Principal by being a push-over. Silas is an intimidating man, by all accounts. Yet Cole sits here, as usual, calm, collected, yet commanding the room.

If everyone has a superpower, Cole's ability is appearing intimidating as fuck all the while maintaining total composure.

"The silica in tires is where the magic happens. Every company has a secret blend, and they guard it like a nuclear code. But the Concordia tires, they're not like any we've seen before. When we blend silica with rubber, generally speaking, we can decrease wear resistance while increasing grip. When we add silane, we can really start manipulating the magic triangle."

"What?" Silas bites.

"The balance between grip, rolling resistance, and wear. Altering the silane levels lets us manipulate the sweet spot. We can have low hysteresis at low frequencies and high hysteresis at high frequencies. That idea blew the magic triangle out the window..."

"I'm losing my patience, Emily."

'I'm sorry, I'm trying to explain it. It's going to take more time to dissect the silica and silane in these tires and identify the other hundred compounds that are bonded together at molecular levels. But I know it has something to do with that."

"Oh, you know it?" Silas asks sarcastically, somewhat pompously.

I'm again reminded that this is a male-dominated sport, and I'm the new, meddling, girl.

"Edmund brought Emily aboard because she's brilliant, and this is her jam," Cole leans forward and interrupts with a booming voice that rocks me back in my chair. "Neither of us knows what she's talking about, but she does. If she says the tires are fucked, the tires are fucked."

My eyes go wide as Cole stares down Silas, who is peering at him through slanted eyes and tapping the table deciding how to proceed.

"Are the tires fucked, Emily?" Silas finally asks.

"Yes sir, the tires are fucked," I answer.

He goes back to tapping the table with one hand, rubbing his chin with the other.

I have no idea if I am going to leave this table with a job at this point.

I do know that I am right, though. I am not some stupid girl, no matter how Olivier or the other chauvinistic pigs walking around this paddock act sometimes.

"Give her time," Cole interjects.

"No more stealing tires," Silas waves his finger between Cole and me. "And in the meantime, figure out how to *unfuck* the tires we do have because we're losing points all season to this shit."

"Yes, sir," I nod.

As soon as Silas leaves the room, I wrap my arms around Cole's sculpted shoulders and bury my head in his neck. I inhale in his familiar spicy scent and feel my blood pressure come back down.

"What's this for?" He wraps an arm around my waist and lifts me off my feet for a second.

"For standing up for me, believing in me."

For always having my back, for being selfless, for treating me like I have a brain in addition to tits, for listening even when I don't make sense, for trusting me even when *I* know I don't make sense, for being the silence and calm amongst all my inner noise.

He kisses me, and I catch a faint hint of the minty hypotonic beverage concoction Liam is always making him drink gallons of.

"As much as I'd like to continue this, you need to get back to Shady Acres," he pulls away and tells me.

He's still ragging on our hideous hotel suite. His righteous indignation over it is as comical as the decor.

I sag my shoulders and pout. "Do I really have to go? I don't think the dress I have is acceptable for a gala in Milan, of all places. You know I hate parties and…"

He stops me with another kiss, which I have to admit, is a surefire way to shut me up.

"Dresses, shoes, all that shit, will be at our room in," he checks his watch, "an hour. Pick whatever you want. You'll be the most beautiful woman there even if you choose a burlap sack."

"Are you serious?"

This is not my life, I work in a lab, or on car parts, with my hair pulled up and often safety glasses.

"Mm-hmm," he nuzzles me. "But I'm going to make it up to you. After the race, we'll be learning to make cheese in the Italian countryside."

"No," I push his shoulders back so I can see his eyes. They tell me he's dead serious, about the dresses, the gala—the cheese!

"Yes," he grins, "*No Reservations*, season nine, episode one-thirty-six."

He slaps me on the ass, turns to leave, and while I stand there slack-jawed, he exclaims for everyone in the hallway to hear, "Wooing, Emily. Prepare yourself."

"I want to find a man who looks at me like that," Dante's younger sister, Angelina, sighs. She points to Cole, who is sitting next to me at our banquet table.

Dante rolls his eyes, "Him? Absolutely not. He looks like he's either going to drag her back to a cave or eat her alive."

"Both," Cole's lips turn up around his glass, and he gives me that smoldering, panty-dropping grin that hooked me nearly a decade ago.

All night he's not taken his eyes off me. Not when he was schmoozing the sponsors who put on this charity event. Not when he let Dante cut in and dance with me. And not even when I nearly tripped in the heels that I'm not accustomed to when Nova the Tennis Bitch strutted past us.

Apparently, she was nearby in Milan, though Cole couldn't guess if it was because there was a sporting event or she's here as someone else's arm-candy.

Didn't know, didn't care, he'd said.

His eyes have stayed firmly on me, in a dress by a designer I can't even pronounce that two Italian bombshells squished me into.

They spoke no English when they rolled a rack of dresses into our Shady Acres suite. But I was able to communicate 'I have no idea, please help me' and help me they did.

It's floor-length, Ferrari red, which seemed appropriate, with a plunging neckline and a slit to the top of one thigh. This is a 'fuck me dress' if Klara has ever seen one. But classy, I was clear, I think, with the stylists who just kept clapping and exclaiming 'si, si' when I put it on.

They came with shoes, make-up, and even jewelry. The diamond earrings they mandated could probably have paid for my college degrees.

I can tell you all about Cole's Brioni tuxedo, though, because holy shit, I don't care what it costs—it's well worth it.

Cole is right. Nice things are nice.

And, watching him command the room all night looking like 007, I am going to do very not-nice things to him tonight.

All the furniture is going down.

"Will you dance with me again, Cole?" Angelina begs. She's fifteen and obviously smitten, not that I can blame her.

With Sophia Loren's cheekbones and long, wavy black hair to her waist, she's going to break hearts one day. Dante is already ready to lose his mind hovering around her like a guard dog. He likes to show it by slugging her in the arm and biting the head off anyone who looks at her, but the love Dante has for his sister is endearing.

And making her crazy.

Cole looks to me to ask if he can accommodate Angelina, and of course, I nod and smile because it wasn't that long ago I was a teenager.

While I didn't long to be at a ball like Cinderella, every girl dreamed of Prince Charming in a tuxedo.

"Stay away from my sister, asshole," Dante tries to smack Cole's shoulder as he helps her up.

Angelina stomps her foot and swats Dante's hand away, so embarrassed by him.

I giggle because I've had umpteen glasses of champagne. Plus, it's utterly adorable that Dante brought his little sister as his date since this is his home country.

Such tough guys, all of them.

"I'll be back," I tell Dante. I don't think he heard me though because he's mumbling threats under his breath as Angelina rests her head on Cole's chest on the dance floor.

I make hand signals to Cole that I'm going to the restroom. He sends me a sexy little wink.

After figuring out the logistics of how to pee in a ball gown, I make my way out of the restroom stall, heady with a delightful champagne buzz and eager to get back to the gorgeous man who is hellbent on wooing me.

As if Cole hasn't owned every piece of me for a quarter of my life and needs to *woo* me.

Rinsing my hands off, I check the makeup job the Italian ladies did on me. It's holding steady.

A stall door opens, and, of course, Nova emerges.

She looks like she just walked off a runway in Milan, her perfectly toned athletic legs jutting out from her silver gown and towering several inches above me in heels I'd break a leg in.

Nope, don't think it. He loves you, not her.

"Well, if it isn't Plain Jane," she snickers in a Russian accent, sizing me up through the bathroom mirrors.

I wonder if she's drunk or just a nasty bitch.

"Sorry, do I know you?" I play stupid, refuse to take the bait.

"Cole knows me *very* well," she fluffs her fiery red hair.

"That's nice, make sure to stop by and say hello," I make my way to the door.

Screw you, fire-crotch.

"You think you can keep a man like Cole satisfied?" She escalates when she hasn't gotten her way thus far.

"He seems plenty satisfied, but thank you for asking," I snip back at her, then kick myself for stooping to her level.

"Please, look at you. Mousey little girl, how long do you think before he grows tired of you? Little brown house mouse," she laughs.

Don't do it, Emily. Walk Away.

Hell no.

"Guess he must like mice since he's asked me to move in with him and marry him," I shrug my shoulders and give her my most phony, smug simper.

Obviously, I lied, but Cole will never know, and my claws are out. He's mine. He's always been mine. Bitch can step off and go back to the frozen wasteland she came from before I shove her own tennis racket up her ass.

"What." Her face becomes as red as her hair.

Oh, did I hit a nerve?

"Enjoy your evening, lovely dress," I examine her up and down as if she's wearing a paper bag. I have no idea what she's wearing, and I can only hope whatever I'm wearing is even better. Hell if I know.

And then I put my shoulders back, beg my feet to play nicely with my heels, and sashay my mousey ass right out the door.

Strolling down the long hallway like I own the place, I have every plan to wrap my arms around Cole and ram my tongue down his throat every time that bitch looks our way.

"I need you, now," A throaty growl whispers from behind me. Before I can turn, strong arms wrap around me and pull me into a tiny, empty coatroom.

"Oh my god, what are you doing," I giggle as Cole attacks my neck and runs his hand up the open slit of my dress.

He tries to kick the door closed, but it's a half-door, and only the bottom slams shut. He pushes me up against it and dives into my exposed cleavage.

I lean my head out the open top half of the door and panic to see Nova coming out of the restroom and locking eyes with me.

"Stop, stop," I push Cole as she gets closer, aiming for me like she's out for bloodsport. "Get down," I push him down to his knees to hide, spinning around just in time for Nova's finger to be right in my face.

Hanging over the closed half of the door, I panic. "Nova, 'wassup."

Wassup? Real cool, Emily.

"You!" Nova starts ranting at me. "You're not special, you're just his latest play-thing. We're just on a break while he gets you out of his system, then he'll come back..."

What the fuck.

Cole's hands slide up my legs, and he pushes my panties aside. I sneak my eyes down, while Nova rants, and I can just make out a huge grin on his face before I feel his tongue swipe through me.

I suck in a breath and slam my hand down against the wooden door. "Uh-huh," I try to keep a straight face as Cole's tongue laps at me and goosebumps race across my flesh.

"...pathetic little American tramp, you're lying, he'll never marry you..."

"Oh god," my head tilts back when Cole sucks my clit into his mouth.

Nova rambles words I can't even understand anymore. Words in English, words in Russian, I can't focus. "What is wrong with you?"

"Too. Much. Champagne," I clench my teeth, Cole plastered against the door on his knees and absolutely devouring me while his shoulders heave in silent laughter.

"You're insane," Nova continues, her hands on her hips and her face pursed up.

"Yes," I moan.

God help me, I'm about to come in this coatroom while the Tennis Bitch stares at me like I have two heads. I *am* insane.

"I don't know what's wrong with you, Plain Jane, but..."

"Jesus god, yes," I grip the door as I come apart on Cole's tongue. My knees start to quicker and buckle.

Cole can't hold it in anymore and lets out a hearty laugh as he grips my hips and then stands up next to me.

My mouth falls.

Nova's about to go supernova. Her eyes are bigger than her fake tits. Rage fills her perfectly coiffed face.

"Nova, I see you've met my fiancé," he grins at her as he wipes off his chin.

"What are you... were you..." Nova stutters.

"Was he," I repeat and point to the floor. "Oh no, he just saw a *mouse*."

Suck it, Tennis Bitch.

Nova lets out a shrieking huff, stomps her foot like a two-year-old, and storms down the hallway.

Cole stands tall and proud like he's just conquered Everest, but my jaw is still hanging open.

"What's this about marrying me, now?"

Oh god.

"I, uh, she… well, I might have…"

He beams at me, his blue eyes dancing and glittering, then his big hands cup my face and his lips meet mine. His tongue spears. He latches on with the perfect amount of suction, holding my head right where he wants it.

Then he pulls away, leaving me in a lust-fueled haze, adjusts himself, fixes my dress, and opens the door.

"Come along, future Mrs. Ballentine," he holds his arm out for me to take, "we have a gala to get back to."

"You're never going to let me live this down, are you?"

"Nope."

Twenty Two

Marina Bay Street Circuit - Singapore

Cole

The Singapore night race is, hands down, the most grueling of the year with its intolerable, stifling humidity.

We've been here for a week sauna training and acclimating to the climate. The street circuit requires exacting concentration and intense preparation and, even then, it's a battle to avoid mental fatigue for the two-hour duration.

So, I cut Liam some slack even though he's been hovering and scolding me all week about energy conservation and filling me up with fluids like I'm a water balloon.

"You can have a banana," he tells me, my stomach growling on the way to the garage.

"I don't want a banana. Or another salad. Or more fish."

I want a good, old fashioned, greasy American cheeseburger and a regular—heaven forbid—full-sugar Mountain Dew. I'd stab someone for a Mountain Dew right now.

"And I don't want to look at scratches down your back from your girlfriend every time I ice you down, but yet, here we are," he tips my water bottle at me.

"Em okay? She's not used to this heat."

"Yeah. Worried about the race, but fine. Heard her on the phone talking to her parents earlier. Nervous about the visibility between it being a night race and now raining. But then it turned into giggling and 'Cole this, Cole that' and I walked away before I threw up," he makes a girly voice and jazz hands.

"Thanks for watching out for her, man," I laugh and slap him on the back. "This will be a big enough shit-show with Edmund out again."

"I haven't heard any updates on him, have you?"

My head drops, and the smile on my face fades. I have a terrible feeling about Edmund and can't stomach the thought of losing him. He started coughing up blood weeks ago. The whole team is feeling his absence as we wait for more news.

"Waiting for more test results," I shrug.

Edmund has always looked out for me, he's guided me around every circuit since I was eighteen. My eyes and ears outside the car, he's kept me safe, led me to victories, and every other Sunday, I trust him with my life.

He's been more of a father to me than Stan ever was, really.

"I don't like that James is your stand-in again. It did *not* go well in Italy."

"No shit," I add.

Italy was a nightmare having to work with James, the junior engineer replacement. I felt like Dante out there, ignoring calls and arguing over the radio the whole time.

I don't trust James. He doesn't know me or how I drive. He doesn't know what I need to hear and how I need to hear it when I have one-thousandth of a second to make a decision.

I felt like I was not only driving the car, but I was also my own engineer, my own strategist, and my own pit crew. I should have been on the podium but finished in fourth, instead.

"Silas and I argued about it, but he won't let Emily stand in for Edmund," I add and hand Liam my empty drink bottle. He immediately gives me a full replacement.

"Why not?"

"I don't know, I think it comes down to the fact that she's new and she's a girl."

"You gotta be kidding me," he squints.

"You know this place, full of swinging dicks."

For one of the most technologically advanced industries in the world, F1 has a long way to go to catch up with the rest of the world. We've never had a woman driver, an openly gay driver, barely any people of color.

"Whole lotta rich white boys," Liam reads my mind and nods as we reach the garage and head inside to start the race.

Of course, I'm now one of those rich white boys, so I'm a bit of a hypocrite, but it pisses me off that Emily has to put up with this antiquated nonsense. Despite her degrees and mind, she still has to prove to people that she knows what she's doing.

As soon as we're in the garage bay, I see her doing just that. She's showing James and Silas something on her laptop. She's been working her ass off trying to improve tire performance and calling her old professor at Cambridge every day for updates on Tire-Gate.

"What's going on?" I ask when I reach the three of them.

"Emily wants to change your Energy Recovery System settings," Silas answers me.

"It's a bad idea," James adds. "You'll lose time."

"The time lost will be marginal in these conditions. We'll save the tire life, *and* he'll be more confident going into the corners," Emily argues.

"And I've changed the camber and toe angles to increase traction. Like I told you," James taps her laptop screen.

"And I'm telling *you*, these tires are not going to hold together if you do that and do not turn down the ERS."

"How long is the rain going to last?" I ask. Maybe we can get off the wet tires altogether soon enough.

"It's going to get worse as it goes on," Silas says, negating my previous thought.

"So we need to be concerned about wear life on these tires. Change the ERS," I tell James.

"No, we can't lose more time. We need the points. We aren't changing Dante's car, and we're not changing yours," Silas issues the final word and walks away.

James does the same. Emily snaps her laptop closed, letting out a huff and gazing up to the ceiling.

This is the problem, James doesn't understand how I need the car set up, how I need the car to *feel*.

Emily does. We've worked in the simulator a dozen times now. She gets it.

And I trust her.

"Cole, time to go," Liam yells across the garage bay.

"If you don't feel like the car is with you, or if it's oversteering, unlock your on-throttle differential. It'll help and extend the tires a bit since you'll come out of the corners a little more slowly," she grimaces at me.

Pulling on my balaclava and hearing the raindrops hit the pavement just outside the team garage, I do my best to distract her. She's nervous about the conditions as it is, and now my car isn't set up how she wants it.

"Will do. Now give me my kiss," I grin, pulling down the chin of my face mask. Emily gives me a PG-13 kiss since half the crew is watching and waiting for me.

"Good luck, have fun, go fast, come back to me, then take me to bed...and the other thing I'm not allowed to tell you because you're stubborn."

"Pretty soon, you'll need to write that all down to remember it," I smile as I pull my helmet on.

Every race, she extends her good luck wish by one new phrase. I'm starting to think she's as superstitious as us drivers are, but knowing Emily, she'd never bank on something so scientifically refuted.

"Nope, it's all up here," she taps her temple then puts her thumb to her lip to chew her cuticle, nervously.

Right, more distracting needed.

"Move in with me when we get home," I blurt out as I tighten my chin strap.

Her hand falls from her face as her eyes flutter.

"I don't like you driving all the way from Cambridge every day, you spend the night at my place every night anyway, and I want you there. Don't argue."

"I wasn't planning on arguing," she grins. "But you should know I'm only using you for your kitchen."

"Just my kitchen?" I pull her against me.

"Maybe other things, too."

"Time to get your ass kicked, lover boy," Dante slaps my helmet as he walks past and starts to climb in his car.

I want to ask her how the conversation with her parents went earlier. I find it hard to believe they aren't making her life hell if they know we're together. Even if they don't know now, they're going to when she moves in with me.

But it's race time, and that's not going to be a quick conversation, by any stretch of the imagination.

We're not even half-way done with this race yet six cars have already retired. They've spun out, crashed together, the track is more akin to a pond, and I'm going to ram my fist down James' throat.

"Change to strat-mode four, please," James tells me over the radio.

"Four? No way, there is no grip now. That isn't going to work," I yell back and try not to hydroplane off the track in a corner.

The rain is coming down in buckets, and it's a wonder the race hasn't been red-flagged yet. We've had safety car after safety car.

"Correct, mode four is faster."

"I won't be going very fast when I'm in the wall," I lose my patience. "I'm telling you, the tires are shot, and there is no grip."

This circuit is unforgiving under the best of conditions. One slip up and you're in the wall with few run-off areas and no margin for error. The storm has made the night race even darker, the rain reflecting off the Singapore city lights makes everything blend together even more chaotically.

"Concordia rated them for another eleven laps. The wear on them looks fine on my end."

"I don't give two shits what Concordia rated them as or how they look on *your* end. Put Emily on."

"Negative. Strat Mode four, please."

"Are you listening to me? I'm telling you, whatever your data is saying, it isn't working on my end. You know, the guy actually inside the car."

Then there's long silence where James simply refuses to answer me.

Another car spins out in the meantime, and, in my side mirror, I see him smack up against the wall, powerless to stop the slide. At least it was a slow impact, not enough to hurt anyone, just enough to ruin your day.

I'm in third place, and I know the team wants the points.

Hell, I want to win more than anyone, but what James is telling me makes no sense. This is the problem when you don't trust your engineer. You're in no man's land trying to navigate, plan ahead, develop strategies, and—minor detail—keep the car on the track in the middle of a monsoon.

I don't have much choice but to switch the engine mode to mode four since James is giving me the silent treatment, and I can't see what's on the engineer's computer screens. My only other option is to box for an unscheduled pit stop, which will piss Silas off *and* I'll lose track position.

Traction is immediately worse.

Shocker, James. You prick.

Just ahead of me, Alessi Cruisinallo, from the Anora team, slides sideways through a corner, which lets me catch up to him, but now we're both coming up to backmarkers.

We're trying to navigate through this traffic—I'm trying to pass, he's trying to defend—and neither of us can see shit through the spray coming off all the other cars.

"Push now," James says.

"Is it clear? I can't see."

I can barely see Alessi ahead, only occasionally the red light on the back of his car that blinks when he slows down, when his car is harvesting energy under braking.

James doesn't answer.

James and I are going to have a little chat about communication as soon as this race is over.

Coming out of turn five, there's a decent passing zone, so I accelerate as hard as I can without losing the car. The tires are slipping, and I'm fighting the steering wheel to stay in a straight line. Visibility is next to zero.

James had better be...

"Cole! Cole!" Emily is screaming in my ear.

I blink hard, turn my neck, wiggle my toes.

"I'm okay," I mumble.

Feels like the wind got knocked out of me, but I'm okay.

Steam is billowing out of my car, the rain hitting hot engine components. Somehow, I'm in the wall, my right front tire is on top of the car and held on only by its safety cord.

I take off the steering wheel and unstrap myself. I need to get out of the car and let everyone see I'm okay.

I'm just stepping out when I see the yellow lights of the medical car approach and I'm grateful I won't have to walk back to the garage in the rain, but it darts right past me.

When I watch it fly past, that's when I see the white carbon fiber car components littered over the asphalt.

My car is black and green.

Alessi.

Oh fuck, what did I hit?

I drop the steering wheel and run toward the medical car's flashing lights ahead as the cars that were behind us slowly navigate the debris field, passing us by.

It doesn't take but a moment to come into view, Alessi's car is on its side up against the wall, the whole front end destroyed beyond recognition.

The underside of his car faces me. I can't see Alessi, only the heads of the medical crew trying to work between the car and the wall.

The Extraction Team car flies up behind me with its yellow lights flashing. The only time they're called is when a driver cannot get out of the vehicle. When he's unconscious or may have spinal trauma or fatal injuries.

No.

No, no, no.

What happened? What have I done?

I try to get closer, but the marshals and a second medical team arrive and force me into their Mercedes.

"What happened? Is he hurt?" I scream at them while they shine lights in my eyes and assess me.

They won't tell me anything.

Twenty Three

Emily

Liam, Mila, and I cram into a private waiting room at Singapore General Hospital Accident and Emergency. Cole is pacing back and forth like a caged lion, still in his race suit and soaking wet. F1 personnel line the hallways and fill every waiting room on this floor.

As soon as the on-track medical crew cleared him, Cole was in a car racing here, where Alessi was airlifted by medical helicopter.

No one will tell us anything.

All we know, at this point, is that a backmarker spun into Alessi, who was trying to pass him. That caused Alessi to lose control, and Cole, who could see nothing and could not have avoided it, hit Alessi. The impact lifted Alessi's car into the air, flipped it, and it eventually stopped a quarter mile down the track against a wall.

The horrifying footage is replaying, over and over, online and on every sports television channel. Liam turned the waiting room televisions off as soon as we arrived.

We've all told Cole it wasn't his fault. While he watched the footage once, he isn't saying much. His every muscle is tense and taut, his fists clench at his sides, his nostrils continue to flare even now, almost an hour later.

I feel guilty to be relieved that Cole isn't hurt because someone else is. Badly hurt.

I feel guilty that my heart is breaking for Cole right now, who will not be consoled. Even though it's not his fault, I know he is blaming himself.

Mila clutches my hand in the chair next to me. A tear falls down her eye beside me, which makes me start to tear up again, too. Liam observes both of us, then stands and has me move one seat over so he can sit between us. He wraps an arm around each of us.

"Just let the adrenaline wear off," he whispers to me as I watch Cole. "He'll be okay."

I nod. "I wish they'd tell us something already."

Anything, any news. Maybe it's good that they haven't updated us. Maybe that means he is alive.

The waiting room door flies open. Everyone turns, praying for a doctor or a nurse who will update us, but it isn't.

"You motherfucker!" A tall twenty-something man storms in the room and screams at Cole in a Scottish accent. He has shaggy brown hair and blue eyes, but unlike Cole's, this man's eyes are dark and dangerous and seething right now.

He shoves Cole, hard, up against a wall as Lennox Gibbes, the other Anora driver, barges into the room. "Jack," he yells at the man shoving Cole.

Mila, Liam, and I jump to our feet when two more people barge in— a blond Scandinavian type who looks ready to murder everyone in the room, and a pretty, dark-haired woman.

Before anyone knows what's happening, Jack rears his hand back and punches Cole right in the jaw. Cole's head snaps back for a second, then his icy eyes return to his attacker's, and he just stands there, not even defending himself.

His chin juts out.

Like he wants to be hit again.

Lennox grabs Jack's arm as he's about to hit Cole again. Now Liam, Lennox, and the blond man are all grappling to control him. Jack is raging and trying to pry his arms free from their grips.

"Jack, stop it!" The woman with Lennox screams.

Cole hasn't moved an inch or said a word. He's practically taunting, begging this Jack person to hit him again even though it's taking three grown men to hold Jack back.

"I'll fucking kill you," Jack screams.

"It's not his fault, mate, it's not his fault," Lennox yells back at Jack.

The woman who came in with them clearly has no fear because she gets right between all the men and puts her hands on Jack's face. "Jack, stop. This isn't helping Alessi. It isn't his fault. Stop, please stop."

I've seen her before, around the paddock, but I can't place her. My brain is hardly working right at the moment.

Lennox Gibbes, everyone knows. He's not only Alessi's teammate, but the points leader this year, and it's all but a given he is going to win the championship.

Jack seems to listen to the woman as he stops thrashing and fighting against the three men, though he is still breathing hard and filled with rage. The pain visible on his face is unmistakable.

"Come on, out. Let's go back," Lennox tells Jack while he continues to stare hard at Cole. Lennox and the blond get him out of the room, telling the girl he'll be back as soon as he can.

Liam tries to examine Cole's jaw, but he shakes his head and turns his back to all of us, going to the window overlooking a dark Singapore sky. I can see all the muscles in his back contracting, his breath laboring.

I can't stand it anymore and make my way toward him. "Are you ok?"

He doesn't look at me. He just stares out the window. "Physically, yes," he answers. What he implies with his answer, how he's *not* okay, guts me.

I reach out to touch him, but he stops me. "Just give me some time. Please."

I pull my hand back and wrap my arms around myself, my heart breaking in pieces for him, for Alessi's teammate Lennox, even Jack, who just hit Cole because I can see how much he is hurting, too.

Alessi was a good person, he had a lot of friends in the paddock. No, he *is* a good person, damnit. We don't know what's happening yet.

Liam takes my arm, and he, Mila, and I sit back down. The woman who came in with Lennox pulls a chair to the corner we're sitting in. Watching her, I suddenly remember who she is.

"You're the Cooper Media reporter," I say to her. I remember now, reading about the scandal she broke last season when one of the drivers was busted for doing cocaine on track. There was something about prostitutes and sexual harassment. It took down an entire team, Celeritas, in the end, and was all over F1 news.

"Yes, Mallory," she introduces herself. Her eyes are red and bloodshot like she's been crying, too.

"Have you heard anything about how Alessi is?" I ask, thinking maybe she might know. Not only is she a reporter, but there were rumors about her involvement with Lennox Gibbes, but then those online news reports quickly vanished.

"He's stable but unconscious, probably some broken bones."

Cole overhears this and turns, "He's stable?"

"Yes. He woke up, but they have him sedated until they can run all the scans, make sure there's no swelling or traumatic brain injury."

"His... spine?" Cole asks, his Adam's apple bobbing as he swallows hard.

"Waiting on tests," Mallory rubs her eyes then gazes up at Cole. "I'll update you as soon as I hear anything. It wasn't your fault."

Cole nods at her, "Thank you." Then he returns to the window.

Relief flows through me that Alessi is alive and stable. I want to start googling medical information on what Mallory has said, but Dr. Google has rarely proved helpful. I'll only scare myself reading about the worst-case scenarios.

"Are you related to Alessi?" I ask Mallory to distract myself. Even for a reporter, she has way more information than anyone else has been able to get.

"He's a dear friend, Lennox's teammate."

"Right, sorry. It's none of my business."

"No, it's fine. I'm sorry about Jack. They're all good friends, and they're understandably upset," Mallory sniffles and takes a few deep breaths.

"You don't have to apologize."

"Mila and I are going to go get coffee. I'll bring one back for you, Em. Mallory?" Liam asks.

"Yes, please," Mallory answers. She takes the seat next to me once Liam and Mila leave.

I'm grateful that Cole has Liam. He doesn't even need to ask him if he wants anything, Liam will just automatically appear with what Cole should be drinking right now. It probably won't be coffee, and it definitely won't have sugar.

If I had Sailor Jerry on me, I'd sneak it to Cole, nonetheless.

"Does that one belong to you?" Mallory points to Cole.

"He does," I look at Cole, his face still blank as he stares at nothing out the window. "Which one is yours? Lennox, right?"

"All three of them may as well be. Can't get one without the other two," she laughs with no humor at all, grabbing a tissue from a box on the end table near us.

"You're a better woman than I am. I can barely keep up with just the one."

"Heh, just Lennox. The other two are just work husbands. I'm so sorry, I never asked your name," she turns to me.

"Emily," I shake her hand.

"New engineer, right?"

"Yep."

"Yeah, I've heard about you. Pissed off Concordia, if I heard correctly."

"News travels fast," I shrug. "You pissed off a whole lot of people if I remember correctly."

"That I did. Well, I'm glad to have another woman around. This circus needs more estrogen. God knows these idiots can't be left to their own devices, going around punching each other all the time like a bunch of primates."

I see Cole watching us out of the corner of my eye.

I'm sure he can hear us. I'm happy to see him returning, ever so slightly, to the land of the living instead of catatonically staring out the window.

Mallory and I chat for a long while until Liam and Mila return with coffee for everyone, and she gets a text from Lennox that the doctors do not suspect spinal trauma.

We exchange numbers, and she promises to keep us updated. I like her immediately and hope we stay in contact. She's right, it's nice to have more women around.

After she leaves, Mila hands me Cole's cell phone. She carries it while he's in the car. I don't even know where my phone is, probably still at the track because we left in such a hurry.

I take it from her but keep it face-down in my lap.

"It's been blowing up," she whispers.

"I don't think he should deal with this right now," Liam adds and turns the phone over in my hands, whispering and watching Cole whose back is still to us.

"Oh," I look at it, though I feel weird about snooping. But with the accident, I'm sure it is blowing up with people worried about him. There are all kinds of texts and notifications.

> **Stan: you're an embarrassment**
> **Stan: I told you this would happen when you let yourself get distracted with pussy. now some driver —a talented driver, unlike you—is probably dead because of your bullshit**
> **Voicemail From: Stan**

Stan: answer your fucking phone
Stan: you best answer me, boy
Voicemail From: Stan
Voicemail From: Ava Walker
Stan: WTF have you done

My blood boils as I read through all these messages from Cole's father. They go on and on. Why is he not blocked? Cole is not dealing with this garbage right now, absolutely not. Liam is right.

Wait, why has my mom called Cole?

Probably because my phone is at the track and she can't reach me. She must have seen the accident on TV and is probably worried out of her mind. I just spoke to her this morning, and everything was fine at home. At their home.

"I'm going to step out and deal with this," I tell Liam and Mila.

Cole sees me stand to leave and breaks his trance from the window to watch me, but I say I'm just going to find a restroom. I'm definitely not upsetting him more with the awful, toxic messages from his abusive, demonic father.

In the hallway, the voicemails start playing. There are a few from Stanley, who is drunk as a skunk, as usual, slurring his words and berating Cole for the accident. I delete them all then block him.

Tomorrow I'll tell Cole he's been blocked so he has one night of peace and then Cole can decide, on his own, if he wants to keep it that way.

God knows he should, but it's his decision.

Then it plays the voicemail from my mother. Her voice is angry, harsh, saying only, "You need to call me. Now."

I don't know what time it is in Delaware, but I call her back since she's obviously worried, and the call was recent.

"Cole," she barks as soon as she picks up.

"Mom? No, it's me."

"Emily? Why, why are you calling from Cole's phone?"

"We're at the hospital, and I left mine at the track. Isn't that why you called Cole's number?"

"The hospital? Are you all right?" Her normal motherly voice has returned, but now I'm confused.

"Yes, we're fine. Cole and I are fine. You saw the accident?"

There's a pause, then she says, "Yes, right. You're both okay?"

Maybe she was asleep, and I woke her up. I'm sure she was

panicking and out of her mind worrying about Cole because she saw the horrible crash footage.

"Yes, we're okay. Cole wasn't hurt. Still waiting to hear about Alessi, but he's stable."

"Thank god," she sighs. "Okay, well, it's late, and I don't want to wake your father. Call me tomorrow, honey."

"I'll try. I'll text if I can't."

I hang up but linger in the hallway. Something doesn't feel right. Mom was acting super weird.

I know I shouldn't—tomorrow, I will kick myself for doing this—but I scroll through Cole's call log and messages.

Dante, Silas, some of the other engineers and mechanics, more trash from Stan, Dante sending lewd gestures and emojis, several from me, of course.

Nothing from my mother, though.

I sigh and kick myself for going through his phone.

I'm not sorry for blocking Stan, though. I have my own issues with the Major General, but my parents are saints compared to Cole's. If I were in his shoes, I'd be a total mess, locked up in an institution or in prison by now. There's no way I could deal with this shit.

But not Cole.

He didn't let his parents win. He's gone on to fulfill his dreams and become one of the most elite athletes in the world, a millionaire, someone who has the respect of all of his coworkers and peers—but most importantly—someone who is selfless and kind, generous and full of love.

He's strong. He's always been the strong one of the two of us.

That's how I know he's going to get through this, through whatever happens with Alessi. Except, this time, he won't have to deal with alone. He will have me by his side.

Twenty Four

Emily

"Is he out for the season, then?" I ask Mallory, who has joined me in the hospital waiting room while her trio of men and Cole visit with Alessi.

The door to his private room is open and, from our vantage point, we're watching them tease and joke with one another as if three days ago Jack didn't attack Cole and Alessi wasn't airlifted to the emergency center.

"There are eight more races, so he might be back before the end of the season. These guys are tough and stubborn, you'd be surprised."

"Tell me about it." I feel like I could write a technical manual on tough and stubborn at this point.

Thank god, Alessi only has bruised ribs, a concussion, and a compression fracture in his neck. They're expecting him to make a full recovery, and he'll be discharged in the next day or two. It could have been so much worse.

We've been back to the hospital every day, but we need to leave for the Russian Grand Prix. So, this is Cole's final visit, for now. These races are back-to-back weekends. There wasn't time to go home, we just extended our stay here in Singapore.

I let Klara know that Cole asked me to move in, officially, not just as an informal post-sex request. She's thrilled for me and will be finishing her master's courses up soon, anyway, so the timing is perfect. She has a few months left, so there's no rush on her end, but I'm not waiting. As soon as we're back home, I want to move in with him.

Enough time has passed between us. I'm not wasting more of it.

"Sometimes I think they have it right," Mallory says, watching the guys through the door. "Just punch each other, get it over with, then move on."

"Could you imagine how much easier life would be?"

"I have a list of people I'd like to test my theory out on," she grins.

Lennox is trying to steal Alessi's jello. The others are throwing plastic spoons at one another, laughing, and acting like this is a frat party. Even Jack, who was so enraged and upset after the accident, has his dimples on full display as he smiles alongside Alessi.

"Honestly, I don't know how they do it," I motion my hand at them. "Cole was absolutely beside himself, worried sick. When we heard Alessi would be okay, he said he got twenty-four hours to wallow, then that was it. Sure enough, twenty-five hours later, he snapped out of it."

"Yeah, that's an athlete thing, Lennox does it, too. They get one day to work through the issue, but then it's time to let it go so they can focus and prepare for the next race."

I don't tell her that Cole actually set the alarm on his phone. The minute it went off, he stretched, cracked his neck, took a deep breath— and moved on. It was one of the most fascinating and disciplined things I've ever seen in my life.

"I need to learn that trick," I sip down the last of my coffee.

God knows moving on past heartache, trauma, or even perceived slights has never been something I could do.

No, I am the girl who remembers random comments strangers made to me years ago or questions I answered in college. I replay them in my head, wishing I had said something different, wishing I had behaved just a margin cooler.

I am the girl whose thoughts and memories get stuck in my mind forever, kicking about and ricocheting into the still of the night.

Except when I'm with Cole, and it all turns off.

"You and I, both. Girl, I can hold a grudge forever." Mallory scans me out of the corner of her eye, wanting to say something but hesitating. We've chatted a lot the last few days in the hospital. I think we're both surprised by how much we've shared so quickly.

Finally, she continues, "Lennox and I kind of broke up after the whole cocaine scandal. We were both stupid," she shrugs. "I went back to New York, and it took weeks for me to come to my senses. Apparently, I should have just slugged him."

"Weeks? Please. I have you beat by over five years."

At that moment, Cole sees me in the hallway, and gives me a little wink that melts my insides, pulls me back from that time warp, hauls me into the present where he is. Where I am. Where we are.

"Years?" She gasps and points at Cole.

"Mmm-hmm, he was my first love, my high school sweetheart."

"Oh, wow. I feel like this is a story that could take hours and multiple bottles of wine."

"Ha, maybe. Boy meets girl. Girl falls in love. Boy leaves girl, breaks her heart."

"And now?" She asks.

"Now, six years later, boy and girl still love each other. Boy wants girl to move in with him," my face flushes from telling someone our very condensed, simplified version of events.

I'm surprised to find myself sharing as much with Mallory, too. It isn't like me to talk about Cole with anyone besides Makenna, but there's something about Mallory that puts me at ease. Like she's been through this before, and part of me is eager to unload on an understanding ear.

"Damn, I hope boy is groveling."

"He says he is wooing." We both laugh and sit back, watching the guys.

I don't know that I can call the last three days 'wooing,' but something intense has been happening between Cole and I in the aftermath of Alessi's accident. His sweet wooing gestures are on point, no question about that, but this is more.

At first, he was so tense and worried he spent hours in the hotel gym working his energy out, taking out his frustrations on the equipment. But then he'd come back to our suite, and we'd have the most intense sex. It was every bit as hard and dominating as always, but extraordinarily intimate at the same time.

The juxtaposition is still bending my mind.

His body took mine easily enough, but it was the slow, teasing kisses that set it apart—the way his tongue licked my bottom lip. The way we shared breaths with our foreheads resting together.

It was like he'd shattered and was giving me every piece to put back together. He was offering me his entire soul, every raw, exposed nerve within him.

And I drank him in. I wrapped my arms around him and let the entirety of his lifeblood flow through me. It crept inside my veins, into the chambers of my heart, and into every recess of my mind

He let me tell him that I love him. Amid mind-blowing passion, I asked if he could believe me now. All he could do was nod, hold me tighter, give me even more of himself.

I can *feel* that he believes me now. He's letting me love him now.

All the demons he's clung to, he's cast them aside and made room for me to move into their spaces. Dark memories and shame have been evicted. I want to spend the rest of my life filling them with the feelings he deserves, instead.

I thought I knew Cole before, I thought I loved him before. I thought I had all of him. But now, he's opened up and given me pieces I didn't even know existed, an expanse greater than the deepest ocean trench.

As teenagers, our love felt dreamy and dramatic. He was off-limits, and I was clinging to him for salvation, rescue from mundane, freedom from perfection. He wanted me for who I was, and I loved every damaged piece of him. We shared components no one else got to see.

But now, it's so much more.

He's protective and honest. He cherishes me and treats me like I am his first priority, like I matter.

He's had me a thousand times, at this point, but he treats every time we're together like it's our first, like he's seeing me for the very first time. He loves me like I am perfect, exactly the imperfect way that I am.

Somehow, the inside of Cole, his beautiful inner workings, shine even brighter and are so much more gorgeous than even the sculpted and perfected exterior.

"Tell me about the Concordia situation, the tires," Mallory interrupts my daydream, and my ogling stare at the way Cole is leaned up against the hospital room wall.

"Are you asking as a reporter?" If so, I don't know what I could tell her. Silas has made it clear that any sleuthing needs to be done quietly and without dragging Imperium through the mud.

"Right now, I'm asking as a woman who has as much to lose as you do. Are they safe?"

Mallory stares ahead at Lennox. I know she feels the same fears, the same oppressive weight in her chest every time their cars pull onto the race track. In truth, nothing about this sport is safe. It's safer than it was years ago, of course, but the word safe is misguided, at best.

Alessi lying in his hospital bed proves that

I shake my head, "Not entirely. Something is wrong. I'm getting closer to what, but everything is such a freaking secret around here."

"That it is," she nods. "You know, if you need help, I have resources through Cooper Media."

"Thank you. I don't want to be a conspiracy theorist or wrap my head in tinfoil, but...something isn't right."

"You don't need to be a conspiracy theorist, Emily. There's so much money in F1, it's impossible to throw a rock and not hit a scam or corruption or something illegal going on. You know what they say, there are no ethical billionaires. And we walk amongst them every single day."

Mallory is right, of course, and I shudder to think of what else she's come across as a reporter with unprecedented paddock access like she has.

"It could be an honest mistake or just an inferior product, though."

"Sure, and Olivier is out marching for women's rights on the weekends," she snickers.

"Oh my god, does he give you the creeps, too?"

"Oui oui. Lennox actually kicked him out of our garage the last time he came calling, but he's kind of a caveman like that."

"Cole's always watching, monitoring, keeping an eye on things. I think he likes watching Olivier sink his own ship."

As I say that, both Cole and Lennox look out the door at us, like they know we're talking about them. And then they start wrapping things up with Alessi, saying their goodbyes, and I know we all need to leave for Russia soon.

Our time is up, and the next race waits for no one. It's there breathing down their throats, and mine, too.

"Mallory," I turn to her before the men arrive, "I can't explain it, and it won't make sense even if I try to, but the rain is making things worse."

"The wet tires, you mean?"

"No, I think it's all the compounds. But they're even worse when they're wet."

Mallory nods. I can see that she remembers all the accidents and blowouts and other unusual failures that have plagued the track this season. And, of course, there's Alessi right before our eyes, who is in a hospital bed right now over another incident that happened under wet conditions.

"Figure this shit out, Emily. There's too much at stake, and I can tell you better than anyone, the truth will never come to light if you don't push for it, drag it into the light. Bad things happen around here in dark corners. Let me know if you need an extra flashlight."

"I will."

Everyone says their goodbyes, Mallory and I even exchange a hug, before we head to the airport to leave for Russia.

Mom and Dad have been calling, but I've been avoiding them. As another call comes in from them now, I reject that, too.

Honestly, I've been plenty busy with Cole and Professor Tillman the last few days, but I still have a nagging feeling about my parents that I can't seem to shake.

It started out as a niggling suspicion, quickly enough dismissed like a breeze passing through. But no matter how much I ignore it, the thoughts are creeping back in and setting up camp in my gut.

Why didn't Cole get the letters I sent? Why did Mom call him, how would she even know his number is the same? Why is the Major General mysteriously silent after years of terrorizing me about Cole?

There may be other secrets hiding in dark corners, but do I want them dragged into the light, too?

Live in the moment, Em. Stop thinking.

Things are so good with Cole right now. Meanwhile, Alessi is in the hospital over something I might be able to help with, something I might be able to stop from happening again. Cole, Lennox, and every other driver on the grid could be in harm's way.

That's my answer.

Any demons who might be lingering in the dark will have to stay there and are probably figments of my overactive imagination, anyway. It's time to put my head down and get to the bottom of Concordia and these tires.

Twenty Five

"Braved the forest, braved the stone. Braved the icy winds and fire, braved and beat them on my own. Yet I'm helpless by the river. Angel, angel, what have I done? I've faced the quakes, the wind, the fire. I've conquered country, crown, and throne. Why can't I cross this river?" Puscifer - The Humbling River

London

Cole

Rain trickles down the uncovered windows that let in a gray haze of dewy morning light. It's silent, save the occasional clap of thunder or a boat making its way down the Thames.

Emily's been pressed into me all night. Every night since we've been home.

She wiggles her little ass into me harder, trying to bite back a smirk as if she doesn't know exactly what she's doing to me.

Reaching between us, I slide my fingers between her thighs, which she so willingly parts for me. "You're always so wet for me, gorgeous girl. You have any idea how much that turns me on?"

"I might need some convincing." Her voice is soft in the mornings, her hair fanned out around the pillows, her body small and warm under my arms.

Angling my hips, I slide into her from behind and groan as her tight heat envelops me.

In Russia, she told me she had a five-year birth control implant and, if possible, the sex is even better between us bare. I'm consumed with filthy thoughts about coming inside her, and she outright demands it now.

As God is my witness, there is nothing hotter than a good girl who gets very naughty in bed.

My hands wrap around her and cup her tits, her hard nipples pushing into my palms as she arches her back.

She turns her head. Our lips meet over her shoulder before she whimpers into my mouth, "Make love to me."

I growl and pull her body in tighter, sinking as far into her as I can get, though it's never deep enough. It'll never be deep enough. "You want it slow, baby?"

I can't stop my smile as she whimpers her 'yes.' This is her new favorite thing, this slow, passionate burn where it feels like we're two candles melting into one. It's her appetizer, as soon as she gets off like this, she begs me to take control, to fuck her hard until she loses herself in the surrender.

Lately, she wants the slow and quiet before the rough and dirty. I want to give her all of it.

Love isn't a sufficient word anymore for how I feel about Em. Love was ten or so steps behind whatever ethereal dimension I'm flying through these days.

"Touch yourself," I breathe into her ear as I take her hand and move her fingers over her clit. With a deliberate and torturous pace, I continue pushing into her, then slowly dragging out.

As if on cue, because I know her body better than I know my own, she rocks her hips and starts pushing, grinding hard backward into me. I'm so turned on watching her, feeling her spear herself onto me, using me to get herself off, that I let her. I guide her hips and help her.

I revel in everything that she is and the fact that she's mine.

Just like old times, Emily was there to pull me out of my depths of despair in Singapore. She drew me back above the surface where buried demons don't exist. It's funny what having someone believe in you can do, how they can salvage you from your darkest hour.

She's the only one who has ever loved me even after I made a mistake. The only consequence was that she loved me even more. It snapped something inside of me, something ancient and frayed that wouldn't believe she could love me.

She lit the wick on fire, and it's burning at both ends, now. For the first time in my life, I feel like I deserve her, that I can be worthy of her. And I will be.

Emily tenses and starts shuddering around me, begging me to come with her, to fill her up. Her words undo me like they always do.

In every way I know how, I tell her how much I love her as she clenches and cries, then collapses in my arms.

As the rain continues to come down and she looks out the windows, safe and tucked into me, I can't think of anything in the world that is worth getting out of bed for.

Except, maybe Em's stomach, which has just rumbled louder than the thunder outside our walls. I chuckle, and she throws the covers back, the loss of her heat and skin making me growl.

"Get up, I'll make you eggs," she starts piling her hair up onto the top of her head, stretching her naked body out before me like the goddess of seduction and temptation and everything that makes men lose their goddamn minds.

"Get back in bed, I'll make you come again," I counter.

"After, today is Eggs 101."

I put a pillow over my head and grumble. She's been on a kick teaching me to cook basic food, forbidding Liam from bringing over the prepped meals I've sustained life on for the past several years.

I have no intention of ever cooking my own eggs, and I'm grumbling about it, but she knows as well as I do that I'll be in the kitchen with her in a matter of minutes.

I can't pin place where it was, exactly, that I handed over my balls, but I haven't seen them in weeks.

Never been happier.

"I'm going to jump in the shower, then I'll be right there."

Fifteen minutes later, I'm in the kitchen, as promised, but paying no attention whatsoever to the omelet instructions.

"You're killing me with these damn pajamas," I kiss her neck from behind while she whisks and talks about Gordon Ramsey's eggs and why they're the best. Something about the heat and the creme fresh, molecular gastronomy.

I'm fondling the penguins on her pajamas instead, which are wearing headphones and eating popsicles. Obviously.

Dressed up to the nines in silk and heels can be hot as hell—but dressed down, when a woman is comfortable and casual, that's another level of sexy.

"You're awfully handsy this morning," she says as she pours the eggs into a skillet.

"Penguins get me hot," I run my hands down her sides and rest them on her hips. The truth is that I just need to be touching her at all times. If my hands are on her, she is real, she's here.

"Uh-huh," she ignores me. "See all the nice, fluffy layers in here?" She slips the omelet onto a plate and makes a point to show me her master creation, her own kitchen-based composite she made out of nothing.

"Everything is an onion to you, layers upon layers, something out of nothing."

"Not nothing, lots of little somethings that are better together. Eat," Emily hands me my omelet, and we sit at the breakfast bar together, watching the lightning outside.

I'm suddenly feeling pretty impressed with myself with a smart, gorgeous woman in my bed every night, our apartment filled with her moving boxes and a damn fine omelet in front of me.

She catches me smirking, so I say what I'm thinking, "All those smart guys in college had you right next to them all those years, but here you are."

"Hmm, I guess you're just lucky," she teases me with a roll of her eyes.

"Nope, luck has nothing to do with it. I won."

"Oh, that's right, because everything is a competition."

"Isn't it?"

She shrugs and swallows down a gulp of coffee, "Maybe. I wasn't exactly putting myself out there, so perhaps they never had a fair chance."

"See, I think they never had a chance to begin with."

"I'm glad your ego is back, and while I am not encouraging it, you're probably right." She starts gathering up dishes, but I put a hand on her wrist to stop her because that's the deal—she cooks, and I clean —so she sits back down to continue.

"No one else ever stuck. They weren't you. When I say I'm not like this with anyone else, I mean everything," Emily waves her arms in a circle to make her point. "I don't feel like anyone else has ever known me or accepted me the way you do."

"I know what that's like."

"I know you do, and I love you for it," she pops off her stool again and kisses me.

"I love you more." Because this is the kind of shit that I say nowadays. I'm never going to hear the end of it from Dante.

"I don't know about that, but I do know if you don't stop strutting around half-naked, we're never going to get all these boxes unpacked.

The living room is full of stacked up moving boxes, each meticulously labeled, color-coded, and organized. Emily has moved so many times in her life that she has a system and, I'm pretty sure, a spreadsheet. I know better than to mess with it.

"Tell me what color goes in what room. I'll move them all."

"You don't have to do that."

"I'm a man, Em. I lift heavy things to impress women. That's my job."

A few hours later, about half the moving boxes have been broken down. The rest are all in the correct rooms, and Emily has been busy unpacking while I worked out and get started on the dishes now.

She has music on throughout the apartment and is bopping around, singing, while the rain comes down hard, the river rising outside.

Dante texts and asks if we're partying tonight, I tell him to fuck off. I am shockingly domestic these days.

"Can I make some space in the master closet?" Emily calls from the bedroom.

I turn the music down and answer her back from the kitchen, "Yep, of course."

She actually doesn't have that much stuff, a byproduct of her professional moving skills, and the fact that she left most of it behind in the states when she came to Cambridge. Klara offered to sell her furniture and anything she left behind, so we had the place boxed up and ready for the movers in one day.

Ninety percent of the dishes are loaded into the dishwasher when I hear a crash in the bedroom, and Emily yells a string of expletives. "I'm okay, just dumped a shelf," she calls.

I dry my hands off and make my way to the walk-in closet to make sure she hasn't killed herself, and sure enough, the top shelf has all but collapsed. There are shoes, boxes, a couple helmets, clothes, shit everywhere on the floor.

She's kneeling on the carpet trying to clean it up, apologizing like it's her fault, while I try and fix the shelf above our heads.

I'm so focused on the shelf I don't even notice when she goes quiet. It isn't until the I register the change in her tone, the breathy whisper of her voice, that fear and panic race up my spine. I don't even have to turn around to know how much I've just fucked up.

"Cole, what is this?"

Don't turn around. This isn't happening.

"What. Is. This." Her whisper isn't just surprise, fear, or panic now. Anger is seeping into her, her voice is shaking.

Despite every cell in my body willing me to keep my back turned and not acknowledge what I know she's looking at, I let the shelf continue to dangle and turn my body toward her. I position myself in the doorway so she can't run.

I force myself to glance down and see what she has in her hands.

Dozens of letters spill out of an overturned shoe box. Articles, photos, and printed emails cover the floor, Emily's hands flipping through them all, trying to make sense of it all.

I wish any of it made sense, that I could explain it away. But there is nothing I can say or do to chase these demons away, this time.

"What the fuck is this, Cole?" She rages at me.

"I didn't want to hurt you," I manage to creak out.

"What are all these letters, why do you have letters from my mother?" She rips one out of its envelope, her hands shaking. I want to pull it away like it's a hot pan that's going to burn her fingers, but there's nothing I can do.

The portal to her hell has just opened up.

I don't even know which letter she's reading right now, and it probably doesn't matter—they're all terrible. She looks at me, her head jerking back, and her face twisted up in confusion, her eyes growing glassy.

"I, I don't understand," she whimpers.

"I never wanted to leave you, Em. I love you. I've always loved you."

"You love me? What the hell is this? Why do you have this?" She holds up a copy of an award she got at MIT for building a mini eco-friendly thermodynamic engine.

"It was," I hesitate because fucking hell, there is no right way to say it, "it was part of the deal."

"The deal?" She says the word like I'm the biggest piece of shit on the planet. "And this?" She holds up a framed photo of her graduating from MIT, her wearing a black gown and waving her diploma proudly over her head on stage.

"I took that picture," I mumble as I stare at the carpet wishing it could swallow me up. It's framed because it sat on my nightstand for so many years until I had to put it away when she showed up at my door.

"What do you mean you took it?"

"I was there."

I was always there, no matter how much it killed me to be so close to her, to watch her, to not be able to be a part of the life she was excelling at. I had to stand back and watch because at every opportunity, there she was, succeeding at everything she ever did because I wasn't around to drag her down. "I was so proud of you," I mutter, and, for the first time that I can remember, I feel my eyes watering.

"You were there, like, like some sort of fucking stalker? And you didn't say anything? Why? Why would you do that?" Emily is shaking, and her face is red. She's breathing hard. All I want to do is hold her and make it go away. Fix it. But it's going to get worse.

"I'm sorry. I thought I was doing the right thing," I hang my head.

She keeps rifling through the box and pulls out packets of "research" her mother sent me. She holds up a psychology paper entitled *Reality Check: Sex Crimes are Genetic,* and then another titled *Sex Offending is Written in DNA, Studies Find.* There's dozens of them. "Where did you get this crap?"

And here's where it's going to get worse for Emily, and thus, for me.

"Your mother sent them."

"What? No, she didn't. Why would she do that? My mom loves you."

I can see the confusion in her eyes, and it guts me. I never wanted to take her family away from her, no matter how much I hate them. No matter how much they hate me.

She goes back to the letters, her hand covers up her gasps, and she wracks with sobs reading the confirmation of what I've been trying to keep from her. All the emails, all the letters poisoning us against each other. Years worth.

"Has she been calling you, Cole?" She looks up at me, tears streaming down her face, daring me to answer.

"Not for a long time, but recently again, yeah."

"I don't understand, this isn't right. Why would my mom do this? None of this makes sense. How could you not tell me this? How could you keep all of this from me?"

"I didn't want to hurt you," I repeat and try to explain, but she cuts me off, caught somewhere between livid and destroyed.

"You were never going to tell me? You were just going to let me go on thinking everything was okay?"

"I tried to warn you, but I couldn't make myself do it, I couldn't make myself hurt you like this. Look at you," I call out what I knew was going to happen, Emily's world is turned upside down, the illusion pulled out from under her.

I can't stomach the thought of Emily experiencing even a fraction of the pain I went through because of my family, much less do it to her. No one should have to feel the kind of pain that comes when your parents willfully destroy everything you love. It's not something you get over.

Emily's voice elevates another octave and her face grows impossibly red, "You could have stopped all of this! Six years ago! We could have worked through this *together* years ago! Instead, you left me. You let me live a lie and you've still been lying to me! Were you ever going to tell me, Cole? You know what, never mind, fuck you!" She screams at me and throws all of the papers, the photos, in their box. She tucks it tight to her body like it's a treasure chest instead of Pandora's Box. "Get out of my way!"

"I know what I should have done, but I did what I thought was best. You were in school. You hated me, but you were doing exactly what you were born to do. You're asking me now why I couldn't hurt you even more? I can't do that, Em. I won't do it."

"Get out of my way," she tries to shove me, but I don't budge. I can't let her go. I can't lose her again.

"I've felt nothing but shame and regret for six fucking years, and I could not hurt you more. Take your family away from you, prove her right that everything I touch is toxic and I'd ruin your life," I point to the letters. "I won't fucking apologize for not hurting you more."

"You promised me! You promised you'd respect my decisions, but you've been lying all along! All of you! You've made a complete fool of me!"

"No…"

"Yes! I've felt naive, ugly, plain, nerdy, a thousand things. But I have never felt *stupid* before. Before now. Let me leave, move."

"I can't, Em. Please." If I move out of this doorway, I could lose her forever.

"Move," she wails at me, her face bright red, a vein in her temple pulsing. "Or are you going to *force* me to stay here *against my will*?"

Her eyes squint. She says the words with so much venom it nearly brings me to my knees.

"Oh fuck, come on, don't say that shit."

"Move."

I step out of her way, willing my bones and muscles to move against everything they instinctually want to do—keep her here safe with me forever—and she brushes past me out of the closet.

Watching her storm away, I chase her down the hallway, my heart racing and panic pumping through my arteries. Her horrible words reverberate through my ears. "Jesus Christ, when did you become so fucking cruel?"

She spins around, strands of brown hair wet from tears, and stuck to her face, "When you ripped out my heart and made me this way!"

"Where are you going?"

"Away from you!" She's still clutching the shoebox full of nightmares and tries to put shoes on with shaking hands before she grabs her car keys off the kitchen counter.

"Don't leave. It's pouring, you're not even dressed," I'm grabbing at any excuse, but it's true, she's still in her pajamas, and the rain is coming down in buckets now.

"I am not staying here with you, stay away from me!"

"Then I'll leave, you stay," I say, putting up my hands, offering her some space to cool down. She can't drive an hour back to Cambridge in this weather.

"Yeah, you've got a lot of experience in leaving, don't you? Do you need my parents to make an excuse for you this time, too?"

I run my hands over my face and bite back the anger bubbling up inside me, my lizard brain desperate to call her out on the hypocrisy, for making me believe she didn't think differently of me, making me think that she could love me despite everything.

When I open my eyes, she's almost to the front door.

"If you leave now, Emily, you're doing it with the knowledge that I don't want you to. When I left you, I thought I was doing the right thing. I know I was wrong, but I was eighteen. I thought I was helping you. Right now, though? You're an adult, and you're walking away knowing you're hurting me. Hurting *us!* That isn't what you do to someone you love." I make air quotes to drive my point home. "There's no way for you to rationalize running now."

Her chest heaves for two breaths, just enough time for the pit in my stomach to consider the possibility that she will stay, and we can work this out. Just enough time to allow hope to sneak in. There's so much more to tell her.

"I was smart enough to make my own decisions then, and I am smart enough to make them now." She reaches for the doorknob as tears run down her cheeks harder than any thunderstorm outside.

"You know what?" I put my hands on my hips, and adrenaline surges through me, knowing this will be the fight of my life. "You want to give up control, surrender to me, make me chase you around, wear you down? Fine. Fine, baby. Let's do it. You will *not* win."

"What? I'm not... you're insane!" She screams. "Do not come to Cambridge, do not call me, leave me alone!"

"No, goddamnit, I will not leave you alone. I lost you once, and I will burn this fucking world to the ground before I let you go again! You can fight all you want, Emily, you can push me away and say terrible, shitty things—and fuck you for that—but I promise you will not win!"

Her eyes are enormous, and she's clutching the shoebox like it's going to save her.

I pace to her, she takes one step back for each of mine forward until her back is up against the door. Resting my elbows on the wooden door aside her head, I look down at her.

"I love you. I have always loved you. I waited six years, and I can do another sixty. You need to run from me right now, baby? Go ahead. I fucking dare you."

Pushing off the wall, I take two long strides back from her. She was out of her mind and not even hearing me, at least now she's caught off guard and might come to her senses.

The look in her eyes says she's thinking about it.

I try to convey with my own that I'm dead serious—there's no fighting this between us anymore, and I will spend my every last day on this earth fighting for her.

Don't think, Em. Just feel.

"I hope you're happy. Now I have no one, just like you." And then she grips the doorknob again, twists it, and shatters my heart into a million pieces as she turns and runs out.

Twenty Six

Emily

The alarm on my phone goes off, the buzzing and noises breaking my blank stare at the bedroom wall. I turn the alarm off and ignore the long list of texts, missed calls, and notifications.

I haven't looked at any of them. I don't need any more lies.

In desperation, I tried the twenty-four-hour trick Cole taught me. I gave myself twenty-four hours to wallow like he did. I barely moved from my bed the whole time, and wallow, I did.

Unlike for him, hour twenty-five feels no better for me. I can't switch it off like he can. I'm not built like that. Maybe I don't have the discipline or the strength, or maybe I just don't have the will anymore.

I have absolutely nothing, now.

I don't even have my clothes or belongings. They're all at Cole's apartment. I'm still in the same pajamas in my empty Cambridge bedroom. If I didn't leave my bed here, I'd be lying on the floor like an even bigger loser.

All the little mementos, photos of him, those are all gone, too. There is literally nothing left to cling to.

I'm too embarrassed to call Makenna. I wouldn't know where to start with Klara. Every few hours, I can hear her stop outside of my bedroom door, listening to hear if there are sounds of life inside, then she moves on, smartly leaving me alone inside my chamber of misery.

My parents—I don't know what to do. All I feel for them is anger, betrayal, rage. I would never believe it if I didn't spend all night reading through every letter and email I found in Cole's closet. They're scattered across my room like shards of broken glass that pierce my skin each time I move.

My whole life, I was the smart girl. I had that going for me if nothing else. It was my identity. But now, I've never felt so stupid.

For six years, I've been played. I've been a marionette dangled on strings, pulled all around the world by puppeteers.

And for what? Why is it so goddamn important to my parents that Cole and I stay apart? How could he let them manipulate us like this? If he loved me, he wouldn't have let it happen.

My skull throbs with every beat of my pulse. My eyelids are swollen and raw. Still, I'm drawn to the letters and emails, the horrible, destructive words before me laid out by the woman who gave me life.

```
Cole,
Or should I call you Stanley? Emily said you called her
last week. We were able to undo your harm, once again, not
that you seem to care. Every time you call, email, text
her, she regresses. YOU ARE HURTING HER. It's not bad
enough I have to live with what your sick family has done
to me, I will not watch Emily suffer, too. Do us all a
favor and jump off the London Bridge while you're over
there. STAY THE FUCK OUT OF OUR LIVES!!
Ava
```

```
Cole,
Attached is a photo with her new boyfriend. He's a PhD
student, will be a pediatrician. Look how happy she is.
She's on the Dean's list again this semester. She loves
her new dorm and has a host of amazing friends in her
life. She hasn't spoken of you in over a year. You're
doing the right thing, I'm proud of you.
Ava
```

```
Cole,
I don't know what game you're playing, but this needs to
end. She cannot work with you. How could you be so stupid?
Haven't you learned anything over all these years? You're
still you, nothing has changed. Stop avoiding my calls,
email me back.
Ava
```

Bile creeps up my throat again as I reread everything for the hundredth time. All these years, it was my dad who was hellbent on keeping Cole and me apart. But even he never said such horrible, manipulative things. Mom was supportive, listened when I talked about Cole, watched his races, kept up with his career.

It was all lies. She was manipulating me as much as him.

Like an idiot, I fell for it. I told her everything about Cole, my new job, and it only gave her intel so she could hurt us worse.

Why? How could she do this? She knew how badly I was hurt when he left. She knew my pain when he stopped calling, when never wrote me back—all the letters he never got. She must have intercepted them after I put them in our mailbox.

My fingers are shaking when I push the call button, but I can't call Ava right now. I don't even want to refer to her as my mother, right now.

I call the Major General.

"Sweetheart?" He answers after two rings.

I can hear sounds of the military base in the background, engines whirring, soldiers barking out orders.

I haven't spoken to him in months, but the sound of his voice enrages me.

"What the fuck, Dad!" I've never spoken this way to my father, no one has. Grown men, battle-hardened soldiers, live in fear of the Major General. But I can't control it, it comes out on its own, like a burst dam.

There's a pause, he's clearly caught off guard, which is unprecedented. Nothing gets past the Major General. No-one gets the jump on him.

"What's wrong? Are you okay? I'm at work, sweetheart."

"I don't give a shit where you are, DAD," I growl the word. He's as far from a father to me right now as Ava is a mother, as far as I'm concerned.

"I suggest you remember who you're speaking to, Emily, and tell me what is going on." I hear him cover the phone and issue an order to someone nearby, then the sounds in the background grow faint like he's walking away to get privacy.

Good.

"I am your daughter! How could you do this to me?" Tears stream down my eyes, my voice shakes.

As angry as I am, I'm so hurt. But I can't deny there is also a little girl still inside of me who is panicked and filled with fear speaking to her father like this.

I have been a prisoner to fear for so long. Fear of disappointing him, fear of hearing his harsh words and tone like I'm one of his cadets who has just screwed up. Fear of any minor imperfection, anything less than excellence.

I feel sick.

"Do what? What are you talking about?"

The Major General is many things, but stupid is not one of them. It infuriates me all the more that he's going to play dumb now, treat me as if I am dumb. "You know exactly what. You and Mom have made me feel stupid for the last time. How could you?"

He pauses, "He told you."

"He told me everything," I lie. I know there's more. The letters prove it.

"I only want what's best for you, you know that."

"I don't believe you. You're lying. You and Mom are nothing but filthy, manipulative liars! For six years, you watched me suffer for nothing!"

"You will watch your tone, Emily Walker," he barks. "It wasn't for nothing, Cole had good reasons for leaving. I have good reasons for wanting him to stay away from you. That's the end of it."

I leap up from my bed, my fists balled. So help me, if he were in front of me, I would pummel my fists into his face. "The end of it? Who the hell do you think you are? You don't get to decide…"

"I am your father, and you will talk to me with the respect I deserve!" There is no longer any 'Dad' on this call, I know. There is only the Major General present now.

"Respect is earned, DAD, and you don't deserve any of it! You or Mom, I hate you both!"

"You will not hate your mother over this. It isn't her fault. You hate me if you need to, not her," his voice drops an octave.

"Why? What the hell are you talking about? What is wrong with both of you?" My whole body is shaking, I don't know if I'm going to throw up or explode.

"You should come home," he huffs, and I can picture him in his uniform, hands on his hips, issuing commands. "We'll talk all of this through."

"I am home. This is my home."

"Your home is with your mother and I. You've graduated, and it's time to come back now. We'll work all of this out."

I laugh, maniacally, "I don't have a home with you. I'm a grown woman, for starters. I don't even know where you might be living this month. Are you still in Delaware, or have you uprooted everyone yet again?"

"Don't be such a child."

The words 'fuck you' hover over my tongue, but something deep inside of me won't let them come out. Years of conditioning, I'm sure. "I'm not coming back home, ever. You and Mom are dead to me," I say instead.

"Don't be ridiculous. We'll come there, then. I can get some time off in the next month or two, I'm sure."

"Oh, how nice of you to prioritize me in the next month or two, Daddy. It's really all you can do, given the fact that you've ruined my life." I have never called the Major General 'Daddy' in all of my years, but it seemed especially hurtful, and I want him to hurt right now, hurt as much as I do.

"No one has ruined your life except that degenerate boy," the loathing in his voice makes my skin crawl.

At that moment, I wish I had no self-respect at all. I wish I was the kind of person who would use Cole because I would run right back to him just to piss off my father at this point.

I'd marry him and get knocked up just to spite him. Have a million goddamn Ballentine babies and ram them down his throat.

They're utterly ridiculous thoughts, and I know it. They're born of panic and rage and the insatiable need for revenge. But I'm not impulsive or stupid, no matter how much they all want me to feel like it.

I won't let them manipulate me anymore.

And I never used Cole, never.

"You will not contact him, or me, ever again. Do you understand me, DAD?"

He chuffs, like I'm nothing. Like I'm silly, frivolous, stupid. "On what planet do you think you live? *You* don't issue commands to *me*."

"I am not one of your soldiers. This is my life, mine! And you are no longer welcome in it. You or Mom. I am blocking you both. I won't see your calls. I will not open any letters you send. If you show up here, I will call the police. You feel me now, Major General?"

My hand covers my mouth, my eyes go wide. I can't believe I just said that to him, I don't know where it came from. I didn't know I had it in me. I am so grateful he can't see me because I am shaking like a leaf, despite the gangster words my lying mouth spews forward.

"Emily!"

I say nothing, and he shouts my name again.

"Goodbye, Dad."

I disconnect the call, and I block him.

I block my mother.

I don't block Cole.

My traitorous fingers won't physically push the buttons, and I hate myself that I can't do it. My fingers grip the cell phone until I think I might crack the screen, and then I scream and spike it into the carpet.

Cole may have been able to flex his shoulders and take a deep breath after twenty-four hours of wallowing, shrug it all off at the final hour.

But for me? Hour twenty-five brings only rage, anger, and an unbridled sense of betrayal.

Twenty Seven

Suzuka Circuit, Japan

Cole

"I can't tell you how glad I am to have you back, man," I clap Edmund on the back and take a seat on the outdoor loveseat atop our motorhome in Japan. Liam and Dante are both here, too, welcoming Edmund back to his first race since he took leave.

"Well, after Singapore, it was clear I'm still needed here," he laughs.

He's lost a bit of weight and looks tired, his complexion is pale, but we're all beyond thrilled that he had a nasty case of walking pneumonia and not lung cancer.

It's taking the sting off, just a smidgen, from the fact that Emily isn't in the garage this weekend. I expected as much, she's a runner, as much as she wants to believe that I'm the one who does the leaving.

Every argument or fight we had in the past, she'd run. And if she didn't run, she'd retreat back inside of herself, which was just as bad. I think she figured if she ran away from the situation, she couldn't possibly be bad at something or fail at it.

I feel Edmund staring at me while I gaze off into the distance. He purses his lips, "I didn't tell her, but she knows how she got the job. HR told her when she put in for leave."

I nod. "I know," I tell him while Dante and Liam sit silent, pretending this isn't awkward as hell. I've dragged them all into our mess, begrudgingly.

Dante showed up unannounced at my apartment, like he's prone to

234

doing, and saw the state I was in. If I wasn't drunk out of my mind, I don't know if I would have ever told him.

But I did, he knows everything.

We've been roommates, we've grown up from gangly teenagers to men together. We were ignorant jackasses racing karts when we met, and now we're both accomplished in F1. But it took this for me to spill my guts. The things I kept secret all that time poured out of me that night over bottles of bourbon.

I'm not sure how I feel about it, but I don't feel ashamed like I thought I would. Maybe Emily broke the seal. I figured, if she didn't judge me, others wouldn't, either.

But beyond that, if Emily can accept me for all the baggage I come with, I don't give a shit what anyone else thinks. As long as I have her, as long as she can love me, to hell with the opinions of others.

I am not Stan, I am not my mother. I am not the byproduct of the two of them, or their combined dysfunctions, crimes, or sins. I know it, and, as angry as I am over the shit Emily said to me, she knows it, too.

She's hurt.

Horrible words come out of everyone's mouths from time to time, it doesn't mean we believe them. Like stubbing your toe against the bedpost late at night, pain lace expletives come out of all our mouths when we're hurting.

Liam knows less. He figured out something was very wrong when I asked him to resume delivering prepped meals for me. I thought about asking him to take some to Cambridge too, knowing Emily won't eat when she's upset, but I didn't want to land him in jail.

Because Emily actually threatened to have me arrested. Or rather, Klara did.

After I gave her a couple days to cool down, I drove there to talk to her, to work this out. Klara met me outside and said she was given orders to call the police if she ever saw a Lamborghini, a Ferrari, a McLaren, a Bugatti, or 'any other car worth six figures' parked outside.

The competitor in me wanted to come back on a motorcycle, or in a thrashed Fiat. But I let her win this round.

I would be more insulted if Klara didn't add that she's to call the cops on any men who show up in US military outfits, as well, so I know we're all on Emily's shit-list.

Then Emily put in for official leave at Imperium.

But she didn't quit.

She hasn't blocked my number, as far as I can tell. It still rings when

I call, I can leave voicemails. My texts say they've been delivered. Google confirms I haven't been blocked.

She hasn't answered.

But this is the game we play.

I know it's anything but a game to her, right now, technically. Of all people, I understand the pain she's going through. It's taken me my whole life to deal with the feelings so I'll give her the time she needs.

But I meant what I said to her. As long as she wants me, and I think she does, there is no corner of the world that I won't follow her to. No amount of time or distance has ever been able to stop it.

I'll be miserable right alongside her, in different corners of the world, for as long as it takes.

"She's still working on the tires, too, with Tillman from Cambridge," Edmund tells me, knowing I'm always desperate for affirmation that I haven't lost her forever.

"Oh yeah?"

"Mmm-hmm, it's the other reason I came back early, even against the doctor's wishes," he coughs and proves his point. He's still on a mess of antibiotics and pills. If I weren't such a selfish prick, I'd feel bad he's here, not home in bed where he belongs.

"She's right about the bloody tires. They've gotten them all broken down and are running computer simulations now. It's not good," he continues.

"What do you mean?" Dante asks. This affects him, too. It affects all of us on the track.

"Not sure yet. Let's pray for dry races, though, boys." Edmund sighs and tries to make light of the situation, but we all know how serious it is. We all know Alessi is still laid up in a neck brace and going through physical therapy right now.

And he got lucky. The incredible safety advances in these cars are the only reason he's alive. The engineering marvels created by people like Emily.

The first thing Edmund did when he got back was cornering me, emphasize the accident wasn't my fault. I knew it, logically, but he knew it meant something to me to hear him say it.

"Is that why Olivier has been hanging around even more?" Dante asks.

"Probably," Edmund confirms. "Emily and Tillman tried going over his head at Concordia. Olivier isn't happy."

"I don't trust him," Dante huffs, crossing his arms over his chest.

"No one trusts him," Liam adds.

I don't know how deep this thing with Olivier or Concordia runs, but Liam is right. Everyone in the paddock is distrustful of Olivier. He's just too smooth, too slick, he gives everyone the creeps and sets off their bullshit-meters.

Twenty grand in tires, per race, per team. I didn't grow up surrounded by this kind of money, I know what it does to people.

And he knows Emily is on to him. Better safe than sorry.

> **Cole: Can you arrange for security for Emily please?**
> **Mila: Yes. One person?**
> **Cole: Two, unless that's too obvious. 24/7. I don't want her knowing they're there. She'll rip my balls off.**
> **Mila: I'm on it.**
> **Cole: Thank you**

She's going to be even more pissed, but I'll take pissed and alive-and-well over the alternative. If they're good, she'll never even know they're there.

"Okay, gentleman, I need to rest. I'll leave you to it," Edmund stands and heads down the stairs leaving Dante, Liam, and I alone on the rooftop.

I lean my head back on the sofa cushion and look up at the familiar stars overhead. It's late morning in London, she isn't even able to see the same constellations as me right now.

I don't know how much time has passed, lost in my thoughts, when Dante interrupts, "It was more fun with the brown-eyed girl here."

"It was," Liam kicks his feet up on the coffee table and settles in like we're going to have a friendly group discussion about this now.

"We aren't doing this," I whisk that notion away.

"I'm not doing anything," Dante quips sarcastically, "nothing at all."

"What can you possibly contribute, anyway?" I challenge, "There is absolutely no sage advice you can offer. You're the biggest whore on the planet."

Liam nods.

"That's true," Dante agrees.

Idiot.

"I'm still jealous I didn't get to steal the tire with you guys," Liam adds.

Dante tells him the story again, laughing and moaning as he impersonates Emily pretending we were having some kind of orgy in the garage restroom.

I feel myself smiling as I remember it.

"Why the hell are you smiling? You're supposed to be miserable. You're supposed to miss her. Hell, *we* miss her. Did you know that she thanks Siri when she asks her phone to do something? Who does that?" Liam furrows his brows at me.

"I'm plenty miserable, thanks for asking." And yes, I know that she thanks Siri, even when she has to push the button a second time just to say it.

I just have enough faith in Emily, in us, that she'll come back. She knows I'm not going anywhere. She now knows I've always been there, even if that makes me a stalker, or whatever she called me.

She forgets she told me she was doing the same thing for six years. Watching all my races, reading all my interviews, prowling the social media posts I made solely because I knew she'd see them.

She's smart, and she has inner strength she underestimates, but she's stubborn. Pushing her now will only make her feel more manipulated and defensive. Even if she doesn't believe in herself, I believe in her, and I have to believe she'll come back.

I just pray it isn't another six years.

More than anything, I hate that she is all alone right now. It's the worst feeling in the world. You can surround yourself with hundreds of people and still feel so utterly, devastatingly alone.

I wish she could see the stars right now and know she isn't.

"If you two want to help, maybe just text her and just let her know you miss her." She doesn't want to hear from me, but she does have other people who care about her. She should know that.

I may have called Makenna a couple of days ago and asked her to do the same. We ended up yelling at one another, but I'm still glad I called because Emily hadn't told her anything.

Makenna wanted to blame me, which is fine. That's her job as Emily's best friend to support her, throw me under the bus, and call me every name in the book. I get it.

It is ironic, though, that those privileges do not extend to men. If men speak that way about a friend's recent ex, they'd expect a swift, blinding, and well-deserved fist to the face.

Regardless, I may have told Makenna off for planting nonsense in Emily's mind about me cheating on her the day she raided our apartment.

The only important thing is that she's not alone, wallowing in despair, throwing up, starving herself, crying all day and night.

Emily and I process pain differently. She wants to sit with her grief and analyze it endlessly, make sense of it. She wants to strategize and plan her way out of it, every move needs to be calculated and precise.

I get pissed.

That's the only reason I've made anything out of my life in the wake of the shitty upbringing I endured. It's my ultimate revenge on Stan and Kristy. Every time they hurt me, I use it as fuel.

So if Liam really wants to know why I'm smiling right now, it's because I'm pissed. Pissed at this ridiculous situation that's been foisted upon us. Pissed that Emily is not beside me right now.

And those responsible are going to pay in the way it hurts them the most—by watching Emily be happy. Doing whatever the fuck she wants, wherever the fuck she wants, and with whoever the fuck she wants.

That's just always been with me.

"You did it. That is P1! P1 for you! Excellent race, just outstanding, Cole," Edmund's voice comes through my helmet as I cross the finish line in first at Suzuka.

"Yes, yes!" I scream, pumping my fists into the air, adrenaline flowing through me like fire blazing through dry brush.

Lennox pulls up beside me on track and gives me the finger, then a thumbs up a second later before he pulls away, and I start my victory lap. We were neck and neck the last ten laps, it was intense and so much goddamn fun.

"Thank you, Edmund," I say through the radio, so grateful he's back with us. "Thank you, everyone. Everybody back in the factory. You too, GG, thank you."

I know she's watching the race, probably holed up in her bedroom right now on her laptop. She's never missed one. I hope they play my audio on live tv for her.

Pulling the car up to the Number One sign in parc ferme, I pull myself out of the car and stand on top of it, pumping my steering wheel into the sky while the fans go nuts. Flags and signs waive in the crowd. The Japanese fans are notorious for being the best in the world, and they don't let me down.

The team sucks me into hugs and slaps my helmet over the crowd barrier. The only thing that would make it better is if she were here, kissing my helmet again, telling me she was proud of me.

The television crew points a massive camera in my face, and I take the lens in both of my hands. I bend my head down in front of it and point my gloved finger right at the spot on my helmet where her initials are printed. This time they're in big, bold, red letters, *EW*, emblazoned across the top.

I tap the initials, pound my fist over my heart twice, and point at the camera.

That's for you, baby.

I'm here.

I'm never leaving.

I'm coming for you.

Twenty Eight

Emily

It's early Sunday morning in Cambridge, but late afternoon in Mexico City and also in Texas, where Makenna is joining us from Skype.

For the first time, I am not hidden in my bedroom while I watch Cole's race. It's playing on the small television in our apartment with Klara by my side and Makenna joining us, virtually.

We have coffee, she has margaritas.

I'm off the Sailor Jerry now, at least.

I'm pretty sure Klara was ready to have me committed if I didn't fess up to what my problem was. I don't blame her. I had to borrow clothes from her, a phone charger, even deodorant—until I was able to drag myself into the land of the living to replace the bare essentials I'd moved into Cole's apartment.

The least I could do was explain to her what was going on with her psycho roommate. That's what I'm telling myself, anyway.

More likely, I finally broke under the weight of having absolutely no one to commiserate with, and I'm only making excuses for my uncharacteristic transparency.

For her part, Klara pulled her shirt up and showed me the scar from her first love—a very, well, unfortunate tattoo on her lower back with his name in script lettering. She said it's been years, but she still can't bring herself to have it laser removed.

Then she shrugged and said she really hasn't had the money, anyway.

But I know what she meant.

Money could rain down from the heavens, yet Klara would not remove that tattoo any sooner than I would block Cole's phone number despite his daily texts and voicemails that I do not respond to.

"He's going to win this one, too, isn't he?" Makenna watches her TV on her side of the world, asking lots of questions along the way. She hasn't invested several years of her life into F1, like I have, to know what's going on half the time.

"Yes, he is," I don't want to jinx it, but I know it in my bones.

Cole has several laps to go, and Lennox is right behind him, again. Lennox only has to finish in fourth or better this race to clinch the championship, but that won't stop him from trying to beat Cole.

It's not in their blood to give up, even when winning is a foregone conclusion.

They simply don't know how.

Edmund and I have been communicating, even though I'm still on leave from Imperium. We've made some setup changes to the car that appear to be working. I can see it in the way Cole is driving confidently, sticking the car exactly where he needs it, trusting it will do exactly what he wants it to do.

And, it's not raining in Mexico City today.

"Did you book your tickets yet?" Klara asks, drinking her black coffee. Since she got fired from the cafe, she says we're off fancy coffee, and she never wants to see a cappuccino again.

"No."

"Come on," Makenna argues. "You know you're coming."

I bite my cuticle and pretend to ignore them while I watch the race. Next weekend is the US Grand Prix in Austin, Texas, an hour away from Makenna. We'd always planned to meet up there this year.

That was before.

BC. Before Cole.

"You're going," Klara agrees. She and Makenna start ganging up on me.

Cole gains another quarter of a second on his lead. Dante may be able to snag third.

"I need to work on the tire models."

"Oh, stop," Makenna rolls her eyes.

"No, it's true. It's important. And look at him. He seems to be doing fine without me, anyway," I wave my hand toward the television, knowing I am acting like a petulant child.

I'm not proud. But I am hurt.

I hate that I say such awful things when I'm hurt. I'm not going to do that anymore, no matter what. I'm better than that. I will be better than that.

"You will go. Or I will kick you out," Klara points her finger at me.

"Kick me out? I pay all the rent!

"Tomato tomato," she replies, using the same pronunciation for each word, blowing the colloquialism again.

I stifle a smile down. I don't want to smile yet. I want to wallow more.

"I wish I had a few days to sit down and think all of this through, but I don't. I've been so busy. We're so close on the tire models."

"For the love of God, Emily. There's nothing to think about," Makenna fixes herself another margarita on screen. I can't see it, but I know she's rolling her eyes at me.

"Nothing to think about? I just lost Cole, my family, probably my job. I need time to figure out what I'm going to do."

I know things aren't over between Cole and me—they never are. I doubt they ever will be. But I still don't know what will happen and now I have no safety net in place, at all.

"You did not lose Cole. The man is like Pepe le Pew chasing you around the world. There's no getting rid of him."

"What is Pepe le Pew?" Klara asks.

"He's a French skunk," Makenna answers. "He's forever chasing a lady skunk around even though she pretends she doesn't want him."

"That's not exactly accurate," I argue. I've always wanted Cole. I can't say it aloud, but there's a single neuron in my brain right now admitting that I like it when he chases me.

Maybe it's my way of seeking revenge on him for leaving. Making him prove that he wants me.

Maybe it just turns me on.

I hate that Cole knew that about me before I was aware of it. And that he called me out on my bullshit. For being a control freak and needing to have everything planned and organized, I feel like I'm being swept out to sea right now.

"He smells bad? Like a skunk?" Klara asks, still confused about Pepe le Pew.

"No," I can't help but laugh a little. Cole most certainly does not smell bad.

"Your mom tried calling me last night, by the way," Makenna lets slip like it's an afterthought.

My smile falls. Now Ava's going to harass Makenna, manipulate her? What's next? Maybe she can try to run Makenna out of my life, too.

"I didn't answer, then I blocked her ass," Makenna adds. "Rotten witch."

"Fitta," Klara sneers. If I understand her correctly, she just called my mother the c-word, in Swedish.

I don't argue with her.

"I still don't understand it all." And since I'm not speaking to my mother, the Major General, or Cole, I may never understand it all.

"Why don't you just ask him for the whole story?"

"Because I don't trust him. I don't trust any of them. They've all been lying to me for years, in cahoots. How can I ever trust any of them again?" I wrap a throw blanket around myself and try not to break down again.

I focus on the race instead.

"Oh look, Dante's in third," Makenna claps, and the television cuts to a shot of the Imperium garage cheering.

I catch a glance of Liam and Mila on screen, big smiles and high-fives going around. I miss them. I miss Edmund. I even miss Dante, as immature and ridiculous as he is.

There's only a couple of laps to go.

Cole's doing it, he's going to win. He's going a million miles per hour, putting his trust in his engineers, his mechanics, his team.

The irony is not lost on me that I am not doing the same.

I look at the phone in my lap and re-read the last message he sent me yesterday.

Cole: Don't think Em, just feel. Your brain is big, but your heart is bigger, let it lead. Just this once.

And then he attached the video we made in his kitchen, but I'm obviously not sharing that with Klara or Makenna. Too much information, indeed.

With one lap to go, Klara, Makenna, and I grow silent then explode into cheers when Cole crosses the finish line. He did it again.

I hold my breath as he lifts both hands off the steering wheel and pumps them into the air, the car still flying around the track.

I will have bloody stumps for fingers if I keep chewing them, put your hands back on the steering wheel, Cole.

They don't play his post-race radio message this time. Lennox has just won the championship, and the announcers are consumed with talking about that, playing Lennox's team radio conversation, instead.

I'm happy for him, and Mallory, but I want to hear Cole's voice. I'm desperate to know if he'd mention me again.

He and Lennox do a victory lap together—it's touching. Then they all pull into parc ferme, Dante in third place, too. They're all out of their cars, hugging, jumping, being swallowed up by their crews who are congratulating them all.

I should have been there.

"Oh shit, he's going to do it again," Makenna whispers.

My breath stills.

Please do it.

But, as the camera faces Cole, he pulls his helmet off instead of pointing to my initials like he did at the last race. His balaclava comes off to reveal his sweat-soaked brown hair and piercing blue eyes. He rips his earbuds out.

As the camera begins to pan away from him, he suddenly pulls it back to him. He shoves his helmet right at the lens. It's a Dia de los Muertos design this week. He points at one of the skeleton characters with a big red heart inside its chest, the initials *EW* inside it.

He did it.

And then...

"Oh my god," Klara leans toward the television.

"Is he..." Makenna whispers.

He is.

Cole is full-on kissing and licking the lens of the camera. Flicking his tongue up and down it like, like he's having sex with it. Everything is blurry on the television now because the live camera is covered in Cole's lips and saliva.

The British commentators on television are laughing and apologizing for the suggestive gesture they've just shown to the entire world. You can hear women in the crowd squealing in appreciation. I'm pretty sure the collective panties of everyone in attendance just dropped.

Then the screen cuts to a second cameraman's feed, one that is not obscured by lips, tongue, and raw sex appeal.

"I'm going to Texas," I state, all of us in a trance watching the television.

I don't say it loud or proud. It's a whimper and not a scream, but I said it.

I have no idea what will happen. No matter how many scenarios I plan for in my head, I can't predict it. For the first time in my life, I am making the decision to walk into the unknown.

I'm terrified.

But I'm even more terrified of what could happen if I don't.

I don't want to go back to my life of hiding, being closed off, never taking any risks because there might be consequences, being so afraid of everything. Being afraid to fail.

What if I fail now, at the thing I care about the most?

Twenty Nine

Emily

This is a far cry from the private jet.

Nice things are nice. Were nice.

"Sir, this plane is not taking off until you turn off your cell phone," The flight attendant chews out a jackass in a business suit next to me. The plane hasn't even taken off, yet he is man-spread into the already cramped leg quarters of my economy seat.

"Yeah, yeah," he waves her off and continues his call with total disregard for the other two hundred people on the plane. With complete disregard for the fact that my flight is cutting it close to race time, as it is.

"Sir!" The flight attendant yells.

I need this plane in the air.

Now.

While waiting to board, Professor Tillman called. It's the unknown type of silica Concordia is using. It's not bonding right with the silane or the rubber. He said he sent me an email with the materials broken down, and now, I just need this godforsaken jackass next to me to get off his phone so that we can take off. So I can connect to the wifi and finally solve the riddle.

Because I put my phone into airplane mode, like a civilized person.

Like a good girl.

"Lady, never mind my phone. Go get me some pretzels or something," the jackass waves his fingers at the flight attendant.

That's it.

Look away, good girl.

"Get off your goddamn phone!" I bark at him.

He wrinkles his nose at me. The flight attendant smirks.

"Hey," he protests when I rip it out of his hands, turn it off myself, and hand it to the flight attendant.

"It's off. Please, can we go now?"

She nods, smirks at the jackass in satisfaction, and continues down the aisle with his confiscated phone in her hand.

"You can't…"

"Sit there and shut up," I kick his leg back into his own seating area.

"Crazy bitch," he mumbles.

Yeah, you have no idea, asshole.

As soon as we hit cruising altitude and are given the all-clear, I drag my laptop out from my carry-on and pay the extortionate wifi fee.

Despite the jackass leering at me the whole time, I spend hours dissecting the raw material composition Professor Tillman sent. I forgo pretzels, free wine, and bathroom breaks. I dismiss the possibility of deep vein thrombosis from sitting in one position for hours on a long-haul flight.

The answer is here, I can feel it. If the wifi speeds weren't so freaking slow, this would be quicker.

Silica is crazy-expensive. Still, I'm surprised to see the lab report showing that Concordia isn't using pure silica from sand. They're using something else, something synthetic. For the price Concordia charges, the tires should be made of gold, diamonds, and unicorn tears.

Googling the only remaining chemical structure in the list of unidentified compounds, I find it.

Corn husks? What the hell.

There's one company that had been experimenting with sourcing silica from rice husks, but that didn't work. And corn is different.

"Lady, let me out, I need to piss."

I think better of it, then I begrudgingly stand to let the jackass out. "Hurry up." Jerk.

Finally, he sits back down and buckles back in. His legs stay in his own area.

Adding the corn husk silica to the computer-simulated tire model, I start running the program. At first, it seems stable enough.

When I throw added heat at it, or wear, the structures start breaking down, though. The molecules in the corn silica start changing, disintegrating, the molecular bonds to the rubber break down.

When I throw water into the mix, I'm not sure if it is my heart that just dropped or the plane.

Real silica reduces chemical incompatibility between the tire and water. But Concordia isn't using pure silica. Concordia is using cheap corn husk silica, its molecules are not as impervious.

The jackass next to me grabs his armrest. It was the plane that dropped, after all.

The overhead seatbelt light dings, the plane rocks.

"Ladies and gentlemen, the pilot has turned on the seatbelt sign. Please return to your seats while we pass through some turbulence. We're expecting some rough weather for the rest of the flight, so please keep seatbelts fastened for the remainder of the flight. We should have you in Texas within the next hour."

Rough weather? Oh, god.

I pull up the weather page on my laptop. There's a huge red, swirling storm graphic circling over the bottom half of Texas.

No, no, no.

I can't call anyone, warn them. All I can do is text or email over this shitty wifi.

> **Emily: It's corn husk silica. It's breaking down in water. You have to warn them!**
> **Doc: Corn? That's unheard of.**
> **Emily: It isn't stable under extreme conditions. It's very unstable in wet conditions. Please, it's raining in Texas. They can't use these tires! DO SOMETHING! I'M ON A PLANE!**
> **Doc: I'm calling Concordia now.**

I check my seatback pocket for the sick bag because I may very well throw up.

"You aren't gonna barf, are you, lady?"

"Shut up!" I scream back at the jackass.

Do not barf, Emily. Pull it together, this is your time. You got this.

I send a group text to everyone in the paddock that I have in my contact list. Cole, Edmund, Liam, Mila, Mallory, Dante, the other engineers, and mechanics. I text everyone I can think of. I email everyone I can think of.

Anyone.

Half of the texts can't be delivered because their phones aren't on global plans, or they can't receive the wifi-based iMessage, but some of them go through. It has to be enough.

I get some replies, mostly all question marks. I mumble to myself, curse at my phone. The jackass next to me is clearly now afraid for his life with me, the crazy bitch, sitting next to him.

I demand someone find Edmund and show him my texts.

Cole, answer me. Please, answer me.

Thirty minutes until we land, that gives me enough time to get to the track and stop this before the race, worst case. I don't know how, but I will make them listen to me.

"Ladies and gentlemen, this is your Captain speaking. Got some bad news for you. It's raining pretty hard in Austin right now, so we're going to need to circle for a bit until conditions settle down. Should have you on the ground safely in a jiffy, just sit tight."

I bang my head onto the seat in front of me and grip my tray table.

Those rotten assholes, Olivier in his expensive suit and Rolex... They have money for that but use cheap materials to save a few bucks in their product. The very product that separates all the F1 drivers from the unforgiving asphalt they speed over at two hundred miles per hour.

I remember what Mallory said—*There are no ethical billionaires, Emily.*

For the next hour, I refuse to have a panic attack. I don't have twenty-four hours, but I set the alarm on my phone, and I give myself five minutes.

When that alarm goes off, that's it. Panic and fear are going to have to take a backseat because I have to prepare and focus on the race.

It goes off just as the flight attendants ask everyone to put their seats in the upright position and stow their large electronics. We're finally descending and landing.

When I push past the crowd on the jet bridge and race through the Austin airport, I feel the phone in my back pocket vibrating and catching up with cell signals, but there's no time to stop running.

Exiting the airport doors, Makenna is waiting for me in her car, just like she said she would be.

"Go!" I cry out as my door shuts behind me. It's pouring buckets, and everyone is driving like a complete idiot like Texans have never seen rain.

"Jesus, I should have brought an arc," Makenna says as she navigates the traffic to the circuit. It's not that far, but with my flight delay, there are only twenty minutes left until race time.

"Go around them, drive on the shoulder, hurry!" We aren't going to make it in time.

Cole has not texted me back. Mila must have his phone already because he's getting ready to get into the car.

I cannot bear the thought of something happening to him, ever. But not like this. Not with us not speaking.

Me, not speaking.

Finally, pulling into the Circuit of the America's VIP entrance, we park the car in a grassy area that is now a swamp of mud and silt, and we race to the Pit Crew security gate.

They scan my access badge, and I fly through the metal turnstile.

"She's with me," I tell security when Makenna tries to follow.

"Badge?" The security guard asks again.

"I don't..." Makenna stutters. We're both dripping wet, waterlogged.

"I said she's with me," I argue.

"Lady, ain't nobody getting through without a badge."

"It's okay, go," Makenna says. "I'll go through the regular entrance."

I feel bad that she will have to now walk half a mile to the regular entrance, in the pouring rain, but there's no choice.

"I'm so sorry," I tell her.

"Go get him," she brushes me off.

Turning away, I slosh through puddles and run through tunnels and service roads trying to get to the team garage. I don't hear the cars on track, yet it's well past the two-o-clock start time.

It's been twelve hours since I left London and days since I've slept. I am frozen to the bone, soaking wet, starving, and exhausted. But, all I can think about when I finally make it to the Imperium garage is that I don't see Cole.

His car is there. So is Dante's.

"Edmund," I cry when I see him sitting on the pit wall under the awning and in his Imperium rain jacket.

"Emily!" his eyes are wide like he didn't expect to see me. "Good lord, you look like a drowned rat!"

"Why aren't the cars running? We can't use the tires, Edmund. The silica, it's corn, they're not safe, where's Cole, the molecular bond..."

"Slow down, slow down," he interrupts my panting.

I'm so out of breath from running so far, I can't get a full sentence out. Edmund starts leading me into the garage, where a couple of mechanics and engineers are sitting around looking bored.

"Cole?" I squeak out, taking deep breaths and trying to suck in oxygen.

"They're all in the motorhome. The race is delayed due to weather."

"Oh, thank god," I put my hands on my knees and bend over. "We can't use the tires, Edmund. We can't…"

"I know, everyone knows."

I stand back up, look to him for explanation.

"Concordia pulled them all, hours ago. They said they just discovered a manufacturing defect. We'll all be running last season's tires."

"What?"

"Then someone showed me your texts a while later. Figured you might have had something to do with that," he smiles.

Professor Tillman. Doc. He got to them. He made them listen.

"Where's Olivier?"

"Haven't seen him since this morning," Edmund shrugs.

As we stand together in the garage, everything catches up to me. I feel like I've just run into a brick wall, stopped dead in my tracks, and got smacked upside the head with a sack of emotions.

My shoulders heave, my eyes start running, and I can't breathe through my nose for the snot. I don't even know what I'm feeling—I'm just feeling *all* of whatever it is.

"Oh, I know that look," Edmund wraps his arms around me as sobs rock through my body. "Your adrenaline just wore off," he chuckles.

I blabber into his raincoat, unintelligible words. I'm so tired.

"Come on, let's get you some tea. You're freezing."

Edmund starts walking me back to the motorhome under an umbrella and supporting me as I walk. I've never felt so exhausted in my life, I don't know what's wrong with me.

Is this how Cole feels? Invincible during a race and then like a limp noodle after? No, he's used to this, trained, and conditioned for it.

When we finally make it into the motorhome, Edmund tells the first person he sees to find Cole. Someone brings me a cup of hot tea, which I wrap my hands around but am too tired to bring to my lips.

"Jesus, what the hell?" I look up and hear Cole yell. He storms into the room, his race suit on but undone to his waist.

"I, I'm sorry. I, love. So. Mad," I manage to squeak out about every third word I want to, but the tears and the sobs are unmanageable.

He's okay, he's safe. He's not in a hospital like Alessi was. It's over with the tires.

But I can't relax because there's so much more to resolve.

He scoops me up in his arms and holds me tight to his chest, starts walking away with me. "Get Liam," he says to someone in passing.

I'm carried up a flight of stairs, and then he puts me down on the bed in his room. He starts pulling my waterlogged, cold clothes off me. When I'm naked down to my bra and panties, he wraps his blanket all around me in a cocoon and runs his hands all over me to warm me up.

"You're okay," I utter as my senses start returning to me again.

"I'm okay," he confirms. "Race hasn't even started."

Liam comes into the room and hands me a huge, warm drink. "Drink all of that," he orders.

I lift it to my lips. It tastes like dirt. It's gritty, salty. My face puckers.

"Drink it," he barks.

Jesus, is this what Cole has to put up with?

I swallow it all down and hand him back the cup because he's standing in front of me like a drill sergeant. He feels my forehead and cheeks, looks in my eyes, checks me out all over. Cole stands a foot back and watches, his eyes worried and following Liam's movements.

"You're a wuss," Liam finally announces.

"What?"

"You're dehydrated and pale and exhausted. Buck up, buttercup. When's the last time you ate?"

Cole snickers behind him like this is funny.

"I don't know, yesterday, I guess?" I've been so busy, the tires, the last minute airplane tickets, buying a suitcase and the things I needed for this trip because I still don't have any of my belongings.

He shakes his head at me like he's disappointed with my non-existent exercise and nutrition plan. "I'll go get you some food. The drink help?"

I nod, hesitant to admit that his sludge water did, in fact, make me feel better.

He closes the door on the way out, and I'm left alone with Cole.

My moment of truth is upon me, the situation I could not predict or plan for. I have no strategy, no contingency plan, no flow chart outlining possible decisions.

"I don't know where to start," I tell him.

He rubs his eyes with the heels of his hands, then gets me some of his dry clothes out of his closet. He silently slips an Imperium hoodie over me and helps me into a pair of sweatpants.

"Are you mad?" I ask. I know he is, of course, he is. If I had scripted this all out in my mind, as usual, I would have had a better line to start with.

"Yes, I'm mad," he answers.

"I'm mad, too."

There's a moment of silence.

"What do you want, Emily? What do you really want?"

"I don't know," I admit. "I'm so confused."

"Confused about me, or the situation?"

"Both." I wish he would touch me, hold me, but he's leaning against his desk watching me, his eyes dark and flickering between mine.

"I'm sorry I said such terrible things to you," I tell him. "No matter what happens, I am sorry for that. I didn't mean it."

"What do you mean 'whatever happens?'"

I wave between the two of us, "I mean whatever happens with us. You're mad, I'm mad, I don't know."

"I love you, Em, but you're pissing me off," he lets out a big sigh.

"Why? I'm just being honest."

"No, you're not. You know as well as I do that there is no 'whatever happens.' You know the outcome here as well as I do."

"No, I don't."

He moves in front of me, bends down and puts his hands on my knees, looking me in the eyes, "Then tell me what it will take to get through to you. Fucking tell me, and I will do it."

"How do I ever trust you again? Can you make me do that?"

"I don't know. Can you believe me that I did what I did because I was trying not to hurt you? Do you know me well enough to believe, in your heart, I would never hurt you?"

"I don't even know the full story, Cole."

"You know the full me, though. Those secrets would only have hurt you. They *did* hurt you. I'm not saying I was right, I'm asking you to understand why I couldn't do it to you."

"But they were my decisions to make. I had a right to know."

He stands back up and puts his hands on his hips. I know he's as frustrated as I am.

"It wasn't my place to tell you. It's my place to protect you, to prevent you from being hurt to begin with. And if I can't, to be there for you and pick up the pieces."

There's a knock at the door, and Liam opens it. "Eat this," he hands me a protein bar. "And umm, security is here to see you."

"Me?" I ask.

He nods.

It must be Makenna. I stand up to follow Liam, but Cole takes my hand and holds me back a second.

"Do you love me?"

"Yes," I tell him. I've never needed to think about that question.

"Then trust me, let that be enough."

I tuck my chin down and head out into the hallway to follow Liam. Cole is right behind and makes me eat the protein bar on the way.

Thirty

Cole

Liam leads us into a conference room on the main floor. A sizable security guard is standing in front of the door.

This is really not a good time for Makenna to interrupt things, but the race will hopefully start soon, anyway, so it's not like this is going to wrap itself up in a neat little package right now, regardless.

I don't know how long I have to wait for the neat little wrapped package anymore.

"Ma'am, these folks say they're here with you," the security guard says to Emily, sheepishly, like he knows better.

"Folks?" She asks.

He opens up the door, and Emily takes a step back, slamming into my chest.

"What are you doing here?" She yells at her parents, who are waiting inside the room like vipers ready to strike.

Jesus Christ, of all the days, of all the times.

There goes all hopes of a neat little wrapped package. Unless I wrap it all up for them. Throw a bright red bow over the sucker, signed, sealed, and delivered.

"Ma'am, are these people your guests or should I escort them off the property?" the guard asks when he sees the look on her face.

I vote for throwing them the fuck out, but...

Not my decision, apparently.

Emily squares her shoulders off. I can see her inner badass rise to the surface. It's always been in there, the snake-bashing, welding, up-for-anything adventurous badass girl inside. It just gets scared and retreats from time to time.

I put a hand on her hip, just letting her know I'm here. I'm not going anywhere. I'd give anything to fix this for her, if only it were possible.

Let the badass out, baby. I'll catch her if she falls.

"They are not my guests, but I'll speak with them," she answers the guard. "Can you wait here, though?"

"Of course, ma'am," the guard answers.

Emily and I walk into the conference room, and she shuts the door.

The Major General is puffed up in full military dress, and Ava stands several feet away from him, her face more wrinkled and aged since I last saw her.

Both of them are standing with their feet out wide like they're here for a fight. If they think they've come to take their little girl home, lock her back up in an ivory tower and clip her wings, they're sorely mistaken.

They'd be underestimating her, as usual.

"Ballentine, leave us alone with our daughter," the Major General orders.

"He's not going anywhere," Emily argues.

Good girl, baby.

"Looks like I'm staying," I smirk.

"You have exactly five minutes to tell me everything and say what you came here for. Or I will have security escort you out, then call the police, like I told you I would," Emily tells them.

She's staring at Ava, though, hard. Like she's going to get the wrath of what's bubbling just below Emily's skin.

I don't know what they've told her, or how much she's talked to them since she ran out of our apartment. But I have nothing left to hide.

Frankly, I want to hear it out of their filthy, lying mouths. I've waited a long time for the satisfaction but was content to never have it if it meant sparing Emily.

"Emily, let's go home and discuss this in private. Please, honey," Ava's fake, saccharine voice makes me cringe.

"Clock is ticking," Emily sneers.

"Your father and I only wanted what was best for you, like we've always said."

"I saw the letters, the emails, the horrible papers you sent him. Give it up, Mother," the word mother practically spits from Emily's lips.

Ava's face falls, and she leers sideways to her husband. His face is steel, unchanging, but he's used to interrogations, I suppose. "I'm sorry you had to see that, but... he... he," Ava looks at me, pure hatred and disgust in her eyes.

I suppose it would be much easier to believe that I'm the degenerate bad boy who stole their untarnished daughter away instead of looking in the mirror. I get it. I've done a lot of looking in the mirror, and for a very long time, I hated what I saw, too.

But, I did the work. Paid the piper. Now it's their turn.

"Oh no, don't look at me, Ava. This is all on you two. Go ahead, tell her," I stand behind Emily and taunt them.

Fuck their shit. After everything, they think they're still going to stand here, in my house, and manipulate Emily?

"Tell me what?" Emily asks. When they don't answer, she slams her hand down on the table, "You have four minutes."

They stay silent. Cowards.

"Either you tell her, or I will," I direct my stare at the Major General. "This ends today."

His jaw ticks.

I push, needle him. "Now or never. You gonna man up or not?"

"What does this have to do you with you?" Emily asks her father, who is standing as still as a statue, but I can practically feel his blood pressure rising from here.

"Emily, no marriage is perfect," Ava starts.

I can't help it—I laugh out loud after Ava starts that ridiculous sentence.

Ava pulls out a chair and slumps into it, so dramatic.

I warned him I'd tell her if they didn't. Guess they think I'm bluffing. "You see, Emily. Your parents, so exacting in their standards for you and me, the ones who spent years telling you *I'd* be the one to cheat on you, ruin your life... Well, it turns out the two of them just like to project their bullshit onto everyone else."

"Stop," her father barks. Apparently, he is going to man up at the eleventh hour. "Emily, I had an affair. I cheated on your mother."

Ava turns away from him in her chair and closes her eyes, playing the victim. She may have been a victim at one time, I'll give her that. But, now she's just as bad.

"What? When?" Emily swivels her head between her parents.

"It was a long time ago, it meant nothing, and it's over. It's all over with now," the Major General says.

"Oh come on now, tell her the rest of it," I add. We're not doing this for six more years. It's all coming out now. I will help Emily get through it, and we'll bury it, bury all of it.

The Major General can't help it and takes one step toward us, arms clenched at his side like he'd like to beat me senseless. I'm sure he would. Good luck, fucker.

"He slept with Kristy," Ava blurts out, but she does it with such malice it's clear she's said it only to hurt her husband, to shame him in front of his daughter.

"Kristy?" Emily exclaims and turns her head to me. "Your mother?"

"Yep," I confirm.

"What the fuck?" Emily roars. "Are you, are you serious?"

The Major General must not feel he owes her an answer because he just locks eyes with her and grinds his jaw.

"What the hell is wrong with you?" Emily barks at him.

"Watch your tone. I am still your father."

I don't know why fathers say this crap as if their sperm entitles them to respect, love, or loyalty even after they treat their kids worse than mafia bookies. Nothing is inherently owed to him, nor Stan.

Emily may share the Walker name, but that's their only claim over her. And even that will one day be changing, if I have anything to say about it.

"When?" Emily asks them both.

"Around the time *he* left," Ava points at me.

Emily pauses and tilts her head, "That's what all the arguing was about back then. You weren't fighting about *me*. You were fighting about each other."

"He humiliated me, Emily. Sneaking around with that filthy home-wrecker for months," Ava's fists are balling up, the real Ava is coming to the surface.

"Months!" Emily shrieks.

"This changes nothing, Emily. Everything I said to you remains true," the Major General attempts to retake control of the conversation.

"You're, you're the biggest hypocrite I've ever met! Of all the people, Dad, Cole's mother? Jesus, just, why?"

"If you had listened to us, to begin with, none of this would have happened, Emily. Your father wouldn't have had to go over there to drag you home, speak to Cole's father. We would never have met them! None of this would have happened if he, and his disgusting family, had never come around. But you had to defy us and go slumming," Ava glares and points at me.

"Slumming?" Emily cries. "All these years, you lied to me, you told me you loved Cole. You were just lying to me, manipulating me!"

"Don't you blame her, Ava," I shake my head at her. That shit is over.

"I don't, I blame you!" Ava roars.

"Me?" I chuff. "From where I'm standing, it looks like I'm the only one of the three of us who isn't a lying, cheating, piece of shit."

The Major General rounds the table and gets within inches of me. I move Emily behind me, instinctually. Unlike one of his soldiers or Emily, I'm not threatened or intimidated by him. Long ago, I stopped being afraid of being hit.

There are worse feelings.

Internal bruises are infinitely more damaging than those on the outside.

"Cole, what do you mean—of the three of them?" Emily asks from behind me.

"Confession time, Ava," I call to her. "And what did you do to get even?"

"Mom?" Emily pops out from behind me and stares, with huge eyes, at her mother. The same mother who dares to call mine a whore.

"I was going to be a chemist, Emily. I see myself in you every time I look at you. I threw it all away, I gave everything up and ruined my life for a man, a cheater. The same as you are doing with Cole. I couldn't let you do it," Ava cries, tears in her eyes now.

"Ruined your life? What about me? You had me! What did you do?" Emily begs her.

"Ava, you stay quiet," the Major General barks, still staring me down.

"Enough goddamn lies!" Emily screams. I'm sure half the motorhome can hear us yelling.

"I got even. I had an affair, too," Ava admits as she wipes tears away. "Are you happy now?"

"With who?" Emily asks, her face wracked with confusion.

Ava can't lift her head and waves her arm towards me then lets it flop onto the table in front of her as her answer.

"Cole?" Emily looks to me with haunted eyes, full of fear at what Ava has just suggested.

"Fuck no," I take my eyes off the Major General to look at Emily and shake my head. Jesus, one thousand times no.

"His fucking father," Ava admits in defeat.

"What? STAN?" Emily lets out a shriek that could break glass.

I don't blame her. It's like her very own episode of Jerry Springer in the motorhome right now.

"It was just revenge," Ava tries to rationalize. "Stan was the person your father hated most in the world at the time. Don't you see? Cole's whole family is toxic, Emily. Everything they touch gets ruined. It's in their blood."

Emily puts her hands over her face and mumbles several words, but few coherent sentences, "I can't, this is, what the fuck…" It goes on for several beats. "This is so messed up."

It's breaking my heart for her to go through this, but it's the only way forward now. No more secrets, no more lies.

Take your Jerry Springer guest star asses home and fuck the hell off.

"As trashy as my parents are, and I do not deny that," I interject, "it seems to me that you two really take the cake. And yet you both *still* sit here trying to blame me, blame Emily. Still!"

"Shut your mouth," the Major General shoves me in the shoulder.

"Stop it," Emily yells and tries to step between us, but I hold my hand up to keep her safely away.

"You had the nerve to nerve to tell me *I'd* cheat on Emily, that *I'm* just like my father. It was always *you two* projecting your shit onto us. Well, guess what? I'm not eighteen anymore, and no one believes your bullshit anymore. I'm not my father, I never have been. I may have left Emily—because of you two sick fucks—but I won't make that mistake again. I had my reasons, what the fuck were yours?"

He shoves me again, harder.

"I'm not gonna hit you if that's what you think you're doing— provoking me. Trying to taunt me into proving your point, like you did," I point to Ava, "Let me tell you, Major General, it takes a lot more balls *not* to hit someone, most days. Maybe you should get some."

The veins on his forehead are bulging. Ava stands up and tries to wrangle Emily out the door while she protests and pushes her mother away.

"How could you do this to me?" Emily shoves her mother away, "You're both sick, disgusting! I will never forgive you, either of you, for what you've done! I was miserable for six years. Six fucking years —it was all because of you two!"

The Major General rounds the table again and tries to take Emily's arms.

"The horrible things you said to Cole, I will never forgive you!" She continues wailing on him.

"Emily, stop this. It's over now, we're going home," he wraps his hands over her biceps.

"Don't touch me," she screams and pulls away from him.

That's all I need to hear.

"Get your fucking hands off her," I warn him.

"You stay out of this. Goddamn it, why won't you go away!" He screams at me.

Emily jerks away from her father, "You have made me feel so stupid, but what you two have done—cheat on one another, lie to your daughter, manipulate me, try to destroy Cole's worth—you two are the stupid ones. All of these years, I lived in fear of disappointing you. Well, guess what, *you're* the disappointments. *You* are the failures. Not me!"

Her fingers poke at them, her face flushes in anger. Her chest is rising and falling. For the first time, the Major General and Ava stand with mouths open. Their good girl has left the proverbial building.

"Security!" Emily calls.

The conference room door bursts open immediately. The guard and Liam both storm in. Other people who'd started congregating around the door, listening to the shouting match, try to disperse like they haven't been caught eavesdropping.

"Emily, what are you doing?" Ava protests.

"Please remove these two from the property, they're trespassing and not welcome," she tells the guard. "Please make a note that this man assaulted Cole," she adds and points to her father.

"Emily, stop this. We are your parents," the Major General argues.

"No," she roars. "Parents don't do this to their children. You were supposed to love me. All you've done is lie, manipulate, hurt. I never want to see you again, never!"

The security guard and Liam start to shuffle Ava and the Major General out as professionally as possible, but I'll have both their asses handcuffed and dragged out of here if I need to.

Emily buries herself in my chest, her fingernails clutching my fire suit.

As much as it pains me to say it, I ask.

"Are you sure this is what you want?" I whisper into the side of her head. "I know you're upset, I'm sorry. I'll support whatever you decide, but be sure. You don't get over having no family, Em."

"I'm sure," she mumbles into me, then lifts her head and looks me in the eye. "Please make them leave."

"Okay," I kiss her hair. "Get 'em the fuck out," I call to security.

The guard nods, and her parents are shuffled out of the motorhome, both absolutely incredulous as if Emily has no right. As if she owes them loyalty in the face of so much selfishness, total disregard for her wellbeing.

Liam comes back a few minutes later. I'm still holding Emily, who is quiet and still in my arms.

I can only imagine how much is racing through her mind right now.

"Hey, I'm real sorry guys. But the rain is letting up, they're predicting we'll start the race in twenty. We need you in the garage in ten."

I nod at Liam, and he gives us a minute.

I keep my arms wrapped around Emily, rubbing my hands up and down her back. No one knows better than I do what she's feeling or the road she has ahead of her now.

"All I ask is that you don't run. Let me help you, in whatever capacity you decide. I can't take it if you run right now in this condition. I'll lose my mind."

She doesn't answer me. Goddamn it.

"Okay, if you really want to run, at least know that I *will* chase you. But is that really what you want?"

She shrugs her shoulders.

"Why did you move to London, baby? Why did you pick Cambridge, of all the schools in the world?"

Emily lifts her head to see me, her eyes are red and swollen, but her tears have stopped. "It was a nine-month master's program. It's one of the best…"

"Be honest," I interrupt her. "Look me in the eye and tell me you didn't move to London to be near me."

She looks away.

So fucking stubborn.

"Em, we can talk until the cows come home, and we will. But you either know it by now, or you don't. I've made it as clear to you as I can." I pull her face to look at me, "I love you. I am desperately, pathetically, hook, line, and sinker in love with you. I always have been, I always will be."

"I know. I love you, too. I just…"

"Just nothing. That's all that matters. Let's lock this shit down."

"Cole, we need to go," Liam announces from the hallway.

"Will you be here after the race? Or do I need to start the search party now?"

She tries to hide her face, but I can see her lips quiver a tiny bit, "I'll be here."

I kiss her head, thankful as hell for her answer, and start heading out of the room.

If she stays, we have a hell of a path to forge to move ahead. But we'll get there. She just needs to stay, to let herself feel, not run from it.

She can crash against me as hard as she needs to, over and over like a wave breaking on the shore. I will be the boulder that is always there to absorb it like she was for me.

"Cole, wait," she calls at the last second.

I turn my head back.

"Good luck, have fun, go fast, come back to me, then take me to bed, I love you, I'll be waiting for you."

Thirty One

Emily

My phone alarm goes off, and I sit up from Cole's bed in the motorhome.

I gave myself thirty minutes. A bit more than five, because I think I deserve thirty freaking minutes to process what just happened. But less than twenty-four hours because I'm done wasting time.

So many years have been spent feeling afraid to fail, hiding away, not really living because I was scared of consequences. For what?

What the hell was the point? Here I thought I was so smart.

Cole has always had far worse consequences to deal with than I ever did. He lives, every single day, despite them. He doesn't hide or cower. He's out on the track right now doing what he loves, in the face of the most significant consequence there could be.

Cole could so easily have taken the bait and brawled with my father, but he's a better man than that. He's experienced so much violence but doesn't resort to it. *He* should be teaching cadets how to be real men.

Throwing his rain jacket over his clothes that I'm still wearing, his pants flopping around my ankles like bell bottoms, I make my way to the garage. I can hear the roar of the cars on the track.

My feet take me there, but my heart leads the way.

It's driving.

I may not always be able to feel and not think so much, but all I have right now are feelings. Because there is no science to truly explain people.

All the psychologists in the world could not put this Humpty

Dumpty family nightmare back together again.

And that's okay.

Because when I walk into the garage and Mila gives me a big hug, when Liam ruffles the hair on my head, zips my jacket up knowing I'm cold and makes me eat another protein bar—I feel it. When I look on the television screen and see Dante and Cole racing around the track neck and neck again—I feel it. When Edmund, the engineers, and mechanics, wave, and welcome me back—I feel it.

I feel it, and I know that family is not your DNA.

When I look at my cell phone, and I see messages from Makenna and Klara and Professor Tillman, I know family is not genetics. It isn't what makes up the cells in your body or the blood that flows through your veins.

Family is the people you choose to surround yourself with. It's the people who are always there for you when no one else is. The ones who accept you, exactly as you are. In your perfectly imperfect form.

A bunch of little somethings that combine to make something greater, something stronger and more stable than any of the individuals.

My family is here, my real family, and it's led by the man currently going entirely too fast on last season's tires that I know absolutely nothing about.

C'est la vie, as Oliver the weasel might say.

Cole knows what he's doing, he'll always come back to me.

And I'm done running from him.

Mostly. Being chased is kinda fun in the right circumstances, like naked-time.

Imagining it, I grin as I grab a set of headphones off the charging rack. Before I forget and turn into the worst friend ever, I ask Mila if she can locate poor Makenna, who is god-knows-where wandering around the track, and she sets off to find her.

Then I throw my headphones on. I don't want to sit at my regular engineer station today, though, and I'm hoping Edmund will humor me.

"Do you think I could pull up a stool?" I lift one side of his headphones off his head and ask him when I reach the pit wall.

"It would be my honor," he winks.

He seems healthier since the last time I saw him thank God.

"Thank you for everything," I tell him.

"We're the ones who should be thanking you. Every driver out there today is safer because of you, because of what you did."

"It wasn't just me," I blush. It was so many people. It was the same family who helped. The ones who believed in my crazy ideas and long-winded tangents about tires, materials, compounds, and chemicals.

"Celebrate the win when you get it, Emily," he reminds me.

"I intend to."

Edmund and I sit together with the other chief engineers and strategists, and we watch our boys on track continue to duke it out. I know they're having the time of their lives doing it.

The track is nearly dry now, and the sun is starting to peek through the overcast sky. It's time for both the drivers to make a pit stop to get off the wet tires and back onto slicks.

"Can I?" I ask Edmund.

"Yes, please. I had hoped for this, you know."

"What's that?"

"I'm old. I want to bloody retire one day. I have a wife I'd like to see more of. Travel with her when we actually have time to stop and see the sights. Play golf or some shit," he laughs.

I grin at him as big as I can. I don't think Edmund will ever be a golfer, but I like the thought of him relaxing and puttering about with someone he loves. He's taken care of Cole and Dante since they were just teens, and I'll be eternally grateful to him.

With that, I cue the pit crew to get ready and push the button on my desk to broadcast my microphone to Cole's car.

"Now that things aren't so wet let's get you slicked up. Box, box, box."

"Emily?" He responds half a second later.

"Copy that. Come in this lap so I can service you."

Edmund lowers his head, and his shoulders rack with silent laughter.

"What if I like it wet?" Cole responds.

"Plenty of wetness forecasted for this evening. Box, please."

"Jesus Christ," he mumbles back.

My face is beet red, and I don't dare turn around to see what's happening in the garage, but I can hear the crew laughing, even over the roar of the cars screaming past us.

The British broadcast networks are probably having a field day over this. I imagine they're apologizing for more suggestive content right now.

Cole's car comes in a moment later, and in the two-point-three seconds he has before the car launches again, he sees me out of the corner of his eye.

We've double-stacked the pit stops, and Dante flies in right behind him, then they're both gone in the blink of an eye.

The crowd is on its feet and screaming for Cole, the only American driver on the grid right now. I know he can hear them inside his helmet, see them waving flags in the stands, as he and Dante make their way through the pack.

We've made good strategy calls on the tire changes, and both have made up several places. They've cleared the back-markers, and their tires are heated up.

"How's the car feeling?" I ask him to make sure everything is stable before I give the next order.

"Car feels better now, feels like it's with me."

"Well, then open that baby up and give me everything you have. Push hard."

There's a long pause. And by a long pause, I mean maybe one-second because, in Formula 1, one-second is a lifetime.

"Uh, confirm if that was real or…"

Edmund laughs and pushes his radio button, "Bloody push, Ballentine."

"Not as much fun when you say it, Edmund," Cole responds.

The laps tick by, Edmund and I watch the data and run all the numbers. If he keeps the pace up, he may be able to win again.

"Can we turn the engine up?" Cole asks over the radio. He knows a win is in sight, too.

"We can. I'm turning it up right now, Cole."

I do actually change his engine mode, give him more power. But I have something else in mind, too.

"How's that feel?" I ask when I see his data change under the extra horsepower.

"Everything feels very right."

"I think it can feel even better."

"Oh yeah?" He chuckles, and I picture him biting his lip as he flies through the chicanes, the asphalt covered in bright red, white, and blue.

"Yeah. I think we should turn it up even more."

Edmund taps me, raises his eyebrows in question, and I give him the gesture for don't worry, I know what I'm doing. I don't mean the engine. He'll see in a minute.

"I think the car might blow up if you turn it on any more, *up* any more, I mean," Cole answers.

"Well, I think you were right when you said we needed to lock things down."

"Message unclear, come again?"

"Yes, please. Just as soon as the race ends."

"Em…" he warns.

I glance up at my television monitor, and I see the networks are broadcasting our radio messages. I can't hear what the commentators are saying, but clearly, they've all caught on to the unusual banter.

I feel like I'm broadcasting a version of Charlotte and Steel's torrid love affair here, but mine's better than fiction.

I check all of his data one more time. Everything on the car looks good.

I check the screen, he's in a good spot on track.

And then I give a huge middle finger to every fear of failure, every consequence, every minute of lost time we've wasted without each other.

"Cole?"

"Yes, GG?"

"The only place I ever want to run again is into your arms. I know what I want, it's the same thing I've always wanted. I'm locking you down, Cole Ballentine. Marry me?"

I can see all the heads in the paddock turn towards me, but I don't hear anything except the white noise in my headphones as I wait for his response. A thousandth of a second, twelve-seconds, four hours, I have no idea how much time passes because my world stands still.

Finally, his familiar, throaty voice is my ear.

"Baby. My gorgeous girl. I'm gonna marry the shit out of you."

I feel like I've just won the race myself because there are hands all over me, hugging me, patting me on the back, fingers mussing my hair up. Someone behind me wraps their arms around me in a bear hug and lifts me out of my stool for a second. The whole crew is cheering, and cameramen are racing down the paddock to capture the moment.

Cole's car zooms past us just in front of the pit wall, and he comes on the radio again, "For the permanent record, I'll be asking you again because I've waited six years to do it. And you're going to say yes."

"I will," I answer him, my cheeks aching from smiling so hard. "Right now, though, you win this race."

"Copy that, baby."

There are a dozen or more reporters and cameras pointing at me when Mallory arrives, pulls me off my stool, and we squeal like schoolgirls. "I get first dibs on the post-race interview," she hugs me again.

"Yes, yes," I laugh.

"Looks like it's going around," she holds up her left hand and shows me a beautiful diamond engagement ring on her finger, gleaming in the light.

"Oh, I'm so happy for you!" I cry and hug her.

"Right back at you."

Makenna and Mila come racing through the garage and join us. "Holy shit," Makenna screams. "It was on every big screen on the circuit!"

"Oh my god," I laugh.

Edmund taps my shoulder and points to the television monitor above the pit wall, "Last lap, bring your boy home."

I jump back on my stool. I've missed how Cole got into first place, but he's there.

"Two seconds to the car behind, Cole. It's yours for the taking."

"Get your ass to parc ferme, this is for you."

Edmund waves his hands at me with a proud smile, "Go, go!"

I give him a big kiss on the cheek, and I race my as fast as my legs will run down the paddock toward parc ferme where the winning cars will be pulling in any second.

The camera crews are chasing me, the other garages are shouting words of congratulations and putting their hands out for high-fives as I run past.

"Permission for celebratory donuts?" Cole asks. I didn't even realize I left my headset on, and I can still hear him, though I can't respond.

"Permission granted," Edmund answers.

I gaze up at a giant outdoor television monitor, and Cole's car is spinning around and around, blue smoke rising up the sides of his car. The engineer inside me can't even cringe watching what he's doing to those tires and his engine life right now.

I'm too happy to care.

Then he takes off like a rocket toward the pit lane and is pulling up to his parking spot before me.

I try to run to him, but FIA personnel holds me back because there are still moving cars, and, technically, no one is allowed to be in that area. But I'm right here, twenty feet away, as Cole climbs out of the car and looks around for me.

"Cole," I scream and wave while the FIA guy keeps one hand on my arm.

Cole's head turns, and he lifts one hand up and motions a finger for me to come to him.

"Oh hell with it, go," the FIA man tells me and gives me a little push on my back.

Cole lifts his helmet visor up a split second before I launch myself at him, wrapping my legs around his hips and my arms around his neck. His strong arms hold me tight while I take his helmet in my hands and try like hell to kiss him through it.

"I love you so much," I keep telling him and trying to kiss him, though the only thing I can connect my lips to is his nose.

He's laughing, and the corners of those gorgeous blue eyes are all crinkled up like he's sporting the biggest grin ever under his gear.

"Get this damn helmet off," I start pulling at his chin strap while the crowd grows around us. I'm oblivious to it, though. I just need my lips on his.

Finally, I loosen the chin strap, and Cole flips his helmet and balaclava over his head, both fall to the ground, and our mouths smash together.

One hand under my ass and one in my hair, he ravishes me hard as I squeeze my legs around him tighter, kiss him like my life depends on it—because it does—and tears start streaming down my face again.

Happy tears.

Incredible, beautiful, happy tears that wash away all the years of the ones that came before.

"God damn I love you," he smiles around my lips as my fingers run through his hair.

"Boy, I kind of hate to break this up," the official podium interviewer steps up to us with a microphone. "Can we cut in, offer congratulations, and get a comment?"

"Piss off," Cole answers, never making eye contact with him and continuing to kiss me.

The crowd roars in laughter.

"Umm, sorry again for the language, folks, hopefully, we were able to bleep that out in time, umm," the interviewer fumbles around.

I pull away and smile down at Cole, unwrap my legs from him, and slide down. He lets me but doesn't fully let me go.

This is his home crowd, this is his race. I want him to bask in it, enjoy it, let all of his fans celebrate alongside him. With his hand in mine, I raise it above us and point at him. The crowd goes nuts.

Cole climbs on top of his car and pumps his fists, waves to all the hometown fans in the crowd, relishes in the glory he's earned. I beam at him from the ground, so proud.

I'm watching Cole so intensely I'm caught off guard when my feet lift off the ground, and I'm being spun around in a circle.

"Making an honest man out of him, huh?" Dante cheers before he stops spinning me and puts me down.

"You're next," I tell him and give him a huge hug.

"Hell no, bellissima."

Cole jumps down from his car, and the interviewer swarms him, "We'll have to check the history books, but I think this may be a first. What an incredible day! We had a rain delay, an absolute stunner of a race, and then this! Were you expecting this at all, Cole?"

"Which part?"

The interviewer laughs, "Well, any of it."

"Then yes, yes, and yes," Cole answers.

"I suppose you wouldn't be an F1 driver if you weren't so confident, but you're saying you knew there'd be a marriage proposal over your team radio today?"

"No, but I did know many years ago that there'd be one, one day," he runs his hand through his hair then waves to the crowd again.

"Amazing, just amazing. Congratulations from all of us, you've given the fans quite a show today."

"Thank you to all the fans, thank you for coming out in the rain today, for all of your support. My team, everyone back home in London, thank you all so much. Now, if you'll excuse me, there's some champagne to be sprayed, and then I'd like to take my fiancé home," he winks at the camera, and the crowd goes wild again.

He walks away from the interviewer and speeds up to the podium ceremony while the other two top drivers answer their questions. I feel a little bad, but not too bad, that we've upstaged the whole thing.

Champagne sprays down on all of us below the podium after everyone is presented with their trophies. I'm drenched in it by the time Cole takes my hand, and we race back to the motorhome.

There's more cheering and clapping as he drags me upstairs and into his room. I expect him to pin me up against the wall as soon as he kicks the door closed behind him, but he's ripping his race suit off and pulling new clothes out of his closet.

"You didn't seriously think I was going to make love to my *fiancé* for the first time in the motorhome?" He asks when he sees my questioning eyes.

"I kind of did, yes," I laugh.

He pulls on a pair of jeans and stalks to me, takes my face in his hands, and whispers into my lips, "You thought wrong, gorgeous girl. I'll be damned if we walked through fire all these years not to do this right."

"Where are we going, then?"

"Wherever you want. I'm thinking we need a hotel suite for a few days, a private jet home, then I intend to do just what I said—marry the shit out of you. Immediately."

"Yes, please."

"Unless you want to get married here, in the States?"

"No, our family is back in London. Take me home."

Epilogue

December - London

Cole

"It's technically Christmas morning."

"It's 12:01 am, Cole."

"Exactly, Christmas morning."

Emily's back is pressed up against my chest, sitting in between my legs on the couch. An oversized wool throw over us keeps her barely clad body warm. Her fingers lazily trace up and down my thigh.

Just outside the windows, the city lights twinkle. Fat, heavy snowflakes have been coming down for hours, coating London in a thick, white blanket. It'll be gone tomorrow, but it's here tonight, and it's perfect.

"You know that saying, excited as a kid on Christmas morning? They're talking about you," she arches her neck backward into my shoulder. I press a kiss to her temple and breathe in the smell of her shampoo.

Even though the whole apartment smells like pine and gingerbread and cinnamon, I can still smell her when she's up close like this.

"We may have gone a little overboard."

"We, nothing. This is all on you. I purchased a *reasonable* amount of Christmas decorations." Her eyes twinkle, reflecting the warm glow from all the strategically placed, battery-powered candles.

We can't have real candles for fear the place would go up like a tinderbox if they got too close to one of the many decorated fir trees.

There's an enormous one—Big Mama—in the living room, before us. Em wants to decorate that one with ornaments from all the countries we travel to.

But there's another tree in every single room, I think. And on the deck.

I may have gone a little overboard, I'll admit it. I may have overcompensated, knowing it was Emily's first Christmas away from her parents.

But she started it, overcompensating for my first real Christmas, period.

Now, between the two of us, it looks like Santa's workshop up in here.

"Want more cider?" She asks before she stands, wraps the blanket around herself, and leaves me naked on the couch.

"Sure. Is there any more of that pudding left?" I ask as she walks into the kitchen. I take the opportunity to pick my pants up off the floor and slip them on.

"Christmas pudding, Yorkshire pudding, or figgy pudding?"

"I'll eat any pudding you bring me, baby." It's winter break, I can live it up. Besides, someone has to eat the metric ton of food in this place.

Emily's been cooking all month, including a few batches of 'healthy' sugar-free cookies that were a massive fail. She fed them to the ducks on the river instead of throwing them straight into the bin.

But food production and experimentation really ramped up earlier today for Christmas Eve dinner. I've never done so many dishes in my life.

I can't say I ever thought I would have a full house on Christmas Eve, but we did. Dante's not flying home to Italy until tomorrow, so he was here. Edmund and his wife stopped over, Klara and her new boyfriend. Emily issued an open invitation to anyone at Imperium who didn't have anywhere to go.

Between everyone who came and went all night long, we demolished a twenty-four-pound turkey and enough liquor to fill a river.

Tomorrow it should be much quieter, and I'm actually looking forward to that. I want to watch Emily and Danica open all the gifts under the tree, the heaping mound she scolded me for adding to every day. I can't help it.

I don't want to help it.

As I polish off another one of the puddings that Em brings me—no clue which variety this one is, but it's delicious—she snuggles back into the couch with her mug of cider.

"Time for presents yet?" I've been harassing her all day, but she's insistent we have to wait until Christmas morning, which it now is. Technically.

"No."

"Just one? You gave me one present already. Fair is fair."

"I was kidding about that being a present," she laughs.

I wasn't. I may not have received too many Christmas presents over the years, but I don't see how it could get any better than the strappy, freaky little lingerie thing she pranced out of the bedroom in once everyone left.

I glance at the three stockings hung up by the fireplace. I just want to give Emily the one little present while we're still alone, before Dante returns home with my sister.

And he'd better return home with my sister, or he's not going to live to see New Year's Eve. If I weren't so determined to finally have time alone with Emily, I would never have let him leave with her tonight. But I was desperate.

Come hell or high water, that ring is going on her finger tonight.

It's been one thing after another preventing it since we got home from the US Grand Prix.

We had races left to attend, all of them on last season's tires, which Emily had to catch up on. Concordia, officially, claimed they discovered a simple defect in their manufacturing process. Their statement was, more or less, a very unsatisfying "Whoops."

Officially, Oliver and a few other executives resigned.

Officially, Emily and Professor Tillman never got credit. Both said they didn't want to be involved in publicity or scandal, anyway. They are writing a new scientific paper about what they learned, though.

But unofficially, and where it matters most to her, Emily has respect from the teams, engineers, and crews. They know.

Then, Emily's parents did not exactly go quietly into the night. There's a Christmas card from them sitting in a kitchen drawer, in fact. It doesn't get displayed with the others, but Emily hasn't thrown it out, either.

Emily is still working through her feelings about them, and she probably will for a long time. She did set boundaries for her parents. Under threat of a total ban on contact, they're adhering to her rules, for now.

Honestly, I don't know if it will work out or not. It's up to Emily.

I don't know that people ever fundamentally change who they are at their cores. Emily is always going to be good, though she lets the bad-girl out frequently and with unapologetic passion these days. Her inner badass flies freer than it ever has.

Everyone has chains around their neck from someone, somewhere, something that weighs them down. Cutting that shit off is the best thing either of us has ever done.

Stan and Kristy, on the other hand, it's been a clean break away from them. Instead of wondering if this is the year either of them would contact me on Christmas, I took control of the situation and made the decision for them. One more weight around my neck fell away.

I won't feel guilty for it.

Then it was Thanksgiving.

It was around then Danica came into our lives. Apparently, I have a younger sister. Half-sister, technically, but that's just semantics. Her mother was one of Stan's hookups, and I never knew about it.

She's only a few years younger than me and, my whole life, I never knew it. Never knew I had other family out there in the world.

She's had a rough go of things and is staying with us for a bit since, like me, she isn't interested in spending the holidays with her biological father.

While I'm glad to have Danica here, I intend to marry my girl before the year is up, and, right now, we finally have the apartment to ourselves.

"If this is really our Christmas and we're doing things how we want, then I'm doing it my way," I tell her.

"I kind of want to keep teasing you, but I also want my ring. Okay, go get it," she smiles.

She beat me to proposing, so it isn't like I could drop to my knee and surprise her with a grand gesture. I'm trying to make up for it in other ways and am nervous as hell about them.

Standing from the couch, I take her hand and pull her up. She's still wrapped in only a blanket, and we move over to the stockings by the fireplace.

"I'm so excited, gimme, gimme, gimme," she squeals.

God, I hope she likes it. I researched and read everything I could find online, but I was on my own for this.

She was so specific on the kind of ring she did *not* want, I may have gone too far. No diamonds because she has ethical concerns about their sourcing, plus she thinks lab-created diamonds are 'cooler' anyway. Nothing too showy because that isn't her. Nothing that can get damaged at work.

The same girl who wanted to ride a beat up Vespa around Budapest was not going to be impressed with a giant rock from Tiffany's.

She also doesn't want a fancy wedding because she's happier covered in tire grime than designer gowns. So, I have a private ceremony scheduled for us on New Year's Eve and then one hell of a party planned afterward at the London Tower Bridge.

Makenna is flying in, Klara and several friends and professors from Cambridge, Liam, and Mila, obviously. Half of the F1 grid and team members, damn near everyone from Imperium, will be there.

It'll be huge, but still intimate because these are friends and family, now.

I'll wear a tux because Emily gets off on it. She can come in pancake pajamas if she wants. But I have stylists with gowns and all the frilly shit on standby if she does want it. I've covered every base.

And then we're leaving for a two week Anthony Bourdain food tour of Vietnam, with a third week at the end dedicated to holing up, just the two of us, along the beaches of Amanoi.

Reaching into her red velvet Christmas stocking, I pull out the obligatory little black box. Her hands are clasped, her eyes are enormous, shiny, and reflecting the Christmas tree lights.

She's the most beautiful thing I've ever seen in my life.

"Gorgeous girl," I bend down because she may know it's coming, but I'm still going to do it right. "You already asked me to marry you, so I'm not going to ask you that again. I'm asking you to give me every single piece of yourself, and I promise to do the same, the good and the bad. I want all of it. I don't remember a time when I didn't love you. Even when we were apart, I was always yours. But we're better together. We're fused, connected, stronger."

Tears well up in her eyes, but I know they're the right kind. "Is there a question?" She sniffles.

"No, Em. There was never any question. It was always you and me. I love you, baby."

She sinks to the floor with me and wraps her arms around my neck, "I love you, Cole. So much."

"Want your ring now?"

"Yes!"

I creak open the box and pray she likes it. I spent weeks researching it, and it took a month to have made.

"Oh my god," she gasps as I slide it on her finger. She spins the black and gold band around and around examining it. "I've never seen anything like it."

"The band is tungsten carbide and rose gold, for you and me, fused together. The engraving is a hexagonal pattern because it's the strongest structure found in nature. And the inlay gems are moissanite because they can withstand anything and still shine."

"You, you... Cole," she whimpers, looking between me and the ring on her finger.

"Do you like it?"

"It's the most perfect thing I've ever seen, it's you and me."

"Yeah, baby," I take her face in my palm. "It's you and me. Always you and me."

Before you go, please consider leaving a review!

Reviews are tough to come by these days! You, the reader, have the power to make or break a book or series! As an indie author, your review would mean the world to me!

Visit my Amazon Author Page: https://amzn.to/2OdDsfv

Kat Ransom writes steamy romances filled with strong, sassy men and women who bring them to their knees. She lives in Cowboy Country in the Southern US with her husband and two janky rescue cats. When she isn't writing, she's exploring isolated corners of the world or curled up with a wool blanket and a stiff whisky trying to warm up her perpetually cold toes.

Continue Reading

The Fast Series
Fast & Hard (The Fast Series, Book 1)
Fast & Wet (The Fast Series, Book 2)

Find them on Amazon: https://amzn.to/2OdDsfv

Kat loves to hear from her readers! Contact her at authorkatransom@gmail.com
Follow along at katransom.com or find her on:
Twitter: @katransomauthor
Instagram: @authorkatransom

Join her mailing list for the latest updates, sneak peeks and fun freebies: https:// katransom.subscribemenow.com

Before you go, please consider leaving a review!
Reviews are tough to come by these days! You, the reader, have the power to make or break a book or series! As an indie author, your review would mean the world to me!

Visit my Amazon Author Page: https:// amzn.to/2OdDsfv

Made in the USA
San Bernardino, CA
10 January 2020